The
Ice Cream
Terrorist

MIKE LEAVER

The Book Guild Ltd

First published in Great Britain in 2021 by
The Book Guild Ltd
9 Priory Business Park
Wistow Road, Kibworth
Leicestershire, LE8 0RX
Freephone: 0800 999 2982
www.bookguild.co.uk
Email: info@bookguild.co.uk
Twitter: @bookguild

Typeset in 12pt Minion Pro

Printed and bound by CPI Group (UK) Ltd, Croydon, CR0 4YY

ISBN 978 1913913 687

British Library Cataloguing in Publication Data.
A catalogue record for this book is available from the British Library.

To   Kate the rugby player
        Kim the rock climber
        Sally the potholing fanatic

Three ladies who showed me what can be achieved
by those who have no fear

ONE

Mr Tebbit could not help admiring the lakeside walk – a rare moment of intelligence from the Games master to introduce competitive path laying as a sport, quickly followed by the true genius of Mr Cranmore, who had obtained a regular supply of gravel from the farmer, in return for the potato-picking lessons. It was a testament to logical thinking, so unlike…

Mr Tebbit's gaze drifted across the old boating lake to where the girls' orphanage was based. "The horror, the horror!" he cried.

Where their path had crumbled into the water, a detour had been roughly made through the woods, and leftwards, towards the dam, everything became an uncivilised riot of vegetation. It was quite obvious the girls did not know how to use brooms, rakes, or shears. All of a sudden, he had a tormented vision of the girls turning up for their first potato-picking lesson, the field newly ploughed. "But they are covered in dirt," they would squeak, "and how do we know there aren't any earthworms?"

Fortunately, Mr Cranmore had built up good defences against such awful creatures, this side of the dam being piled high with iron bedsteads, now overgrown with brambles. Why the other side had thought it necessary to roll out coils of barbed wire he had no idea, but it was like that all the way along the frontline – an arms race backed by fear, greatly helped by the English master, who thought any boy who used the words 'girl' or 'pink' in a story was fundamentally unsound, and needed to be ridiculed in front of the class.

Mr Tebbit lifted his gaze from the chaotic path, to survey the dense woodland that rose up the enemy hillside. Gripped in a perpetual Winter of disobedience, it offered a perfect habitat for those wishing to hide from their lessons, domestic duties, or any other form of useful endeavour. At other times, they would come right down to the water's edge, stick out their tongues, and waggle fingers against the side of their ears. The first time it happened, he had rushed straight to tell Mr Cranmore about the outrage.

"The first batch were war orphans," Mr Cranmore had replied, "the street urchins and ragamuffins nobody else wanted, some living completely wild on the bombsite where their house used to be. Hence, 'over the lane' quickly established itself as the world's leading university of juvenile delinquency, a place where all later arrivals could study the subject from those already there."

Thinking of the unspeakable horrors that lurked across the water caused Mr Tebbit to snort with such contempt that his nostrils lifted on a cushion of air. When he had first practised this as a five-foot-four teenager, he had used the upwards force to stand on tiptoe, so as to look down on the lower life form. Now, at the age of twenty-five, three inches taller in Cuban heels, the snort came naturally, and he found it more convenient to use his neck as a shock absorber, thus giving the object of his displeasure the delight of looking up his nostrils.

When looking across the lake, his snorts always lifted his gaze to the skyline, an untidy bobble of trees of such differing heights that it was impossible to work out where the actual summit might be. Only well to the left, roughly above the dam, did the hill begin a continuous descent to the lowlands, where good honest folk tended their farms. To the right, the hill merged with the upland plateau, where the girls had turned a once-grand Victorian mansion into a temple of disobedience.

The house! The house! Why did his thoughts always drift towards the house? It should not be there, with its upper storey poking above the trees. Did it not say 'look at me, with my folly of corner towers, and unnecessarily tall chimney stacks?' Yet, what had happened when he had surveyed the upper storey with binoculars two years ago? He had received the shock of a telescope looking back. He had rushed straight to tell Mr Cranmore about the outrage.

"It's Miss Buckley," he had responded. "She has a telescope in her study to search for any girls who manage to cross the frontline, also a panic button wired to the fire alarm. It lines them up for a head count, you see, but she also takes great exception to binoculars, because the upper floor is part-occupied by…the senior dormitory, I believe."

Mr Tebbit did not have the confidence to say he knew this because sometimes they forgot to close the curtains. He had only recently finished his National Service, and knew how his fellows would have reacted to such a disagreeable circumstance.

According to legend, Miss Buckley had not set foot outside her fortifications since prehistoric times. Others claimed to have seen her inside the telephone box by the village post office during the 1940s, the operator accidentally overhearing the caller make repeated attempts to contact Winston Churchill about the new army base being built over the lane. Apparently, it was possible to see men, often inadequately dressed, and frequently doing unnecessary, vulgar exercises over a vaulting horse. When the blackout curtains arrived, Miss Buckley assumed they had been sent in response to her telephone call. Hence, their purpose was to hang over the military fence directly opposite her gates, and she only agreed to remove them after the army constructed a towering wall of corrugated iron for the same purpose. Anyway, with the army came the telephone lines, and Miss Buckley was seen no more.

The location of the new secret army base made perfect sense to everyone, except Miss Buckley. The only access was down a dead-end lane that left a country-bumpkin village by squeezing between a lopsided cottage and run-down blacksmith's shed. To an enemy spy, it would have looked like a peculiar English eccentricity, unsignposted and without any pretensions to be anything other than a cart track. Only when clear of the ancient buildings did the lane widen out, so that two cars might pass with difficulty. It then meandered between fields and woodland for two miles, at which distance the army base was to be found on the left, a hundred yards before the entrance to the girls' home on the right. Miss Buckley's comments on hearing that the army base was, in 1947, to be taken over by a boys' orphanage went unrecorded.

Given all the insanity that existed over the lane, Mr

Cranmore, the first headmaster, obtained two gallons of white paint, and gave it to the Art department for a white-line painting lesson. The lane was really too narrow to be divided, but it established a frontline, until they ran out of paint after a quarter of a mile. But that was far enough; Mr Cranmore could get to and from the boys' orphanage keeping to his side and, with care, make certain his tyres never touched the white line. The stand-off with a mistress, who insisted on staying on the left, lasted for two hours, until a message arrived from Miss Buckley stating that, henceforth, mistresses would be expected to remain on the girls' side of the lane, irrespective of direction of travel. For the benefit of a birdwatching society who sometimes came to visit the lake, Mr Cranmore erected a sign stating '*Oncoming vehicles in middle of road*'. The true meaning of the sign remained a mystery to them, but equally the birdwatchers remained a mystery to him.

The entrance to the boys' orphanage was entirely practical – a lift barrier with a large '*Halt*' sign in the middle. The drive was cast of wide concrete slabs in a perfect straight line, so that wartime aeroplanes could use it as an emergency landing strip. The main buildings were well to the left – an odd assortment of low wooden huts clustered haphazardly around a central exercise yard, together with some outlying workshops of semicircular corrugated iron. The grassy area on the right of the drive was known as the lower playing field, and was sufficiently large to accommodate separate pitches for cricket, rugby and football. It was all very manly, and therefore entirely functional – so unlike the girls' home.

According to the large-scale map on Mr Cranmore's wall, their drive took the shape of a back-to-front question mark, the gates occupying the space of the full stop. The house was situated just above the crest of the question mark, depicted by a drawing of Miss Buckley sitting astride a broomstick wearing her witch's uniform. Mr Cranmore had absent-mindedly doodled this while in the public library, which is why they had made him buy it from their reference section for ten shillings.

While the map gave Mr Cranmore's office a basic military decor, it did nothing to convey the frenzied activity expected of a frontline command centre, these requiring a good display of top-secret reports to be scattered about the place. Mr Cranmore preferred the 'top secret' to be stamped using red ink, but grey stamps would do; anything was better than gazing across a naked desk. It gave visitors the impression he had no real understanding of what was happening behind enemy lines – sadly true. Indeed, the sergeant major who had suggested he start an orphanage at an abandoned army base even failed to mention the enemy camp across the lane existed.

In the beginning, or to be more precise, on the day Mr Cranmore first arrived at the abandoned army base in July 1947, he had spent the spent the morning wandering about the derelict buildings muttering '*Where*'. This related to the absence of a working gas stove, or frying pan, that would allow him to make a bacon sandwich. Realising the uncooked bacon he had bought with him was pretty useless without these items, his muttering changed to '*the rotters*'.

At two o'clock in the afternoon, he stood outside an abandoned hut to munch a chunk of dry bread. It reminded him of the war, eating whatever was available, as his regiment fought its way across Africa. Thinking of this brought his mind to the obvious question. '*What is the purpose of this latest mission?*'

Eventually, he decided to drive to the village at the top of the lane. Here he could buy some stamps, which would allow him to send a letter to his commanding officer to ask *'why'*. Obviously, while undertaking a secret mission, it would have to be in code. Nothing complicated, just using the Latin word, spelled backwards, in this case, *'ruc'*. It was a system they had devised when at public school together, mostly to exchange notes about their masters, be it hairy nostrils, or the silly hats they use to wear – these having a dangle of rope, like the dangly participles they were suppose to be learning. It served them well as, later, they had fought their way across Africa, knowing their code would totally confuse Hitler. Though, if it was really top-top secret, like notes regarding matron's bottom, they further converted it to Morse code.

On entering the Post Office, Mr Cranmore found a gossipy old woman behind the counter.

"You not from round these parts," she said.

He was on a secret mission, so merely shook his head – then asked if she knew where he could buy a bacon sandwich…or a frying pan.

She responded with an equally secret nod, which did not help him a great deal. However, skilfully he began extracting local knowledge from the daft old bat, before accidentally talking about his his own secret mission. It was then that the true horror of the situation become apparent.

"I think you are so brave," she muttered, "going down there. I still remember the great escape of 1944…"

Her 'intelligence report' so traumatised Mr Cranmore, that he forgot the stamps; also that his car was parked… somewhere in the village. Indeed, the image of 150 girls rampaging up the drive so closed his brain to any other business, that his walking became a series of reflex actions, until he went off course, and stumbled onto the verge.

After one such stumble, he realised that he had somehow found his way back down the lane, and was now within sight of the ex-army base. Cautiously he advanced to the entrance, where he stopped to peer at the lane's continuation. To the untrained eye, it gave the appearance of being a long-forgotten byway, the sort rarely used since the days of horse-drawn carts. However, his acute military training allowed him to identify a straggly hawthorn hedge, growing above the right-hand verge, as the enemy frontline. After estimating its height to be a little over eight feet, he lowered his gaze to study the numerous gravel-filled potholes of the lane, these reminding him of a minefield he had once crossed in Africa. Then, looking left, he discovered the lane crumbled into a muddy ditch, its far bank rising to a thin strip of woodland. From this, many ancient trees cast a dense weave of branches over the lane, thereby creating a gloomy tunnel, supporting the postmistress's 'intelligence report' that 'the lane was a place the villagers dare not enter, some because they were scared of ghosts, others because of dangers, far more real...'

But none of these military observations answered Mr Cranmore's question as to why the army had sent him to a place beyond the known civilised world?

Eventually, he just accepted that he had been selected to carry out a top-secret reconnaissance mission, yet to be revealed. Thus he bravely entered 'the tunnel', carefully watching his feet to make sure they did not step on any of the mines, at least until it became so dark he had to stop. Here, looking up, he saw a towering wall of corrugated iron. He realised the army had needed to build this to defend itself from attack, which rather implied he was on the wrong side of it. Now on full military alert, he turned quietly to discover the opposite wall; what had happened to the hawthorn hedge?

Oh, never mind, the relevant fact was that the enemy frontline was now a wall, that curved inwards to hang a pair of cemetery-style gates some twenty feet back from the lane. Gazing skywards, he saw the thick iron bars ended in a crest of sharp spikes, these used to display an interesting selection of rats, their tails all neatly dangling down on the far side. This meant their collective stare of death was focused directly at himself.

'*Visitors are not allowed,*' it seemed to say.

Presently, he realised that whoever prepared this gothic display must have access to a double-extension ladder, so it was obviously a hobby of their caretaker…or window cleaner. Lowering his gaze, he discovered the ground beneath the gates was a mixture of mud and rotting animal remains that had presumably fallen from the spikes.

'*Go away,*' said the bones of the fallen, '*look what happened to us.*'

He decided to call the muddy ground between the entrance walls 'No Man's Land'. Then, on hearing a noise, he looked up to see a tiny distorted face trying to push itself between the thick iron bars. Slowly a tongue appeared, and it was pointing directly at him. He fled, and never went to look at the gates again; the experience was too traumatic.

Later that evening, Mr Cranmore found a pile of old armchairs in a storeroom and, selecting the best one, dragged it to a shed with a rusty wood-burning stove at one end. After using it to boil a kettle, he sat with a mug of tea, occasionally gazing up to the great curve of corrugated iron from which droplets of condensation fell as light rain.

Dejected, he opened the road atlas on his lap, to see where civilisation might begin. Using a finger as a measure, he identified three lowland villages within a road distance of ten miles. It was then he realised the base was too isolated to be part of any wider plan. For the first time, he accepted the truth: his sergeant major, with whom he had been friends at boarding school, had sent him here as a practical joke. The gentleman's handshake between them had been that of Judas.

Thinking of the war reminded Mr Cranmore of all the times he had set up camp, with the enemy just over the next ridge. Was the girls' orphanage fundamentally different to this? Did it matter if the threat of invasion came from a line of tanks, or a load of girls rampaging up the drive? He had survived the former, and could always hide down the air-raid shelters from the latter.

In the next instant, he was wide awake with a startling idea: what if he turned this isolated place into the best orphanage for boys there had ever been? A safe environment, where they could develop healthy minds, free from the torments suffered by those on the outside. All he had to do was employ men who found girls terrifying; that would show the rotters who had sent him to a place beyond the known civilised world.

Over the following months, Mr Cranmore discovered that finding men who shared his vision proved surprisingly difficult, especially after he mentioned their pay was essentially board and lodgings, plus a little pocket money. Only in the third year did he sit down to interview the final applicant: a man recommended by an ex-army officer who now did something important for the National Service programme.

According to him, Mr Tebbit had 'unusual' characteristics that made him 'just the ticket'. Still, Mr Cranmore was quite surprised when, on being told about the girls' orphanage across the lane, the applicant had leapt from his chair to give a determined salute.

"Yes, sir," he barked. "I shall investigate the situation immediately."

Five minutes later, Mr Tebbit found himself standing on the far side of the exit barrier to stare down the lane. He knew it was important to appear brave, otherwise the men would laugh at him, like they did during his days of National Service. But, on this occasion, he decided to tell Mr Cranmore he had been to inspect the enemy camp – without actually doing so. Then he caught sight of his new commanding officer watching him from the driveway. Thus he saluted, and walked into the unknown.

Over the following weeks, Mr Tebbit discovered the importance given to holding regular air-raid drills, the aim being to get the boys down the shelters within three minutes of hearing the siren. This proved very difficult, especially at night, given their matron's extreme teeth-cleaning regime, beginning the moment her victims got out of bed. Indeed, the first midnight drill sent three infants running directly to the wash-house, toothbrushes at the ready.

"But they will fall out anyway," Mr Cranmore shouted as he waved the government booklet about nuclear war before their eyes. "Three minutes, that's how long you have to save yourself!"

Then he saw Matron running towards him, all excited, and wearing a dressing gown. He circled behind the boys, pushing the tallest forwards to act as a defensive shield. On her arrival, Matron shouted something, but the air-raid siren was of a military specification, and sufficiently loud to drown out her actual words.

Mr Tebbit escaped the confrontation by sneaking into the under fives dormitory. On hearing great gulps of misery coming from underneath one of the beds, he bent down to discover a boy curled up, hands over his ears.

"There are thousands of them," Mr Tebbit shouted, "all coming to take you away and make you eat earthworms, then laugh as they wriggle about inside your tummy!"

Mr Tebbit knew punishment was essential, helping the boy understand the fundamental association between girls and pain, a lesson that would serve him well in later life. He reached under the bed, grabbed an ankle, and dragged it to the middle of the room, the boy bouncing behind. However, before caning could begin, Matron threw open the double doors to stare at him. And inside that dressing gown was an awful lot of woman waiting to escape.

He fled via the fire escape, then crept quietly along the outer wall to peep around the corner, where he saw Matron leading the boy towards her surgery.

On that occasion, getting the boys down the shelters, with all hatches secured, had taken eighteen minutes, thirty-one seconds; even then, six were missing. Mr Cranmore had gone to peep through Matron's surgery window, and thought he saw two of them, both with mugs of steaming drinking chocolate. The other four were found the following morning hiding in the coal cellar, so covered with black dust, that any girl who saw them would immediately run away screaming, leaving Mr Cranmore totally baffled by Matron's reaction.

Having exposed the vulnerability of the air-raid shelters,

Mr Tebbit realised it was his duty to observe the enemy camp for any developments and, where necessary, report his findings to Mr Cranmore. This demonstrated great bravery, which meant he felt the need to keep going back, at least if the weather was nice.

When standing in the shadow of the corrugated iron, it was possible to peer across No Man's Land, and look between the bars of the enemy gates. Just behind the left-hand gate pillar, he could see the blackened foundations of the gatehouse, mysteriously destroyed by fire during the late 1940s. Behind these, a vast expanse of grassland frequently included the displeasing sight of girls playing hockey, on three separate pitches. He had no idea why they did not have proper PE kits to wear. Any boy running about in his underpants after the age of five would be severely caned.

To the right of the gates, the drive was edged by a line of trees and dense vegetation, hiding the boundary wall, thereby making the estate look bigger than it actually was. Not that the exaggerated grandeur meant anything to the war orphans. To them, the vegetation was only there to provide a corridor of disobedience through which they could scamper unseen, the first batch using it to take control of the adjoining field, thereby getting within twenty feet of the entrance to the army base. They never got over the hawthorn hedge guarding the lane, but Mr Cranmore had once found a paper aeroplane bearing a frivolous message, and there was no saying the infamous 'trampolinist incident' of 1958 was just another of the English master's hallucinations.

A financial arrangement with the farmer, to keep a solitary love-sick bull in the field, was completed in 1962, after which time Mr Cranmore was often seen walking along the lane, holding a fishing rod over the hedge. A red skirt fluttering on the hook caused furious snorts from the other side, so there was no way anything in a skirt was going across that field again.

In the modern sense of the word, the lane ended at the entrance to the girls' home, its continuation being nothing more than an ancient drovers' route that descended into a wooded valley, without any great sense of purpose. Once it had been the main route to the lowlands, but now it came to an abrupt end above the quarry after half a mile.

"It's where the bad men live," their English mistress would whisper as she brought the five-year-old girls out of the gates for their first supervised walk. "Oh look, you can see one of their tents hidden between the trees."

A hairy vagabond would then leap from the tent, and run up the lane screaming, "I am the bad man, I am the bad man, and I want to gobble you all up!"

Mr Cranmore took a more pragmatic view, and told their caretaker to erect a line of 'snake sanctuary' signs on the boys' side. Then, in a moment of true genius, he had a word with the 'bad' man employed by Miss Buckley to leap from the tent. His other acting job was Father Christmas at a big department store and, as a result, he had a particular dislike of small children. For the cost of a double brandy, he took great delight in running up the lane waving a grass snake in each hand. They were three feet long, one painted yellow and red; the other, magnolia dusted with flour. Throwing them at the English mistress was, he claimed later, an impulse caused by all the shrieking she was doing.

That evening, Mr Cranmore called a meeting in the staff room, or, more precisely, a semicircular tunnel of corrugated iron lacking any windows or architecture, except a rusty wood-burning stove towards one end. An odd assortment of well-worn armchairs was clustered around this, each specific to an individual master. Mr Cranmore seemed to be glowing with contentment.

"Miss Buckley," he said, "has telephoned me to ask what I am proposing to do about the English mistress, who has climbed on top of the wardrobe in reception." He paused for dramatic effect. "'I don't know', I replied, 'what do you normally do when she climbs on top of the wardrobe?'"

The masters thumped the arms of their chairs in appreciation, except the English master who gave a slight squeak. To him, upsetting the enemy was akin to poking a sleeping bear in the ribs.

"Of course," Mr Cranmore continued, "I did not tell her about the poster paint. I said the man in the pet shop thought the red and yellow one might be a corn snake. If so, it climbs trees and eats rats – big ones!"

Mr Cranmore acknowledged their adoration with a nod, then leaned forwards, as if in deep thought. His audience knew this meant he was going to say something really important, but were too excited to settle. After the fidgeting stopped, Mr Cranmore coughed.

"Gentlemen," he whispered, "I am pleased to inform you that my snake sanctuary has resulted in the other side refusing to do any more supervised walks, or anything else that involves crossing No Man's Land on foot. The 'Great Catastrophe' has been averted. In future, a boy who arrives here as a baby might complete his entire childhood without ever seeing a girl…"

"But…" interrupted the Games master.

Mr Cranmore appeared not to hear. "And," he continued, "this is just the beginning. We must all strive to ensure the snakes take on the image of great wriggling beasts, hiding under bushes, fangs bared, crazy for the taste of human flesh!"

"But the boys know girls exist," said the Games master. "The older arrivals might have bad memories of the outside."

Mr Cranmore blinked. "What?" he said. "Oh yes, but knowing they exist does not mean they are going to like it."

He turned to the English master. "Do you think," he said, "it is possible to tell the boys that girls are pink, always carry a doll, and stand on one leg to do ballet dancing? Perhaps they could write a story about it?"

"It's not natural," replied the English master, "for boys to write stories about not-boys."

"Quite so," said Mr Cranmore. He turned to the Art master.

"Do you think," he said, "you could make a scale model from papier-mâché, something permanent for the corner of your art room? Use marbles for eyes, set in a cross-eyed squint."

"The one leg would require a lot of coat hangers," he replied, "but yes, so long as it's not me who has to go into a namby-pamby shop to buy a pink ballet skirt."

Mr Kent, the Music master, coughed. "And what about underneath," he mumbled, "if the model is…as you describe?"

"Perhaps," said the Games master, "we could make underneath…you know…a boy?"

"Might lead to awkward questions," said Mr Cranmore. "Some late arrivals might already have…unfortunate knowledge?"

"Pink pants," mumbled the English master. "Wash boy pants with the red skirt you got for the bull, then we can tell the boys…well, it's pink, they would never dare ask questions about it."

Mr Cranmore walked to the blackboard that he used for his talks, and wrote: '*Girls stop developing in mind and body when they are ten.*' He then turned to face his audience.

"True," he said, "and if the boys never see any modifications, I am sure they would never invent them."

Mr Tebbit thought Mr Cranmore was no longer bringing the necessary gravitas to the situation, but could not find the words to explain girls that were not confined to physical boundaries; rather, they took flight to visit the heads of boys as they lay awake in their beds. "Oh, look at my modifications," they would squeak. "Now try again to make it stand up."

The Games master raised a hand. "But…" he began.

"There are no buts," interrupted Mr Cranmore. "My snake signs have secured the lane, and have I not personally chosen you from all over England so that boys can grow up in a safe environment? It would be a shame if any of you were…no longer here."

The masters instinctively folded their arms and tried to look innocent, except the Games master, who seemed to be having a fantasy about playing basketball.

"Well," said Mr Cranmore, "what is it?"

The Games master looked up at his hand, apparently confused as to why it was still waving about in the air.

"Oh," he said, "I was only going to say that, if the snakes prevent girls attacking from the lane, they will surely find a way to cross the lake."

"The only water girls like," said Mr Cranmore, "is the sort that increases their pinkness, and comes out of a hot tap with ten per cent bubble bath"

"Air beds," said the Games master. "They must have them for all the sunbathing they do. They could use these to paddle across."

"Ah," said all the masters.

Mr Brown, the Mathematics master, instinctively twitched. "As it happens," he said, "I have done a trigonometrical survey of the other side." He removed a book of trigonometrical tables from his pocket and flicked through the pages. "I have to report," he continued, "that a girl paddling an air bed at one mile per hour could cross the narrow part of the lake in ninety-three seconds."

"But the top end is filled with silt," protested Mr Cranmore. "All we need there is a sign to warn about the bog snake. I see a really big advertising hoarding. If you can get it out of the art room, without removing the door frame, then it is not big enough. The artwork is to be in the style of a poster, representing a film about flesh-eating dinosaurs. If the under tens who see it do not run away screaming, then it is not scary enough!"

The masters instinctively knew it was best to keep their actual thoughts secret, except the Art master, who fell from his chair to kneel on the floor, gazing upwards, where he saw the painting on the ceiling of the Sistine Chapel…except it was his work, featuring magnificent flesh-eating dinosaurs.

"It will be a masterpiece of creation!" he cried.

Mr Brown gave a deeply troubled frown. Trigonometry was far more important than splashing a paint brush about, and to prove it he waved his trigonometrical tables in the air.

"Or," he said, "they could launch from the peninsula near the dam. The curve of the valley means the bottom end cannot be seen from the telescope window."

"It's half a mile wide!" exclaimed Mr Cranmore. "And we are talking girls, not Olympic airbed paddlers!"

"Eight hundred and sixty-one yards," said Mr Brown, triumphantly waving his trigonometrical tables in the air. "That's the hypotenuse from the peninsula to the corner of the dam by the bedsteads."

"If you walk back from there," interrupted Mr Tebbit, "it's twenty-three paces before the first chimney appears over the tree tops."

"Now even I am confused," said Mr Cranmore. "Why are we talking about chimney pots?"

"Miss Buckley's madness goes far beyond anything a man can comprehend," said Mr Tebbit. "I have no difficulty in seeing her sitting astride a chimney pot with a telescope in one hand."

Mr Brown furiously scribbled down some figures. "If we allow for extreme telescope observations," he said, "and an airbed-paddling speed of one mile an hour, the safe crossing time is twenty-two minutes."

"There is no need for any of that," said the Games master. "Logically the girls…"

The snort from Mr Tebbit's nostrils was so fierce that it caused him to stand.

"If there was any logic to this," he roared, "the enemy camp would be attached to the side of a zoo, with proper bars to keep them inside, instead…"

He pointed vaguely in the direction of the opposite hill, an action that appeared to drain him of the will to live.

"I expect," he said more weakly, "the word 'logic' has been cut out from their dictionaries. I imagine the girls are told it's something boys do, and not anything they need to worry about."

A murmur of approval filled the room. Mr Tebbit realised this was in response to his words of wisdom. In the next instant, he saw himself looking down from a high podium, a crowd of supporters all chanting his name, as would happen in the years to come. Sadly, on this occasion, he could not think how to continue his speech. On hearing Mr Cranmore's serious cough, his mind reluctantly returned to the staff room.

"It is true," said Mr Cranmore, "that girls have their logic back to front, and is therefore anti-logic. Any boy would know the snake board came from a zoo. Whoever heard of a thirty-foot anaconda living in a ditch alongside a country lane? But, it is their complete lack of thinking power that keeps us safe."

Mr Tebbit realised this is what his audience had wanted to hear. To claim joint ownership of the idea, he tried to copy Mr Cranmore's serious cough.

"Their thinking power has been plugged in back to front," he said.

"Really?" said Mr Cranmore. "Is that so?"

Then the Games master interrupted. "They do not need to paddle air beds at one mile an hour," he said. "All they have to do is wait until the wind is in the right direction, and sit on them. A whole Spanish Armada could be blown across in minutes."

The English master threw his head between his knees. "They are coming, they are coming!" he wailed.

Mr Cranmore tapped a finger against the side of his head, as if shaking up his thoughts. Then he looked in turn at Mr Tebbit, Mr Brown, and the Games master. Finally, he nodded, as if something inside his brain had been resolved.

"So," he said, "the matter is settled. Mr Tebbit, I am putting you in charge of monitoring any suspicious airbed activity in the vicinity of the lake. This is very important work, so I will take you off five teaching periods a week, in order that you can give it adequate attention."

Mr Cranmore then settled back in his armchair, folded his favourite newspaper from 1952 over his face, and began to prepare for his snooze.

"Or," he muttered to himself, "the girls could just steal Miss Buckley's broomstick and fly across."

*

Mr Tebbit had left the meeting beaming with pride at his promotion, but now, as he patrolled the lakeside walk, he felt mildly disappointed by the arrangement. Nothing interesting had happened in the five weeks since the painted grass snake release, added to which there was the beady eye of the witch possibly watching his every move. He was in a birdwatching sanctuary, for heaven's sake, of course it was legal for him to carry binoculars. Defiantly, he raised the 'illegal' instrument to his eyes.

Today, the narrow end of the telescope was occupied by the cardboard cutout Miss Buckley used when not in personal attendance. Without binoculars, it was impossible to know this, but magnification showed it to be a much younger image of herself, with what looked like a large black spider sitting on her head. The real thing now had white hair, and a facial expression to suggest she had a cattle prod up her bottom.

Giving a dejected sigh, he turned around to gaze up the boys' side of the valley. It was hunting territory, with ancient oaks carefully spaced to allow horses to thunder through at full gallop. Along the edge of the plateau, just visible on the skyline, ran the ex-military fence. Once it had done an excellent job at keeping the boys within the top playing field, but now sections of barbed wire had rusted away to make it more of a theoretical notion. Slowly, his eyes were drawn to the staff gate. He fiddled with the key in his pocket; he was only fifteen minutes away from a nice cup of tea in the staff room. But his work here was important; Mr Cranmore was constantly reminding him to be vigilant for the airbed armada.

In the hope of motivating himself, he closed his eyes to daydream about Mr Cranmore's Utopian vision of a boy completing his whole childhood without ever seeing a girl, except for the model in the corner of the art room, a thing so hideous, three under twelves had woken up in the middle of the night screaming that it was coming to get them. And one day they would come...it's what girls did – torment boys.

Reluctantly, his mind returned to the task of defending the frontline from enemy attack. His National Service training had taught him this required a lot of marching back and forth with clean boots. He looked down to make sure his shoes would pass the inspection and, finding them nice and shiny, gave a satisfied nod. He then looked to where the gravel path crossed a boggy inlet a few yards ahead. The boys had built this, carrying the rock from all the abandoned dry-stone walls of the area, then using the caretaker's heavy roller to get the gravel surface nice and level.

Not that it had always been so logical; the rare moment of intelligence from the Games master being so brief, it did not consider how the individual path-laying teams might join their sections together. When the discrepancies had been raised at a staff meeting, the Games master had looked genuinely puzzled.

"Did you never do ditch jumping as a boy?" he asked.

The remark seemed to catch Mr Cranmore off guard, but it did not matter because the Games master was too excited to stop talking.

"In Holland," he babbled, "they do it all the time, and Somerset where I grew up. Can you imagine a whole ditch-jumping course? Two of our boys can already do the fifteen-footers. Next week they are going to try the monster. Eighteen feet, can you imagine that! Let them Somerset lot laugh at me now. Pushed, I was…"

It was an unspoken rule that you never talked about whatever had happened before, on the outside. It was obviously a girl who had pushed him, probably as part of a more general campaign of torment, and now he was falling back into the dark place, but fortunately Mr Cranmore came to the rescue.

"Do you think ditch jumping will ever be made an Olympic sport?" he asked.

"Oh yes," said the Games master. "I have designed our course for that very purpose."

The masters relaxed. The dark side had been defeated.

The following morning, Mr Tebbit sat the Games master down for a little talk, but quickly came to understand that in a county with a lot of ditches, the ability to jump them provided a reliable method of escape from those who wanted to torment him. However, this did not solve his problem of how he might visit the hillside, without getting his shoes dirty.

Two weeks later, Mr Tebbit's brain was still occupied on the problem as he supervised the weekly detention session. Then he noticed a boy fidgeting – strictly forbidden, detention being a punishment, not a visit to a holiday camp. He walked down the aisle with the intention of correcting the disobedience, but stopped after two paces as his cane began to twitch. It was trying to tell him something. Then his vision arrived, fully formed in black and white, as in the way of an old photograph depicting convicts building the great highways of North America. He was surrounded by criminals. In future, the path-laying programme would be undertaken by 'detention gangs' supervised by himself. His dream of marching places with clean shoes suddenly became his mission in life.

Over the following months, the lakeside walk had been corrected, after which came the more complex problem of getting a path from the staff gate to the lake. The steep bits required zigzag cuttings, with the spoils taken away in wheelbarrows to fill the hollows where a future network of paths would be laid. These were all to be a standard width of three feet, with no gradient greater than one-in-ten. And, all the time, the boys were turning into proper men with big muscles, like in his days of National Service…

Thinking of his National Service caused Mr Tebbit to start marching. On approaching the head of the valley, he looked up to confirm he was no longer on telescope, but had not yet worked out what to make of a periscope that had recently poked itself out of a chimney pot. It was easy to imagine the daft old bat sitting in a fireplace with the soot falling on her head. After giving a snort of contempt, he stepped up from the path to hide behind a bush. Here, looking down, he was pleased to discover his shoes were still nice and shiny, like his drill sergeant would expect.

Having established the civilised nature of his post, he turned his gaze to the quarry at the head of the valley, a sheer cliff where he had recently seen the Games master dangling from a rope as he tried to fix the snake board to the rock. Mr Cranmore had seemed quite hurt by all the negative screaming the master was doing regarding his logic.

"But it is exactly the sort of place a bog snake might live," Mr Cranmore had called back. "Up a bit, down a bit, not level…"

The Games master had then taken a pendulum swing on the rope, slowly bouncing towards a central point that left him gazing down into the swamp beneath the cliff.

"It is pointless," he had screamed. "The girls will see your magnificent snake signs, and all run away screaming, whatever their angle."

"Quite so," shouted Mr Cranmore, as if something had been resolved.

Then Mr Brown had splashed furiously towards the bank on the rubber dinghy that had started to hiss air. His attempt to leap over the muddy bank sent the dinghy shooting back into the lake, but left him in much the same place, except the dinghy was no longer there.

Mr Cranmore had looked at the dinghy hissing its final death throws in the middle of the lake.

"Bet you are glad you are not on that," he had said.

Mr Brown, standing knee deep in mud, appeared to be suffering some sort of inner turmoil. Then he threw his trigonometrical-dangly-thing into the water.

"On seeing your magnificent snake sign, the girls will all run away screaming," he gasped. "Compared to your logic, trigonometry is pointless."

Mr Cranmore gave a satisfied nod. "Perhaps there is something Mr Tebbit would like to add?"

Mr Tebbit had no understanding of trigonometry, and certainly had no wish to talk about it in front of an audience.

All of a sudden, Mr Tebbit's daydream vanished. Two units of 'disobedience' had emerged in a little clearing near the base of the quarry.

"The horror, the horror," he mumbled, thereby giving numerical accuracy to the situation.

Then he realised that after a particularly dry Summer, the swamp had contracted to half its normal width, the peripheral mud now forming a solid crust on which an infant might walk. He looked up to the top of the quarry, this being the terminus of 'Bad Man Lane'. Normally, the ditch discharged slimy green water over the trailing vegetation, but today it merely dripped from leaf to leaf, finally ending up in a little splash pool at the bottom. From this, a stagnant stream wandered aimlessly about the swamp, until it seemed to find the lake by accident. He decided this alone was sufficient to swallow a girl whole, and that was all it required to keep the boys safe, which begged the question, what were the girls looking at? No, one girl, the other presumably having gone back to play with her dolls.

Then he became aware of a slight disturbance in the bulrushes that grew against the cliff on the girls' side. A hand appeared, followed by an entire unit of disobedience, which then climbed to the snake board and, using its left side for extra handholds, quickly wriggled around to stand on top. Here, she used the frame to scrape the mud from her pumps.

Strange, he did not think girls wore these, but there were a lot of things about this situation he did not understand. Anyway, when the girl seemed happy with her footwear, she traversed the top of the board to reach a narrow, vertical crack, into which she stuck a set of fingers. She then leaned outwards to look at the cliff above.

How…? Why…?

The girl then put both sets of fingers into the crack and began to climb, apparently walking up the blank wall with her pumps in various strange positions to either side. Soon, she reached a place where even the bravest boy would get the shakes, but she did not seem to care, instead climbing higher until the crack ended beneath a great overhang of rock. Now all that remained to happen was her descending scream, followed by a splat. Mr Tebbit imagined the mud oozing into the girl's mouth as she vanished into the bog forever. At last, he had something about which he could write a top-secret report for Mr Cranmore to put on his desk. His promotion to deputy head now seemed a formality. Then his frown returned. The girl had wedged one hand into the crack, allowing her free arm to dangle down, and shake about. The boys sometimes did this before a boxing match, the Games master saying it was to improve circulation, but a girl would never be able to understand such a complicated idea. So why had she now swapped hands to shake the other arm? Then, using holds too small for him to see, she swung across an apparently blank wall beneath the overhang, her feet not even touching the rock. On clearing this section, she stood on a little ledge to look up at the path, cut through the brambles by the Games master to get himself and the snake board from the lane.

Panic!

Mr Tebbit raced from his hiding place, knowing only that he must defend the lane from attack. But the vegetation forced him to leap chaotically in a series of high kicks, at least until his right foot disappeared into a muddy hole. After this, his entire brain became focused on the need for vengeance, thereby losing its ability to synchronise limb movements. By the time he reached a solid stone slab, one arm was pointing to the sky, the other trying to remove tangled vegetation from his knees. Having done this, he looked up the stone steps that ascended the hill beneath the reducing wing of the quarry wall. They were rough, unpredictably spaced, and, more importantly, great in number. Reluctantly, he began to plod upwards, all the time getting slower until he stopped, bent double, his lungs gasping for air. Then, putting both hands on his knees, he pushed himself up to count the remaining steps – ten. He counted them again, but there were still ten.

Next, his attention turned to the path above the quarry. This was so badly eroded that many of the fence posts, designed to stop people falling into the bog, were hanging in mid-air from just the wires. With increasing discomfort, he struggled up the remaining steps, then turned left to follow a path of loose gravel, until it took flight above the terrifying drop. From here, he continued on all fours, grabbing any exposed tree root that presented itself, until he was able to lunge upwards to hug a stile. Here, his eyes focused on a brass plate a few inches in front of his face. This told him the stile had been made by the birdwatching society in memory of one of their members, who had fallen over the cliff while spotting… He did not read any further; his life was hanging onto something cobbled together by lunatics. He was over the top and standing in the lane before the full horror of his near-death experience had time to sink in.

It was the first time he had been to the bottom of the lane; some of the birdwatchers were female, and he frequently imagined them hiding in the bushes, waiting for a man like himself to get within grabbing distance. Then he looked down at the loose gravel that represented the lane. The white line had been made with a wheely thing like the caretaker used to mark out the games pitches. A line of chalk! What use was that? One scuff with a shoe and it would be blown away in the wind. Nervously he advanced towards it and, keeping his feet firmly on the civilised side, leaned forwards to peer, but it was hopeless. He tried to step over, but could not, causing him first to stand on one leg, then the other. He looked down, but did not see gravel, just a pit of disobedience into which he would surely sink.

"Are you doing a dare?" came a voice.

He gazed into the opposite undergrowth. Arggghh, it was even more horrible than the bog snake. Near the ground was a tangled mop-top of mousy hair with two enormous eyes beneath. Slowly, the creature used its front paws to gain a little height.

"I dare you," it said, "to step across the line. There, you have to do it now or you're a cowardy custard."

It was the closest he had been to a girl for many years. Instinctively, he stepped backwards, then remembered the stile, and took a step forwards. The creature smiled, giving a horrible display of dimples.

"I'm doing a double dare," it said. "I bet you've never done one of those."

The creature wriggled from the undergrowth to reveal a shabby grey jumper, so extensively darned that she could be six feet away, yet still remain unseen due to the camouflage it provided. His brain could not handle such an overload of disagreeable information and, as a safety measure, it shut down, only re-engaging when the creature was no longer opposite. Looking up the lane, he saw 'it' climbing over the fence. He raced to the white line opposite, and stuck out his arms like a goalkeeper who had developed a fear of the ball.

The girl giggled, then stepped sideways, forcing him to follow her lead. But she kept getting faster, her direction changes more unpredictable. Soon she was sprinting uphill, while he was still sidestepping down. The girl did a kangaroo jump across the line.

"Double dare, double dare," she shouted. "Tra-ra!" she added, taking a bow.

He raced towards her. But, at the last possible moment, she jumped back with a scream. Before he could stabilise, she was over the fence.

"I'm the best at doing dares," she said. "You must be the worst."

The fact that she was now retreating, and behind a fence, allowed him to feel a little more confident. He straightened up, standing to attention as in his days of National Service.

"Name, rank and number!" he demanded.

The girl shook her head. "Are you going to stand like a stork again?" she asked. "I think it's funny."

"No, I want your name."

The girl rested her chin on the back of her hands. "Spot," she said.

"Real name."

"It is my real name. I was a foundling, so Matron called me Spot, because I was spotted. She's weird."

He could not argue that matrons were weird. "Number?" he asked.

"One hundred and one," said the girl.

"Senior dormitory, I take it?"

The girl shook her head.

He looked to see if she had developed any modifications, but her jumper was so ill-fitting, it was impossible to work out what shape she might be.

"I think...I think..." Why was he stammering? "You are not...junior dormitory," he said more positively.

"Nope, I live in a little shed outside the back door, and sometimes Cook feeds me sausages. Though you could save yourself a lot of time if you read *101 Dalmatians*. It's a really good book."

He took a notebook from his pocket to write down the details. "You will be punished," he asked, "for coming into the lane?"

"Not if I don't get caught, which we never do!"

He looked up to discover the girl was also making notes, only in a less civilised way, using a scrap of paper and stubby pencil.

"Is this where the bad men live?" she asked.

"Yes, and they might catch you."

The girl looked up the lane. "So that goes up to our gates," she said, "and the path above the quarry goes to where we can see boys chasing a football...interesting."

"No!" he gasped.

The girl ignored him, instead noting the facts before putting the pencil into her hair in the region of her ears, and pushing the paper down her jumper. He stared in horror. She must be wearing a brassiere and, by pointing this out, was tempting him, talking inside his head.

"The snakes," he shouted to drown out her words. "If you ever come over here, they will gobble you up!"

31

"Miss Jones says they will gobble us whole," said the girl.

"Yes, that's it, whole, in one gulp. You will be in their tummy, slowly dissolving in acid."

"Miss Jones thinks a lot of things want to gobble us whole. The under tens are always running from her class, screaming. But I think, for a snake to eat me in one go, it would have to be two feet wide and a hundred feet long. Then you would not be standing on that side of the line."

Suddenly, the girl jumped up to grab an overhanging branch, and swung herself up.

"Don't move," she said, "whatever you do, don't move!"

"Surely you don't expect me to fall for that?"

"No, no, it's blotchy brown with a 'V' on its head. I've never seen one like it before, not a hundred foot long. Maybe thirty? The man who came down here with a big box labelled 'snakes' must have released it, probably because it's a snake sanctuary."

Mr Tebbit began to feel the fear in his tummy. And, all the time, the girl's eyes were opening wider, fixed on the ditch behind him. Slowly, they moved towards his ankles.

"It's got fangs," she whispered, "great, big, yellow fangs. "Oh, I can't bear to look."

Mr Tebbit spun around to discover absolutely nothing. And, when he turned back, the girl had gone. He immediately raced up the lane to tell Mr Cranmore about the outrage. He burst into his study without knocking.

"The girls," he gasped, "they have found a way to climb the quarry!"

Mr Cranmore responded by scratching his chin. "Do you recall the 'trampolining incident' of 1958?" he asked.

"You think I am hallucinating!"

"It is how parthenophobia begins."

"You think I am like the English master, scared of girls. He was sent to us by a 'nut' doctor!"

"A hospital certainly. Perhaps you would like me to arrange a visit, while you are still able to function in the outside world? Thing is, girls do not like mud, climb rocks, or repeatedly pop up from behind a hedge. It requires too much effort – like airbeds."

Mr Tebbit realised he would have to make the situation seem more real. "The girl," he gasped, "said I could feel her chest development for two shillings. There, what do you say to that?"

"And did you," he asked, "inside your head?"

Mr Tebbit stared at him in disbelief.

"Oh, come now," continued Mr Cranmore, "we all know modifications can turn a young man from sensibility. When you are older you will learn to overcome such difficulties, or perhaps remain here, where it is safe."

Mr Tebbit rushed from the study, just in time to direct his explosive snort across the central parade ground. On reaching his room, he threw himself to the bed; Mr Cranmore wanted to send him to a 'nut' doctor. Henceforth, he would be put into the same category as the English master, a man most famous for his hallucination of a girl repeatedly popping up from behind a hedge.

As the first light entered the sky, Mr Tebbit realised that, disagreeable as it was, he needed the girl to do a repeat performance. No, that was not good enough, she could outrun him. The girl had to reveal herself at a place where she could be trapped. Given this, he realised that his fate lay in the vagaries of the weather. It must not rain, the swamp must not expand.

Mr Tebbit then remembered how the girl's camouflage clothes had allowed her to hide in the bushes without being seen. Likewise, he had only witnessed this incident because he had been hiding behind a bush. Then he had an idea: the birdwatchers could bumble about the hillside completely unnoticed. After breakfast, he would drive to town to buy the sort of clothes they wore, then exchange his existing binoculars for a really big pair.

That afternoon, Mr Tebbit bumbled across the hillside, occasionally stopping to make notes, or exclaim things like "A great spotted woodpecker!" In this way, he got to within forty feet of a group of out-of-bounds boys, who had lashed a six-year-old to a low, springy, horizontal branch. They all hung from it, letting go at the same time to send the little one accelerating into the canopy. Mr Tebbit realised they were paying him not the slightest regard; he had become invisible.

The following week, Mr Tebbit lay in a wedge of fox covert that came down the hunting hillside to terminate just above the bog. Only his green binoculars poked from the thicket, held by brown woollen gloves, his entire face hidden by a grey balaclava. He trained his binoculars across the lake to where...

Arggghh...with these new binoculars, the girls looked really big, almost as if he was among them. He lowered the glasses, closed his eyes, and tried to stabilise his breathing. To panic in the face of the enemy showed cowardice, but he would not run away. Instead, he crawled closer to the edge of the covert to look at the scene, without the horror of magnification. It seemed Spot had the entire orphanage as a fan club. He wriggled back to risk the binoculars again. What they showed him, no man should ever have to see...

They were all wearing shabby grey jumpers, seemingly of a standard size. This meant the younger girls wore them down to their knees, while the bigger girls…He blinked, confused by the prefect badges – six blue shields lying at a most disagreeable angle.

What on earth were the prefects doing? Instead of taking a cane to all the disobedience, they were jumping up and down with excitement. All the bouncing was making him nod in sympathy, so he raised his binoculars to study a girl at the back, who stood perfectly still. Her badge was different, a yellow shield…Head girl, possibly? Ah, most satisfactory; she was mouthing the words 'fall, fall'. But nobody was paying her any attention, and she backed away into the woods unnoticed.

Mr Tebbit did not want the girl to fall. To the best of his knowledge, this was her fourth ascent, each time pushing her boundaries just a little bit further. Soon, she would go through the narrows at the bottom of the fox covert, a place where he could cut her off, and…he had not quite worked that bit out yet, but he knew it to be important.

Mr Tebbit was so disorientated by all the bouncy jumpers, that he forgot all about Spot until she came into his line of sight, on the boys' side of the lake. Here, she waved to her spectators, generating a slow chant of "Double, double-double dare." Slowly, Spot edged along the path, all the time looking towards the house. Then she stopped, placed a stone, and walked backwards up the hill to place another. She was obviously marking the limit of the telescope observation, and generally assessing the hill…

And all the time, Mr Tebbit was wriggling towards her on his tummy. He could see her ankles, or at least the mud that covered them. Then the ankles disappeared and, looking above the thicket, he saw the girl racing up the hill towards the fence. Here, she pushed her fingers between the wires to waggle them about like insect feelers. Naturally, the boys on the other side ran away, the rim of the plateau preventing him from seeing to where. He then became vaguely aware of a bell ringing in the distance, followed by a cry of "Come back!", but Spot was too far away to hear. Turning around, he saw the last of her audience disappearing into the woods.

Confused by all the activity, he looked around for an explanation, only to receive the hallucination of a mistress running along the death path above the quarry, a thing he knew to be impossible. After blinking, he returned his gaze up the civilised side of the valley. To his astonishment, a boy of about thirteen was now standing by the fence, a mere twenty feet from the girl, and slowly he was sidestepping towards her. Then, after closing the gap, he reached out, fingers exploring fingers, both looking curiously at the other's face. Presently, a more normal boy appeared, kneeling behind the first to pull down his shorts, then underpants. The normal boy looked up to see the reaction, but obviously thought the girl-creature was too frightening, so he ran, once again out of sight beyond the ridge.

Through his binoculars, Mr Tebbit could see the boy without his pants was actually smiling…or hypnotised, the girl having taken control of his brain. Then the mistress, who had previously been a hallucination, came running around the bottom of the fox covert, followed by two more. Puffing and panting, they continued up the hill, stopping twice to hug convenient trees. The first mistress to reach the girl pulled her back. The location of the boy's underpants then became noticed by the girl, who screamed "Pig!"

Mr Tebbit threw aside his camouflage to reveal his crumpled clothes beneath. He marched up the hill to…

How on Earth had she managed that? She had only been holding the boy's hands at shoulder height, while putting her horrible face a few inches from his, yet somehow she had managed to affect his plumbing all the way down there…it was even poking upwards through the chain-link fence! After a moment to recover, Mr Tebbit marched the final four paces to reach the scene of 'disobedience'.

"Daughter of Eve," he boomed at the girl, "temptress, who God has so wisely provided with an exceedingly ugly face…"

He pointed his cane at the displeasing sight poking through the fence.

"And what," he asked, "is the meaning of that?"

The mistresses looked to where the cane was pointing, screamed, then threw their hands over their eyes. In so doing they released the girl, who took the opportunity to start running. But downhill, Mr Tebbit's longer legs gave him the advantage. Within thirty strides, he tripped her up from behind. As soon as she stopped sledging down the grass on her tummy, he put a knee on her back and, after removing a rope from his pocket, quickly secured her with a handcuff knot. Let Mr Cranmore say he was scared of girls now; he had even captured one and tied her up. Indeed, Mr Cranmore would probably make him the deputy head that afternoon.

Mr Tebbit stood up to watch the girl wriggle around, and then with even greater difficulty sit up.

"I know you," she said, "you're the man who guards the lane."

"Child," he boomed, "I am a master at this place of civilisation."

"Then you have the power to let me go, because you are very important."

"Of course."

"If you let me escape, I promise to run away for ever. You will never see me again."

"Because you have been caught and will be punished?"

"Yes…er…I bet they won't even give me any bananas with my custard tonight. It will be like that for a whole week probably."

He snorted with such contempt that he found himself looking at the sky. Lowering his gaze, he saw the girl had somehow escaped and was running towards a line of trees that came up the hillside from near the dam. But with hands tied behind her back, it was a pathetic attempt. He quickly caught her, holding the rope to wrench her shoulders back, causing her to squeal with pain.

"Pig," she screamed, "man pig!"

"Dog," he boomed, "girl dog, and now it's time for your walk!"

"You can't. If I go back, I'll tell all the others how to get across the quarry. There will be thousands of us, all climbing over the fence to steal the boys' trousers!"

Mr Tebbit realised the other girls had not shown the slightest inclination to go climbing. This girl was a freak of nature. Yes, he remembered it now: an entire family of climbers had been wiped out in an avalanche, but for one surviving girl-child, who had briefly become famous for getting down alone in the dark. Her arrival at the orphanage had brought the press down a couple of times, but they never got past the gates. That was two years ago, plenty of time for her to increase her level of disobedience to what it was today. The Matterhorn, that was it – father, mother and older brother all swept to their deaths.

"You're the 'Matterhorn Girl,'" he said.

"So people say," said the girl.

He gave the rope a tug to wrench her shoulder blades. "No more cheek," he said. "You are, or you are not."

"It happened in Greenland," she said. "Mountain with an unpronounceable name. When the press learned we'd done the Matterhorn the year before, they decided to call me that instead. But my parents would never have got killed on that, it's only a mountain for tourists."

She looked up, tears in her eyes.

"They would have liked my quarry climb though," she said. "It was interesting…a bit, anyway. When I was up there, I could feel them watching my back from heaven. That's all I wanted. The boy thing was just to stop the other girls thinking I am weird. Let me go, and you will never see me again, I promise."

Mr Tebbit decided not to tell Mr Cranmore he had captured the 'Matterhorn Girl'. If he thought there was a possibility of a more general attack, he would be more agreeable to letting him become the deputy head. So, instead, he marched up to the mistresses, and held out the end of the lead.

"I believe this belongs to you?" he said.

But the women were paralysed with fear, so he threaded the rope through the fence and, lifting the girl's foot, tied her ankle at waist height to make it look as if she was ballet dancing. Then he looked towards the boys in the middle of the football pitch. As expected, the prefects had taken a firm hold of the idiot boy, whose shorts and underpants were still around his ankles.

39

"Don't you know girls always carry diseases?" he boomed. "Or perhaps you want to be covered in pimples and smelly scabs. Prefects, take him for a long, cold bath immediately. Rapid shrinkage sometimes destroys the germs, other times it does not."

He turned his attention to his wider audience of fascinated boys.

"You will know this," he shouted. "If your wee turns black, this is dried blood. Eventually, the scabs will come away to block the tube, and you suffer a long, painful death as your bladder explodes. Before this happens, go to see Matron. She has a special brush to poke down the tube, and give the inside a good scrub."

The boys all began to agree that the creature was indeed very ugly.

"Go to the caretaker," he continued, "and get a bucket of water with disinfectant and a scrubbing brush. I want this section of fence decontaminated. If the girl is still tied to it, throw the water over her when you finish."

Mr Tebbit marched back to his room, where he changed into black robes and mortarboard. He then recovered a long mahogany box from his bedside locker, and marched to Mr Cranmore's study. He found the occupant staring at the big black wartime telephone on his desk.

"That woman," said Mr Cranmore, "is quite mad."

Mr Tebbit knew this to be one of those statements that did not require an answer, since it applied to all women. He stepped to the bookcase and reached up to recover a six-inch box platform kept on top. He placed this carefully on the floor.

"She has just spent fifteen minutes talking to me," continued Mr Cranmore, "and I still have absolutely no idea what she was trying to explain. Apparently, a trouser problem has attempted a code green, then she started talking about the Devil."

"A girl has climbed the quarry," responded Mr Tebbit, "then raced to our fence, where she played with a boy's plumbing, the chain-link fence between them having no ability to prevent such a thing."

Mr Cranmore gave a strangled cry of horror, then leapt up to stare out of the window. "Our fence!" he gasped.

"Indeed," said Mr Tebbit calmly, "for girls have the most horrible, spidery fingers, always up to mischief."

Mr Cranmore shivered, but did not reply.

Presently, a knock on the door announced the arrival of the prisoner. The boy, naked after his bath, was shivering so intensely it could have been an epileptic fit. The prefects dragged him to the corner, then retreated to guard the door. Mr Tebbit swept towards the boy, growing in height as he stepped onto the box platform. The boy, now in the shadow of the robes, cowered back, dropping to one knee.

"I am the Vanquisher of Disobedience!" boomed Mr Tebbit.

"Yes, yes," said Mr Cranmore, "but there's no need for any of that. I have telephoned the borstal and they have a place for him. They have better medical facilities, so that he can be flogged across the back every day until he is corrected."

"Ah," said Mr Tebbit, "but did you not say all the girls were laughing because of what they had done to him?"

"I could only hear them down the telephone. More like hysterical delight, I would say."

"Because they are deceitful creatures who like nothing better than to make a boy cry?"

"Of course."

"Well, I witnessed the event, and strongly believe the girl used her deformed mind to hypnotise the boy. This makes him extremely stupid, but not criminal."

"The borstal will still need to correct his stupidity."

"And when he is eighteen," interrupted Mr Tebbit, "he will be transferred to finish his sentence in prison. Indecent exposure, they will call it, ten years at least. No allowance will be made for the hypnotism."

"True...but surely you are not suggesting we keep the crime quiet from the police?"

Mr Tebbit bent forwards, so the light bulb behind his head dramatically cast the shadow of his mortarboard over the boy's face.

"Do you think," he asked, "the model in the art room is exactly like the creature you have seen? Perhaps you also noticed the awful stink?"

The boy began to cry.

"You are in great danger of turning into a girl," said Mr Tebbit. "You should not have let her touch you. But if you saw her again, what would you do this time?"

"Punch her in the face," sobbed the boy.

"Scabs and diseases," said Mr Tebbit. "There should be no contact."

"I want no part of this," said Mr Cranmore. "If the police come, I will say I know nothing."

"But the boy will need to go down the air-raid shelter for three days, while I cure his insanity," replied Mr Tebbit. "They will not look for him down there. You could tell the police he escaped."

"Eight hours' detention is the maximum I can give without informing Matron, of all people."

"We must never tell Matron about this, you know what she's like with that brush of hers. She'll want to poke down the tube, in case he has the scabs. Anyway, this is quarantine. If the scabs start to develop, we will send him to hospital, where they can do the procedure under anaesthetic."

"Quite so," said Mr Cranmore. "Matron turns into a raving-mad woman if she finds out a boy has even been interfering with himself. Getting a girl to do it…through a chain-link fence…she will scrub so furiously, we will have to send him to hospital anyway!"

"Then it is agreed," said Mr Tebbit. "I will do my best to correct the boy here."

Ceremonially, he removed a cat-o'-nine-tails from its box, then applied oil and salt to the whips, necessary to keep torn skin sterile. The boy whimpered, his eyes bulging at the dangling whips.

"Smash her in the face with a brick," he gasped, "that's what I would do if I saw her again!"

Mr Tebbit heard a trickle of urine dripping to the floor. He glanced down to see the boy's plumbing had almost vanished from the outside world. Finally, the boy understood the torment girls could bring into his life; all that remained now was to rebuild him with a defensive shield.

"We can talk more about this when you are in quarantine," he said. "In the meantime, I feel a single lesson will be sufficient to correct your stupidity…Prefects, the boy across the desk, if you please. Hold him firm, don't want him wriggling all over the place if he has been infected with girl-germs."

*

Meanwhile, in the girls' orphanage, anarchy ruled, the rumour being that their senior dormitory had barricaded themselves in, and were threatening to throw burning blankets from the windows, if the flogging of the girl went ahead. But the locals got to hear the most awful stories of that place, and it was impossible to know what was true.

Anyway, the following week, three uniformed nuns arrived, rosary beads already drawn, crosses held out before them. After taking their bare-faced prisoner to the village at the top of the lane, she was marched around the green – twice – this being the custom with trollops since the stocks had been removed in 1914. From within the crowd of spectators, Mr Tebbit stared incredulously at a large wooden tally tied to the girl's wrist. On it was branded the number '86'.

"Your mouth is full of foul lies," he boomed, "waiting to spew forth odious vomit common to your kind!"

Mr Tebbit was so impressed by his dark Shakespearian proclamation, that he took three dramatic strides to stand on a park bench, allowing his audience to see him better.

"She said I could feel her chest development for two shillings," he boomed, throwing wide his arms.

"Two shillings!" exclaimed a voice from the audience. "What a waste, sending her to live with the nuns."

Furious at the intervention, Mr Tebbit marched towards the scene of disobedience, until he realised the individual was about eighteen, with tattoos covering his muscular arms. Mr Tebbit swerved to stand beside Mr Cranmore, once more an anonymous member of the audience.

Across the green, the girl walked, head bowed, looking down to see where her next uncertain step might land. Mr Tebbit thought how different she looked now her hair had been shaved to a stubble. Then a nun pushed her shoulders, causing the girl to scream with pain as she dropped to her knees before the gates of the church.

"Pray forgiveness from our Lord!" screamed the nun.

Then they all stepped back, holding out their crosses at arm's length to protect themselves.

"Satan! Leave this child!" they screeched.

Almost immediately, the girl's body went limp, falling forwards to lie motionless upon the ground, her face squashed into the wet turf.

"Good acting," said Mr Tebbit.

"I'm not so certain," replied Mr Cranmore. "What we believe and what we observe seem to be in contradiction. Miss Buckley, we know, is quite mad, and therefore unpredictable where Devil worship is concerned." He shivered. "Through a chain-link fence…" he muttered.

Slowly, the mood of the audience changed, until one of the spectators shouted for an ambulance. The nuns sprang into life, quickly dragging the girl into the back of a big black car, into which they all piled, before driving away at high speed.

"Well," he said, "they certainly did not want the girl to be seen by a hospital."

Spot's border crossing proved to be the turning point in Mr Tebbit's fortunes. Mr Cranmore said he could call himself the deputy head and, while there was no actual pay rise, it did mean he could ensure the weaker masters maintained a healthy-boy environment. Boxing and rugby were increased to ensure all the boys went to bed exhausted, seeing only the image of a funny-shaped ball or boxing glove whizzing towards them. Cricket was dropped from the games lesson;

too much standing around allowed young minds to wander into dark places. Meanwhile, the boy who had been 'corrected' down the air-raid shelter, after allowing his plumbing to be exposed, started to write *'Kill all girls'* manically and repeatedly across his exercise books. He was given intense training in the boxing ring, quickly advancing his position to number ten, automatically making him number ten prefect. With this authority he was given special responsibility for identifying boys who showed frivolous tendencies...

And on the seventh day, Mr Tebbit walked about the games field to observe what he had created, and saw that it was good...

Now all the boys understood that if they saw a girl again, the only sensible thing to do was run away.

TWO

If Mr Cranmore had any religious belief, it was that a low-mileage car did not need to be taxed. More people believed in this than went to church on Sunday, greatly encouraged by the Government, who, in 1960, tried to stop ordinary people buying tax discs by inventing the MOT certificate.

Mr Tebbit followed the same religion, at least until he became deputy head. This, he understood, was the first step on his path towards becoming a great leader. Thus, no longer an ordinary person, he bought an MOT certificate from the man in the village for £10, then drove to town, where he gave the post office a further £15 for the status certificate to put in his windscreen. After displaying this to the rest of the world, he felt the universe beginning to change, twisting into weird shapes that re-formed not as before. He seemed taller and, looking down an alleyway, saw dark clouds of 'disobedience' hovering above the cars parked in the street beyond. He decided it must be where the ordinary people lived. As in a dream, he walked towards them, bending at the waist to inspect the tax discs until one turned out to be a Guinness label. He gave a loud snort of disgust, then marched on until he found a disc four months out of date.

Furiously, he returned to the high street, then up the steps of the police station to tell them about the outrage. But once inside, he stopped abruptly; a girl behind the counter was pretending to be a policeman. He looked around to see if a real policeman was coming to arrest her, but his gaze immediately focused on a woman sitting on one of the blue plastic chairs. Across the top of her head was a crest of purple spiky hair, to either side of which, she was completely bald. A ring in her nose reminded him of a bull, causing his imagination to see her charging across the room to spear him against the wall, so she could expose his manhood. Looking down to check his buttons were secure, he noticed a really ugly baby with a messy nose crawling towards his nicely pressed trousers. He tried to push it away with the bottom of his shoe, but this only swivelled the nappy end even closer. Fortunately, his foot was in the right position to give the smelly bottom a good shove...after which the baby howled, and all the women sitting opposite started screaming. Mr Tebbit forgot all about the tax discs, and fled.

Mr Tebbit realised the explosion of 'disobedience' at the police station was like the one described in a government booklet, explaining what to do in the event of nuclear war. This knowledge sent him racing over the pavement in great leaps, scattering pedestrians, many of whom ended up in the road to the accompaniment of blasting car horns. This only confirmed his belief that a great mushroom cloud of 'disobedience' was rising up behind him to spread darkness across the kingdom, a circumstance that turned his car into an escape capsule, which logically meant the Highway Code no longer applied. Hence, by a combination of skidding and taking bends on two wheels, he screeched to a halt on the driveway of the boys' home, eight minutes after the initial explosion. Here he mistook the smell of burning rubber for the 'fallout' of 'disobedience' dropping from the sky. In an effort to save himself, he raced to the old tank workshop next to the drive, this a windowless dome of corrugated iron that he knew to be reinforced to withstand any bombs that did not arrive as a direct hit. Once inside, he bolted all the doors, then collapsed on a metal chair, head between his knees.

Mr Cranmore's inability to drive backwards in a straight line meant he had sole use of the shed, so when Mr Tebbit finally looked up, he was not at all surprised to see his car parked at a funny angle somewhere in the middle.

Obviously Mr Cranmore could never talk about whatever had happened before, on the outside, but it was generally understood that he had learned to drive as his regiment fought its way across the North African desert. For this, going backwards was not particularly important. After arriving in Italy, his life became a mystery, until he turned up here. Clearly the Italy bit contained a girl who had completely disorganised his life. Also his general conversation held clues that a bus shelter was involved.

Mr Tebbit stood up from his chair to give the untaxed car a severe look of disapproval. Then, understanding how important it was to know what his commander-in-chief was doing, he walked across to inspect the car's milometer. This showed 3,018, proving Mr Cranmore's last trip to the outside had been his normal, monthly visit to the village to buy the luxury items not provided by the home, in particular, mints and shaving foam. Three times a year, Mr Cranmore drove to the nearest town to get his hair cut, a round trip of sixteen miles. Whether this allowed the vehicle to be considered low mileage, Mr Tebbit was not certain.

Presently, Mr Tebbit stepped back to give the car a confused frown. Those who did not believe in road-fund tax always drove anonymous-looking cars, so as to blend with the background traffic – except for Mr Cranmore. Everything about his pre-war Jowett said, 'look at me'. Most noticeable were the great sweeping mudguards that flowed back to become running boards on which an old Esso petrol can was strapped. If this failed to attract attention, a starting handle sticking out of the radiator grill was designed to trip people up. He guessed that when Mr Cranmore had first trundled up the drive in 1947, it would have been just another old car. The 'look at me' status probably arrived around 1960, by which time starting handles had given way to electrical motors.

Eventually Mr Tebbit looked away from the car towards the garage doors, beyond which lay the outside world…no it didn't. Beyond the doors was the safe sanctuary of the boys' home and its dining room. Then all his decision making diverted to his tummy.

Whenever Mr Cranmore returned from his travels, Mr Tebbit went to look at the milometer of his car but, as the years went by, he found it made him rather cross; having taxed his car once, the Government wanted him to do it again, every year. Unwittingly, he had taken out a lifetime subscription, not helped by the man in the village now charging £30 for a certificate, and what did Mr Cranmore pay? Nothing, except for two gallons of petrol a year, because that was all a low-mileage car needed, apparently.

*

Four years after becoming the deputy head, Mr Tebbit watched the Jowett trundle down the drive, until Mr Cranmore stuck out his right arm to indicate he intended to turn into the lane. This caused Mr Tebbit to feel a powerful force surging through his body, the one that meant he was turning into a headmaster, at least for the afternoon. However, on this occasion, a few seconds after the Jowett had turned from the drive came the sound of screeching tyres. Mr Tebbit waited for the crunch, but it never came, so he walked quietly to the hedge that fronted the lane, and peeped over the top. The Jowett was bumper-to-bumper with a Land Rover. Mr Cranmore had wound down his window to shout that the other side was for girls. The assumed birdwatcher had also wound down his window to shout he was an off-duty policeman, and that he (Mr Cranmore) needed to move his bottom immediately.

Mr Tebbit was surprised the policeman had not actually used the word 'bottom' to describe what Mr Cranmore was using to sit on. More importantly, the birdwatcher did not seem to understand the impossible situation in which Mr Cranmore found himself. Obviously, he could not go onto the girls' side of the lane, nor could he go backwards without ending up in the ditch. The policeman seemed equally determined to stay put, even using his radio to call for backup. Soon, the lane was alive with blue flashing lights, but Mr Cranmore was stuck, so that seemed to be the end of the matter…until something else happened.

Mr Tebbit realised a situation like this needed a strong headmaster to take control of things. He marched to his room, changed into his most powerful Cuban heels, then went to do some classroom inspections, correcting any 'disobedience' the weaker masters might have missed. After his cane had done its work, Mr Tebbit returned to peep over the hedge to discover the stand-off had become an argument about who was best suited to use the girls' side of the lane.

It was obvious Mr Cranmore was going to spend at least one night in jail. Mr Tebbit rushed to the headmaster's study, then stood nervously outside the door as he built up the courage to enter without knocking. Soon, he would be sitting behind the big oak desk, waiting for a prefect to bring him a disobedient boy who needed to be punished. Then he heard a cough, and spun around to discover Mr Cranmore standing behind him.

"Going somewhere?" he asked.

Mr Tebbit realised he was still wearing his Cuban heels, so bent slightly at the knees.

"Have you ever wondered," continued Mr Cranmore, "why we never get a bus service down here?"

Mr Tebbit was too disoriented to answer. He could not understand why Mr Cranmore was not in prison.

"I have measured the lane by the blacksmith's shed," continued Mr Cranmore, "also a bus, and found it to be six inches narrower. The driver took great pride telling me how he negotiated narrow lanes to reach isolated villages, sometimes just a few houses, yet down here, with over 300 souls, they do not venture. Have you never wondered why this might be so, given that our entrance could serve as a turning point?"

Mr Tebbit tried to back away while still keeping his knees bent, but Mr Cranmore followed, the distance between them uncomfortably close.

"The lack of a 'fornication shelter' opposite our drive was the first thing I noticed when I came here in 1947," said Mr Cranmore. "Buses were even narrower back then, a dangerous situation, don't you agree? Well, I researched the matter. In Victorian times, the lane was part of the estate, possibly designed for horse and carriage. By 1945 it had been removed from maps altogether, presumably so Hitler would not be aware of our existence."

All that worried Mr Tebbit was keeping his knees bent, so that Mr Cranmore would not realise he was wearing headmaster shoes.

"You will also have noticed the lane is made of concrete slabs," continued Mr Cranmore, "presumably laid by the army. In consequence, the Highways Agency have no interest in adopting two miles of crumbling lane. The council would also like to pretend we do not exist, since it is where they send all their unwanted children for storage. Hence, no buses. Also, cars using the lane do not need to stay on any particular side, or display a tax disc. A point I needed to prove to the police officer, don't you think?"

Mr Tebbit had now retreated thirty yards to a corner, all the time stooping lower while Mr Cranmore stared directly at him. He decided to make a run for it, before his knees gave way altogether. On reaching the open air, he risked a quiet snort. He knew Mr Cranmore did not stop at the end of the lane, and therefore needed to buy a tax disc.

*

In 1968, Mr Tebbit inspected the milometer on the Jowett, to discover it had advanced by eighty-three miles. He rushed straight to the Geography master to tell him about the inexplicable event.

After frowning, the Geography master put a compass on the home to see where you ended up after 41.5 miles, which happened to be nowhere in particular. Then the Geography master remembered roads were not always straight, and in any event, Mr Cranmore probably got lost if anything complicated like a traffic island was involved. And there it was, a city, thirty-five miles distant.

Mr Cranmore's epic journey to the big city caused much speculation, increasing to fever pitch after he called a special staff meeting for the following Friday. After the masters had assembled, he put a chair under the door handle to stop anybody else coming in, then turned dramatically to address his audience.

"Gentlemen," he announced, "we are at war!"

He dropped an Act of Parliament on the chair. The actual title had been crossed out, and replaced with the words, '*The Namby-Pamby Act of 1967*'. He gestured for his audience to read it. Among other things, it said the cat-o'-nine-tails was no longer allowed, however serious the offence.

"It can't be true," gasped Mr Tebbit.

"That was my first thought," said Mr Cranmore. "I mean, when Matron first told me about it, I thought it was something her delusional friends had invented to spread chaos and disorder. So last week, I went to Her Majesty's Stationery Office in the city. They actually sell copies to the general public. When this information gets out, the proper education our boys have known will become a thing of the past. Instead of sitting silently at desks with straight backs, they will be huddled in groups to plan their next raid on the tuck shop."

Mr Cranmore blinked in disbelief as he looked about his stunned audience.

"So what will happen to the facts they are required to learn," he continued presently, "which, as we have established, takes ten years? Do you suppose they will be required to spell fewer words, or fail to learn logarithms? No, the namby-pambies will increase the school-leaving age yet again, to allow for proper juvenile delinquency breaks, I expect. But we will not allow such things, so will be left with a lot of bored fifteen-year-olds, who have learned all the required facts and are ready to start work."

The History master shot up his hand. "There were twenty kings before 1066," he said, "I could talk about those."

Mr Cranmore gave him a hostile look. "So you are no longer content with just adding more history at the front end?" he said.

Mr Brown put up his hand, though a bit more carefully.

"There is something called quadratic equations," he said. "I can't remember what they were for, but I could look them up."

"The boys have managed quite well without quadratic equations until now," said Mr Cranmore. "My thinking is we should teach them something useful, so I am proposing to convert the old ammunitions hut into a metalwork shop. I know a chap who works in a factory, and he wants to come to a place where his dragon-wife will never find him."

The audience nodded wisely, except for the Woodwork teacher, who felt mildly threatened by the prospect.

"And," continued Mr Cranmore, "shed number six can be used as a senior-senior dormitory…"

"But that's where we live!" cried a chorus of masters.

"Exactly," said Mr Cranmore. "I can still remember last Winter, looking up at the ice that had formed on the corrugated iron ceiling above my bed."

With a dramatic gesture, he tore a sheet of paper from an easel by his side, to reveal a drawing of a two-storey brick building. Above this was written the heading:

'*The New Masters' Block*'

"If the namby-pambies want us to supervise boys of working age," Mr Cranmore continued, "we will need somewhere else to live, preferably with windows. I thought about commandeering the wasteland in front of Matron's prefab. It will make her place...less interfering." He turned to the Woodwork teacher. "And do you think fifteen-year-old boys could do the woodwork?" he asked. "Kitchen units, window frames, that sort of thing, assuming builders constructed the main shell? Yes! Good man! Henceforth, you are to be known as the Carpentry master."

The Woodwork master beamed with pride. It was only later, alone in his bed, that he wondered how such things might be carried out. He liked making parrots cut from plywood that swung back and forth when you rested their feet on a dowel perch. He felt certain books would have been written about more difficult things, but it would mean going to the big town, and groups of teenage girls gathered on street corners were just too terrifying. If he wanted Polo mints, Mr Cranmore would collect them from the outside, but how could he ask him to collect a carpentry book, when he was the Carpentry master? Eventually, he closed his eyes to pretend fixing a window frame to a brick wall, which he found remarkably easy.

*

The way Mr Cranmore outwitted the namby-pambies had amazed the masters. By 1974, two years ahead of the school-leaving age rising to sixteen, they had moved into the new block. But the central heating did not work, so when the weather was cold, they still came to huddle around the wood-burning stove in the staff room. It was on one such afternoon that the Carpentry master had rushed in, unable to speak, but pointing wildly in the direction of the gates. Curiously they followed, stopping of one accord to stare in disbelief. A van was parked on the drive and, from this, an electrical television was being unloaded. Another man had put a long pole on the roof of Matron's prefab onto which he was now fixing an aerial. Then Matron emerged from her front door.

"*Coronation Street*," she said. "I have taken a fancy to seeing what it is all about."

The masters had no idea what 'Coronation Street' was, nor did they want to know. In all probability it contained girls, here, on this side of the fence. That evening, as soon as it got dark, they all gathered on the thin strip of wasteground that remained between their block and the prefab. There was a grey light flickering on the curtains.

"It looks like a spaceship," said Mr Cranmore, "with that antennae sticking out of the top."

"Perhaps," said Mr Tebbit, "now might be a good time to implement your genius plan of getting a man-matron?"

Mr Cranmore shook his head, a pointless activity in the dark, but such an abomination needed action.

"The council won't let me employ just a sensible man," he said. "Apparently matrons have to be qualified, a man-matron would therefore be a doctor – far too expensive. No, the only way to deal with that abomination is to build a security wall around it, to give Matron a bit of garden."

He looked at the Games master, again, a pointless activity in the dark.

"I want the wall to be so high that boys can only gaze skywards to see the spikes running along the top," he continued. "The gate will be solid steel, and made in our own metalwork shop. That place is seriously out of bounds until the awful television contraption explodes, or whatever happens to them when they die."

*

Towards the end of 1977, Mr Cranmore called a staff meeting, the special sort that everybody was expected to attend. The masters viewed these with increasing alarm, especially those that began with Mr Cranmore waving his arms in the general direction of the lane. The only meetings worse than these were those he began by saying "It..." before walking off to pace the floor.

"It..." he began, before walking off to spend a few minutes at the dark end of the room. On his return, he remained standing, in case another wander proved necessary.

"As you know," he said, "I have recently had a few problems with the council. I am now given to understand it all stems from a letter they received, stating that we still use the cat-o'-nine-tails. May I point out that since the Namby-Pamby Act, no such correction is allowed, and that its use typically leaves scars for two years."

Mr Cranmore stared directly at each master in turn, then shook his head in disbelief.

"I explained all this to the man at the other end of the telephone," he said, "but he was of such limited intelligence he could only ramble incoherently, and made no sense whatsoever. Anyway, it seems my military service record no longer carries the weight it once did, so I have approached five outstanding members of the community, who are in a better position to pull strings in high places. They have agreed to act as governors, translating the demented ramblings of the council into something that can be understood by sensible men. These governors have agreed to guarantee all our well-disciplined boys a job on completion of their education, and while the council might like to see herds of unemployed teenagers roaming the streets with cans of spray paint, those who aspire to own a Rolls-Royce do not, which brings us to our governors. One you already know, since he kindly lets us use his farm for potato-picking lessons. Also, there are two big-whig builders, and somebody else who owns a chain of man shops. Tools, paint, wood, that sort of thing…"

The English master shot up his hand. "They are called hardware stores," he said, apparently excited by his better understanding of words.

"I am quite aware of that," said Mr Cranmore, "I was merely pointing out they are the sort of places where a boy can go about his duties without being traumatised by disagreeable situations, as would happen to you if this sanctuary of common sense ever fell to the dark forces that surround us. I expect you would end up living in a bus shelter, with all the girls asking you to move over so they can try for a free council house with their delinquent boyfriends."

Having sown the seeds of despair, Mr Cranmore settled himself into his armchair to give his audience time to refocus on his plans for salvation.

"I have shown the owners of the building companies the

wall we built for Matron," he said presently. "All they could do was stare in astonishment. Then I took them to see the paths we laid across the hunting hillside; they were quite incredulous that we achieved such a network using only shovels, buckets, and a wheelbarrow. As a result, their vans will sometimes be seen coming up the drive at six in the morning. These will be taking boys for their work experience. I explained that we could not have them traumatised by girls parading back and forth to flaunt their modifications. They have assured me that all work will take place in discrete locations, such as the back of farm buildings, hill tops, indeed anywhere that can only be accessed by a wheelbarrow."

Mr Cranmore turned to the Games master. "Of course," he said, "the fortifications around Matron's prefab are only a triumph to those who do not know they are twice the size I intended. I quite definitely remember using the phrase 'a bit of garden', not something the Queen might like to have around Buckingham Palace! When I send you to supervise a body-building lesson on a building site, perhaps you will remember this."

"But the marking stakes did move," spluttered the Games master. "I measured everything with tape and string."

"Possibly, but you forgot about the fairies who go about doing mischief in the middle of the night. Perhaps next time you will check the measurements, before you actually start sloshing concrete everywhere. Our governors will not take kindly to financing another 200 bags of cement to make a silage clamp twice the size the farmer expected."

One by one, the masters looked up from their despair, the uncoordinated chant of "Mr Cranmore, Mr Cranmore" eventually becoming a harmonic chorus of hero worship.

With some reluctance, Mr Cranmore silenced them with a gesture of his hand.

"Also," he continued, "you might see the odd monk wandering about. Do not let them trouble you. They simply need a place to sleep when travelling, and to them heaven is a bit of floor on which to unroll a blanket. Needless to say, the Abbot was delighted to hear of there being no disagreeable temptations for his novice monks to worry about. He is the fifth governor I was referring to. The council are not going to poke their noses in, if there is a religious connection, which I presume is how the daft old bat over the lane gets away with her witchcraft, completely unhindered by bureaucracy."

"We are saved!" cried the Geography master.

"Mostly," responded Mr Cranmore.

His audience looked around nervously. How could you be mostly saved?

"The council cannot argue with the logic of the situation," continued Mr Cranmore, "but I still needed to guarantee certain things. The first of which is of no great concern: I have simply agreed to take any boy up to the age of eight, but no older because of the psychological damage they would have suffered on the outside. We are no longer a general orphanage, but a storage facility for unwanted 'bus-shelter kids'. The governors have advised me to avoid using this term, though I have no idea why, it is where such things begin. Anyway, there will never be any shortage of supply, because out there hundreds of teenagers are doing it in bus shelters as we speak. Our jobs are safe."

The masters thumped their chairs in approval, slowing down only when they realised Mr Cranmore had his head in his hands. After things became silent, he looked up, his face deathly white.

"The governors," he said, "only managed to sell the idea to the council on the basis of stability, in the form of Matron. She is to have complete control of the boys up to the age of five. She will obviously fill their heads with namby-pamby ideas, but fortunately, the governors have agreed to fund a proper boxing gym down the big air-raid shelter, where any damage done can be corrected. There will be hot lamps and proper ropes for sweaty bodies to bounce off. Here, the over fives can relearn how to be proper boys, strong in mind and body. Also, as luck would have it, I have measured the access manhole and found it to be twenty inches square, and Mr Brown's excellent trigonometrical survey has already shown that Matron's bottom needs twenty-six inches of clearance – more, if we allow for the wobble factor."

Mr Cranmore allowed himself to blink.

"Anyway," he continued, "what was I talking about? Ah, yes, the new boxing gym. It will have to be delayed, because first we must pay for the extra sand, cement, and fencing needed to complete Matron's grand enclosure. But this is only a temporary problem, the real difficulty comes from Matron's second demand. Under the disguise of stability, she wants a twenty-year lease on her prefab. The wall so extravagantly constructed by the Games master is to be the boundary. Inside this will exist a new country of namby-pamby land."

Mr Cranmore glanced at the Games master, who gave the appearance of having his entire brain occupied on the task of keeping his mouth shut. Looking at the rest of the audience, it was obvious they had not understood the hidden meaning of his speech, so he gave an embarrassed cough.

"We can sack Matron for gross misconduct," he said, "but can never ask her to leave the premises. We are stuck with her for twenty years. That is the deal with the council anyway. To the new intake she will be their mother."

The masters left the meeting so traumatised that they struggled to make it back to their rooms without bumping into things – mostly each other. Once inside, they lay on their beds to consider the nightmare Mr Cranmore had described. Then, as frequently happened, they remembered that out there, in the darkness, lived the insane Miss Buckley, with the power to release 156 girls onto an unsuspecting world. Never had their civilisation seemed so fragile.

The following morning, the English master was discovered inside the central chalk circle of the lower football pitch, periodically jumping around to see what was behind him. At other times he would push away objects that only he could see. Mr Cranmore understood the logic of the situation.

"Girls can't play football," he said, "so the pitch gives him a force field of protection. I expect yesterday's meeting pushed him over the edge of…"

"…reason," mumbled the Geography master.

All the masters understood the comment, but it was only Mr Kent who decided to resolve the situation by stepping into the circle.

What he intended to do remained unclear, because the English master immediately punched him on the nose. Mr Kent rolled back out, screaming for help. However, the English master showed no inclination to pursue him over the chalk line, allowing Mr Kent to crawl away from his near-death experience, and join the others, who had regrouped at a safe distance. Then Mr Cranmore remembered the breakfast man would stop serving porridge in five minutes, after which he would tip the leftovers into a bucket. He would then take this back to his house in the village, where he kept a few pigs in the garden. It was an unofficial arrangement, balanced by the equally unofficial return of two hot bacon sandwiches, delivered to their rooms, twice a month; but that was not important, the important thing was that the English master would no longer be needing his.

Mr Cranmore hurried back to discuss what alternative arrangements might be made for the sandwiches, the outcome of which put him in such good humour, that he could see no particular reason why the English master should not be allowed to continue his silent contemplations unhindered. Thus, he instructed the Woodwork master to fix a couple of pram wheels to a scaffolding plank with a laundry basket screwed to the other side. This could be rolled into the circle to deliver a tent and meals. Having sorted out the practical problems, things soon settled down, with the English master acquiring the status of a hermit. This lasted until the first monk came shuffling up the drive, whereupon the English master ran wildly across the playing field. The monk must have been very experienced, because he did not seem at all frightened by the silent, hairy man who had thrown himself across his feet. Instead, the monk just brought his hands up to his chin, and began to nod.

"My son," he said presently, "follow the path of righteousness and you will be saved."

Whether the monk intended the word 'follow' to be taken so literally was open to question, but the following morning, he left with the English master clinging to his robes. A week later, the Abbot telephoned to say the English master had found peace within the walled garden, and that a donation of £100 would be sufficient to cover the first month of his apprenticeship.

And Mr Cranmore knew exactly who to call if he had any problems with the council in future, because arguing with an abbot was completely impossible.

*

Their new English master had something to do with the governors, but nobody seemed to know what it might be, until the day he arrived, when it became obvious he was an embarrassing relative who needed to be sent away somewhere secluded. You could tell from his car; it was yellow with a missing roof. On the back seat were four large suitcases. How could anyone own so much stuff? That evening the existing masters gathered in the staff room to discuss the matter. The Geography master said the cases probably contained a stamp collection, which he would quite like to see. The History master put the view that, if he had not been told the home provided all the necessities of life, they might contain blankets and saucepans?

"Nappies," said the Games master, "if you know what I mean."

"It's called a metonymy," said a voice they did not recognise.

They all spun around, immediately turning back to shield their eyes. The new English master was standing in the doorway, his yellow shirt exactly matching the colour of his car. When they cautiously looked back through spaced fingers, they realised he was still there, staring into the room with a vague expression on his face.

"Oh yes," he said presently, "I was wondering where I can get a key for the gate in the fence?"

When the masters emerged from their state of shock, they realised the yellow shirt had gone. Surely he was not planning to go outside, dressed like that? With people watching.

The Games master hurried to the door. "He's wearing gymnasium pumps!" he cried. "Makes him walk like a nancy boy. It's how he was able to sneak up on us!"

All the masters filed out to look, then hypnotically followed the yellow shirt to the bottom of the drive, where it turned left. On reaching the exit, the masters spread out, the adventurous standing just before the white line, the more timid remaining inside the lift barrier.

"If we don't give him a key for the staff gate," said Mr Tebbit, "it's only a matter of time before he falls into the swamp."

Mr Cranmore looked puzzled, but he never went down the lane, so Mr Tebbit realised he would not know about the death path above the quarry. He decided to let his ignorance continue; it would make things a lot easier when the English master simply vanished without trace.

The following morning, Mr Cranmore telephoned the governors to find out to which of them the new English master belonged, but they were all too embarrassed to admit it. However, they were obviously trying to hide something, because they all said that under no circumstance should he speak to the council about it – or anything else for that matter.

Mr Cranmore understood the governors liked to deal with the council themselves and, since they controlled the supply of cash needed to purchase a set of golf clubs the Games department needed, it was important not to upset them. However, the mental damage being done to the boys by the 'namby-pamby extremist' was too great to be ignored, so he telephoned the council anyway. The man seemed quite flummoxed by the description of the yellow shirt, and merely rambled on about the English master having very good 'A' level results.

"The fact that he is related to the Lord Mayor," he added, "is not relevant." Then the telephone went dead.

Mr Cranmore put his head into his hands. The Lord Mayor; how was he supposed to deal with somebody that important?

As soon as Mr Cranmore told the others about the new arrival's fancy qualifications, they immediately gave him the name of 'Old Clever Clogs' – at least behind his back. Each word was carefully chosen to mean the opposite. 'Old' he was not; 'Clever'...he even lacked the basic intelligence to understand Mr Cranmore's reading list of approved books. As for 'Clogs', what he did in the privacy of his own room was anybody's guess, but nothing actually clumped across the floorboards in the night.

Mr Cranmore's list of approved books was entirely sensible, and included works like *Treasure Island*, *The Pilgrim's Progress*, and the one about the Cyclops. In short, any book that did not contain girls, at least after the offending page had been removed, which realistically limited their appearance to a single visit of no consequence. Then came Old Clever Clogs, pushing a trolley containing three large suitcases towards his English room. The masters all tried to follow without being seen, at journey's end spreading out to crowd around the outside of the windows, periodically peeping over the sill to see what he was doing. There were books everywhere, many of which had modern-looking covers.

"We could always lock him down the air-raid shelter," said Mr Kent, "before his namby-pambyism causes the boys any more harm."

Mr Cranmore shook his head. "If Daddy comes visiting, it would be too difficult to explain," he said. "Hopefully, putting him in the monk's room will be sufficient to make him leave less dramatically."

And there it was, out in the open: the connection to the Lord Mayor put the English master beyond the law of sensibility. As if to emphasise this, when he noticed a face peering through his window he came across to open it.

"Here's a good one," he said, holding out a book. "*Fair Stood the Wind for France...*"

Then he realised all the masters were crouching beneath his windows. It made him think about the trenches of the First World War, with the men waiting to go over the top. Finally, something he had been told at his job interview made sense. "A challenging assignment," the most important man had said. "I can only advise you to make it up as you go along. The headmaster will get to hear a rumour that you are related to somebody very important. It might help? This conversation never happened."

The interview committee members had then filed up to shake his hand, in a way that suggested they were saying goodbye to someone they were sending behind enemy lines, and never expected to see again. Now, looking out of his English room, to see all the men huddled beneath his windows, he realised why he had been offered the job without the need to do formal teacher training. Anyone with preconceptions about how things should be done, would leave within the first week. Also, the contract had a 'live-in' clause, without specifying the one-room accommodation was essentially unfurnished, with all the plumbing, including toilets, on the ground floor.

To sort this place out, the council needed to knock everything down and start again – an unlikely level of expense, given that Matron still lived in a prefab designed for emergency accommodation after the war, now frowned upon since they were made almost entirely of asbestos sheets. And what would they do with 150 boys in the meantime? In truth, the council were stuck with this place, lost in its time bubble of the 1920s. Here, not even the invention of the wind-up gramophone had made it through the time wall; the only music the boys ever heard came from the worn-out piano in the assembly hall, more sensibly viewed as a collective punishment to prepare them for the vicissitudes of later life.

But the privilege of experiencing a world Jane Austen would have recognised, had done nothing to prepare him for the reality of facing his first classroom full of boys. Only on seeing all the men pinned down, as in a trench, did he remember the First World War poetry of Wilfred Owen. And from this came the inspiration for which he had been waiting. He turned to face the audience of silent boys.

"Words…" he said,

"Drifting in the air…

"Like a gas attack holding down an army, the unseen menace."

He displayed the book he was holding to the boys. "Bullets can kill," he said, "but words can change minds."

The boys looked at him without comprehension. They always had a spelling test on Monday.

Outside, the masters were too preoccupied with the horror of what they had just seen to register mere words. The book had a photograph of an actual real woman on the cover. They all scuttled back to the safety of their own classrooms; there were girls here, on this side of the fence.

And that night, the new English master stood in his small room to gaze down at the three scaffolding planks supported by breeze blocks. "Bed," he said, as if learning a new language. Then he looked up at the single light bulb hanging from a wire in the middle of the ceiling. It swayed in the draught coming through the ill-fitting window frame. Did he really want this challenge? He had only applied for the job after his girlfriend had smashed up all his Doris Day records. Ex-girlfriend; how could anyone dislike the gentle voice of Doris? And what did he have now? Mr Kent terrorising the piano. Then he remembered his ex-girlfriend throwing his favourite Doris Day poster out of the window into the rain. By the time he had caught up with her beautiful image, both himself and Doris were equally soggy. On returning home, his mother had tried to hide a dustpan and brush behind her back, and he just knew it contained the remains of a broken Doris Day lampshade. So he had applied for a job here, not realising it was so isolated from the rest of the world, that the masters had evolved a new 'normality': feeding each year on each others' growing insanity.

Then his thoughts returned to his humble bed. The forced sleeping posture would be excellent for his back. Also, there was all the fresh air coming through the gaps in the window frame, and a fully equipped gym awaiting his pleasure. He too could have a body like Rock Hudson, whom Doris seemed to find irresistible. Next time she came to England, he could get her attention by doing one-arm pull-ups from a lamp post – the old cast-iron type that had ladder rests for the man who came to light the gas.

Presently, his attention turned to a soap box beside the scaffolding planks. He wanted to say 'bedside locker', but the combination of furniture made him think about a go-cart he had once owned – the sort steered with the feet – then his happy childhood memories turned to sadness, for he knew it was a place to which he could never return.

Subconsciously, he lifted his gaze to the window, the darkness better suiting his mood. Then he noticed a solitary light shining back. He decided it must be coming from Matron's prefab – the gentle lady whose only interest seemed to be looking after the boys. Perhaps his life might also be dedicated to a similar purpose? Tomorrow, he would invite her to the tearoom in the nearby village, to see if they might begin a joint project with the aim of helping the boys develop into well-balanced men. He could teach them to play table tennis – properly. At the age of fourteen he had been ranked number one in the youth club – leaping gracefully around to make successful returns fifteen feet away from the table – before his ex-girlfriend had crashed into his life, and expected him to do discotheque dancing instead.

*

In the Winter of 1978, Mr Tebbit realised that what Mr Cranmore had predicted many years before had come to pass. He no longer thought about girls, at least not in a way that involved wondering what their biological variations might look like. When he saw Matron bending down to tie a boy's shoelace, he merely wondered if he could get away with giving her bottom a good kick, then running away to hide, before she had chance to recover herself from the floor. He told Mr Cranmore about this, who nodded wisely.

"I have often thought the same myself," he said, "and may I say how pleased I am to hear that you have overcome your unfortunate thoughts of long ago. Women no longer have any relevance to our lives. Matron's bottom is merely enormously funny, like the bottom of an elephant, lacking only a tail."

Then they sniggered, men together, both hoping that one day the other would have the courage to do the kicking deed.

*

In the Summer of 1979, Mr Cranmore walked into the staff room looking like a man who had just witnessed his own funeral. Unable to speak, he paced the length of the corrugated-iron tunnel three times. Each time he emerged from the dark end, he said, "It...", but each time felt unable to continue the sentence.

It made the masters very nervous. Staff meetings that required a lot of wandering about were always called in advance; it gave time to build up the dramatic tension, which Mr Cranmore would then resolve to gasps of admiration. But this meeting had been called without warning. Then, after his third visit into the darkness, he collapsed in his armchair to stare at the floor.

"A girl has become Prime Minister," he said quietly.

The masters took a moment to adjust, then roared with laughter. It was Mr Cranmore's best-ever joke. Only after realising Mr Cranmore did not appear to be a man who had suddenly mastered the art of comic timing, did they fall silent.

"It's not legal," gasped the History master. "There has never been a girl prime minister."

"The logic of history is not in doubt," said Mr Cranmore, "but I was in the barber's waiting room this morning, when I noticed the man opposite reading a modern newspaper, and there it was in black and white. It happened last month apparently. There can be no doubt about it, a girl is namby-pambying the country!"

Mr Tebbit felt himself turning into the Vanquisher of Disobedience. He got up from his armchair and paced the tunnel three times; no more, because that would put him senior to Mr Cranmore.

"The boys must never find out about this great catastrophe!" he proclaimed.

Mr Cranmore mumbled something incomprehensible, most probably a Latin quotation to make it sound more important. However, Mr Tebbit did not allow himself to be distracted.

"But think how the news will be greeted in the enemy camp," he continued. "There will be great cheering, with double bananas and custard for tea to celebrate."

Mr Tebbit glanced at Mr Cranmore to see how his speech had been received. After a few moments, he decided to play it safe, and returned to his chair to await developments. Presently, Mr Cranmore looked up, his haunted eyes focused on something not in the room.

"I can't get this vision out of my mind," he said, "that of the Cabinet Room where Winston Churchill once sat...only now there is a girl with her feet resting on two stools, legs wide apart, facing the door so as to disorientate any man who enters, by showing her underpants. All her namby-pamby advisers are gathered around drinking milkshakes through pink straws!"

Mr Tebbit interrupted the incoherent rambling. "Namby-pamby extremists don't drink milk," he said, "they think it upsets the cows. All they drink is cabbage water."

"Ah," said Mr Cranmore, "I remember cabbage water from the war. Mother said it was good for us, but it tasted disgusting."

Suddenly, Mr Tebbit realised the girl prime minister had seriously affected Mr Cranmore's brain. This situation needed a strong man like himself to take control, like Churchill during the war.

"Ever since 1941," Mr Tebbit proclaimed, "the enemy camp have been sending out newly trained agents to spread chaos and despair. The first batch have now acquired the perfect disguise of becoming wrinkled old prunes. Any moment now a spy can push her bicycle up the drive, pretending to be a postman. But we will never surrender – never!"

He thumped the wartime office desk with his fist, but since it was not there, only succeeded in doubling up with pain.

"Well," he continued, a slight squeak to his voice, "it seems that our first problem is the enemy within. Where is Old Clever Clogs during our darkest hour? Has he even once used the armchair vacated by his predecessor? No, because he spends all his time in the gym!"

"Climbs the ropes," said the Games master, "but not properly, just using his arms with legs sticking out sideways, and now all the boys are trying to copy him."

"And I've seen him dancing around like a fairy," said Mr Tebbit, "when he's playing table tennis."

"And now all the boys are trying to copy his girlie prancing about," interrupted the Games master.

The horror of the image opened up the floodgates of despair.

"Last week," gasped Mr Kent, "I saw him talking to Matron, when he did not have to!"

"He must be a namby-pamby spy," gasped Mr Brown, "sent by those who want to destroy us!"

"There might be other places," said the History master, "scattered here and there, behind high walls, down long-forgotten lanes? The Tudors did that sort of stuff while awaiting the return of the king."

"Perhaps," said Mr Tebbit, "history should end when Churchill was prime minister."

"Yes, yes," said the History master, "and begin a bit earlier, perhaps when Ethelready burned the cakes in…Saxon times, I think. You only got kings back then, the first queen was Jane in 1553, and she was beheaded after nine days."

"Off with her head," mumbled Mr Cranmore, "yes, yes, off with her head!"

Mr Tebbit had quite forgotten Mr Cranmore was in the room, but fortunately so had Mr Cranmore, his brain having drifted away to a dark planet. Very slowly, he rose from his armchair.

"As to the spies within…" he said. Then he gave Mr Tebbit a slight nod, and walked into the night…

And Mr Tebbit knew from that moment he was now the real headmaster, with Mr Cranmore becoming the feeble old man who rarely left his room. The governors would not interfere, because someone from the outside might not understand the financial arrangements associated with the work-experience lessons. Nor was there any need to tell the council, at least not until he had got the home running with perfect discipline. Then they would kneel before him, fully understanding that he was the Vanquisher of Disobedience.

THREE

Mr Tebbit needed to take a pee. Throughout his teenage years such events were like breathing; they just happened as the need arose. Now, well established in middle age, the activity made him feel vulnerable, especially since their fat matron had started spying on him. If she saw his exposed manhood, there was no saying how her lustful thoughts might develop.

Deciding to play it safe, he hurried along the lakeside walk towards the thin strip of woodland that descended the hillside towards the bog. Once there, he scrambled up from the path towards a great oak tree, where he looked in all directions to make sure Matron was not hiding in the bushes, because once started, you could not simply put it away without getting wet trousers.

After a few minutes, he decided it was safe, and looked down to watch a trickle of wee dribbling down the rough bark. It was only after he shook away the final drops, that he became aware of a faint 'brm-brrr' sound drifting about on the breeze. Slowly his walking cane pointed up the hill. 'Boy flesh,' it seemed to say, 'let me taste the boy flesh…'

Mr Tebbit showed no emotion, he never did; not since reading the Namby-Pamby Act of 1967, the shock of which had caused his face to set into a permanent expression of strict authority. The boys knew that when he dabbed the side of his nose with a white handkerchief, he was feeling mildly displeased, but mostly he expressed his emotion with a cane, of which a wide selection hung on his study wall. This morning he had been in a dark mood, so carried the 'Savage Beast' – a rod of great craftsmanship that he had rescued from a second-hand shop twenty years before. It was ebony, with a tiny ivory insert in the crook, stating '*Upper Thomas Street School 1898*'. This stick had been teaching discipline when Queen Victoria had been on the throne, a time when fit, healthy boys left school ready to serve the Empire.

Mr Tebbit looked to see where the Savage Beast was pointing. It seemed most uncivilised, with slippery grass and rotting leaves blown against untidy brambles. Probably much the same as it had been twenty years before, but he had long since given up wild walking, and any search would now require a prefect to do the flushing-out. Oh, let the Neanderthal boy continue his foolish existence. But the Savage Beast was having none of it. Furiously, it stabbed the air, sadly still in the direction of the hill. It then planted itself firmly on the first grassy step, and refused to move.

'We can do this thing,' it said. 'The disobedience needs correction.'

With the Savage Beast leading the way, Mr Tebbit reluctantly stumbled fifty paces up the hill, where he steadied himself against a tree. Having recovered his breath, he looked left to discover a tangle of brambles surrounding a shallow hollow, at the bottom of which patches of mud and water loosely joined together as a stream. Something moved; sitting in one of the puddles was a boy, his back hunched over a fallen tree, along which he was pulling a rusty toy car.

"Screeccchhh," said the boy as the car met a lorry he was pulling with his other hand.

That boy, thought Mr Tebbit, *is just not normal.* He often thought this about the under tens, but today it seemed to have a special relevance. That boy was the place in the universe where disobedience and insanity came together in a perfect storm. Such a boy could only be number thirty-seven.

Number thirty-seven had been trouble from the day he arrived, found just inside the barrier, clutching a paper bag and wrapped in a strange newspaper. Every page seemed to have a girl exposing her modifications, and why on Earth would people want to know a lady from Bristol liked to do her housework wearing just her underpants? Mr Tebbit had taken the pornographic 'blankets' straight to the incinerator, then went to find Matron, who had been especially trained to deal with ugly babies.

On their return, they discovered the baby had removed a toy car from the paper bag, and now gurgled away as it chewed on a wheel. Only when Matron tried to take the car away, did it make a most displeasing howl, causing her to make stupid noises while patting the baby on the head.

Astonishing, Mr Tebbit had thought. *She is presented with a colostomy bag that will require emptying for the next two years, and all she can say is 'choo-choo-chubby cheeks!'*

That afternoon, Matron had guessed his age at ten months, tagged him number thirty-seven and, like all other unspecified arrivals, called him David after her favourite Bible story. But, as the months went by, muscles eluded him, so the other boys came to call him Scrag. By his fifth year this became reinforced by his terror of snapping scissors. As soon as Matron put the pudding bowl on his head, he screamed and wriggled with such determination that it invariably slipped, to leave his haircuts lopsided with scraggy bits. But the most obnoxious thing about the boy was his general stupidity. Like last week, his daily chore had been to sweep the dormitory before lessons, yet he was found two hours later standing on a chair to sweep the ceiling, carefully collecting the spiders into a little box. When Matron arrived at the scene of disobedience, she placed her hands on her hips, and actually laughed.

"But I did ask David to sweep the dormitory," she said, "which is exactly what he is doing."

Mr Tebbit had wanted to tell her that she was a raving namby-pamby extremist, but his strict authority seemed less impressive in the presence of a twenty-stone woman. He looked at the same child now.

"Fox!" he boomed.

'Fox and Hounds' was a game he played quite often, with himself using a stopwatch to record how long it took the 'fox' – a boy – to get from its place of discovery to the nearest section of the out-of-bounds fence. For every minute, or part thereof, he would give one stroke of the cane. Sometimes the prefects joined in, trying to stop the 'fox' and sit on its head until they had counted six minutes. They would then shout, "British bulldog, six, six, six!"

As Mr Tebbit looked at number thirty-seven sitting in the mud, he came to realise that, from his current position, there was no way an under ten could reach the fence in six minutes. This meant the game would be void, and could therefore be replayed every Friday night for many years to come. Such entertainment would be a useful way of persuading normal boys not to increase their out-of-bounds activity beyond a distance that their physical ability sensibly allowed.

"The Savage Beast wants to be your friend," said Mr Tebbit presently, "to taste your blood. Would you like that, eh, to be friends?"

The Savage Beast gave a nervous twitch. 'Mud,' it whimpered, 'too much mud.'

Mr Tebbit nodded. Caning the boy anywhere on the body would send up great dollops of the stuff. He looked at the Savage Beast.

"Perhaps we should give him a good scrub-down in the yard first," he said. "Use a hose pipe and long-handled broom."

He would call it an 'elephant wash', and the boy could bend over with one arm pretending to be a trunk, the other, a tail. He would have to get some prefects to do it, because Matron was quite likely to leap from her hiding place to spout some nonsense about an 'elephant wash' being illegal.

The sight of number thirty-seven sitting in the puddle was so disagreeable, that the picture faded from his mind; all he could see now was the Savage Beast slicing into cold white skin, as it would after his 'elephant wash'. Then he had a brilliant idea: the insanity of number thirty-seven was no greater than the boy who, twenty years before, had put his fingers through the fence to actually touch a girl. Yet, after three nights down the air-raid shelter, just showing him a pink card made him leap backwards. Pushing the card closer to his face had made him scream in terror. "Smash her in the face with a brick!" he would shout over and over again. His brain had been completely re-educated. Mr Tebbit realised number thirty-seven was not beyond redemption; the only question was, could the necessary work be done without Matron finding out? All he needed was seventy-two hours down the air-raid shelter...

Without warning, Mr Tebbit's thoughts were interrupted by something quite astonishing: number thirty-seven had collected his cars in a carrier bag, and was now slithering on his tummy beneath the brambles. All the boys knew the 'fox' could not begin its run until after the master of the hunt had set the stopwatch. Surely not even this specimen was stupid enough to think he could walk halfway up the hill, before shouting back "You can start now!"

Fortunately, the Savage Beast had quick reactions and, as the boy emerged from the undergrowth, it swivelled around to hook his neck. But the stick must have gone into dog excrement when climbing the hill, for Mr Tebbit now stared at smelly brown goo oozing between his fingers. In complete panic, he grabbed the boy's sticky-out ear to turn him around, the other sticky-out ear being covered by his lopsided hair.

"Your jumper," he boomed, "give it to me now!"

But the boy just looked down at the stick beneath his chin. Frustrated by the boy's stupidity, Mr Tebbit wrestled the jumper from him, then used it to wipe his hand, which became increasingly covered in mud.

"Your shirt," he boomed, "and no more tricks!"

Unlike the jumper, which had many repairs in its dark material, the shirt was theoretically white, and you could see a clean bit near the shoulders. Mr Tebbit used this to wipe his hand then, thinking more rationally, took the boy's vest to polish the Savage Beast. The gentle rubbing always gave him pleasure, and some time passed before he looked up to notice the boy's bedspring ribcage was shivering. From beneath his short trousers, two scraggy legs trembled with the extra weight of goose pimples. Strangely, he seemed to be missing one sock. Tears trickled down his ash-white cheeks, and his lips were quivering in a most horrible, girlie way.

"What a cry baby you are," Mr Tebbit taunted. "I do believe you are turning into a girl. Shall we send you to the other side of the lake, so you can wear a pink ballet dress and play with dolls all day?"

But the insolent boy was not listening. Though his face looked up, his deceitful eyes were actually focused down on the bag of rusty toy cars, cast aside during the struggle to remove his jumper. Mr Tebbit stabbed the bag with the Savage Beast, then marched back down to the lakeside path, where he gave the stick a good swish. The bag flew off to land in the middle of the lake with a great splash. Soon, all that remained were a few bubbles. Then, to Mr Tebbit's astonishment, there was a much greater splash: the boy had dived in after them.

Mr Tebbit realised such an extreme level of disobedience would need to be corrected down the air-raid shelter, without Matron finding out. But annoyingly the boy did not re-surface. Could it be that the disobedient child was about to drown? He looked down at his fine tweed jacket, neatly pressed trousers and highly polished shoes. It was an outrage; a master could hardly be expected to strip to his underpants. He turned to walk away, then remembered the birdwatchers hiding in the bushes, and Matron, or the English master, who frequently ran around the hillside, as if he were training for the Olympics. He was surrounded by spies; he had no choice but to wade into the lake to a depth commensurate with any namby-pamby forms he would be expected to fill in. This happened about halfway across. There he stopped, lifted up the flaps of his jacket, and peered into the depths ahead. Then his tummy got cold and, looking down, he discovered that the water had risen halfway up his nicely ironed shirt.

David knew grown-ups thought him to be a clumsy child with a strange haircut, but it was all part of his clever disguise. Secretly, he was a superhero known as 'The Seal'. He had realised this after the older boys had thrown him into the lake for a game of 'Fireman'. This was something they played quite often but, on this occasion, a magic force had arrived from his home planet, giving him the power to swim underwater. Thus, he popped up some distance along the shore, to climb the bank unseen.

The Seal was born!

After that, his greatest challenge was not letting the others know how much he enjoyed it, because it was the only time they ever wanted to play with him. It seemed they never tired of running along the bank with sticks to try to stop him climbing back out, while he would twist, turn, and generally outwit the evil ones who wanted to destroy the universe. How he laughed at those who won breath-holding competitions at a mere thirty-five seconds. Sitting on the quiet hillside, he could sometimes count to eighty-six, but today, as he swam through the murky depths, he knew he could do better. If he did not, his cars would sink into the gooey mud forever and, truth was, they were made of 'Sealonite', a special metal that could only be found on his home planet. Then he saw the bubbles and, finding the bag, felt about for any cars that had fallen out. Only after his fingers had collected every one, did he reach up with his free hand, and gratefully break the surface to gasp for air. Then he stared in astonishment, because no more than ten feet away, Mr Tebbit was staring back.

David was amazed to discover that Mr Tebbit went swimming in his hat – the silly one, with a feather glued to the side. It looked so funny that he could not help laughing. Then he did the only sensible thing he could think of: he put the bag between his teeth, and swam like mad towards the far bank. Here, he reached up to grab an overhanging branch, along which he squirrelled to cross the mud on which you could not walk.

All superheroes needed a secret headquarters. His was hidden in the forbidden forest; the space aliens that lived in the deep, dark centre did not frighten him too much, because he also came from a different planet. Also, the forest creatures always made such a horrible, squeaky noise when they went places, it was quite easy for The Seal to plop back into the water and disappear. It was thus, he dropped from the branch, and raced along secret tracks that only he knew. Then he lay on his tummy to wriggle beneath the undergrowth, emerging in a clearing surrounded by dense vegetation. To one side lay a tangle of branches, and he pulled these apart to crawl into his secret headquarters. Sitting on the warm leafy floor, he gave a shivery laugh. The shock of almost losing his cars was over; now all he thought about was how funny Mr Tebbit had looked going swimming in his silly hat.

Taking the cars from the bag, he carefully inspected them for damage, then brushed away some leaves from the floor, to uncover a broken plank, beneath which was a very secret hole. It contained a hessian sack that had once belonged to a pirate, who had crossed the seven seas in an old sailing ship. But now, it contained his treasure, including seven marbles, three dinosaurs and, sitting on top to guard it all, a rubber grass snake. He drove the cars down the sides of the hole, then covered them with the sack. Only when everything was hidden under a pile of leaves, did he notice a faint cry for help echoing through the forest.

He left his den, and followed the noise until, peeping out from the bushes, he saw that Mr Tebbit was still swimming in the lake. Now all that remained above the surface was his face, and floating nearby, his hat. Grown-ups lived in such a strange world, he never knew what to make of it, or what they wanted him to do. Then he saw Matron standing on the far path.

"Get the fire brigade," she was saying, but not very loudly. A few older boys emerged from their hiding places to stand beside her, but nobody actually ran back up the hill to get the fire brigade. Of course, they were playing the Fireman game! Now everything made perfect sense. David took two socks from his pocket, and put them on his hands to disguise the fact they were turning into flippers. Then he brushed his hair to the other side to become The Seal.

The Seal could do things much faster than humans, and soon he was swimming across the lake with a blue plastic rope coiled over his shoulder. Then he stopped to tread water. Mr Tebbit looked very strange; his face seemed all teeth, so it was difficult to tell if he was smiling, or wanted to play 'Crocodiles'. Not wishing to get any closer, David swam to the walking stick floating nearby, and tied the rope to that – a difficult thing to do with flippers. But, after making the correct number of 'oink' noises, a knot eventually formed. Then he pushed the stick towards Mr Tebbit, and swam back to the bank. What happened next was really good: Mr Tebbit wanted to play 'Tug of War'.

Across the water, everybody began to run around the lake until the boys skidded to a halt by a wooden jetty. This projected about ten feet from the bank, a few blackened stumps beyond indicating where the boardwalk had once crossed the bog, until it had been blown up by three mysterious night-time explosions back in the 1960s. However, the official-looking cast-iron sign over the entrance was still there, only now turned at ninety degrees to face the path. In raised black letters it stated: '*Any boy proceeding beyond this point will be flogged*'. Fear, inbred over many years, kept the boys' feet rooted to the ground. But there was something else, something they found difficult to put into words. Then Zak, a boy who Mr Tebbit liked to cane at least twice a week, held out a leathery palm.

"Two," he said, "times fifty-two, equals 104. Multiply that by six…that's how many times I'm going to punch anyone in the face who tries to pass."

The other boys began to mill around, working out their own mathematics.

"Three hundred and seventy-eight," said one of them. "That's how many times he's caned me."

"That's not so many as two times fifty-two, times six," said Zak.

It was finally agreed that Zak would always be number one, due to the water now lapping Mr Tebbit's shoulders. Then one of the boys noticed Matron running along the path above the quarry.

"Don't know where she's going," he said, "but wherever it is, the less help she gets the better."

Matron had been given a spare set of keys to the girls' home after the great hockey stick battle of 1968, the scale of the injuries scattered about the pitch having completely overwhelmed their own medical resources. Since that time, it was understood that Matron of the boys' home was available to help out with any serious medical emergencies that might arise across the lane.

On reaching the bottom of Bad Man Lane, Matron ran up the hill towards the girls' entrance. Here she fumbled with her bunch of keys, then onwards, into a world where no male doctor could ever go.

Back at the lake, the boys were quite excited by the prospect of seeing Mr Tebbit's face disappear below the surface of the water. Then they noticed Scrag, high in the tree tops, hanging onto a rope, feet kicking in space. Slowly, Mr Tebbit rose from the water, as Scrag began to descend.

"Bugger," cried Zak, "he's got a rope looped over the branch!"

Mr Tebbit, on the downside of the pulley system, finally cleared the mud, and began to travel through the water like a turbo-charged fish. Scrag, the most hated boy in the universe, was reaping his terrible revenge.

As soon as David dropped to the ground, he pulled the rope with all his strength, until Mr Tebbit slithered onto the muddy bank. There was a long silence until a breathless Matron came running along the path.

"Boy," she spluttered, "brave, brave boy!"

Mr Tebbit lunged clumsily through the mud. The Savage Beast was demanding boy flesh, to be bathed in blood, as in the days of Queen Victoria. It sliced deep into the back of David's legs.

"Mr Tebbit," yelled Matron, "what on Earth are you doing? This boy is a hero!"

Mr Tebbit flicked the cane behind his back for a second swish. Matron saw what he intended to do, and pushed his chest, catching him off balance so that he toppled backwards to land in the mud with his arms outstretched.

David thought it had been the best game of Fireman ever, but now he did not understand what was happening. Mr Tebbit was pretending to be a prehistoric fish with bulging eyes, struggling to escape the swamp. He was trying to say something, but it was difficult to tell what because a great dollop of mud oozed into his mouth. Then David noticed Matron staring at her muddy hands. He knew what was coming next; she was very frightened of mud, so he ran into the forest, before he could be undressed further.

Twenty yards along the path the leaves closed over a pair of bright blue eyes. "Mmm," whispered the bush.

*

Back at his headquarters, David played a really good game of Fireman in his head, only this time there were crocodiles, and he had to prop their mouths open with Mr Tebbit's stick so they could not eat him. Suddenly, there came a terrible noise; it was them, the things that lived in the middle of the forest. His bravery vanished with the reality of a pink, bony hand crawling towards him on spidery fingers. Soon it would emerge from the undergrowth to grab his ankle, and drag him to the dark place. He took flight, the unimaginable horror getting ever closer; now all that mattered was reaching a wide open space where daylight would make the creatures cower backwards, shielding their faces.

It was a different bush, on a peninsula of land near the dam, but the eyes were the same. Curiously, they watched the ripples spread across the lake. Time passed, then some more ripples as a nose appeared some distance from the shore. It seemed to sniff the air then, all of a sudden, there was a great cascade of water from which a boy magically appeared. He seemed to be climbing onto something, because the next moment the water only came up to his knees.

The eyes in the bush grew a lot wider; far from being frightened by his situation, the boy carefully adjusted his hair. Then he splashed carelessly to the middle of the lake, where he turned towards the dam. Here, he stepped to a fallen block, and reached across to a pipe that took the water away. He crawled into this, and disappeared.

"How very curious," said the bush.

*

David's second best subject, after being The Seal, was climbing the out-of- bounds fence. If a master turned his back for five seconds, he could be over the top and standing dead-still on the playing field to innocently gaze up at a cloud. After his reappearance, they would sometimes walk towards him, and even though the fence was still shaking, he only had to say, "It looks like a camel holding a balloon," and they would walk away shaking their heads.

On this occasion, David was distracted from his cloud-gazing by a great stampede of boys heading towards him. The first to arrive punched him on the nose, and the second pushed him to the ground so the others could kick him. Only his head was spared, due to an infant who knelt over him to bite his ear. After everybody had taken their turn, he was picked up, and hurled against the fence. He vaguely saw Zak's outraged face shouting a lot of numbers, but mostly he saw fists. Then David found his neck grabbed by a senior prefect named Morris.

"Back off," he shouted. "Don't want fatty Matron putting him in sickbay where I can't get to him. This one's mine!"

Of one accord, the boys took a step backwards. Senior prefects could administer punishment any way they wanted, and it was silently understood that one day Morris would get too carried away, and be tried for murder.

"Anyway," said Morris to his gang of four, "head wants to see him now, to give him his teacher's pet medal, I expect."

David became vaguely aware of a bouncing sensation, until Mr Cranmore's study door loomed up before him. A moment later, just on the verge of fainting, he was left to stand before a desk.

"He's been climbing trees again," said a voice beside him. "Must have fallen out, isn't that right, Scrag?"

After the boys had gone, David noticed Mr Tebbit sitting on a side chair. He looked very odd, his face twitching as his hands fumbled with three canes on his lap. They had German names, but David knew them as 'The Ride of the Valeries' because it was easier to say.

"*Schlecht, Junge,*" spluttered Mr Tebbit. "*Mutter eine Hexe.*"

Mr Cranmore took a standard-issue cane from the back wall, handed it to Mr Tebbit, then prised 'The Ride of the Valeries' away.

"It's the thirty-inch Dragon Smoky Malacca," he said. "You like those."

But Mr Tebbit seemed lost in a world of his own, and merely stared blankly at what he had been given.

Mr Cranmore turned back to David. "So," he said, "Mr Tebbit informs me that you were in the boating lake this morning, screaming that you couldn't swim, and when he came to save you, you laughed, then swam away, making 'oink' noises."

David froze in terror. Mr Tebbit had seen through his disguise; knew he was The Seal, and would now tell the evil ones, who wanted to destroy the universe. They would beat him up forever and ever because they did not like boys with superpowers.

"He needs to be flogged!" exploded Mr Tebbit. "We could hang the Devil child from the rafters. I'll put a bucket underneath to stop the blood dripping on your carpet. I still have a cat-o'-nine-tails, and a special licence from the Government to use it."

Hearing that Mr Tebbit had a special licence from the Government to use the cat-o'-nine-tails was enough to make David's legs give way, and he crumpled onto the carpet. Above him the voices went on.

"Have you any idea why he is only wearing his shorts?" asked Mr Cranmore. "You know how Matron fusses."

"For his swimming, I expect. I bet you never wore girlie vests in the trenches."

"You would have to ask my father. But the boy, I don't understand why he went swimming in February."

"Because he's not normal; because it was the Devil himself who dumped him at our gate. Quite an embarrassment to any parent, I expect."

David could not remember being in this much trouble before. Mr Tebbit was going to use the cat-o'-nine-tails, and 155 boys were all waiting outside to beat him up. The time had come to run away – now, before any more pain arrived. Slowly, he struggled to his feet, then staggered about the room in seemingly aimless circles. But each stagger took him closer to the open window, where he pretended to lean against the sill for support. Having got his bearings, he dropped his belly onto the ledge and somersaulted onto the grass below. The fear of the cat-o'-nine-tails made him scamper away, straight through some flowers, then up the side of the caretaker's shed. Once on the roof, he looked back to see what was chasing him.

Mr Cranmore was staring out of the window, apparently quite unable to believe how easy it was to make a path through a lot of flowers. Mr Tebbit was trying to push past him, and had managed to get one leg out of the window, but seemed to have his trousers caught on the prong that held the latch in place. There was blood running from his nose, probably because it had got in the way of his somersaulting feet. David turned, ran along the roof, and leapt clean over the fence, to land in the undergrowth beyond. Not an out-of-bounds he knew, but it seemed far better than the place he had just left.

*

Matron watched Mr Tebbit running down the corridor, his uncoordinated snorts squirting blood across the front of his shirt. He looked exactly like a murderer might look just before committing one of his foul deeds. Fortunately, his overhanging belly did not take well to running, so he was relatively easy to follow to the lower playing field, then to the line of trees and bushes that separated it from the top. From here, she watched Mr Tebbit running around the outside of the fence.

How irresponsible; he had left the staff gate open with his keys dangling in the lock. The under tens could easily wander down to play near the water, into which they would surely fall, and pick up some terrible disease. She went to lock the gate, and put the keys in her pocket. Then she saw a line of splashes making their way across the lake, made by a boy swimming at such speed, he obviously thought a crocodile was chasing him. Strangely, he was heading towards the far bank. The only way out of there was through the girls' home, or by swimming back.

It was not a sight a matron should ever have to see, but she forced herself to watch until he was out of the nasty water. He was too far away to identify properly but, since he was only wearing shorts and one sock, it seemed reasonable to assume it was David. Next, she turned to look towards Mr Tebbit's last-known location, which appeared to be in the general direction of the lowlands. She felt certain that in some strange way it was connected to David, who had now disappeared into the woods opposite.

Matron hurried back to Mr Cranmore's study, which she entered without knocking. Fortunately, Mr Cranmore was outside, and too busy talking to his daffodils to notice her arrival. She turned to the large-scale map on the wall. This told her the peninsula of land down which Mr Tebbit was running became increasingly narrow, disappearing into bog after about a mile. Hopefully, this would be Mr Tebbit's fate also. She frowned; men disappearing into swamps were not the sort of thoughts a State Registered Nurse should be having. Then another thought popped into her mind: *Exceptional boys sometimes need exceptional solutions.* She decided to call Mr Tebbit's swamp disappearance, plan 'A'.

The map also told her that a pony track descended the girls' hillside to become a wavy line, which somehow found its way through the swamp to reach the first lowland village of Little Morton. No, that could not be right; Miss Buckley would never allow such a thing. A second glance explained everything: the map had been printed in 1938. Whatever Mr Tebbit thought he was doing took no account of anything that might have happened since the war.

Matron decided that a situation like this required some seriously exceptional thinking, which could best be done across the lake, where she might find David.

*

As soon as David knew he was safe in the forbidden forest, his various recent beatings caught up with him, making him so dizzy that he needed to sit on a log to have a good think. Presently, he began to nod; what he needed to do was hide until it got dark, then escape, walking only at night. After travelling for many days, he would sit on a doorstep with his sack of cars, and wait for some new grown-ups to find him. If they asked where he had come from, he would say nowhere. Ah…but his clothes all had numbers sewn into them. He got up and went to a little jetty, where he pulled up a rotten plank with a rusty nail sticking out from one end. Fortunately, he only had three items to deal with. Unpicking the number from his shorts took ages and, by the time he had finished the sock, he was shivering with cold. He never saw the point of underpants anyway, so threw them into the bushes. Then he went to climb his favourite trees, for the last time, before it got dark, when he would begin his escape to faraway places.

*

A little later, Matron arrived at the same jetty where a rusty sign told her that: '*Any girl proceeding beyond this point will be sent to live with the nuns*'. Slowly, the memories of twenty-five years before re-formed in her mind...Back then, the jetty had been the start of a boardwalk along which the birdwatchers would often run in pursuit of whatever it was they were trying to achieve. Matron visualised herself as a thin young woman walking across it to take tea with the previous matron of the girls' home. Once, she had even managed to persuade a group of girls to stick out their tongues and waggle fingers towards the funny-looking man jumping up and down on the other bank.

"If you listen carefully," she had whispered, while hiding in the bushes, "you will hear him snort."

For a time, seeing who could get him to snort the loudest became an accepted way to spend an odd half-hour. And what was she now? A 'slightly' overweight, middle-aged woman gazing to where the boardwalk had once been. Even after the first, relatively minor explosion of 1962, she had managed to balance across the scaffolding planks the birdwatchers had lashed over the gap in the middle. Arms outstretched, giggling...Yes, there she was, free to come and go as she pleased, without Mr Cranmore finding out. The second explosion had made the crossing impossible, and the third, at two o'clock in the morning, had sent planks flying into tree tops 600 feet away. The following morning, Mr Cranmore had come to look at the result, nodding quietly to himself in satisfaction.

Back then, even Mr Tebbit had been easier to deal with. Of course, she knew he had modified detention to resemble a forced-labour camp, but all she saw was healthy boys with great big muscles. As to incubating their sense of social responsibility, she often thought about it as she walked towards the boardwalk along neat gravel paths. *My boys did this*, she would think, *the little ones carrying small stones in buckets, the older ones rocks that a full-grown builder could not have managed without cursing.* But her boys did not know any bad words, thanks to the English master with his eye for detail, and careful use of scissors.

More recently, Matron remembered the wonderful time when her boys had built the concrete wall around her prefab. It had been lovely sitting in a deckchair to watch all the muscles rippling in the sunshine. "Now there's a fine wall," she would shout to the Games master, "that's never going to move!"

At first, she had only intended to adjust the stakes by a few feet, so as to put a washing line between the wall and her prefab, but then she remembered the boys saying the Games master was practically blind when it came to refereeing football matches. Most probably, he did not want to make his weedy image even worse by wearing goggle glasses, so she had measured a tennis court with her feet, and moved the stakes accordingly. Soon, the boys were sloshing concrete everywhere and, whenever a section of wall was completed, she got up to hang a wrought-iron basket on one of the spikes. Of course, she knew they had been made in their own metalwork shop, but had bought them from the hardware store, just to keep everything in good order. After hanging a basket, she would fill it with earth that had been dug out to make the foundations. "Now, which of you boys would like to help me to choose the flowers?" she would ask. They would blush and pretend not to hear.

Teasing was not something she normally did, but was just so happy that the boxing gym had been postponed to pay for her wall. To her, every bag of cement represented one less boxing glove smashing into a boy's face. Of course, there would still be boxing, but only with benches pulled around to make a temporary ring in the general gym. Here, the masters never knew when she might turn up, and it was generally possible to enforce the no-under-eights rule. Down the air-raid shelter, she felt certain the weakest boy would be pinned to the ropes, the prefects crowding around, screaming for more blood.

As the project had continued, she came to marvel at the way a fixed idea in the Games master's brain had set like concrete, as permanent as the structure he was building on land. Only towards the end did his face show moments of doubt, and it was not until there was just a brown patch of grass where the materials had been, that he finally accepted the truth – the wall was only half complete and, repeatedly looking around corners, would not make any more cement materialise.

"Now, there's a mighty fine wall," she had called across. "Don't it just hang my baskets lovely."

Then the boys had fallen about laughing, so she had taken them homemade lemonade and apple pie.

Sadly, after the wall had eventually been completed, a terrified boy could no longer tap nervously on her prefab door late at night, however serious his injury or general misfortune. Also, the previous construction of the new masters' block meant the residents no longer remained within the general cluster of buildings at night. Without exception, they left the dining room after tea, and were not seen again until breakfast the following morning. Between these hours, the running of the home was left to the prefects – a system similar to that of the girls' home. But all their appointments were made by Miss Buckley, who frequently began her sentences with the phrase "Jesus has told me that he wants…Bla, bla, bla…" As a result, girl prefects vaguely fitted in with something good she had read about in the Bible. On the other hand, boy prefects were ranked entirely on their ability in the boxing ring. This brought order, in the sense that disputes never escalated beyond the weaker having a quiet grumble, since continuing the disagreement would only mean being humiliated in the ring. Then came Morris, who loved fighting, particularly older boys, the demolition of whom gave him a status far beyond his years. When Morris reached the age of thirteen, Mr Tebbit had entered him for the big match. It was all the boys talked about for the preceding week – the masters also – and somehow the governors got to hear about it because, on the day of the match, the drive was lined with expensive-looking cars. Matron had no interest in watching such things, but made a point of staying in her surgery, waiting for Morris to be carried in on a stretcher, his opponent being well into puberty with muscles to match. Then her nose began to twitch and, looking out of her back window, she saw an overweight man emerging from a Rolls-Royce, clouds of smoke rising from an equally overweight cigar. Blocking his advance was Mr Tebbit, a slight bow bringing his nose closer to the man's chest.

Boxing matches were always based on the original rules: namely a fight was never stopped until somebody got 'knocked out'. In practice, this meant the weaker pretending to be knocked out, and lying on the floor until the ten seconds were counted. It established a pecking order, and reluctantly she had to agree it meant wild scraps rarely happened. But the match with Morris was to prove different; even after the adult-sized boxing gloves had been smashing into his face for two hours, he refused to lie down. Then, slowly, the prefect's arms became fatigued. Morris did not waste any time exploiting the weakness, hitting back with such force that his opponent's white skin became a bruised canvas of blood.

But, the rules of boyhood meant a fifteen-year-old could not be beaten by somebody so much younger. Only after three hours did the laws of biology take over, the brain of the older becoming unconscious, leaving the body to fall over. Ten minutes later, the old number one was carried into her surgery, nose smashed to one side, eyes completely closed by the puffed-up flesh that had once represented his face. On leaving the surgery, five days later, he was allocated the slot of number ten prefect, Mr Tebbit telling the other boys he was a delicate child who should not be exposed to rough games. To emphasise this, Mr Tebbit gave him a pink cane that he had to carry at all times to warn 'normal' boys not to get too close. The message was simple: you did not mess with Morris, who was now Mr Tebbit's personal property.

And that is when it had finally gone wrong, when Mr Tebbit found himself commander-in-chief of a ruthless organisation, a situation that seemed to make him believe he was God. Then, today, his insanity finally manifested itself in a belief that, as God, he would have the power to walk across water.

Thinking of Mr Tebbit's increasing insanity allowed Matron to reach the necessary, exceptional decision: she would sneak David into her compound under cover of darkness and, for the time being, keep his whereabouts secret. All she had to do was find him first…

Then she noticed the underpants thrown into the bushes; the monster had taken his pleasure, and thrown the body into the bog. But he had become careless with the underpants.

But, even if she managed to persuade the fire service to dig David out of the bog, the monster would still get away with it. The boy had been seen swimming in the lake, so they would not be surprised by the gruesome discovery. Her television was always going on about the dangers of wild swimming.

*

After David had climbed all his favourite trees, he felt a lot warmer and generally much happier, now he no longer had a number sewn into his clothes that would allow the grown-ups to send him back to be flogged. Then, just as it was starting to get dark, he returned to his secret headquarters to collect his treasure sack. Halfway through the entrance, he came to a sudden halt. A space alien was sitting cross-legged on the floor, looking at his toy cars.

"Urk," it said, "you're all wet…and smelly!"

David could do nothing but stare, unable to believe how horrible it was.

"I expect you've been swimming again," it said. "Is this your changing room?" The thing squeaked a horrible giggle. "You can change if you want to," it said. "I promise not to look. See, I'm playing with your cars."

A Ford Escort careered across the floor and crashed into a lorry.

"Whoops," it said, "and here comes the ambulance. Is this how you play with cars? I'm not quite certain."

David looked at the horrendous accident; the thing

obviously didn't know how to drive an ambulance. It was making a noise that sounded more like a donkey.

"Mine," he said, trying to snatch it away.

The thing took his hand and began shaking it. "I'm Mandy," it said. "How do you do."

The thing couldn't even talk sensibly.

"You can kiss my hand, if you like," it said.

The thing made a move to punch him on the nose, from which he only just managed to back away.

"My den," he managed to stammer.

"I know, I was watching you in the lake this morning, and saw you run into the woods carrying a bag. You came back without one, so I knew you had a den, in my woods – the cheek of it. But, if you like, it can be our den, then I can bring my tea service, and we can play 'Mothers and Fathers.'"

The Mandy-thing held out its free hand to show him a wooden peg. It had a face painted at the top, and a handkerchief wrapped around the bottom. The thing put the peg to its ear.

"Pegatha says she is very pleased to meet you," said the Mandy-thing. "Pegatha says you can hold her, if you want?"

It was the most frightening thing that had ever happened to him. He made a fist with his free hand, and stuck the thumb into his mouth.

"Pegatha is very upset," said the Mandy-thing. "If you want to be her friend, now you will have to give her a kiss."

The Mandy-thing opened its eyes wide, then turned to the peg.

"Naughty Pegatha," it said.

The Mandy-thing turned back to him. "She grew up with the gypsies," it said, "and knows the ways of magic. When a boy kisses her, she will turn into a princess, then she would want to live with you, and I would be left all alone. But you can kiss me instead, and I can tell her what it is like."

The Mandy-thing looked at him for a long time before saying, "Huh," as if it was annoyed about something. Then it let go of his hand and looked at his treasure sack.

"I wonder what you have in here?" it said.

The Mandy-thing plunged its fist inside, only to take it straight back out with an ear-piercing scream. As it opened its fingers, the rubber grass snake continued upwards, bouncing off the bush ceiling to land in its hair. Shrieking hysterically, the thing leapt forwards, knocking him flat on his back. Knees and elbows sunk into his body as it clambered over him to the exit. Once in the clearing, it made grasping movements towards its head. The snake came out and, after a short flight, bounced into the undergrowth. The Mandy-thing then closed its eyes, waved its arms about, and screamed until it was empty of air.

Suddenly, there came a great crashing through the undergrowth, and Mr Tebbit burst into the clearing.

"Filthy, disgusting, Devil child!" he yelled.

David found himself dragged out of the den, then twisted around until he was upside down, with Mr Tebbit's knee pushing into his tummy. A moment later, a stick began to slice into the back of his legs.

Mandy stopped screaming to look in horror at the beating that was taking place before her eyes. She realised the attacker was the strange man she had seen earlier, taking a bath in the lake. Letting out her loudest tonsil-waving scream ever, she dived forwards to grab the man's hair, using it to swing her feet off the ground.

Mr Tebbit forgot all about the boy. Never had he known such pain. He staggered backwards, his hair being pulled out by the roots. Then, realising a Devil child was responsible for the pain, he used the crook of his stick to fish her over his shoulder. Now she was upside down, the pain left his hair, but a set of teeth sank into his hand, while nails clawed across his face. It was like wrestling a wriggling tiger cub. He dropped his walking stick, grabbed the girl's leg, and spun around to make her fly outwards. It confused her enough to stop biting his hand. Then his overwhelming strength took over and, spinning faster, he sent her flying into a great mass of brambles.

Mandy looked up from her bed of thorns to see the man advancing towards her. He grabbed her ankle and tried to drag her back to the clearing, but the brambles tore into her clothes and twisted about her arms.

"You evil child!" yelled the man. "How dare you attack a master!"

David saw the brambles tearing into the girl's skin. It was completely mad, but he could feel the pain of the thorns in his own flesh, and the girl's sobs seemed to be coming from his own throat. What was happening? His whole body seemed to be taken over by something inexplicable. Then he realised he was turning into The Seal. Why? This had never happened on land before. Perhaps it was because he had recently seen Mr Tebbit slithering from a swamp as a fish monster. Anyway, some special force had arrived from his home planet, making him pick up the stick, and bring it crashing down on the fish monster's head. But the fish monster did not seem to notice, so he put the hook into its mouth, and pulled. Slowly the fish monster's neck twisted around until its bulging eyes were staring down, and once more David felt very small.

Mandy knew she had to break free, and struggled upwards with the thorns slicing her skin. Still trailing bits of vegetation, she ran to the man, kicking him on the back of the legs, until he let go of the boy's throat.

"Run!" she yelled.

For a moment, Mr Tebbit found himself alone and disorientated. Then he saw the two Devils crawling under the vegetation, which would only admit his head, not his shoulders.

*

Matron was still holding the underpants to remind herself of David's passing, when she heard the scream, a girl this time. The monster was about to strike again. She turned to look in the vague direction of the scream.

"Scream again," she whispered.

Then a girl burst from the undergrowth, her clothes dreadfully torn and covered in blood. She was half dragging a boy, easily recognisable as David because he was only wearing one sock.

"My boy!" she cried.

Then the children started to run side by side. She was going to stop them, but Mr Tebbit fought his way from the bushes, advancing in great strides.

"The man in the woods tried to look up my legs!" screamed the girl as she ran by.

Matron let them pass, then braced herself for Mr Tebbit. At the last moment, she moved her considerable weight sideways. She was knocked backwards to sit on the grass, Mr Tebbit veering in the opposite direction, which happened to be the lake. As soon as his feet sank into the gooey mud, he stopped running, to dive face down into the water beyond.

By the time Matron was back on her feet, she realised Mr Tebbit wasn't moving. *How very interesting*, she thought. Given Mr Tebbit's habit of swimming in the lake, who would question such a gruesome discovery? Certainly not the fire brigade; the driver of his earlier rescue had been quite cross at the thought of reversing his engine all the way back up the lane, because there was insufficient room to turn it around. The two men who had carried the dinghy from the top of the quarry, had been even more cross. But this was nothing compared to the commander, who had done the actual rescue. His lecture to the mud-covered man climbing into his clean yellow dinghy could be heard across the lake. Apparently, it was quite dangerous for fat, middle-aged men to do wild swimming. You could almost hear the officer thinking that, if there was a next time, it would be a dead body they would be hauling over the side.

For a few moments, Matron watched Mr Tebbit sinking into the mud. Then she realised this was not just a rather nice fantasy, but something that was actually happening. Reluctantly, she grabbed his feet and dragged him to the path. After clearing the mud from his mouth, he coughed a breath, so she rolled him into the recovery position. Then she stood back to look at him. His trousers were torn to ribbons, while the rest of him was just a great big wobble of mud – a mere extension of the bog. Next, she looked at her own muddy hands, and began hurrying back towards her surgery, where she intended to take a long, hot bath. A moment later, she returned to shove David's underpants in Mr Tebbit's pocket.

If the police got involved, it would be useful if he had some explaining to do, while she worked out what to do next.

*

At first, David was happy to be dragged away from Mr Tebbit, but then realised he was holding hands with a girl, and tried to escape before anybody saw. But she would not let go, and pulled him to a secret track that he thought might go to the dark place.

"Hurry," she screamed, "he's just behind you!"

He tried to look back, but a branch hit the side of his head, and he staggered on, before the Mandy-thing pulled off his arm. Eventually, she ducked into the undergrowth, then scampered through a hole in the fence, to stand up in the bushes beyond.

"Go away," she yelled into the trees. "Don't hit him!"

The fear of Mr Tebbit made David do something extremely silly. He scrambled through the hole to stand beside the Mandy-thing.

"The man won't get through there," she said, "he's too fat."

Then she put a hand over the blood that ran from the slashes on the back of his legs, and smeared it over his body, patting his face just below some embedded tree bark. Taking his hand, she then dragged him to the middle of an open field. Looking about, David saw what he had most feared. He was surrounded by things, hundreds of them, some trying to chase a ball with sticks, others chanting silly rhymes as they jumped over a rope. Then, for the second time that day, he found himself the target for a great stampede, but this time they stopped a few feet away, the ones at the back crashing into the ones at the front.

"The man," gasped the Mandy-thing, "in the woods, tried to look up my skirt!"

The audience took a collective gulp, leaving David terrified that they were filling up with air to do screaming in his ears.

"But this boy saved me," said the Mandy-thing. "He was ever so brave. He nearly died!"

The audience let out a collective sigh. Then one of them reached out to touch him, but the Mandy-thing pushed her away.

"Get off," she said, "he's mine. I found him."

"But you're only eight," said somebody else, "you wouldn't know what to do with him. I'm ten."

The speaker lunged forwards, her mouth like a giant goldfish. David managed to jump sideways, closer to the Mandy-thing, who seemed to be the only one who was trying to protect him. Their shoulders were actually touching, but it wasn't so horrible as being sucked by the goldfish.

"There," said the Mandy-thing, "he likes me better than you, and you're not ten anyway."

Then David heard a whistle, followed by a grown-up's voice. The crowd parted, and before him stood a woman in a PE kit.

Miss Williams, the PE teacher, stared at the blood-splattered girl with the dreadfully torn clothes.

"The man in the woods tried to look up my legs," wailed Mandy. "This boy saved me, he was ever so brave."

"The man," stammered Miss Williams, "did this to one of our girls?"

Then she saw the boy, and the girls had to jump aside as she fainted. At the same time, Mandy limply raised her arms and fell against him, sliding down his body, smearing gooey blood as she went. Once lying across his feet, she secured him with a double ankle lock.

"I'm getting Matron," shouted a voice at the back.

Three or four of the audience broke away to follow; the others just fainted or stood watching, as befitted their mood. Only a group of three girls showed no obvious emotion. They looked at the boy for some time, before pushing their way forwards.

David recognised their attack formation from a picture he had seen in a book about fighting aeroplanes. The thing on the left began to snuffle his arm like a curious pig.

"This one won't take up much room in the cooking pot," it said. "We'll have to put loads of spiders in to get more meat."

The thing on his right poked him in the ribs.

"I'm playing the xylophone," it said, in an ever-more squeaky voice. "Doh, ray, so, fah…whatever."

But it was the one in the middle that filled him with the most terror. It said nothing, just looked at him in a way that said, 'I could turn you into an earthworm if I wanted, then eat you for my tea.' Suddenly, she grabbed his armpits and lifted him skywards. She appeared to do this without effort, even though the Mandy-thing was still hanging onto his shoes. Now her face was close up, he realised that it was the most horrible thing he had ever seen, shaped like an upside-down onion, with eyes so big they could easily belong to a cow.

"We're The Three Musketeers," it said, "and we need a boy to…"

Then her face changed shape, and she looked down at the Mandy-thing.

"You say the man in the woods did this?" she asked.

The Mandy-thing gulped, then nodded.

David found himself returned to the ground.

"Musketeers," said the most fearsome thing, "there is work to be done."

The three of them ran towards the fence, retrieving catapults from their skirt waistbands as they went.

"Till we meet again, my little weed!" shouted back the most horrible.

Then they were gone, and their matron stood before him. He knew this because she wore a white apron but, besides this, she looked nothing at all like a matron. She was thin, not incredibly old, and had a lot of yellow hair sticking out from her white matron's hat. She fell to her knees to look at the Mandy-thing lying across his feet.

"My poor thing," she said, "what happened to you?"

David had that funny feeling in his tummy again. Matron had called her a 'thing'. The others, altogether, yes they were 'things', but to wake up with the words 'get out of bed, thing' must be really horrible.

Mandy turned around to look up. "I'm OK, Mummy," she said, "the man in the woods tried to look up my legs, but this boy saved me, he was ever so brave."

David stood bewildered. Why did the Mandy-girl keep going on about the man trying to look up her legs – they were just legs – and why had she been using both of them to stand, and not doing ballet dancing to get from one place to another? In fact, she looked nothing at all like the model in the art room. Indeed, the only thing that identified her as a space alien was that she could send brain thoughts directly into his own head, making him do strange things like hooking Mr Tebbit in the mouth with a walking stick.

Thinking about Mr Tebbit made David remember why

running away was so important. He looked around for an escape route, but every direction had pink, bony fingers snapping towards him like the claws of a crab. Then the Mandy-girl stood up to look directly at their faces, making them back away, frightened by her magical powers. Subconsciously, he edged towards the Mandy-girl, who responded by putting an arm around his shoulder. He wished she would stop doing strange things, it always got him into bigger trouble. He tried to wriggle free, but the grasp tightened, like one of those knots you could never undo.

Matron got up from her knees. "Follow me, whoever you are," she said. As soon as Matron's back was turned, the Mandy-girl punched the nearest girl on the nose, then took a swing at a second, missing only because they had all leapt back to a safer distance. On hearing the squeals, Matron turned around, but the Mandy-girl was already halfway to passing out.

"I've lost too much blood…" she mumbled.

Matron quickly got both arms underneath the Mandy-girl, and lifted her into a carrying position. Immediately, the Mandy-girl reached back to grab his neck, and David found himself pulled forwards like an unsuspecting railway carriage snatched by a train engine.

He staggered across the lawn until the shadow of a towering stone castle fell upon him. Knowing he was being taken to the dungeons, he tried to look back, but the Mandy-girl grabbing his neck made this too difficult. Then he had to stagger up some wide stone steps, at the top of which Matron turned around to open a huge set of wooden doors with her back. Nobody seemed to worry about what all the pulling was doing to his neck, but as he twisted around, he saw all the snapping claws had given chase and, being lower down the steps, were almost grabbing his legs. Escape did not seem an option.

Once inside the dark place, David found his gaze drawn to a picture of a funny-looking woman hanging on the back wall. Even though she was pretending to smile, he knew it was the sort of grown-up who might enjoy eating children. Underneath was a little gold plate that read, '*Miss Buckley – 1940–*'.

He knew all the years were numbered, and so far they had counted 1,982. It was difficult to imagine back to year number 1,940, but it was certainly a time when wolves and dinosaurs lived in the surrounding woods. It made him shiver to think that the woman in the dark picture might still be here, perhaps kept in the dungeons, and fed through a hatch because she would bite anyone who came near.

"Don't like it," he managed to whisper.

"Neither do we," said the Mandy-girl. "The picture comes alive at night to stop the girls escaping."

Then his neck was pulled again, forcing his legs to give chase. Slowly, the noise made by the things faded, until there was just the rhythmic clicking of Matron's shoes on a white stone floor. He thought he might be travelling down a long corridor that smelled suspiciously of flowers. Then a door was opened, and he found himself in a narrow passage that smelled of disinfectant.

Finally, he was pulled into a little room that had one desk and a single hospital bed. Here, the Mandy-girl let go his neck.

"I'm OK, Mummy," she said, "I feel safe now."

The Mandy-girl was allowed to stand, and immediately put an arm about his shoulder.

"The man attacked us both," she said, "but this boy managed to hold him back, while I escaped."

For the first time the matron looked at him closely. "Oh my goodness," she said, "it looks as if you've been through a combine harvester!"

"The man," said Mandy, "really wanted to look up my legs, and when I wouldn't let him, he threw me into the brambles, then this boy started hitting him with a stick, so the man attacked the boy instead. He nearly died."

"Brave, brave boy!" said the matron.

It was the second time he had been called brave today, both times by a matron. He wished they wouldn't; it was quite obvious that if a matron thought you brave, it meant a whole lot of other people wanted to beat you up! He thought about the enemy, all roaming about outside. *Matron thinks he's brave*, he could imagine them saying, *let's put him in a cooking pot, and suck him like a goldfish.*

Nervously, he watched the matron pick up a telephone and push a button.

"Becky," said the matron, "please come to the surgery at once." Then she pushed another button. "This is Matron," she said. "Code red, make sure none of our girls leave the premises. I'm in the surgery dealing with a code yellow."

She put down the receiver, and turned to David. "Miss Becky will look after you," she said. "Do you have a name?"

He shook his head. He did not want anybody to find out who he was; he needed to escape, before Mr Tebbit caught him. Slowly, he began to stagger in circles, once again getting ever closer to the window. He dropped his tummy onto the wide stone ledge, only to freeze with fear of everything that waited below – hundreds of 'things' all staring up at him.

Three jumped up to touch his hair, landing back down with excited giggles.

"You're not safe out there," said the matron. "You might be the first boy they have seen, so there's no telling what they might do. My assistant's very gentle, she'll have you sorted in no time. We'll have to take you out under escort."

He retreated to sit on the bed. He was in a prison, like Mr Tebbit had said. From this place there was no escape, until the grown-ups said so. Then a lady entered the room.

"Good heavens," she said, "a boy…please tell me you're playing a make-up game?"

"It's really blood," said Mandy. "He nearly died saving me from the man in the woods."

Listening to Mandy made the lady start chewing her fingers. Then she took David into the next room, which had two hospital beds either side of a large wooden table. The lady told him it was the sickbay, where the girls stayed if they couldn't sleep in the dormitory.

"When they have chickenpox?" he asked.

"Yes, that sort of thing."

He relaxed just a little. It was a place where you could not have visitors. His fear that a group of 'things' might suddenly burst through the door to do their goldfish impressions faded.

The lady sighed. "I wish I'd had somebody like you to protect me when I was little," she said. "That was so brave."

He frowned, then told the lady what happened the last time a matron called him brave.

"But it's OK when I say it," she said, "because I'm not a matron. If I let you into a secret, will you promise never to tell?"

He nodded.

"Proper matrons," she said, "have to wear white hats all the time, even in bed. I'm only wearing a black band to stop the hair falling over my eyes. Sometimes, I even put the hairband on my wrist, and I bet you've never seen a proper matron do that with her white hat?"

The lady twisted the band on her wrist, then tried to walk away, but crashed into the table, because she never got her hair cut, and now it covered her eyes.

"And would you like to know another secret?" she asked.

He nodded.

The lady bumped into a chair. "I can't see if you nod," she said, "not until I put my hairband back on."

He said he would like to know another secret.

"Two years ago," said the lady, "I was here as one of the girls. I stayed on to learn how to be useful and, in return, they send me to college at night. I am training to be a nurse, and when a nurse says a boy is brave, everybody must agree, even the Queen."

He thought the lady was the nicest grown-up he had ever met. As she checked him over, he kept giggling to himself, thinking about his matron sitting in the bath, wearing her white hat."

"Well," said the lady, "over the past two years, I've learned quite a lot about child-like injuries, and you seem to have them all at the same time. But there is nothing that will not mend itself within a few days. Now, follow me for an extra-special treat!"

Opposite the sickbay there was a short corridor, blocked off at the bottom, but with three doors set into the wall on the left. It was only when David was taken through the middle one that he realised he had been tricked. It contained a pink bath and had a lot of yellow towels.

Why grown-ups always wanted to give him a bath was a mystery. It made no difference to them if he had a bit of dirt behind his ear. He looked about the torture chamber that had two other doors.

"What's through there?" he asked, pointing to the door on the left.

"That's Matron's room," said the lady.

"Huh," he said dismissively. He pointed to the door on the right.

"That's where I live," said the lady. "Would you like to see?"

He thought this sounded a better escape route, so nodded. The lady slid back the door bolt, and he poked his head into the most stupid room he had ever seen. The ceiling was so high that no broom could ever sweep it, yet the walls so close together, a narrow bed only just fitted between them. By his right hand was a door, which he opened, only to find himself looking into the blocked-off passage.

"Huh," he said. Then he looked back into the room that had a door halfway up the wall on the right. He thought it might be where the woman in the dark picture lived, it being too high for her to jump down. When she needed feeding, the caretaker probably arrived with a ladder. Explaining this to the lady made her laugh, which he liked, even though he had not been trying to tell a joke.

"The woman in the picture," said the lady, "mostly roams about the top floor, looking through telescopes and stuff. She has her own apartment and office up there, it's all very scary." The lady pulled him back into the room. "In the old days," she continued, "we think this space had a flight of stairs that started from the end of the corridor, then rose ever so steeply to the door that's halfway up the wall. Perhaps they were used by people who weren't very important."

"Where to?" he asked.

The lady looked confused. "Where to what?" she replied.

"The people who weren't very important, where did they go to?"

"Don't know," said the lady. "The door is screwed shut, I made sure of that before I moved in. Matron says it's always been that way, and she came here as a teenager, twelve years ago. Anyway, I need somewhere to live more than the house needs a fourth set of stairs."

"You could live wherever the stairs go," said David stubbornly, "it might be more interesting."

"I expect they go to the back of a bookcase on the second floor," said Becky. "It's where the mistresses live. I never go there because they still consider me a girl, while the girls think I'm…weird, for going to college, and wanting to be Matron's assistant. Perhaps you would like to be my friend?"

David didn't think a boy could be friends with a grown-up, but nodded anyway. Then he began to think about his escape plans.

"The 'things,'" he said, "are they outside all the time?"

"Things?"

David knew the 'G' word was very bad. Even Matron had called them 'things'.

"Yes," he said, "things."

The lady scratched her head. "What do these 'things' look like?" she asked.

"You know, not boys, and they look at you in a horrible way."

The lady laughed, then knelt down to get really close to his ear. "An extra-special big secret," she whispered. "When they look at you, it means they like you, and I bet they all want to kiss you after you saved Mandy from the horrible man."

"I don't like them," he said.

"But you must like Mandy, you saved her from...and don't you think she's pretty, with all those golden curls? I keep expecting three bears to turn up to make enquiries about their porridge!"

David put his thumb into his mouth. Why was the lady being so horrible to him, he had not meant to upset her. Anyway, Mandy had yellow hair, a missing front tooth, and a squiggle for a nose that she wriggled like a witch. The curls were probably a spell that went wrong.

"I don't like Mandy," he muttered.

"Bet you do really," said the lady. "I think one day you will want to play kissing games with her all the time."

David understood this to be the 'Goldfish' game. To demonstrate he had no interest in such things, he turned to face the wall. Then he felt two hands pushing him gently sideways. He thought it best to look where he was going, only to find himself staring down into the pink instrument of torture. After being submerged into a nightmare of bubbles, things got much worse. The soap smelled of flowers and, when he tried to push it away, the lady bombed him from the air. "Wee," she said, changing hands to whizz it about his body. It was almost as if she was not a proper grown-up at all.

After the torture session was over, the lady asked if he

would like some bandages, because it would look good, and she needed the practice. It sounded like a girl game, so he shook his head.

"Oh, go on, please," said the lady. "I've never had a boy to practise on."

He did not seem to have any choice. When it was done, she led him to a mirror.

"There," she said, "you look like a war hero, and so clean I could hug you forever!"

*

Mr Tebbit could not understand what was happening, or even where he was. His mouth tasted of something horrible, and a snort produced a great quantity of mud from his nostrils.

"See," said a voice, "I told you he wasn't dead."

"Mister," said another voice, "can you run around for a bit, it's no fun using you for catapult practice if you are just lying down."

"The birdwatchers always used to run around," said a third voice, "but they don't come here anymore, so I think you must be a bad man. I bet Miss Buckley would let us use a bad man for target practice, even if he was lying down."

There seemed to be a lot of voices floating about in the darkness. They told him he was lying down, but he still could not understand why.

"If he's a bad man," said one of the voices, "Miss Buckley would think it our duty to stand on his head, and I've always wanted to see what a dead person looks like."

It was then Mr Tebbit became vaguely aware of an outboard motor putt-putting towards him.

"Ooh," said one of the voices, "men, I mean proper men with uniforms and everything, not like this muddy hippopotamus."

Presently, Mr Tebbit felt a shadow.

"You again," said a very cross voice. "Perhaps next time you want to watch girls playing hockey, you will do us all a favour and buy a copy of *Bunty*, or at least learn to swim properly!"

Mr Tebbit realised he was shivering. "The horror, the horror," he gurgled incoherently, taking a pair of boy's underpants from his pocket to wipe his face.

*

Back at the surgery, Matron looked at her patient with concern. Some of the scratches were deep, and really needed a visit to the hospital. But the trauma of getting there to be seen by strangers would make it a daunting prospect for Mandy. Also, the girl kept calling her 'Mummy' and, while this was not the case, it did make her feel more protective towards the confused child. And so, with a roll of sticking plaster and six bandages, she was mended, at least on a temporary basis.

When Mandy heard the door open, she looked up to see Miss Becky had entered the surgery. She was now pulling one of those funny faces grown-ups did when they wanted to have a talk somewhere else. Mandy gave a look back that meant she understood. Two minutes later, they had all resettled, with Mandy listening through the keyhole of the storeroom.

"Mine's not too bad," said Becky, "though he really needs a couple of days before he's fit to be playing rough games. I've put him in the sickbay with a jigsaw puzzle for now. Don't worry about the bandage on the head, it's just for dramatic effect."

"Well," said Matron, "Mandy's got some deep scratches on the back of her legs. I'll keep her in sickbay until I'm sure nothing's going to turn septic. The boy is from the home, I suppose?"

"Difficult to tell, because he's only wearing two items of clothing. If he came from over the lane, they would have a number on, which they do not. As for the complete lack of underpants…Hilda would be horrified by the very idea!"

"Hilda?"

Becky wondered if now was a good time to talk about her secret; it might be important.

"About Hilda," she said, "the matron at the boys' home. Well, last year I was walking down the lane after college, and she stopped to give me a lift. Then she took me back to her surgery for tea and biscuits. I think she struggles sometimes, being stuck over there without a female friend."

Matron coughed. "So long as it was under escort," she said, "though I hope Mr Cranmore did not see you, because he is quite mad, you know."

Becky turned away to avoid eye contact. Matron was not yet ready to hear about anything that happened on the other side of the fence.

Mandy found the grown-up conversation very confusing; they were only talking about stuff she knew already, so why they had wanted her to hear it through a keyhole, she had no idea. Then she had the most awful thought: if her boyfriend was from over the lane, he would be sent back, so she might never see him again. Something needed to be done. She then saw the door handle beginning to turn, so scampered back to the surgery.

Becky remained in the storeroom counting bed sheets, and generally trying to make herself useful. After five minutes Matron returned, closing the door behind her.

"Their matron's in a right state," she said. "Mr Cranmore's threatened to sack her for pushing one of the masters into the boating lake this morning. All she kept saying was, 'My boys, my boys, who will look after my boys?' I explained that we had found one, wearing only one sock. She said that whatever happens, we must keep him over here for tonight. He goes by the name of David."

A squeal of delight came through the keyhole.

"Mandy," called Matron, "come in here, please."

The door opened, and Mandy walked in.

"Anything you would like to tell me," asked Matron, "to explain their matron's extraordinary request for David to be kept in the girls' home?"

"I was playing in the woods…"

"…out of bounds!"

"Only a little bit. Anyway, the man who tried to look up my legs was chasing us, and this lady let us pass. She was as wide as a bus, easily able to stop the man. But I've seen him swimming in the lake before, so he might have dived in by himself."

"So," said Matron, "their matron has either thrown two different men into the lake, or the man who attacked our children is also a master. Becky, go see what the boy has to say for himself, then we shall compare stories, so no making things up, Mandy. If there is any exaggeration to be done, I shall attend to it later."

David looked up from his jigsaw puzzle, slightly nervous in case one of the 'things' had broken through the defences. On seeing the nice lady, he just hoped that she did not want to give him another bath.

"I need to ask you something," she said. "In the woods, did the man really try to look up Mandy's legs? It's very important you answer truthfully."

"He put her knees around his neck, so she was hanging upside down…"

"Stop, I don't want to know any more, it's too horrible, you brave boy. Heaven knows what he might have done had you not been there. Carry on with your jigsaw puzzle, I'll be back."

Becky burst into the surgery where the Mandy interrogation was taking place. "Stop," she cried, "it's a code black!"

"Surely not!"

Becky went to a drawer, and took out a card. "Code black, I tell you, he had his head between her knees, and was trying to…Oh, it's all so horrible, the boy saved her from…"

Two pairs of sympathetic eyes turned towards Mandy.

"Told you," she said, "and the boy saved me, told you that as well."

"And their matron saw them as they tried to run away," said Matron. "That's good enough for me. Becky, look after these two, meals in here tonight. I'm going across the lane to see what's happening. If the bad man is still on the premises after lights out, I'll…well, I'll do something when I've had time to think about it!"

Mandy realised that letting the grown-ups believe that the man had been trying to do a code black was a good way of organising them. And it meant they would not ask her any more questions, because grown-ups did not like talking about where babies came from, and that was only a code blue. Then she saw how worried Miss Becky looked.

"Don't get upset," she said. "As soon as the man got his head between my legs, I bit his hand, and the boy started hitting him with a stick, before he could do anything really naughty!"

For some reason, Miss Becky pulled a horrified face. Mandy decided she needed to be distracted from her bad thoughts. "Can I have a dramatic-effect bandage to go around my head?" she asked.

This done, she asked for a sling, then went to stand in front of the full-length mirror. "Now," she said, "can I come with you to the dining room? I can carry a tray with my right hand, it will look amazing!"

Becky led Mandy along the corridor, slowing down when her patient developed a limp. Then Mandy asked to go back to the surgery to get the little crutch she had seen in the storeroom, presumably to put under the arm that didn't have the sling.

"Go ahead," said Becky, "I'll wait here. And I expect you want to see how David is doing, but remember, you might be the first girl he has ever seen, so you mustn't frighten him by...well, being a girl."

"Uh," said Mandy.

Becky had no idea what that meant, and Mandy was too wrapped up in bandages for any body language to take place. She turned away from her patient to think about what would happen next. She concluded Matron was very naive to consider any attention would be given to the word of a child. When the boy was returned, he would be locked in the cold, dark air-raid shelter to be 'corrected'. This sent her mind drifting back to the time Hilda had given her a guided tour of the ex-military buildings. There were four air-raid shelters, each a great mound of earth, their flattened tops containing a steel hatch, each secured by two massive padlocks. Hilda had awkwardly explained it was where the boys did detention, officially never more than four hours. Becky had picked up on the word 'officially', to which Hilda shook her head. "I don't know," she had said, "I can't prove anything…"

But the size of the padlocks had told Becky everything she needed to know about the cold darkness that waited below. And now, as she thought about David hitting a master with a stick to protect Mandy, she realised sending David back to do detention was unthinkable; there had to be some other way.

Just then, Becky glanced up the stairs to see the slightest glimpse of ginger hair disappearing from view. She quickly climbed to the landing where the stairs doubled back. Here, she discovered a girl huddled in the corner with her head buried in a book. To anybody who knew about such things, she was obviously a lookout.

Becky did all the hairdressing, and could identify every girl from just seeing the top of their head. The mass of ginger curls belonged to Jackie, a girl who would always walk with a slight limp due to a severe beating she had once received from her stepfather. She was well protected by The Three Musketeers and, in return, was very good at doing their bidding, because her nervous disposition meant she could infiltrate and look innocent, if caught. Becky found herself coming to an awful, desperate decision.

"Jackie Smith," she said, "I will remember your name."

It was meant to sound menacing, but she could never quite get the hang of that, so she knelt down beside her instead.

"You will tell me," she said, "if there is anything I need to know."

The girl nodded.

Then Becky heard the sounds of a one-legged girl hopping from the surgery, so went back down, the sickness in her tummy changing to a dread in her heart as she followed Mandy into the dining room.

*

At the boys' home, Matron marched furiously to Mr Cranmore's study and entered without knocking.

"Is the bad man still on the premises?" she asked.

Mr Cranmore lowered his spectacles so as to look disapprovingly over the rim. "Do I know you?" he asked.

"Matron at the girls' home. One of my girls has been attacked, and I want to know what you are going to do about it."

"Never mind that, one of our boys has been seen holding hands with a girl. A girl!"

"You don't understand. The man who attacked our girl was your Mr Tebbit. Now, what do you say to that?"

"I trust she is to be severely punished for telling such terrible lies."

"You are from a different planet!" she snapped.

"I certainly hope so," he replied with equal indignation. "You are from planet 'ga-ga', I presume?"

"And you are a pig-headed donkey!"

Matron stepped back to recover her breath, allowing Mr Cranmore time to stare in disbelief.

"Fah," he said presently.

"Huh," said Matron.

"And now the boy has disappeared," said Mr Cranmore, "quite contaminated with sissyness, I expect. At this very moment, he is probably walking around namby-pamby shops looking for a pink ballet dress."

Matron realised that Mr Cranmore did not know where the boy was, and, until something could be done with the bad man, that is how she wanted it to stay. She turned on her heels, slamming the door behind her.

Mr Cranmore stared at the door. "They are quite mad," he muttered to himself, "all of them."

Then his frown deepened. Having witnessed their true level of insanity, he no longer felt able to dismiss the theory put forward by the Games master many years before; a 'flotilla of air beds being blown across the lake in two minutes', he had said. Tomorrow, he would get the Woodwork class to make a lookout shed, which could be sited on the outcrop of land that projected a little way into the lake. It would them give advanced warning of any attack; one-way glass, that was the answer, then he might go there occasionally to find solitude, while observing the enemy shore without being seen. Thinking about a Thermos flask of steaming tea, he began to nod. He must remember to tell the Woodwork master to put the mirror glass quite low down, so he could observe while sitting in an armchair.

*

On reaching the exit barrier to the lane, Matron was astonished to hear Becky walking up behind her.

"Where did you come from?" she gasped.

"Nowhere," answered Becky. Then she looked down at her feet. "Thing is," she added quietly, "it is the boy. He has…er… disappeared."

FOUR

At the girls' home, Matron's life had always followed a well-organised path, circling each year in much the same way, except for last Winter, when she had started taking a hot water bottle to bed – the result of a stiff shoulder, and the caretaker turning off the central heating at 10.30pm. Then David had come along.

Miss Buckley mentioned several times that 'losing a trouser problem' was exceedingly careless. Mandy remained in the sickbay, and at the end of each day, made a point of saying, "Goodnight, Mummy." Becky became increasingly nervous, and even made excuses to miss her night school in case something happened. But nothing did happen, Miss Buckley saw to that, announcing to all the staff that a mass hallucination had occurred.

"Because if it were otherwise," she explained, "a lot of 'police trouser problems' would come up the drive to ask questions."

This caused three full-scale panic attacks, and the Games mistress to faint, sitting up with the hallucination theory fully formed in her mind. From that moment, any mistress who admitted to seeing the hallucination was labelled as mad, and therefore not suited for continued employment.

Matron could not understand how one small boy could make her life so untidy. But, however hard she tried, she could think of no other explanation.

*

Meanwhile, at the boys' home, Mr Cranmore recovered number thirty-seven's file to study it carefully for clues. The opening was straightforward enough. It read:

A strange boy who seems to live in a world of his own.

There was also a note stating that his malnutrition was the result of missing meal times – presumed out-of-bounds. There followed two pages of punishment – a remarkable achievement for a boy of eight. Mr Cranmore read the list of offences, of which there were three types:

Missed head count, presumed out-of-bounds.
Found out-of-bounds.
Lost item of clothing – sock.

As to other offences, there was not even a hint, with the exception of using this place as a hotel, and treating socks as disposable items; number thirty-seven followed an exemplary existence. His next offence, that of attempted murder, did not sit well against his previous crime of losing a sock. There must be some information missing.

OK – facts. Mr Tebbit liked to cane number thirty-seven at least once a week, nothing unusual about that for a boy he was trying to correct. The difference came with number thirty-seven's response; could it be the boy had actually worked out that while he could tread water at a shallow depth, somebody taller would get stuck? To understand this at the age of eight indicated the mind of a genius, albeit an evil one.

Fact number two: the boy clearly understood that swimming worked a lot better if you were only wearing shorts, while Mr Tebbit always wore long trousers. The events of that day had all the hallmarks of a well-planned crime.

Fact number three was more complicated. Deep down, he knew Mr Tebbit had continued to use the cat-o'-nine-tails long after the Namby-Pamby Act had come into force. He was also fairly certain it was Matron who had sent the anonymous letter to the council; she would see the marks of disobedience as she went about her daily business. Was it just coincidence that she was also at the lake, or was it all part of a well-rehearsed plan?

Thinking of Matron made him shudder. During the Summer months, he would sometimes look out of his window to see her sunning herself in a deck chair, wearing not many clothes. It was terrifying. There was also the problem of her £30-a-week wage packet. Compared to the masters, this made her extremely rich, but it was a condition of service that she kept a reliable car on the road, in case she needed to take a boy to hospital. She could do this because of a widow's pension she received on account of her husband being killed in the Korean War. But anybody else doing the same job? A State Registered Nurse would cost an absolute fortune, meaning the governors would get involved, and their preference would be for something with a wiggly bottom. Then he remembered the rule that matrons were expected to cover for each other in emergency situations. If Matron left, he would get the one from over the lane until a replacement could be found. Whatever Mr Tebbit was doing to upset Matron, he needed to stop it – now, before any more mad women arrived in his study. When the boy returned, he would be punished for what he had done to his beautiful daffodils. If Mr Tebbit thought it was for what had happened in the lake, then let him. Then his mind began to wander, as it often did nowadays. He thought about his retirement in two years' time; yes, that was the important thing, a nice little cottage near a municipal golf course…

*

Ten days after David's disappearance, Becky was walking along a corridor when she noticed Jackie Smith limping towards her. As they met, Jackie reached out to use her shoulder for support. Her face was deathly white.

"There is something you need to know…" she said.

Ten minutes later, Becky walked into the surgery and sat on the bed, biting her nails.

"It's all gone horribly wrong," she mumbled.

Matron made comforting noises, but Becky only put her fingers further into her mouth.

"To some of the older girls," she mumbled, "I am still one of them. I learn things, though I have to promise not to tell."

"You'll have to take your hands out of your mouth," said Matron, "I can hardly hear what you are saying. But I can't imagine it's that bad, I haven't seen you trying to eat your fingers since you were twelve."

"Oh, but it is, and now I'm in so much trouble I expect Miss Buckley will ask me to leave. Thing is, I didn't like the idea of the boy going back over the lane. Hilda can't watch over him all the time, and he'll be beaten up forever and ever. Truth is, from what I hear, he never actually left the building. Apparently Cynthia's sex lessons…Now…"

"Sex lessons?"

"Well, yes, hand over your bar of chocolate and you get instruction, complete with dirty magazines for pictures, or at least it used to be magazines. Apparently you now get to see a real live boy 'doing a wet.'"

A gasp came through the keyhole.

"Apparently," continued Becky, "the under tens can now do kissing practice."

The door burst open, and Mandy rushed in.

"He's my boyfriend," she gasped. "The Three Musketeers will stop at nothing, my poor, poor David!"

"I've heard," said Becky, "that he might be living in the caretaker's cupboard. It's next to the toilets, in case he wants to do anything more than a wet."

"The caretaker only has the workshop in the boiler house," said Matron.

"No, the old caretaker, who fell off the ladder while clearing the guttering. There's a space behind the bath-house where he could look through a peep hole."

"I know nothing of this," said Matron.

"No need, like I said, the girls sorted it, but the cupboard's still there – or at least it was two years ago."

"Still is," said Mandy, "The Three Musketeers captured it last year."

"Well then," said Becky, "I wonder if you would come

with me to watch my back, in case they are on the loose. But if you see any magazines, don't look! They belonged to the old caretaker, and are not exactly legal in this country."

Matron thought Becky had developed an overactive imagination. Quite apart from anything else, the girls did not know about where babies came from. Miss Buckley had a strict rule about it: no new admissions from the over tens, in case their minds had already been disturbed. But in order to humour Becky, Matron allowed herself to be led to the junior bath-house, then three paces further on to a cupboard.

Becky opened the door. "You'll have to do it," she said to Mandy, "my hands are too big."

Mandy put her hand through a tiny mouse hole in the back wall, and was then lifted to do the same at the top.

"Internal bolts," said Becky. "I expect the caretaker had a special tool, but the under tens can normally manage it. Now we'll have to close the outside door, there's some chain mechanism that stops them both being open at the same time."

Matron did not like being locked in a dark cupboard, and was just about to tell Becky to stop being ridiculous, when the back wall swung open, to leave her staring into a small room with a single light bulb hanging from a wire in the middle of the ceiling. David sat on a chair, completely naked except for his bandages, that had been used to tie him up.

Becky gasped in horror, not at the similarity to a torture cell, but because the girls had been trying to do something with his unusual haircut. He was now mostly bald, except for three little tufts that stuck up like clumps of grass, though why they had used knicker-green dye she had no idea. Perhaps it was all they could find.

"Oh, my poor David," wailed Mandy. She threw her arms about Matron's waist. "Oh, Mummy," she cried, "what have they done to him?"

David said nothing, just gazed ahead with a blank expression. Becky knelt down to untie his bandages, which were not only wrapped about the chair, but also back and forth to the various pipes that went into the next room.

"I expect they only took your clothes to stop you escaping," she said, more to make Matron feel better than to describe anything that might happen in the real world. "Mandy," she added, "go steal some more. We can't take a naked boy along the corridors!"

"Wa-ah," wailed Mandy.

She ran out of the room, and a moment later there came a great crashing sound from the bath-house next door. This was followed by a scream.

"He's my boyfriend," came a muffled voice, "now hand them over."

"But I love him," came the reply, "arghh!"

"Well," said Becky, "I was rather thinking of the cloakroom, but I suppose Mandy has her own way of doing things."

Mandy returned with a skirt, ankle socks and a pair of shoes.

"Toni's just fallen off the chair," she said, "then accidentally got her hair tied around a bath pipe, so I couldn't get her jumper."

Mandy turned towards David, Matron leaping forwards to cover her eyes. Becky more calmly threw the skirt across his lap.

"Mandy," she said, "go wait in the corner, and pretend not to look."

The boy broke from his trance, leaping backwards until he crashed into the wall. His eyes bulged in terror at the skirt now lying on the floor. Becky did not understand why the skirt so terrified him, but kicked it aside, and took off her own pullover to drop over his shoulders. The hem fell to his ankles like a baggy dress, but it seemed to pacify him a little. She knelt down to put on the grey ankle socks and buckled shoes. In this fashion he was half dragged down the corridor to the surgery.

"Thank goodness that's over," said Matron. "You're quite safe now, David, just lie down on the bed."

This statement appeared to give the boy superhuman strength. He twisted free, ran to Mandy, and threw his arms around her neck.

"Oh, don't let them do it!" he wailed.

Then he noticed the open window, ran across, and jumped out. Mandy's reactions were so quick, she gave the appearance of leaping out at the same time. Becky took a moment to recover, then climbed out, followed shortly afterwards by Matron.

Halfway across the lawn, David swerved to avoid an astonished prefect. Mandy, holding his shoulder, then kept him running in the changed direction, which happened to take them to a tiny gap in the fence, through which they wriggled before Becky could reach them.

"Rats," said Becky, "it's the under-tens hole, we stand no chance!"

Becky tried to remember where the senior hole in the fence might be but, since going to college, such current affairs had passed her by. Then the prefect came running up.

"I promise never to tell," she said. "We all know about the girl who climbed the quarry. She was flogged on stage, and that was for only holding hands with a boy. Mandy running into the woods with a boy would get her sent to live with the nuns for sure!"

Becky noticed the prefect was talking directly to Matron in a way that gave an awful lot of historical information for a panic situation. Then the prefect turned to herself.

"You can see where the boy is going from the bottom of the lane," she said. "If he swims across the lake, you could run down and stop him. The boys' home would flog him for sure. Otherwise, Matron can meet you at the bottom of the lane."

Becky sprinted diagonally across the hockey field, thereby taking the shortest route to the gate at the bottom of the drive. Matron stood bewildered. Why was everybody shouting at her, then running away? She was the matron, she should be giving the instructions.

Becky had no particular plan, only a vague hope that the insurmountable defences to the lane would look less severe when viewed from a grown-up perspective. Arriving at the gates, she studied the vertical iron bars, only to realise they ended in sharp spikes. Looking right, her gaze followed the high stone wall, beneath which the caretaker maintained a border of brambles and barbed wire. Then the prefect came running up.

"Code llama," she shouted.

Miraculously, three girls dropped from an overhanging tree branch, and raced directly to the right-hand gate pillar. Here, the tallest stood before the coils of barbed wire, holding out both arms, then, fell forwards to make a bridge over the top. With military precision, the shortest, and presumably lightest, climbed to stand on the shoulders of the first, where she hugged the pillar. The third got down on all fours, becoming like one of those steps people used to get into caravans.

"Only you can save the boy from being flogged," said the prefect. "As you climb, hold onto the hinge. Let it take some of your weight."

"Please," said the girl hugging the pillar.

Until this morning, Becky's existence had been entirely predictable: get out of bed, wash hands and face – especially behind the ears – scrub nails, clean teeth, comb hair, and so on for the rest of her prescribed day. Climbing trees or any other childhood adventure had just never happened. In short, since becoming Matron's assistant at the age of twelve, she had behaved entirely as grown-ups expected – sensible, and without any code llamas being involved. Then what the prefect had said about David being flogged completely overwhelmed her sensibilities. She climbed the girl-stairway, after which two hands pushed her feet even higher, until her belly flopped over the top of the pillar. Then the hands disappeared, leaving her legs dangling in space.

"Swivel," said the boss girl, "then drop down on the other side."

All four spectators screamed with hysterical laughter as she dropped down in much the same way as she had fallen from a vaulting horse during her last PE lesson, aged twelve.

"Give us eight chocolate bars," howled one, "then we won't tell the others you still wear gym knickers!"

*

A little way up the drive, a 'bush' with a wayward strand of ginger hair gave a little giggle.

Presently, a car could be heard coming around the copse, and Jackie hopped from the bushes to begin a slow limp towards the gate. On hearing the toot of a horn, she turned to make sure it was a green Morris Minor, then stumbled to fall across the gravel, with a scream of pain.

*

At the age of sixteen, Becky had been trusted with a big grown-up secret: the snake board opposite the gates had been provided by a zoo. But Matron's conspiratorial whisper had not inspired her to venture into the gloomy tunnel beneath the trees because there were still snakes, albeit small ones. But today was different; the children needed her! So here she was, at the bottom of Bad Man Lane, in the depths of snake valley, and facing something the prefect had forgotten to mention: a narrow path above a vertical quarry wall. All things considered, Becky stood astride the stile, which gave her a good view of the valley, while keeping her feet off the ground to protect her from the snakes. If David tried to throw himself on the mercy of the boys' home, she would race down the path to intercept him, just to see if something more sensible might be worked out. If he did not break cover, well, that was less important. All that really worried her was the pervert, the cold dark air-raid shelter...and the path above the quarry. If David took a course of action that meant all three could be avoided, she was quite happy to go along with it.

Becky let her mind drift to other things, in particular how David had broken through the defences in the first place. This was a hot topic of conversation with the girls, the most agile of whom had searched the woods until they discovered his den, complete with toy cars. It rather suggested there was a more regular and easier crossing.

"Oh my lord," breathed Becky. David had been taken prisoner by The Three Musketeers, and held for ten days. It did not seem credible that Cynthia, their leader, had not tortured him for information, and then…

On the way to the caretaker's cupboard, there had been no guards, no decoys, and Cynthia did not make careless mistakes. Sweet, innocent Jackie was just one of her agents, who did exactly what the boss wanted, which had most likely included opening the surgery window, after they had left for the caretaker's cupboard. Cynthia had arranged David's escape, before he could tell anybody else his secret information. Then Becky remembered the prefect telling her about the girl who, many years before, had climbed the quarry. After her capture, she had been stripped to the waist on stage, Miss Buckley being so terrified by the presence of the Devil that she forgot to count the whips tearing apart the girl's flesh. It was said that only a quick-thinking Music mistress, armed with the piano stool, had saved the girl's life. And if David went back to the boys' home, he would suffer a worse fate, because his punishment could be done secretly in a cold, dark air-raid shelter. She was glad the prefect had mentioned such things; it would get Matron thinking sensibly about the need to protect the children. The only confusing thing was that the statements seemed rather rehearsed, without any gaps for thinking.

Becky had never owned a watch, but thought half an hour might have passed since she bravely climbed over the gate pillar. What was keeping Matron? Trying to follow the children now was pointless.

Becky was walking back up the lane when a green Morris Minor came around a bend at about five miles per hour. Matron, driving it, looked terrified; going fast was not something to which she was accustomed, but it made the emergency stop almost instantaneous.

"Have you seen them?" Matron cried.

"No," responded Becky, "and I was above the lake within five minutes. If they crossed the frontline, I would know. My guess is the boy will keep running through the woods on the girls' side, directly away from whatever gave him his superhuman strength to leap clean out of the window. And after the way he defended Mandy from the pervert, she will follow him to the ends of the Earth!"

"Get in," said Matron, "we'll cut them off at the bypass."

On reaching the nearby village, they turned right to follow a country lane that circled around the back of the boys' home. And still Matron drove as if she expected to find a car coming towards her on the wrong side of the road. Then they descended a steep hill, to reach a dual carriageway where Matron turned right, pulling into a little lay-by after a mile or so.

"They've got to cross this road," she said. "We'll park here and wait for them."

Becky got out of the car to study the hill that rose up from the swampy ground on the other side of the highway. Why the English mistress used a picture of the Canadian Rockies to illustrate her story of grizzly bears, who liked to eat little girls, was a complete mystery. The way down from the uplands was so covered with spiky vegetation, it would be impossible to get out of the woods while wearing a skirt.

Becky located the line of the dam, which took her gaze to the boys' side of the valley. Here, a good path descended open grassland all the way to the bypass. Running downhill, David could have crossed this highway half an hour before. But that would mean swimming across the lake, which he had not done. And how did Mandy fit in? They must still be hiding in the woods, but that did not make sense either. David clearly had no plans to stop running anytime soon. Some important information must be missing.

Becky decided it best not to get Matron involved; she was only programmed to deal with nice grown-up thoughts, and not…well, whatever was going on here. Something like this needed Cynthia, a girl who feared no one, and had a remarkable ability to make things happen.

Becky was distracted from her thoughts by a great rumbling lorry pulling away from the opposite lay-by. It made her feel restless; by nightfall that driver could be halfway across England, on a ferry even, yet here she was, seventeen, undertaking her first journey from the uplands. She visualised the secretary counting out the exact number of coins into her palm for her college bus fare. Where could she go with 23p, except to her 'O' level classes?

Becky got back into the car to discover Matron fiddling nervously with a pen. 'Click click' it went, before swivelling around, then again, 'click click'.

"I can't do it," said Matron, "tell Miss Buckley what has happened."

"Never crossed my mind that you would," said Becky.

"How am I to explain that we found a naked boy?" asked Matron.

Becky thought Matron sounded confused, as was to be expected.

"Officially, David is a hallucination," said Becky, "so there is nothing to tell. Mandy going missing from her bed is no big deal."

"No, no, we'll have to leave, and send Miss Buckley a postcard to tell her what has happened. She's bound to sack us anyway."

Becky looked at her incredulously. "You are not proposing to tell Miss Buckley that Mandy has eloped with a boy?"

"But we must!"

"Must!" screamed Becky. "You know what the prefect said. Does running into the woods with a near-naked boy even have a code? Mandy will be flogged on stage to deter the others, then packed off to live with the nuns without so much as a digestive biscuit."

"I would never let such a thing happen."

"But you won't be here. I will do anything to stop Mandy having the skin torn from her back, do you understand? Anything!"

"Calm down, let me think."

Becky had no intention of calming down, and got out of the car to stomp along the edge of the roadway. Matron might be stubborn, but she would not drive back on her own.

Eventually, Becky looked over a crash barrier to discover she was on a little bridge above a stream. Here, she waited until the Morris Minor pulled up. She watched Matron get out and gaze across the lowlands.

"It's OK," said Becky, "the children did not need to cross this busy road, there's a tunnel underneath. It's the overflow from the dam, I expect. The water's not deep, it only comes halfway up the shopping trolleys."

"Shopping trolleys?" said Matron vaguely.

"I don't understand either," said Becky. "But the children are safely away, and that's all that matters. Our job is to make it safe for their return when cold and hunger...I mean, eight is too young to run away forever."

Matron gave an involuntary nod. "The nuns have a convent in Scotland," she said. "Miss Buckley has some association with it, but nobody seems to know what. Children who have acquired forbidden knowledge...apparently the outer compound has twenty-foot-high walls. Nobody ever escapes."

Becky considered the prefect's promise to keep 'the secret' to be such an obvious statement, it had only been made to conform to the rules of 'polite' conversation. However, on observing Matron's general reaction to the event, Becky was reminded that grown-ups sometimes did silly things, so needed to have things explained to them in simple stages.

"A far greater problem," said Becky, "is the pervert who comes from the boys' home. The only organisation strong enough to deal with such a man is The Three Musketeers."

Matron went stiff. "You can't mean Cynthia and company," she gasped. "She's in much too much trouble over the boy already."

"Not if we don't tell anybody," responded Becky. "Anyway, Cynthia grew up in a brothel, she probably saw naked men tied to chairs all the time when she was a toddler. She might think they like it. OK, wrong boy, and probably five years too early..."

"Becky, really, such a wild imagination. Her file clearly states that her origin is unknown. All we know for certain is that Social Services found her sitting on a bench eating a raw cabbage she had stolen from the greengrocers."

"The amnesia was just her way of not being sent back.

Though she'd been living wild in the woods for six months, so the actual address might have been forgotten."

"A six-year-old cannot survive on her own."

"But Cynthia's not normal. She cannot die, or at least that's the impression she likes to give. Anyway, you dated her from her teeth, she might be older. A girl that scraggy was bound to have stunted growth. As to being found, Winter had arrived. She made certain the greengrocer saw her take the cabbage, then sat on a bench opposite waiting for the police to take her to prison." Becky looked in the direction of the home. "Long sentence," she said. "Ten years for stealing a cabbage. Anyway, don't you remember the day she arrived? The awful ragged…no longer a dress, and unravelled jumper. I hid in the bushes when she got out of the social worker's car, thinking, what is that?"

"Well, it certainly wasn't human! What she did in the caretaker's cupboard…I shall never forget the terror in David's eyes when we took him back to the surgery!"

"Actually he seemed rather more frightened by us. His cry of 'don't let them do it' tends to suggest he thought the worst was yet to happen. Let me speak to Cynthia. If only we can get her onto our side we have an army of 156 girls against one weedy pervert. But the less you know the better. Cynthia will want to work without grown-up…sensibilities."

"But Becky, Cynthia's the Devil in a skirt."

"Exactly, and she can be bought with bars of chocolate!"

*

That evening, Becky sat in her room, biting her fingers, and trying to get the courage to face Cynthia. Then, with a box of twenty-four chocolate bars under one arm, she made her way up to the senior dormitory on the top floor. Lying under one of the beds, she pushed a panel on the back wall that lifted up on string hinges. She wriggled through the hatchway into a tiny triangular passage beneath the roof timbers. A second Musketeer, who went by the name of Tod, was sitting on the floor to watch a spider walk around in circles, presumably because she had pulled the legs off one side. On hearing Becky crawling towards her, she looked up.

"You're dead, you are!" she snapped.

"I need to see Cynthia," replied Becky.

"Stay there," said Tod, "and don't go wetting yourself. A damp patch in the ceiling will bring the caretaker up here as well."

"Matron hasn't told anybody about the cupboard," pleaded Becky. "I made her promise not to tell."

"Uh," said Tod. Then she reached up to open a skylight, long since forgotten in the adult world.

This is madness, thought Becky. Six months before, Beryl, the newly appointed head girl, had come this way. Aged fifteen she had been full of enthusiasm for life and the enforcement of Miss Buckley's laws. After spending the night lashed to the chimney stack, she had dripped water into the surgery, and mumbled something about falling into the lake. That afternoon, Cynthia had come to visit the sickbay with a gift of ten chocolate bars. Beryl had pulled the blankets over her head, and refused to come out. Whatever had happened on the roof, it was not something she could ever bring herself to talk about, though it probably did not comply with the Geneva Convention.

Tod dropped back from the roof. "Cynthia will see you now," she said. "You're dead, you are."

Becky decided Cynthia had a sort of terrifying charm, whereas her number two was just the most obnoxious child she could ever imagine. This idea was reinforced by Cynthia, who, being well settled in a lead gully, looked up to give an encouraging smile.

"Very brave of you," she said, "but those chocolate bars are for me, so I assume you need my help."

"But you never make mistakes," gulped Becky. "The boy would not have escaped unless you wanted it."

"Not just a pretty face then," said Cynthia. "Every girl under the age of ten had fallen in love with him. It had become a cult thing not even I could control. It suited me for somebody else to take the rap for his unscheduled departure."

"In return for telling you how to cross the frontline."

Cynthia lifted her eyebrows, and was obviously impressed. She reached up to take the box of chocolate bars, and expertly weighed them in the palm of her hand to make sure it was full.

"And what do you expect in return?" she asked.

"The pervert over the lane – we want him gone, after he admits to attacking the children."

"He's just a slimeball, quite easy to outwit, but I will need you to sign a confidentiality form."

"But secrets learnt on the roof are forever," said Becky, "otherwise we fall over a cliff and die."

"In the grown-up world," said Cynthia, "I expect things to be more legally binding. Wait here."

Becky felt herself going red. Cynthia might be thirteen, but to consider her a child was foolish. In fact, watching her scamper away up the slates gave her a mythical quality, like an elf going about her mischievous business without obeying the laws of gravity.

Then, suddenly, Becky had a gag pushed into her mouth. It was quickly tied with a bandage, and she was forced down, her face held firmly against the slates.

"You broke the rules," snarled Tod. "Time for your 'flying lesson'!"

Another pair of hands pulled down her knickers, and twisted them about her ankles.

"Don't want them getting wet," said the third Musketeer.

Becky wanted to scream in pain as her arm was twisted behind her back, but could only panic-breathe in and out of her nose.

"I say we dangle her nude from the gutter," said the third Musketeer. "If she manages to climb down the drainpipe, we'll let her go."

"To sing to Matron...No, this one's strawberry jam on the tarmac."

Through a veil of tears, Becky noticed Cynthia sit beside her, apparently quite unconcerned by her torment.

"From where you are," she said helpfully, "your best bet is to stick the fingers of your free hand up Tod's nostrils. Though I must say it would have been better not to let them sneak up on you in the first place."

Becky was too paralysed with fear to do anything.

"Alternatively," continued Cynthia, "you could give them two chocolate bars each – with interest, pay me back six."

Becky nodded.

"I shall take that to be your consent," said Cynthia.

The fearsome hands let her go to grab the chocolate bars Cynthia held out. Then her tormentors left as quietly as they arrived. Cynthia reached across to untie the gag, then pull the handkerchief from Becky's mouth.

"They were going to throw me off the roof!" gasped Becky.

"Learn to assess your situation better," said Cynthia. "If you were strawberry jam on the gravel with a gag in your mouth, you'd be telling Matron about our roof as well, which, may I remind you, is a level-two secret. Up here, you were quite safe. The first floor is your most dangerous place. From there you can be thrown out of a window into the big dustbins by the kitchen. You did, after all, break the rules. Monday's a good day because there's plenty of rubbish to soften the fall, and it's easier to climb out."

Becky staggered to her feet and, overwhelmed by her humiliation, bent down to untangle her knickers.

"I'm sorry, I came to the wrong place," she sobbed.

"On the contrary, if you wanted the slimeball dealt with properly, you came to the right place. If you wanted a poetry lesson, well then, yes, you came to the wrong place."

Becky stood bewildered by her strange environment. It took all her effort to cry silently, and not make any silly noises that Cynthia would not understand.

"As to Matron knowing a level-one secret," continued Cynthia, "well, it is true I did not realise how tied you had become to her apron strings. Perhaps you are now the enemy. It's difficult to tell, because your complete lack of tits makes you look about fourteen. A double agent, maybe, but whose side are you on, really? Well, I suppose you climbed over the gate pillar, and a true grown-up would have waited for the key. Anyway, the police haven't been to the caretaker's cupboard yet, so I don't see how Matron can tell them about it now. This puts Matron into my care, like yourself, since getting back down involves getting past Tod, who is no doubt waiting for you in the narrow passageway. You do know Social Services found her living in her uncle's back yard with two Alsatians? Some drug dealer or other. She's a trained attack dog. If she smells fear on her territory, she'll get her teeth into your leg and won't let go until she hears her master's voice…which happens to be mine."

Becky turned around. "This is the worst moment of my life," she said.

Cynthia looked confused. "But you are an orphan," she said. "Would you not play Tod's little game every day of your life to have one more hour with your parents? Now sit down, and stop being silly about trivial things."

Becky did as she was told. "I can only just remember being five…" she began.

Cynthia held out her hand. "Don't do counselling," she said. "I was merely pointing out that bravery often comes from keeping things in perspective. With the right state of mind, you could beat Tod and her helper in a fight, but you became paralysed with fear, and, of course, let them sneak up on you. Now to business: do you have a boyfriend?"

Becky's tears slowly turned to embarrassment. "No," she said, "it's this place, it takes years to recover."

Cynthia held out a pen and clipboard.

"Then you are to write this letter to your imaginary boyfriend," she said. "Begin, '*Dear Passion Pants…*'"

Becky began to write, slowing down only when it got to a bit about 'poking' herself with a carrot.

Cynthia continued her dictation "*And because I am Matron's assistant, I can sneak them back into the kitchen afterwards – it is the best fun ever to watch Miss Buckley eating her dinner…*"

Cynthia looked up. "I'm sorry," she said, "you have stopped writing. Am I going too fast?"

"I can't do it," said Becky.

Cynthia took the clipboard, then handed back the letter together with the box of chocolate bars – minus six.

"Give these to Tod on your way out," she said. "It might stop her biting you."

"But the pervert…You will help me?"

"Such business requires a confidentiality agreement, sorry."

Becky sat on the slates, biting her lip. "What happens to the letter?" she asked.

"If you betray me, ever, about anything, your prefect messenger will hand it to Miss Buckley, before your boyfriend gets to see it. Imagine that!"

"Oh my God! Is this what you did to Beryl when she was lashed to the chimney stack?"

"Personnel records are never discussed. Now, if there is nothing else, I have things to do."

Becky reached out for the clipboard and, after two minutes of total humiliation, signed the letter '*Bonking Becky*' as instructed. Cynthia then held out a roll of Sellotape and a pair of scissors.

"Your fanny hair is to go above the 'y' of your name," she said. "There is to be enough sticking out for your boyfriend to tickle his nose."

"No!" screamed Becky.

Cynthia stood up and began to walk away. "I'll escort you safely past Tod," she said. "I expect she was playing with that spider when you came up. Her greatest desire will be to make you eat it."

"Please," said Becky, "I promise I won't betray you – ever."

Cynthia turned, then held out the scissors and Sellotape. "Of course you won't," she said.

Becky preferred not to think about the next two minutes of her life, or the terror she felt following Cynthia across the slates. Then she peeped over a ridge to see her guide waiting by a skylight, through which she disappeared by means of a bed sheet.

"Take off your shoes," said Cynthia from below. "We are above the library, and are not allowed to make a noise."

Becky descended to stand in a large triangular attic. It seemed to be the old servants' quarters because there were still some bits of furniture scattered about a threadbare carpet.

"This place is not even a rumour," whispered Becky.

Cynthia held up the letter. "And so it will remain," she said.

Becky felt her lips sealing tight. But it was more than just the consequences of the letter. Now her torment was over, she quite liked the idea of being Cynthia's friend.

"Now," said Cynthia, "in war the first thing to do is dehumanise the enemy. So no more talk about perverts. The boy told me the enemy is called Mr Tebbit. So, 'The Teapot'. Do you see? A familiar piece of harmless domestic equipment with a droopy spout."

Becky nodded.

"Except for me," continued Cynthia, "I have a particular dislike of perverts. To me, one less pervert means one less customer going down the brothel to get a hand relief from a little girl."

Becky noticed Cynthia subconsciously wipe a hand on her pullover; also that her speech was rehearsed, and did not require any thought. Possibly it was part of her sex lessons.

"In fact," Cynthia continued, "the more perverts you bring me, the better I shall like it. I only wish I had been in charge of this place when the old caretaker discovered it. The slimeball actually told the girls he would keep their 'little secret' quiet, if he could watch them do a naked snog. So you see, he had to take a flying lesson. Quite a panic, apparently, all the girls running about to find a ladder, then block up the guttering so he had a reason to be on the roof."

"I don't want anybody dead!" gasped Becky.

"In war such things are often unpredictable, but there's nothing to worry about, because it can all be done in a way grown-ups expect. Like before, to them a dead caretaker with a ladder made perfect sense. And The Teapot has a history of swimming in the lake, so if he is found floating face down... well, it is to be expected...of course...*Bunty*, it's exactly what the grown-ups would expect."

"What you have just said makes no sense whatsoever," said Becky. "For one thing *Bunty* is not a sort of comic where people end up dead."

Cynthia smiled, and was clearly pleased by something that was going on inside her head.

"I know how to sort it," she said presently. "My only worry is that you lack the bravery to carry out your part."

"To save the boy, I would do anything."

"And if The Teapot ends up dead?"

Becky bowed her head, using her hands to cover her face. Then she looked up to stare directly into Cynthia's eyes. "Anything..." she said.

Cynthia nodded, then walked to a large ancient chest, and fiddled with a combination lock. She lifted the lid to reveal a great quantity of neatly stacked chocolate bullion. An individual bar could sit comfortably inside the fist of a twelve-year-old, yet the shiny blue wrappers nearly reached the rim. The additions seemed insignificant.

"A payment of twenty-four every three months ensures the border crossing remains a secret," said Cynthia. "This is an agreement between me, you, and Matron. The other two Musketeers don't know about it. I employ them for muscle, not brains. You will find some hostility from them, but I am always on the lookout for intelligent double agents, and it matters not that they tell the girls you wet the bed."

"It does matter," Becky retorted.

"I'd be more worried about the under tens if I were you. They all think you're the most evil person in the universe for stealing their David, and you know how unpredictable they can be."

Becky reflected on the unfairness of life, while Cynthia went to another chest to undo its combination lock. She dropped the letter inside.

"I shall remove it to a safer place later," she said. Then she recovered a little eye-drop bottle.

"Chloroform," she said. "In the old days people used it like sleeping pills. I read about it in the library."

Suddenly, Becky had a most awful sequence of thoughts: the old servants' quarters, the attic…

"…the fourth set of stairs!" she gasped.

"Keep your voice down," said Cynthia. "But yes, the stairs come up in the next room and, with a bit of wriggling, we can monitor the whole top floor, including Miss Buckley's apartment. Like the boy said, grown-ups do not want children to go exploring…"

"What the boy said?" Becky interrupted.

"We needed to monitor his location. We have some earpieces from the old-fashioned telephones to listen through doors."

Becky gave her best horrified look, but Cynthia only shrugged.

"Listening to your bedtime prayers lets me know how your mind works," she said, "and now I am here to answer them, albeit in mysterious ways."

Becky decided her look of horror was not good enough, and tried to increase it, but Cynthia did not seem to notice. Instead, she reached into the chest to recover two padded tea cosies held together by catapult elastic.

"For 'Operation Teapot' you'll need tits," said Cynthia, "or he'll be treating you like Mandy."

Becky gave up on looking horrified in favour of a gasp.

"Nice intake of breath," said Cynthia, "but I saw your tummy expand." She put one hand firmly on Becky's spine, and pressed the other into her tummy. "Breathe in," she said, "all the air into the lungs, nipples out. Now snatch that tummy, I want the illusion of a pelvic thrust."

Before Becky could get an explanation for Cynthia's extraordinary transformation into a demented PE teacher, there was a slight rustling noise from the skylight. Becky turned around to stare in mutual astonishment at the girl who had just descended the bed sheet.

"Miss Becky," gasped Beryl, "you too…Oh my God, you were not re-educated by…"

"No," said Becky, "I have always known Miss Buckley was a daft old bat."

Cynthia smiled her approval. "Miss Becky is my most secret double agent," she said, "a honey trap no man can resist!"

"Wow," said Beryl, overcome by admiration.

But Beryl had always been very gullible, her head filled

with magic butterflies, which is why Miss Buckley found her so appealing. Then Becky thought about the unspoken thing that must have happened to her, in order to be trusted with level-three secrets, and wanted to be her friend also.

Meanwhile, Cynthia reached into her chest, and divided fifteen chocolate bars between them.

"To success," she said, "and may we never know hunger again."

*

Becky's college studies included one very hard subject: learning not to be scared of the dark. Throughout the Winter months, she got off the bus knowing that her two-mile walk down the lane would be lit only by the stars, at least until she came to the overhanging trees, beneath which she had to navigate by occasionally touching a foot to the grass verge. However, none of this prepared her for what she faced staring into the boys' home, at the start of 'Operation Teapot'. This was just a black void waiting to swallow her up.

Then she remembered how Cynthia had described the darkness David would face, if locked in an air-raid shelter, all alone, knowing only that the monster was waiting to get him. As a reflex action she ducked under the barrier, and took two steps forward, after all, her own safety was a trivial thing compared to what David would face, if she did not carry out Cynthia's insane plan.

Beyond the barrier, the ground became an imaginary concept until her foot landed upon it. How long this nightmare lasted she could not say, but eventually her outstretched hand made contact with a concrete wall. Reaching up, she failed to feel the summit, confirming she had located Matron's fortress. She then felt her way around this, until her fingers touched a steel security door. Here, she turned to face the masters' block, a place so terrifying even Hilda refused to go, on the grounds it was full of fuddy-duddy old men. However, Becky had managed to initiate an apparently casual conversation on the subject, and learned that downstairs contained everything to do with plumbing and cooking, while upstairs had eight bedrooms. Apparently The Teapot had the room at the end, and at last she saw a light, apparently in the sky, in the place of terror.

During her early years, Cynthia had become accustomed to moving about in dark corridors without being seen, and later, living in the wild, her senses had developed to those of a nocturnal animal surviving by instinct, and perhaps a hint of starlight beyond the clouds. She was, therefore, slightly bemused by the image of a grey jumper moving chaotically in a zigzag line, though she did not need any visual clues to follow her agent, since she clumped along like a noisy hippopotamus. If she ever had the misfortune to find herself in a brothel, she would be cornered within seconds, and her agility to escape slobbering old men was pretty much zero. Well, it was not something you could teach, certainly not in three days; it was just an instinct for survival that Becky had never needed to learn. In truth, Becky was the worst double agent of all time. Her only chance of success was that all the talk about flogging had generated such a passion for protecting David, that she would battle on, regardless of how hopeless it all seemed. Also, her agent did not know there was a backup plan, and hopefully this would help her find some inner strength when the need arose.

Cynthia watched her agent standing by a wall for a few minutes, then turned her attention to the line of trees near the perimeter fence. Deciding this was the best place to observe developments, she headed directly towards a tree that allowed her to sit comfortably astride a branch some twenty feet off the ground. This gave her a good view into the bedroom where the action was going to take place. If things went wrong, she could be there to hit the pervert over the head with her croquet mallet within two minutes. But anything that involved a rescue mission from a man's bedroom was pretty much the same as complete failure; Becky would instantly be made homeless. Herself – well, that was less important, she could run directly away from The Teapot's bedroom, and for this outcome she carried a satchel full of chocolate bars.

On reaching the rear entrance of the masters' block, Becky stopped to recover her balance. No, it was not herself standing at a funny angle, but the stairs, and the handrail wobbled because it was not attached to anything at the top. After bravely ascending to the higher floor, she stopped to study the short corridor ahead. There were four doors on either side, but thankfully a brass name plate confirmed The Teapot's room was on her immediate right. She began to prepare herself for the ordeal ahead, pulling her hair forwards until it became a curtain cascading over the mountainous woolly jumper. Then she dropped her shoulders, and tilted her head submissively. Cynthia had called this the 'Maid Marian' attack opening, with a sixty-inch double 'D' bazooka variation. Apparently, it was ideally suited to real virgins, because being shy and clumsy helped the acting.

"If you really can't cope," Cynthia had said, "just pretend you have seen Robin Hood's dick for the first time, by accident, and run!"

*

Mr Tebbit sat in his armchair to gaze unhappily at the old trousers Mr Cranmore had given him. They had two enormous turn-ups, and were clearly pre-war. His jackets might have survived the boating lake experience, had the washing machine not switched itself to the sterilisation temperature that Matron used for the nappies. Now all he had was Mr Cranmore's old threadbare blazer. Mr Tebbit used the boy's underpants to stroke the Savage Beast lying across his lap. "There, there," he muttered, "the boy will return."

The Savage Beast gave a twitch of indignation. 'I want to taste the blood,' it said.

"The boy is recorded as missing," responded Mr Tebbit, "but when he returns, he will go down the air-raid shelter for the rest of his days. And, for each of those days, you will taste the blood."

On hearing a slight tap on the door, his spirits rose. Hopefully it was Morris holding a disobedient child who needed to be punished. Opening the door, he received a hallucination that had no explanation.

"If you please, sir," said the hallucination, "I was wondering if you are the Mr Tebbit who knows about improvement?"

He took a step backwards. Hallucinations did not speak. Whatever was standing in front of him must have escaped from somewhere. Perhaps she was one of the mad women from over the lane?

Becky looked around the room for escape routes, just like Cynthia had instructed. There were only two: the doorway in which she was standing, and the theoretical one that involved jumping out of the opposite window. Then she looked at The Teapot to discover her unexpected appearance had thrown him into total confusion, very much as Cynthia had predicted. This gave her the confidence to enter the room, and go directly to the window. She opened the curtains, and released the catch. Cynthia had associated this with something Jackie Smith had done in the surgery so the children could escape, though what good it would do so far from the ground, Becky had no idea. Leaving the window slightly open, she turned to face the room.

"It reminds me of the time I climbed Miss Buckley's drainpipe to put biscuit crumbs in her bed," she said. "Custard creams, they are just the worst."

"Miss Buckley?" said The Teapot, as if confused by something.

"Yes, I'm an assistant at the home, but it's so horrible. The girls are completely out of control, they run this way and that, and the other day...No, it's too awful, but I hear you know about improvement, and how to stop them calling you 'Donkey Face'. Not that you have a donkey face, but it's what they call Miss Buckley, and do you know what she says?"

"I cannot begin to imagine."

"She says the poor little darlings are just going through an awkward phase, and the other day they Sellotaped a tail to her dress, and started making hee-haw noises as she walked down the corridor."

"That is very much as I imagined, but I do not see how I can help."

"But it doesn't have to be this way. Next year I am to be made a full mistress, and I thought you might be able to give me some advice on how to stop the class throwing stuff at me." Becky gave an exaggerated shiver. "Is it true that over here you still use the cane?" she asked.

"Obviously."

"You know, Mr Tebbit, sir, throughout my school days I was never caned once. I think that is why I can't help being naughty sometimes." Becky gave her head a good shake to indicate despair. "When I am made a full mistress," she continued, "what if I caught one of the girls climbing a drainpipe, how could I stop her from being so naughty?"

Now the woman was talking about punishment, Mr Tebbit found the courage to construct a full, logical sentence.

"It has gone too far for that," he said. "The whole establishment needs to be disciplined before you can correct the behaviour of any individual."

"But how? I believe you are only allowed to cane children six times, however naughty they have been."

"Put their hand in jugs of iced water until their skin becomes really cold, then use a thin cane across the fingers. By the third stroke, even the hardest boy is blubbing like a baby. For the other hand, you will need at least three prefects to restrain him. In Winter, make them hold snowballs until they have melted. Do this, and the girls will not be disobedient again."

Mr Tebbit was very pleased with the woman's reaction; she showed total submission to his wisdom, by putting her fingers into her mouth.

"It must be illegal," she mumbled. "I mean the do-gooders, you know what they are like."

161

"Indeed, very small brains, but there is no regulation to say what temperature a hand must be at. I have checked."

"But I was thinking more about...but I see, is there any regulation that prevents me from making them sit in a bowl of ice water?"

Mr Tebbit inexplicably found himself thinking about the bottom he had just seen when the girl looked out of the window.

"Bottom," he said vaguely. "Oh yes, I suppose you could... but over here we have a problem with Matron, she keeps interfering. I believe yours is much the same?"

"Completely off her trolley! Last week a girl was given ten lines for doing something unspeakable. But do you know what happened? Matron wrote the lines for her."

"Well, you must not let her get involved. You might think about a prefect, somebody you look after in return for certain...services."

The girl stared at him with beautiful brown eyes, then put her hands across her mouth. Her submission to his wisdom was total. He forced himself to look away from the prettiest face he had ever seen, his gaze following the line of hair... Phew! What a pair of modifications; her jumper had ridden off her hips to provide the extra material required to cover the bulge. His toes miraculously curled up, causing him to lean forwards slightly.

Faced with the reality of a man staring goggle-eyed at her tea cosies, Becky lowered her gaze. This led to a most remarkable discovery: underneath his bed was a chamber pot. How? Surely a man would have things dangling in the wrong place? Did he kneel before it, as if it were a god, or stand up, holding it to the top of his legs? Even considering the question made him seem less scary, more 'teapotty' with a droopy spout. She moved from the window to fall onto the bed, using the correct etiquette Cynthia had described. After counting two seconds, she sat up, and pulled a handkerchief from the top of her jumper to dab her brow. She wriggled slightly because something Cynthia had said was very important, as it suggested her knickers were uncomfortable and needed to be removed. In this case however, it was more to do with the full-length swimming costume she was also wearing beneath her clothes that was really uncomfortable. She was certain Maid Marian would have been provided with something metallic.

Cynthia had told her to make sure he had a trouser bulge, before saying anything too unbelievable. "His brain needs to be in his pants," she had said, "then you can make him believe the Royal Ballet are using real swans to dance *Swan Lake*."

Becky forced herself to look at the place; either he had a very small brain, or her presence was not having the desired effect. Perhaps his brain had got lost in his overhanging tummy. And what extraordinary trousers; he obviously put them on to sweep the carpet as he walked along. Then she saw something even more peculiar: on a little shelf was a photograph of himself, stripped to the waist, a pair of binoculars in one hand, the other pointing to something in the far distance.

"So heroic," she mumbled, pointing to the photo. "I'm sure if I took off my blouse, people would only laugh at me."

Mr Tebbit had been so transfixed by the brief sight of her underpants as she sat down, that his brain had got stuck on the image. Now it leapt backwards to a universe of long ago, when he was fourteen, and Sally Parkinson had let him feel her chest development for two shillings.

"It was a tiger hunt," he babbled incoherently. What had made him say that? There was a telegraph pole in the background, and he didn't think they had those in Africa, or wherever tigers came from.

"Oh," said the girl meekly. "You know so much. If only I could learn I'm sure I wouldn't have any problems with the 'orrible lot they have given me."

Mr Tebbit fiddled with his collar, then went to the cat-o'-nine-tails drawer.

"What you want is one of these," he said.

The girl gasped. "I didn't think they were legal anymore. I mean, hasn't some do-gooder stuck her nose in where it's not wanted?"

"I have a special licence from the Government to use it…"

He wanted to correct himself, but was too overwhelmed by her delightful look of astonishment to do anything that might reduce her admiration. All that mattered now was that the goddess sitting on his bed knew him to be incredibly powerful. He brought the whips snapping down beside her.

"Of course," he said, "the fat matron does not know about it. You need to keep special licences secret from the namby-pambies."

Becky took a moment to recover from the shock, then, overwhelmed by anger, leapt up for the final attack. The tea cosies rammed into his chest. An astonished Mr Tebbit bounced back to the wall.

"Oh," she said, "so clumsy…I've never tried to hold a man before, I was quite overcome by the improvement of it all. With you as my master…Ooooh…I'd better go before I do something I might regret. But thank you ever so much, I shall…I shall…Oh, it's all too much to take in!"

Then she fled, leaving him in a trance. Those breasts were so firm, and she had just confessed no man had yet got close enough to play with them. Then his eyes caught something glinting on the bed. When she had pulled out her handkerchief, a key must have fallen from somewhere. He smiled; now she would have to come back, and he had so enjoyed talking to her. Then he realised the photograph was missing. How delightful; tonight she would be gazing at his image...lying in the bath, perhaps, stroking herself with the soap...

He had never quite managed the 'hydraulic function', but in the 1950s it was not something one talked about. Now, something peculiar was happening. Frantically, he tore at his trouser buttons, until it sprung out – the most beautiful thing he had ever seen – demanding to be stroked until he moaned with the pleasure of it. It was a miracle! Where Sally Parkinson had failed – the cow! – this goddess of perfection had cured him.

*

Outside, Becky stopped shaking to glance up at the first-storey windows. "Oh my lord," she breathed, "he can't even control himself for a moment."

In a nearby tree, a little soldier gave a nod of satisfaction, then retreated as silently as she had arrived.

*

The following day, Mr Tebbit became the centre of much speculation. Hilda watched in astonishment as he climbed a ladder to inspect the drainpipe outside his window, through which he then climbed. Later, three prefects hid behind a bush as he walked by, not as before, in the middle of the path, but awkwardly to the side, apparently talking to someone who was not there. And Mr Cranmore sat in his office to ponder the legality of making a boy sit in a bowl of iced water, prior to caning.

By the second night, Mr Tebbit could do nothing but sit in his flat to gaze at his beautiful manhood in the mirror. Let the girls at his old school call him 'Mr Softy' now! As to the one who had leapt from a cupboard with a camera, and pinned the resulting photograph on the school notice board – well, if she saw his manhood now, she would be begging to touch it!

*

The following night was so dark, no shadow could exist. Only bats with their sonar could have detected a disturbance in the blackness. Then the starlight seemed to catch a movement on the side of the masters' block – or maybe not, for the phantom dropped to the ground, and vanished as silently as it might have arrived.

Mr Tebbit had stopped sleeping in his pyjamas; the cool sheets against his skin helped him imagine his special friend lying next to him. Then, in the morning, he could sit on the edge of the bed with his eyes closed, his erect penis accidentally on display. "Oh," would gasp a soft, gentle voice inside his head, "what is that enormous thing between your legs, sir? Why, it quite covers your belly button." And this morning, the dream seemed particularly real. He opened his eyes to see his special friend holding a packet of custard creams, which slipped from her fingers to land on the carpet next to three copies of *Bunty*. Huh? He dropped to his knees to pick them up. They were real! He could feel the paper.

He flipped through the pages, mostly brightly coloured drawings of girls skipping, until he came to an insert of a naked woman with her legs apart. Until that moment, he only had the vaguest idea of what a woman looked like, but now he found it unbelievably beautiful – all of it – even the next photograph with three naked girls in a group hug, when all you could see was their bottoms – three of them, since a man in the background happened to be holding a full-length mirror…

At school, the boys only ever talked about the front view; bottoms were just a variation of something you could see in the showers, and not particularly interesting. The realisation that his special friend had a bottom like these sent his brain into complete chaos. In the next instant, his imagination saw her lying face down on his bed, naked, nervously patting her bottom to show him what he had to do.

"Are you sure?" he whispered.

"Don't know," replied the girl, "this is my first time."

A moment later, he was using her bottom as a pillow, while her exceptionally long arms reached down to play with his manhood. The resulting explosion was so massive that only by grabbing a *Bunty* with his free hand did he avoid the need to take a bath.

Two hours later, he stood in front of his class, his brain unable to see anything except for his special friend standing in the aisle, her naked body now fully modified by the magazine pictures he had just seen. The next instant they were on the floor, she screaming in agonised pleasure as his enormous manhood tore apart her virginity. From that moment, he understood that fulfilling his sexual destiny was the only thing in the universe that mattered.

He did not remember walking out of the classroom or driving to town, only sitting obediently in his bank manager's office to beg for an increased overdraft to help his aunt who had been robbed of her pension, and could not pay her heating bill. Half an hour later, he was at the tailor's, throwing aside his pre-war rags to emerge a gentleman, with a neatly folded handkerchief in his top pocket. With his last 50p, he went to the barber's to point to the rubber things he had seen displayed on the shelf. She would so enjoy putting those onto his erect manhood, because whenever he thought of her, that is what it became.

On reaching the home, he got out of the car, and immediately made his way down the lane to stand beneath the towering wall of corrugated iron. Here, he carefully arranged the expensive binoculars around his neck; his special friend thought they made him look heroic, after which she had said something about taking off her blouse. "Bouncy, bouncy, swing, swing," he muttered, swaying his head from side to side.

Presently he looked at the white line in the middle of the lane, but only saw his special friend lying naked on the tarmac. He circled around the image, then went to where he could stare down at a dungeon-style padlock.

"You need a key," said a voice.

A pair of buckled shoes was standing the other side of the bars. He had no interest in looking any higher; all that mattered was searching his pockets for the key his special friend had lost. Soon he brought it to the lock, but it seemed to have no connection to the hole.

"Different locks have different keys," said the voice. "We have been doing about it in class, it is very hard to understand."

"Because girls have very small brains," he said.

"I know," said the girl.

Mr Tebbit felt a twitch of anxiety; he was able to agree with something a girl had said. It made him look up, and realise her face was completely covered with strawberry jam.

"I've just come from make-up class," she said. "Do you like it? Only I'm worried Miss Williams might have had one of her funny turns, and got carried away with the lipstick."

"It looks ridiculous," said Mr Tebbit.

The girl turned around, and made such a horrible wailing sound that he had to put his hands over his ears. In the background, he became vaguely aware the girls had stopped playing hockey to charge en masse across the field to disappear behind the copse. Then the chain-link fence that divided the grounds from the woodland seemed to be alive with girls, some climbing over the top, others crawling underneath. These also ran in what he assumed must be the direction of the house. "Time for their bananas and custard," he mumbled to himself. Still, it meant he could get to the reception without being seen...

...Except his key did not work, and he had no other plan to get inside. Or anything really, just an overwhelming need to see his special friend – naked. He grabbed the bars of the gate with both hands, and banged his head against it.

The girl turned back. "Doesn't that hurt?" she asked.

Mr Tebbit realised she was such a simpleton, there was still a glimmer of hope.

"I need to give this key to one of your mistresses," he said. "Quite young, waist-length hair, and..."

"That would be Miss Linda," said the girl. "Wears a funny-shaped jumper."

"Yes, that's her. Do you think you could bring her to the gate?"

"No," said the girl, "Old Donkey Face has locked her in the wine cellar."

"What…when…why?"

"Miss Linda was caught gazing at a photograph of a man not wearing a shirt. Donkey Face went berserk, and the nuns are coming to take Miss Linda away. It's why I'm waiting at the gate, I've got to let them in."

Mr Tebbit had never experienced such anger. Then came the panic; he would never see his special friend…Linda…again. Then he realised the girl was staring at the key in his hand.

"Does that have 'WS' painted at the top?" she asked.

"Yes," he said.

"Then it is for the wine cellar," said the girl. "It's where we do detention. Miss Linda goes there when she needs a quiet place to think. I expect that's why she has a key."

Mr Tebbit struggled with everything he was being told. The girl could clearly not answer difficult questions.

"Where is the wine cellar?" he asked. "The place where you go for detention?"

"In the woods at the top of the drive. In the old days it used to be the ice house with all the wine on shelves around the walls…except now it's mostly empty bottles. Senior girls do a lot of detention."

Mr Tebbit looked at the key in his hand, then at the key in the girl's hand.

"Now," he said, "this is very important, I want you to listen carefully…"

The girl shook her head. "Not unless you think my make-up looks nice," she said.

Mr Tebbit easily outwitted the simple girl. After letting him through the gate she relocked it to keep out the nuns, then walked up the drive by his side, forcing him ever closer to the grass verge to escape the terror of all the jam getting on his nice clothes. On reaching the place where the drive turned left, she leapt in front of him.

"It's Old Donkey Face," she said. "Quick, run, hide!"

She then disappeared between two trees on his right. Mr Tebbit panicked; he could not lose sight of the girl, because only she knew the location of the wine cellar, and the slightest delay would mean his special friend would be taken by the nuns. He raced after the girl…into the woods.

*

Little Maisie ran across the clearing with her head down to increase her speed. The Teapot was two paces behind, but an almost-invisible fishing line tied between two trees meant only his legs kept running forwards, his chest somersaulting backwards until he landed chaotically in a pile of rotting leaves. Immediately, three girls with pillowcases over their heads dropped from the branches. The leader placed a towel across his face, and put a knee either side of his head to stretch it tight. When she was happy with the clamping arrangement, she began to drip chloroform onto the fabric just below the nose bump. The other two simultaneously hammered croquet hoops across his arms.

It took a long time for the legs to stop kicking, probably because the man seemed to be confused, and was not breathing deeply enough. But the futile struggle eventually became nervous twitches, then nothing in particular. The leader removed the towel from his face, and gently tapped the side of his head with the croquet mallet. Then she removed her pillowcase to become Cynthia. She looked at the identification photograph Miss Becky had given her.

"It's him," she said. "Well done, Maisie, that was very brave of you, but this next bit's for the older girls only."

"Aw," said the lead actress, "I'll let you off the chocolate bars you owe me for guarding the gate – honest."

Cynthia shrugged. Anything that reduced her outgoings was to be gratefully accepted during these expensive times.

Maisie smiled; at last she had tricked Cynthia, because they had used a whole pot of jam to complete her decoy disguise. She leaned against a tree and, rubbed a cheek with a finger. It must be like this going to the picture house, she thought, waiting for the show to begin while licking strawberry lollipops. Whatever was left, she could put back into the jar, so she wouldn't need the extra chocolate bars anyway.

With varying degrees of confidence, twenty or so girls emerged from the bushes to look down upon the victim. Cynthia removed his binoculars, and hung them around her own neck. Tod, being two years older, glared at Cynthia. The great trophy of the binoculars should be hers by rights.

"For today's sex lesson," said Cynthia, "we have a man and, though he is not a very good specimen, he will do for demonstration purposes. Assistants, please remove the croquet hoops."

None of the spectators dared move, as the man's jacket, tie and shirt were removed and placed in a bin liner. Then he was laid back down, and the croquet hoops hammered back across his forearms.

"Now he is safe," said Cynthia, "I shall endeavour to remove his trousers."

Two of the shyer girls took a step backwards, but nobody actually ran away.

"He's a bit hairy," came a voice from the crowd.

"This is why we need to shave our boyfriends every week," said Cynthia. "Anyone who missed my lesson on the subject should see me later –with their chocolate bars – otherwise your future boyfriends will end up looking like this. The only bristles we want to see should be on the shaving brush."

Slowly, the girls inched forwards to look at what happened if you did not shave your boyfriends. Cynthia used the distraction to study the packet she had taken from his jacket pocket. She had no idea what condoms were, but instinct told her they might be important, so tucked them down her bra. Then she looked at the audience.

"And now," she said dramatically, "the underpants!"

Some of the girls started flapping their arms; others threw their hands over their face, looking through the gaps in their fingers. Cynthia tried to keep the impression of being in control, but even she put a finger and thumb over her nostrils as his strange, hairy thing made its first appearance into fresh air. Eventually, she put the underpants into the bin liner, together with the pillowcases, old gym towel, and photograph.

"The evidence," she said, "is to be weighted down with stones and thrown into the boating lake."

Two girls stepped forwards with their eyes closed – or at least, mostly closed. Then they snatched the sack and disappeared into the woods.

"Now," said Cynthia, "the most important thing to remember is that a man will always follow his 'tentacles', as grown-ups like to call them. They cannot help it. Where the tentacles go, he will follow. Tod, the fishing line, if you please."

"Uh," said Tod, as if she was annoyed about something. Then she picked up a long stick to poke the shrivelled organ.

"It's nothing like the pictures we saw in your magazines," she said accusingly, "it won't even stand up. And why has he only got one ball-thing? The men in your magazines had a cucumber and two potatoes."

Cynthia knew this was just Tod's way of saying that she could do even braver dares. Ignoring her intervention, she knelt down to attach the fishing line. Then she caught the awful smell of dirty old men, and found herself back in the dark corridors of her childhood. A big house, where horrible giants shuffled through the shadows with their horrible slimy tongues always hanging out. Instinctively, she reached down to protect herself, but fortunately the audience were too excited to notice, and she carried the move on to wrestle the stick from Tod. Then she looked down to discover that the man did appear to have one very large 'tentacle', at least the size of a grapefruit. She needed to think quickly.

"It's just his monthly cycle," she said, "the small tentacle's resting underneath, the big one's full of stuff ready to impregnate Miss Becky!"

There was a collective gasp of horror. Cynthia felt her courage return.

"You might want to stand back," she added. "If he's dreaming about Miss Becky this tentacle could squirt off like a whale at any moment!"

Tod jumped back with a scream. Cynthia looked around to find her hiding in the bushes with a jumper pulled over her head. That's why Tod would always be number two; when she was released next month, she would probably work in a flower shop or something.

Cynthia put a slip knot around the hideous deformity, then stood up to offer the coil of fishing line to anyone who would take it.

"Whoever is on the end of this line will have total control of the man," she said. "I suggest we roll out a hundred feet, and withdraw to a safe distance until he wakes up. Assistants, remove the croquet hoops, everybody else to battle stations. Emily, tell Miss Becky it is done."

*

Matron walked along the corridor, quite horrified by all the things that Becky had just told her. She reached the spare room on the third floor, and gazed out of the window. A girl was loitering near the trees, while two more played a game of catch near the corner of the building. It looked very peaceful; surely Becky had got it wrong.

Soon a prefect stood beside her. "I'm your personal assistant," she said. "Sorry I wasn't here to meet you, but there was a problem with sector three – sorted now."

"So," said Matron, "you want me to imagine a naked man in the woods as well."

"If you like," mumbled the prefect, going slightly red, "though personally I'd be happy just to imagine a boy walking up the drive to give me a massive snog."

Matron half noticed the girl at the edge of the copse pick

up a tennis racket, and begin to wave it about, as if directing an imaginary aircraft across the lawn. The girls at the corner of the building immediately changed to a game of bounce-catch. Suddenly, the tennis-racket girl dropped her arms by her sides and, in this new form, vanished behind a tree. A moment later, a naked man leapt from the bushes, a look of absolute terror on his face.

Astonished, Matron turned to run, with the intention of getting something heavy with which to hit him over the head.

The prefect pulled her back. "No," she said, "watch the signals officer."

"I want that man stopped before the under tens see him!" shrieked Matron.

"They only have to run about in a mass stampede. They'll have a great time…wait, look there."

Matron watched the man run across the croquet lawn, but the prefect redirected her head to the girl with the tennis racket, who was now swinging it like a golf club.

"Good," said the prefect. "That means the tree lookout has just reported Miss Buckley is still at her desk."

"It's not good," said Matron. "There's a naked man running about the grounds!"

"Not anymore. The signals officer has just reported that he has managed to climb in through the window."

*

Mr Tebbit was finally able to stop running. He looked down to discover a loose length of fishing wire tied around his testicles. Quickly, he opened the loop, and with great relief saw it drop to the floor, snaking away to disappear around the corner. He turned to run, but the door through which he had come was locked. Turning again, he realised he was facing a long, windowless corridor, brilliantly lit by fluorescent tubes. It reminded him of his own school days but, after he had smacked Sally Parkinson in the mouth for putting the photograph of 'Mr Softy' on the notice board, he had been expelled. So why was he now completely naked, and looking at something that reminded him of his youthful embarrassment in the showers?

*

On the third floor, Matron felt her face being fanned with a towel.

"You're starting to overheat," said the prefect. "When you go to see Miss Buckley, you need to be as cool as a cucumber."

Suddenly, the girl with the tennis racket gave a tremendous serve, the ball flying off towards the hockey pitch.

"You're on!" said the prefect. "Remember, walk, don't run, otherwise you'll put our timing out."

Matron felt the perspiration being dabbed from her forehead with the towel. In a dazed state, she was escorted to Miss Buckley's office, where the prefect opened the door, then retreated unseen. Miss Buckley looked up from her crossword.

"I did not say you could come in," she snapped, "though I expect you have come to resign. There can be no other explanation for such insubordination. It has been the same ever since your hallucination of a 'trouser problem.'"

Miss Buckley used the phrase 'trouser problem' to cover anything to do with reproductive biology, men in general, or what might happen on a honeymoon. As a result, working out what she was talking about often required some guesswork, and it was generally easier just to accept something she found displeasing had happened. In complex cases, her demented rambling could be expected to last five minutes and, according to the prefect, it was most important not to stop her, since backup would not arrive for eight minutes.

"...So I accept your resignation," concluded Miss Buckley.

Matron turned her attention from the ancient clock on the wall. Only three minutes had passed; the timing was all wrong. Then the reality of the situation sank in: she had been drawn into a child's game, and would now be cast into the wilderness. The only way to save herself was to follow the Games mistress's example: a full lie-down, before sitting up with the collective amnesia that had affected the rest of the staff.

Matron found herself trying to faint, but her legs refused to collapse. She knew the boy was real, and his injuries were not imaginary. Her only option was to follow the prefect's battle plan, and hope for a miracle. Reluctantly, Matron tried to remember the prefect's script.

"Sorry," she said, "but to me a code black is serious. I want something done about the bad man."

Miss Buckley made a jerking motion, as if to throw her hands over her ears. Instead, she confined herself to a nervous blink.

"We all know that such a trouser problem is just a fairy story," she said.

"From the poor child's tormented nightmare, I think she was describing a code black. But even if it was a code blue, I really don't think such a thing can be overlooked, even if the master is your special friend."

Miss Buckley stared at her with an expression of disbelief.

"Why else," continued Matron, "would you be shielding him from the police…unless, of course, he is paying you to provide him with little girls?"

Miss Buckley went into a state of shock, which thankfully made up for her 'trouser problem' ramblings only lasting three minutes. But, as time passed, Matron came to realise the fantasy was over; this was a child's game gone wrong. Then a twelve-year-old girl rushed into the office to jump up and down in the middle. She tried to speak, but only managed to gulp mouthfuls of air as she flapped her arms like a fledgling bird learning how to fly.

"Miss Buckley," she gasped eventually, "there is a nude man in the corridor playing with a funny sausage. It was 'orrible!"

Then she threw her arms into the air, and crashed to the carpet in a dead faint.

Miss Buckley looked down at the child, then contorted her previously shocked face into one of disgust. She picked up a cane from the umbrella stand and rushed out of the door. The girl on the carpet opened one eye, then lifted herself onto one elbow.

"Now can I take the lead in the Christmas play?" she asked.

Matron felt quite faint, and sat down.

"I hope you really didn't see the bad man," she said.

"He was funny, but I could never do what Cynthia did. She actually had to touch it…and it was all ready to impregnate Miss Becky as well!"

Matron looked at the girl, who was now standing and reaching towards the big black wartime telephone on the desk. Strangely, she seemed to smell of strawberries. Then Matron felt the telephone receiver being pushed to her ear.

"Emergency," said a distant voice. "What service do you require?"

*

Miss Buckley made slow progress along the corridors due to the numerous stampedes, or the odd girl fainting at her feet. But she persevered, swishing her cane, and twitching her nose in disgust. Then she came around a corner to find the 'trouser problem' standing six feet away. It was the first time she had seen a naked 'trouser problem', and it made her mind go completely blank. Then dear sweet Beryl came upon the scene...

"Oh," she said, "I have often seen that man jumping out of the woods on the other side of the lake without any clothes on. Why do you suppose he glues that extraordinary thing to the top of his legs?"

Miss Buckley remembered what her mother superior had told her many years before. Down below was where men kept their evil thoughts. Giving a fearsome cackle, she brought her cane swishing down onto the 'trouser problem'. The man screamed, and bent over to play with himself. Six fearsome swipes across his bottom made the unprotected 'trouser problem' reveal itself. Miss Buckley knew what she had to do next. Glued on indeed! Well, she would soon cure him of that!

There are two ways of dealing with the excess water that can build up in the testicular membrane of older men. The first, favoured by those who do not have girlfriends, is to ignore it. The second is to go to the doctor, where the fluid can be removed with a sterile syringe in ten minutes or so. Miss Buckley used a third way, unbelievable anger sending her claws tearing into the flesh, the water spurting out, as if squeezing a wet sponge. Her belief that she was holding a cupful of warm 'trouser problem' made her stare with horror, as did Mr Tebbit, who had a similar belief, especially since he was deflating. Their screams, perfectly synchronised, caused many faces to appear from every doorway, mouths dropping in astonishment at the cascade of water. Thank heavens Cynthia had warned them; impregnation was far more spectacular than they had ever imagined.

And quietly, down below, a million germs that had been living a precarious existence in the dirt beneath Miss Buckley's fingernails beheld paradise.

*

Cynthia decided that the time had come to acquire some medical knowledge. Her payment for dealing with the pervert was therefore a fully illustrated, grown-up, medical textbook. For this, she had provided one Swedish magazine, and some fishing line at no extra cost. Matron had not known about the deal until she noticed an empty space on her bookshelf. What was Becky thinking of? Her assertion that *Anatomy and Physiology for Nurses* was very educational was clearly nonsense. Cynthia just wanted to look at the photographs. And what about the chocolate bars? Her entire three-month discretionary supply gone, and for what? Protection against some childish nonsense. Secret crossing of the lake indeed. Well, she had put her foot down over that.

That night, Matron lay in bed with various images of the day floating through her mind. Miss Buckley's efforts to separate Mr Tebbit from his 'trouser problem' had apparently almost succeeded. Then she remembered the pitiful way Miss Buckley had got down on her knees in her study, begging forgiveness, and shaking at the prospect of their 'little' conversation being passed on to the nuns. Such idle thoughts continued to drift about, until Becky's voice crashed into her mind. She sat bolt upright in bed. Chloroform, what chloroform? In a state of panic, she got dressed and made her way along the corridor to bang on Becky's door. After some time, there were indistinct noises, and the door opened.

"It's three o'clock in the morning," mumbled Becky. "What on Earth has happened?"

"Where did Cynthia get the chloroform? I want it taken from her now, before she kills someone!"

"Sounds expensive. If I were you, I'd be more worried about the condoms."

"What!"

"That's just what I said when she showed me the packet. Apparently the pervert was expecting to do it three times. Anyway, now she has the knowledge of how to cross the lake, and all the equipment necessary to do a code blue. It's only a matter of time before a girl climbs back over the fence with a great big smile on her face…"

"Stop," demanded Matron. "I want the condoms taken from her now!"

"She thought you might, so for you she'll do a special deal. A hundred chocolate bars for all three."

Only as the first light entered the sky did Matron realise this was something Becky would have to sort out. It was just not dignified for a matron to be negotiating with one of the girls for condoms. Besides, Cynthia knew too much; maintaining good order largely relied on her keeping her mouth shut.

After breakfast, Matron went off to take out her frustration on Mr Cranmore. Without knocking, she walked into his office, causing him to leap from his chair, then attempt to hide behind a cupboard.

"I hear your special friend is in prison," said Matron. "I hope you haven't left any of your special edition *Buntys* lying around where the police can find them. And what extraordinary stains! I do believe a top psychologist is coming from Germany to study him."

Mr Cranmore edged to the window, where he started to nibble his tie.

"But the real question is," she continued, "shall I tell the council that you knew he liked to look up the skirts of little girls, and threatened to sack Matron if she told of your little secrets?"

"No! I beg you…my pension. I'll do whatever you ask!"

Matron stepped across to tear down the large map from the wall.

"You won't be needing this again," she said. "Any further problems and I shall send Miss Buckley to deal with you. She likes to cane men on the penis, you know. Apparently your friend did a lot of screaming when the doctors told him it would never rise again."

On reaching the door, she turned to find a broken man, head buried in his hands. *There*, she thought, *that was much better. I should listen to Becky more often.*

Back at the girls' home, Miss Buckley was also having difficulty adjusting to the new realities of life. That man had

183

no right to come over here with his 'trouser problem'. Yet why did she keep thinking about him, sitting all alone in his prison cell, perhaps taking off his clothes in the hope that his next visitor would want to play with his…Oh, the Devil, the awful Devil, showing her temptation in her sixtieth year! Then she looked at her hands, slightly arthritic, skin the texture of dried Autumn leaves, and quietly began to sob. Finally, she got up, moved the telescope and, through a veil of tears, watched Mr Cranmore walking about his bedroom in his pyjamas.

FIVE

Becky was worried about the under tens, or, more precisely, their ability to throw potatoes covered in gravy that kept hitting the back of her head. How? Their Games lessons produced only noise and chaos, both of which increased if any sort of ball was involved; yet a slimy hand grenade covered in gravy could be launched to hit a moving target with silent accuracy. She didn't turn around to identify the culprit anymore; fifty per cent of their diet was potato related, and you could not argue with that much ammunition. Even Matron, who was largely preoccupied by her own problems, had mentioned she was starting to smell of lunch.

Cynthia had not been much help either, her suggestion being to sit on their faces and give them a good blast of 'bottom trumpet'. "They absolutely hate it," she had said, "legs a'kickin' and everything. And the really great thing is that it leaves no evidence."

Becky sat on the edge of her bed to ponder a more matronly solution. Given the narrow room, this put her face a few inches from the wall, with her legs all bunched up and uncomfortable, so she manoeuvred to lie on her back. But that wasn't much better, looking up from the bottom of a dark pit, the only window being twenty feet up, presumably to light the landing that had once been there. How she wanted to be free to walk the grounds without risk of persecution, to be like Cynthia, and have the confidence to gas the little horrors within an inch of their lives.

Eventually, she began to think about the boys' side of the lake. It was not a place she had ever been, but Hilda reckoned it was very pleasant, with neat paths crossing all the muddy bits. Perhaps the time had come to start exploring the big wide world. It certainly seemed better than lying at the bottom of a pit, or being covered in food, though it really depended on what was for dinner – not breakfast because that was always porridge, and therefore difficult to manipulate into ammunition. She got up, and went to the kitchens on the pretence of doing a vitamin survey for Matron.

"It' a nice one," replied Cook. "Boiled potatoes and sprouts, she'll like that."

This told her all she needed to know. Five minutes later, she was hurrying down the drive, when she noticed a now slightly podgy Beryl hovering near the gate. As head girl, she was allowed to do this, however Miss Buckley's idea was that she police the area, not mope around looking totally fed up. As Becky approached, Beryl gave a depressed sigh.

"Do you think they will like me," she asked, "the boys?"

"For sure," replied Becky.

"When you go to see Matron," she asked, "do they ever chat you up?"

"I would call it more running away to hide behind things,"

replied Becky. "Apparently it's what their brains have been trained to do. Once Hilda managed to drag two fifteen-year-olds from behind a tree; one trembled with fear, the other just giggled. Emotionally they had a mental age of eight, though since The Teapot's gone, things seem to be changing. Now if I walk up the drive, the older ones stare at me from a distance, then put a hand into a trouser pocket. Cynthia reckons it is a reflex action, but their brains lack the basic information to understand why it might be so. She has some plan to sort it. Apparently it involves parting the waters of the lake as she leads the girls to paradise, you know, like in the Bible."

"It will come too late for me," replied Beryl. "I am to be released in two months – staying in a hostel, working in a canning factory…I can't imagine what life on the other side could be like. I arrived as a baby. I've never seen a boy."

"Then you are one of the chosen ones. At the last moment, Miss Buckley will offer you the escape route of becoming a nun. A car with blacked-out passenger windows will take you to Scotland. Two years later, you will be back here as a mistress. You absolutely need to come with me now to look at a boy. Hide behind a tree, if you must. At least it will give you the option of letting Miss Buckley know your mind has been corrupted, and she'll send you to the canning factory without a second thought."

But Beryl was already backing away from the gate.

"I'm not ready," she said.

When twenty feet away, she turned and walked slowly towards the house with shoulders bent…

…And Becky saw how it would be in fifty years' time, Beryl walking up the drive as a nun, her submissive posture hidden by black robes.

*

"SNAKES…"

In all probability, this was the first word a baby heard as it lay in a cot with the fuzzy face of a mistress hovering above. On reaching the age of five, the resulting child would understand they were messengers of Satan, waiting to slither up legs and bite bottoms. Only on becoming teenagers did the girls start to diverge on how these facts should be dealt with. Cynthia applied her knowledge of 'special brothel customers' to the subject, including them in her lesson on 'multiple organisms'. Since nobody had heard of such things before, the mispronunciation went unchallenged, but it was generally seen as a good thing. But whatever they thought about snakes, nobody disputed the sanctuary was a slithering mass of creatures all hypnotically drawn to climbing legs.

The first time Becky had entered snake valley, she was too worried about protecting David to think about the danger. This time, her plan was to run as fast as possible, and complete the journey before the snakes knew she was there. On reaching the stile, she found it much the same as before. No, the snakes worried her less this time; indeed, had she been wearing trousers tucked into wellingtons, they would not have worried her at all.

Ten minutes later, Becky was walking down a flight of steps beneath the quarry wall, when she noticed a thin strip of wild meadow opening up on her left. It looked very pretty, and she made her way across it, careful not to tread on any of the flowers, or step into the muddy holes. Slowly, a smile spread across her face. She had reached a different country by her own efforts – an exciting world, where her new life was about to begin. As if to emphasise this, looking towards the lake she saw the back of a large metal sign, obviously marking the official border crossing. On reaching the nearest post, she swung herself around it, feeling slightly guilty at behaving like a twelve year old. She then realised the sign was telling her that '*Any boy proceeding beyond this point will be flogged*'.

"The monster," she muttered, remembering how The Teapot had brought the cat-o'-nine-tails snapping down on the bed beside her. On her next visit to the college library, she had looked it up; flogging was definitely made illegal in 1967. She had no doubt the nuns still used it with wayward girls, but they had God telling them what to do. This, in any event, is what Miss Buckley told the girls, the threat of being sent to live with the nuns being the same as saying they would be flogged. As to the boys' home, was it just The Teapot who did such things, or were other masters equally insane? She decided to ask Hilda about it; if flogging still went on, something would need to be done.

"Uh…"

This was something Cynthia had been saying for the past week: that something needed to be done about the boys' home. It seemed that, given enough time, Becky found herself agreeing with pretty much everything Cynthia said.

As Becky continued her walk, the girls' side of the lake became more distant, like her childhood. What mattered now was getting her 'O' levels, after which the home would start paying her actual money. It would be the first time she could go into a shop to buy something. What did not matter, the important thing, was that she could return to the pavement and think, This *is mine*. In addition to all this adventure, Matron had made certain she was taking all the right 'O' levels to get on a proper nurses' course. An auxiliary nurse they called it, which probably meant bedpan duties for a year. But it still represented the start of a new life, where all sorts of exciting things might happen in the distant future. However, before she could imagine herself wearing a nurse's uniform, her thoughts were distracted by a bench, set into a little cutting to the left of the path. She threw her coat over one end to indicate it was now her private space, then sat down to gaze across the lake to the far shore. It looked very pretty, with a narrow path occasionally emerging from the woodland to dip gently into the rippling water. It amazed her how any life could improve so quickly. Not one hour before, she had been a prisoner inside her claustrophobic room, staring only at a blank wall no more than six inches in front of her face.

Now she lifted her gaze to the skyline, where the top storey of the house poked above the tree tops. It was then that she finally understood why Cynthia kept going on about separating actual danger from something that was merely imagined. The periscope sticking out of the tallest chimney was simply psychological warfare; not even Miss Buckley was mad enough to sit in the fireplace with the soot falling on her head. Anyway, the periscope had come from a toy shop; the picture on the dining room wall was clearly a film poster about submarines.

Having resolved the periscope issue, Becky began to think about all the terrors that had haunted her childhood. Snakes, she decided, did not crawl up legs to bite bottoms. Bad Man Lane did not contain any men, except for birdwatchers who paid little attention to anything without feathers. The telescope…Ah, that was a real danger, even more so now

Miss Buckley had bought a new one. It had arrived as a parcel with an astronomical society logo label on the side. It was six feet long and had required two girls to carry it up the drive. With a telescope like that, Miss Buckley could not only see any girl who crossed the frontline, but in all probability, the identity number sewn into the back of her jumper.

The realisation that Miss Buckley might be watching her now made her feel awkward. Thus she looked further along the path, to where a cluster of bushes grew on a little outcrop of land that extended perhaps twenty feet into the lake. On a practical level, the protective vegetation might allow her to poke out her tongue in the general direction of the telescope.

After walking to the outcrop, her frown deepened. Between the leaves, she could see a timber panel. Why? After finding a break in the vegetation, she stepped through to find herself looking at a garden shed. Walking around the outside made her jump – her mirror image looked equally surprised. Instinctively, she stepped to one side to consider the extraordinary circumstance, then turned around to gaze across the lake. Slowly things began to make sense…one-way glass! Any occupant of the shed could stare directly across to a girls' home. How dare they build such a monstrosity! She decided immediately the time had come to do her third brave act of the day. She returned to the mirror, and used it to comb her hair into the Maid Marian attack mode. It made no difference to her if a prefect was on the inside, fiddling with himself through a hole in his trouser pocket. Then she imagined Cynthia staring at her from the far bank, quite unable to believe how brave she had become. Inspired by this, she went around the side, and opened the door – to see something quite astonishing.

Hilda reckoned Mr Cranmore had become quite odd after the pervert arrest – more sort of bumbling, and very nervous of anything resembling a matron. And now here he was, sitting in an armchair, quietly dozing. On his lap lay a golfing magazine, and by his side a Thermos flask. He had clearly forgotten to shave recently, and looked quite crumpled. Becky twisted her hairband around his Thermos flask, then retreated.

On leaving the shed, she realised something very important had just happened. She had done something brave, not to protect David, or because she wanted to impress Cynthia, but just because it was fun.

Walking with loose hair was something she had invented to make David laugh. But now, in her new rebellious state, she quite liked it…and thinking about Mr Cranmore leaving his slumber to reach down for his flask made her smile. Also, she liked the way her depression of the morning had made her take hold of her life, and give it a good shaking. It had brought her here, where she needed to be – a place where she had come to realise that this year was going to be much better than anything that had gone before: apart from vague images of the very beginning, when her parents had been alive.

Becky's walk came to an end beneath a mountain of iron bedsteads, the rusty metal overgrown with brambles. Annoyed that the once-circular walk had been so vandalised, she looked towards the woodland that descended into the river valley, beneath the dam. After deciding it was too jungley to be of any interest, she looked up the hill towards the boys' home. There was no actual path, but the battlefield shoes the home provided could cross more or less anything.

As she walked upwards, the woodland to her right became less dense, with speckled sunlight breaking through the narrowing line of trees.

"You're on telescope," said a bush.

Becky jumped into the air, then looked down to see the broken outline of two enormous saucer-like eyes poking from the undergrowth.

"Put a hand on your forehead," said the bush, "then scan the hillside for any girls. It will give you a reason for being here. Good, Miss Buckley's nodding to herself. Now go for a dallying wander in the same fashion, then make your way down to the big oak with a yellow cross on the trunk. That marks the safe zone. There's a gap in the vegetation ten feet further down. Crawl through this, then come back up between the trees."

Becky was confused by many things. Why was she talking to a bush, and why did she need to look for girls, who could not possibly exist on this side of the lake? "Curiouser and curiouser," she said as she got down on hands and knees to look down a foxhole. She then went for a dallying wander to the gap in the vegetation that the bush had told her about, and began to follow a surprisingly well-worn path upwards.

"Curious things, boys," said a voice. "Do you suppose they have a leader, or do they like being so disorganised?"

Becky jumped sideways with a scream. Then the bush by her side poked her leg with a twig. After her heart rate stabilised, she realised the bush was a brown blanket, to which a wide assortment of twigs and dead leaves had been glued. The other side was pointing a rather expensive pair of binoculars towards the boys' home.

"You're going to be in so much trouble if you get caught,"

gasped Becky in terrified admiration. "You'll get sent to live with the nuns!"

"Do I look scared?"

"No, because you look like a bush."

"Exactly, a bush with binoculars, quite normal on this side of the lake. Now, tell me about the boys. Do they have a leader?"

"Er…prefects, and as far as I can tell, they operate above the law."

"Like Beryl."

"Not exactly, they report to the masters."

"Hate them already. Suppose The Teapot got David beaten up, then?"

"Yes, he admitted it when he wanted to get his hands on my tea cosies."

"Slimeball. And the head?"

"Bumbling, ever since The Teapot arrest, I think."

"Good, it's starting to fall apart, and therefore in need of a leader, once I've got their prefects thinking correctly, that is."

"Er…ex-military fence, very high, and you happen to be a girl."

"Bush," corrected Cynthia, "but I was checking the fence for emergency escape routes. What do you have to do to visit Matron – the sensible one who pushed The Teapot into the lake?"

"Be eighteen, seventeen-ish if she meets you at the gate, because her prefab's not exactly part of the boys' home."

"I am only a simple bush. My roots are either in one place, or I am somewhere else. 'Not exactly' is beyond my understanding."

"It's on some sort of lease from the council."

"If you just heard my leaves rustle it's because I'm shaking my head in disbelief. It's obviously the way in I was looking for."

"Only if you have a parachute. It's surrounded by the boys' home, and her wall is…like, really high."

"Ah, that would be the fortress I passed on my way to deliver *Bunty* to The Teapot. Any more questions?"

Without waiting for an answer, the bush grew in height, with two legs underneath. Using these it weaved its way down the hillside. On reaching the birdwatching hide, it opened the door, and stepped inside.

"I fit in here," said the bush. "I was speaking to a man earlier, and he seemed to think me quite normal."

The blanket was removed to reveal Cynthia's smiling face. "This is a very good lookout," she said. "If anybody comes, I shall go back to being a bush. My name is Sharon, and I'm down from Newcastle to spot the great crested grebe. I've been reading about it in the library."

Becky could never remember laughing, at least not to the point where her ribs hurt. Then she threw her arms around Cynthia to give her a big hug.

"My friend," she wailed, "my best ever friend. Please don't let the nuns take you."

Cynthia wriggled free, then went to sit in the corner with her arms about her knees.

"I don't do hugging," she said. "It's weird. Tod beat up two girls last week for being lesbos, and they were only holding hands. Have you any idea what she would make of hugging? And if I'm sharing your room…"

"Share my room? Where did that come from? It's only five feet across."

"Bunk beds. Matron's second assistant can hardly sleep in the dormitory."

"Matron's assistant? That's about fixing arms, not breaking them."

"The humorus, radius, and ulna."

Becky looked puzzled. "The anatomy of the arm is nowhere near the chapter on sexual reproduction," she said. "How could you know what the bones are called?"

"Making babies is quite interesting, but then I realised so was the whole book. When Beryl started moaning about the canning factory, I thought in two years' time that could be me, so I decided to become like you instead. When I go to college next year, do I need to remember the 350 bones we are born with, or the 200 permanent bones into which they fuse?"

"Wait...college? Miss Buckley won't let you out of the gates until you are sixteen, certainly not to study Biology. And you're not really the sort of weed Miss Buckley likes."

"I can learn, and I already know Matron's weak point. I was talking to her about sex earlier, and she tried to hide in the corner."

"Because she considers you a child."

"No, it's more than that, but I can't quite work it out. I'm sure she's a virgin, but I didn't like to ask."

"She'd hate you forever if you did."

"But you're a virgin, I'm a virgin, and I'm sure Miss Buckley's a virgin. It's just this place, it needs sorting. Anyway, does Matron ever go out at night?"

"Too busy looking after you lot."

"Does she ever leave this place at all?"

"Every Thursday afternoon – to the library, shops, and tearoom in the village. She invited me sometimes, but I found it very dull. Not when I was fifteen though. She sneaked me out under a blanket. It was exciting then."

"And are there any men at the tearoom?"

"Only old ones munching wartime buns with false teeth."

"So she only goes to shag-free zones."

"No…yes…I never really thought about it before."

"You must learn to be more observant about what is going on around you. For instance, David's escape, have you not wondered why we posted you at the lake?"

"You didn't."

Cynthia raised an eyebrow. "OK," she said, "for whatever reason, you were at the best place to stop David running back up the hill to be flogged, if things went wrong."

"But he stayed in the woods…maybe swam across later. Which means Mandy got left behind."

"What very confusing things to say. Perhaps it might help if I ask an even easier question? How could I be so certain David was going to jump out of the window?"

"Because you got Jackie Smith to open it."

Cynthia put her head into her hands, and gave a heavy sigh.

"Observe the world around you," she said. "What else did we get Jackie Smith to do?"

"Nothing."

"She's very good at that, it's what grown-ups expect because of her limp. But did you not notice the tray of scissors laid out in the surgery?"

"I thought it odd. I had to put them away."

"What if David thought Matron was going to cut off his winkle to make another girl? She might even keep a jar of pickled winkles locked in her special cupboard. Do you think such a thing might give a certain predictability to his actions?"

"He will be traumatised for life!" gasped Becky.

"More importantly, it doubled his running speed. He has gone to a better place, and is not coming back. If it helps, think about the story of Jesus in the tomb, when the disciple comes out and says, 'he has gone'. You should learn to quote some Bible stuff, it will help you control Miss Buckley. But Matron's brain, that is seriously weird. How did you get in with her?"

"I just followed her around like a spaniel, and left her little notes. I remember using different colour crayons for every letter. Then, when I was twelve, I woke up to find a great red spot on my chin. I ran to the surgery in floods of tears, and Matron started telling me about vitamins. She's just crazy about them, it took her a week to get to B6. By then, I was her assistant, and I had decided to become a nurse. So how did you make friends with Tod and Sharon?"

"Two years back I was climbing trees when Tod and Sharon walked below. I got Tod on the back of the head with an acorn from my catapult, so they invited me down for a scrap. My first punch came upwards to Tod's nose. Even before she fell back, I was ready to start jumping up and down on her face. Sharon immediately decided she liked me better, though personally I think Tod's nose looks better now it's a bit wonky – a 'don't mess with me' sort of look. Anyway, Sharon decided she wanted to keep her hideous button nose, and I decided Tod did not look scary enough, so we went off to collect spiders that we made her eat when she regained consciousness."

"I remember it," gasped Becky. "Tod came back to the

dormitory in a right state, wouldn't tell anybody what had happened."

"I was eleven, I expect she was embarrassed. You do realise she's just a great big sissy who only eats spiders to frighten the under tens. Sharon is the one you want to be careful of. If you end up being pushed from a window, it will be her who does the deed."

"I see," said Becky, "and this is because I have upset them in some way?"

"You took their place, together with Beryl, but she's Miss Buckley's way of getting anything done, so they can't beat her up without there being consequences."

"Stop! Enough! I want all your bravery lessons, and I want them now! I want there to be consequences if I am attacked! I want not to smell of lunch!"

Cynthia nodded. "And in return, I want your best ultra-sissy lessons. I need Matron to like me. To get inside her head, and understand what she is thinking. What do I have to do?"

"Well, there are a lot of baths involved. Haven't you noticed the way Matron always smells of carbolic soap; me, of wild flowers, before I started to smell of lunch."

"I didn't like to say. The prostitutes at the brothel always used to splash stinky stuff over themselves. I thought it was a bad thing."

"I have absolutely no answer for that, I just happen to like smelling of wild flowers. Matron buys me a special bar of soap every month, as a treat."

"I just thought you were advertising that you were available for a shag."

"No, wild flowers is a nice scent."

"Because it makes you a virgin – and more expensive?"

"It's not about money. Being nice is about all sorts of things."

"So what's it going to cost a man to get his shag?"

"Nothing. When the time is right, married maybe."

"So in the meantime you expect him to use the brothel, spending all his money that he could be using to buy you fancy soap?"

"You assume all men use brothels because the only ones you met were so repulsive they could never get a girlfriend. Here we don't meet any men, except for The Teapot, who I expect also had to pay for such things. What is waiting for us on the other side of the wall, I have no idea. I just believe not all men are as you say. College doesn't really count because, to the outside world, I am dressed in rags, and it took me three months to realise they were all laughing behind my back because I curtsied to the teacher. Eventually, one brave boy explained girls did not curtsey anymore, but all I could do in return was eat my fingers. When I am properly on the outside…well, men are a complete mystery."

"Not really," replied Cynthia. "There are three kinds. First, the complete perverts who want to slobber all over you, and for that the girls always charged double. Second, some men are happy just to do the business, and walk away doing up their flies. Then, third, there are those my mother called 'special customers'. I never really believed I had to be naked to help the lesbians take a bath because my clothes would get wet, but I got used to it and afterwards the men who paid to watch the show gave me so much chocolate, I could have it for my tea."

"My friend," wailed Becky, reaching out to give her a hug.

"Gerroff," screamed Cynthia, dodging away. "If you ever

try that when I'm getting out of the bath, I'll smack you in the mouth now I'm bigger."

Becky looked down at her feet, ashamed at her insensitivity. Then she glanced at Cynthia, who had returned to sitting on the floor in the dark corner, with her arms around her raised knees. She doubted if the girl had ever known any physical contact, except for fighting, and whatever she was expected to do at the brothel.

"There is a book I have heard about," said Becky. "It might help…and I bet Matron would swap it for your magazines. It's about…well, I don't know exactly, but I think it covers what normal people do in bedrooms."

"And…?" said Cynthia.

"We'd have to tell Matron I was getting you a book on boy psychology," responded Becky. "The book I am thinking about is called *The Joy of Sex*."

"No," said Cynthia, "I mean I have twenty magazines, which sounds a bum deal for one book. But at the brothel they had a reading room for customers who were waiting for a specific girl. There was one very popular book called *Lazy Chatterly's Mother*. One of the girls was using it to teach me to read, but the words were too big then. Now though…"

Becky could stand the distance between them no longer. She knelt down and gently put her finger on the tip of Cynthia's nose. "You," she said.

Cynthia leapt up in alarm. "What was that for?" she gasped. "I thought you didn't do fighting – psychological warfare."

"It's like ringing a doorbell," said Becky. "It means let me in, I care about you, and want to be your friend…please."

"Oh my God," said Cynthia, "it's worse than I imagined. It never crossed my mind that ultra-sissies made friends by pushing each other's noses. I'm astonished that you are not all cross-eyed!"

*

The following week, Matron and Becky were sitting in the surgery, an awkward silence between them. Both were trying to get the courage to broach a difficult subject. Matron had noticed Becky had stopped wearing a hairband, even when she was outside the gates, where a boy might see her. Becky's awkward subject was the magazine deal.

"About the magazines," she mumbled.

"What? Oh, those. I've already signed an IOU for fifty chocolate bars, with interest of ten per cent APR, to get the condoms from her. It was the interest that confused me. But I thought about it after: have you any idea what Miss Buckley would do if she found the piece of paper telling her what I bought with my three months' supply of discretionary chocolate bars?"

"Have a heart attack, die, and you'd have to explain it all to a judge in front of a load of men. But fear not, I happen to know Cynthia wants to be your friend…"

"No! It is too horrible!"

"Better she likes you than to go down The Teapot route. Now, about the magazines, I really think they should be taken out of circulation, they give the girls a weird view of things."

"Aren't they all training to be prostitutes?"

"No, but the connection between love and sex has been lost, even if they could read Swedish. You probably don't realise just how illegal these magazines are."

"Code blue, but the girls seem to know about it already."

"These magazines deal with codes we cannot even begin to imagine!"

Becky removed a brown envelope from beneath her jumper, and took out a glossy picture of a girl accommodating five men at the same time, an acrobatic manoeuvre that required both hands clasping two quite enormous penises, possibly on the down-stroke. After a moment to stare at the picture, Matron leapt from the chair and ran into the bathroom, where she could be heard being sick into the toilet bowl.

Becky glanced at the photograph taken from near the woman's feet. The anal insertion looked disgusting, but it was no worse than the rat dissection she had done at college. As a student nurse, Matron must have seen car-crash victims all the time, but the poor woman had been completely destroyed by this image. When Matron came back, she looked deathly white.

"What does she want?" she asked quietly.

"All the magazines for a book on boy psychology. I'll go and get it."

Like an old woman, Matron shuffled for her purse, and took out a £10 note, then emptied the change on top.

"Will that do?" she asked. "It's all I have."

Becky gave the near-sobbing Matron a comforting hug.

"I'm sure it will," said Becky. "Do you want to see the magazines, before I destroy them in the incinerator?"

"No," said Matron, "just deal with it, and tell me when it is done."

Two days later, Matron looked up to see Cynthia standing in the doorway of the surgery.

"It is done," said Cynthia. "The magazines are smoke."

Matron sensed a wave of evil spreading across the surgery,

and backed away, turning to stare out of the window. Presently, she heard the door close, and looked around to make sure Cynthia had really gone. On the table were three eye-drop bottles and, twisting off one of the tops, Matron caught the familiar whiff of chloroform. Then she noticed a little card, designed to strike terror into her heart. On it was written a single word – 'Friend' – but not properly, more in the manner of a deranged killer who had just discovered crayons. Every letter was a different colour. What did it mean, and why had Cynthia painted a rainbow over the top?

*

Becky was lying in bed, when a thought unexpectedly popped into her head. It told her exactly where Mandy was. She was with David! Every under ten in the home understood this; it is why they liked to see her covered with food. The next thought came quickly: they were not in the woods. David would never allow such a thing, because of Matron and her scissors. Then something the prefect had said came floating into her mind. "Matron knows she has to meet you at the bottom of the lane," she had said. And there it was; her second role in the escape was to delay Matron while David and Mandy ran down the exposed hill to clear the bypass before they arrived. After that, things became uncertain. Perhaps they found a barn in a distant wood? But the boy was quite hopeless on his own; he would surely die of starvation within a week. The whole escape only worked because Mandy was there to protect him. She could manipulate grown-ups, and was almost a second Cynthia. But Cynthia had not known Mandy would be with David, it had just sort of happened…

But things did not just happen when Cynthia was involved. Mandy was part of the plan, but how Cynthia had organised their joint escape was a complete mystery.

*

Becky had been invited to...what, exactly? She wasn't certain, because she had never been invited anywhere before. Anyway, it brought a new problem into her life: what to wear? Her duffel coat would keep her warm, but it was the only coat she had and, if it got torn, it would give the snooty girls at college something else to snigger about. On the other hand, her jumper had been rescued from the hand-me-down bin after her official issue had vanished along with David. It was so extensively darned that, if torn, the additional repair would not be noticed. Eventually she decided Miss Buckley truly believed a coat should last forever, so the jumper seemed the obvious choice, albeit a slightly cold one. She then went to the bathroom to stare momentarily at the soap. A good double agent did not arouse suspicion by behaving differently. To wash five times a day was to make Matron feel safe around people she understood.

When Becky knew herself to be a walking monument of hygiene, she returned to her room, then opened her bedside locker to recover a key. To this was attached a brown parcel tag, on which were written the words 'Danger –Do Not Use – Ever'. It was the key to the staff gate in the fence, beyond which lay the deep, dark woods. It was a place where nice girls never went. To her the word 'nice' always seemed so much better than the word 'sissy'.

Fifteen minutes later, Becky was standing on the hockey

field to stare at the gate. She had passed through this many times during her nightmares; the last time, Tod and Sharon had tied her to a tree, naked, so the under tens could throw potatoes at her. And now, reality was even worse, because since The Teapot incident, the house went into lockdown an hour before sunset. If she vanished, there was no way any mistress would undertake a rescue mission.

How Becky wished she had managed to persuade Cynthia to meet her on the games field. But the girl had just replied it would not do for Matron's assistant to be seen using the senior hole in the fence, any more than she could use the staff gate. Apparently, it was all to do with the position you held in society. But now, as she looked at the gate that led to the dark side, the finer points of social etiquette did not seem that important.

Then Becky remembered Hilda had used the staff gate to get to the girls' side of the lake – twice – and nothing bad had happened to her. Oh, this was going to be one of those imagined dangers. After all, they were just woods, a place where all the blackbirds would be singing to each other. She unlocked the gate, stepped through, then studied the line of gravel that suggested further progress was made by pushing apart two bushes. On the other side of these, she found a scrappy path that turned left to descend three stone steps in the general direction of the lake. Following this soon brought her to a tree with a metal road sign nailed to the trunk. It had a picture of a catapult, while the plate below stated:

CAUTION – BIRDWATCHERS WILL BE USED FOR TARGET PRACTICE IN THIS AREA.

Becky had heard about the signs. Apparently, Miss Buckley had got the caretaker to put them up after the boardwalk had been destroyed. It made sense, because fifty per cent of birdwatchers were men. Also, all their tramping up from the lowlands kept the path open, which gave Miss Buckley a problem. You could not sensibly contain 150 girls inside the fence that surrounded the games fields, without the whole lot exploding. So Miss Buckley had bought a load of catapults, and told the head girl to sort it – unofficially. That was the deal anyway: the girls made it impossible for men to get to the woods, and she ignored the holes in the fence – unofficially. In essence, the woods had been captured in an act of war, and were now their territory.

Becky had a brief moment of panic. She was now standing in a place the rest of the world had forgotten about, a place where the laws of England had no meaning.

Becky was distracted from her nightmarish thoughts by the sight of three teenage girls walking up the path towards her. What was supposed to happen now? Should she say, "Hello," or pretend not to see them? It was, after all, on the out-of-bounds side of the fence. To Becky's astonishment, the first girl to arrive nodded.

"Respect," she said.

The second also nodded. "Matron," she said.

The third, being a little younger, merely giggled, and hurried to stay close to her friends. Then all three girls formed a neat line, and disappeared into the bushes.

"Uh," said Becky to herself. Before, she had just been one of the inconvenient necessities of life. She handed out plasters, put on bandages...not really a person, more a vending machine. And now, one of the girls had said, "Respect," and there seemed to be a promotion to the role of matron. It gave her a rather warm feeling, increasing her bravery to the point where she continued her walk with the intention of reaching the lake – at least until Cynthia dropped from the trees, landing on the path two feet ahead.

"I didn't see you at all!" gasped Becky, after her heart rate had stabilised.

"Given my past," said Cynthia, "it often pays not to be seen."

"Well, just for me, would you mind giving me a bit of warning before you keep appearing from the vegetation?"

"No," said Cynthia, "I want you to learn to be more aware of what is going on around you. I can't watch over you all the time, and there's no telling what Tod and Sharon might do if they are able to sneak up on you out here."

"Tie me naked to a tree?"

"That sort of thing. But I'm worried they might get carried away, and throw you into the bog to see what a dead person looks like. If things turn out that way, don't scream that it's messing up your hair, because ultra-sissyness drives Sharon insane. Hopefully, my bravery lessons will sort this, but first we must deal with the laws, the most important of which is that what happens here stays here. If a girl gets injured, we take her to the hockey field, where Matron can ponder how such an accident happened. Or, at least, that is how it used to be. I have let it be known that, over here, you are now the matron. Things on this side are mostly back to front."

Cynthia pointed at a grizzly bear sign nailed to a tree.

"Nothing to do with Miss Buckley," she said. "Senior dorm put them up to keep out the under tens. It works. They rarely venture more than half a mile from their hole in the fence. Except for Mandy, who, it seems, lives in a world of her own."

Becky nodded. "The girls also said something about respect," she said.

"Probably because you showed The Teapot your fanny to entice him across here. They think that was quite brave."

Becky gave Cynthia her best horrified look. "I did not do that!" she said.

"Of course you did, inside his head, it's why his brain descended into his pants. Once down there, anything remotely sensible ceased to exist, at least after seeing the special-edition *Bunty*. OK, perhaps I forgot to tell the girls about The Teapot only seeing your fanny inside his head but, if we are to be seen together, I want you to have some credibility, and you know what gossip is like. Last time the story came back to me, you had let him give it a lick. Another month and you'll have shagged him senseless."

Becky opened her mouth to protest, but no words came out. At college, being a virgin was considered embarrassing, but fortunately the other girls never included her in their conversations. Possibly having an identification number sewn onto the back of her jumper told them all they needed to know. And now, even after she had unpicked it, you could see where it had been, because the material that had been underneath was less faded. Anyway, even this was not as embarrassing as her new image of letting The Teapot venture down below.

"You shouldn't walk through the woods with your mouth open," said Cynthia. "To a flying insect it looks like a safe place to hide."

Becky had been walking with her mouth closed for about

fifty yards, when Cynthia got down on all fours to crawl underneath a bush. Becky bent down to discover a natural break in the vegetation.

"Are you expecting me to follow?" she asked. "And balance across that fallen tree over the ditch?"

"You know the answer to that," Cynthia called back, "so why ask?"

"Just checking, what with me being a grown-up and everything."

Becky was so surprised by her ability to balance across a fallen tree, that she returned to solid ground with a secret smile trying to make its presence known. She even stopped to take a bow to an imaginary audience.

"And," she said, "I have worked out about David and Mandy."

Cynthia gave her a questioning look, but was quite happy to nod at everything she said.

"Good," she said at the end of Becky's rehearsed speech. "We are making progress. Things had to be organised so David would overcome his natural instincts to run away from any girl. For this to happen, we had to make Mandy special – the one who rescued him from his harem of devoted admirers, and assorted barbers."

"That is the one thing I don't understand," said Becky. "Mandy had only just found out, listening through the keyhole."

"You only see her 'Little Miss Innocent' act," responded Cynthia. "In the real world, Mandy overheard a group of girls arguing about which of them David wanted to marry, and crept away to have a good think. Eventually, she decided it was going to need grown-ups to make it work properly, so she asked me what it would cost to buy David, and for lessons on how to survive in the woods. She knows to avoid the normal childhood mistake of thinking ten miles is a long way, and they needed to be far enough away not to be identified as local missing orphans, if caught. The sort of thing that happens when you climb into the back of a lorry, while I distract the driver. 'Pervert, do I look sixteen?' But it was OK. After I left, he closed the curtains around his cab to sort himself out. This is surely a sign of sissyness – helping others."

"Let me see, you sent two children off in a lorry, with a pervert, to heaven knows where, but with the general plan of living in the woods, with no teeth-cleaning, baths, or central heating."

Cynthia nodded, and seemed to be waiting for an answer.

"Well," said Becky, "for David I can see your options were limited, and I suppose we do know he can build a den…"

"I told Mandy they needed a hole in the roof to let out the smoke from the fire, before they used it for cooking. Also, that rubbing two sticks together doesn't really work, and they needed to nick some matches."

"I see," said Becky, "and you think stealing stuff might be sissy?"

"No, my lessons on how to survive in the woods are just sensible. My sissyness was letting Mandy buy David for a hundred chocolate bars, and to settle for the twenty per cent deposit she was able to get from terrorising the under tens. And I was sort of helping you, because the chocolate bars had been saved to pay Tod and Sharon for throwing you out of the window."

Becky's secret smile had gone, to be replaced by a frown. "That does not make sense," she said.

"Of course it makes sense," said Cynthia. "The under tens think you ruined the rest of their lives."

"Not that," said Becky. "There's something not right about what you are telling me. I think my brain has finally started to consider how other brains might be working. For example, Mandy got the boy at the end of the day, also she probably knew about the secret crossing of the lake from David. I reckon she planned the escape with her future husband, and you had to go along with it because she knew too much. And why would she pay you in chocolate bars for doing something you needed to happen?"

"To be out-blackmailed by an eight-year-old girl is the most embarrassing thing that has ever happened to me," said Cynthia. "In fact, if you ever breathe a word of it to anybody else, I will have to kill you. But put your mind at rest, they have food for three days – assuming they eat chocolate for breakfast, dinner and tea. This is perhaps a good thing, since the lorry I put them on had a French sticker on the side."

"I don't think Matron would be impressed by all the chocolate, even if I told her, which I never will, because keeping secrets works better if we become special friends…"

Cynthia bowed her head, lifting her hands to cover her face. Becky thought this a good sign, since it was a gesture obviously copied from herself. Any moment, Cynthia would look up to stare directly into her eyes to indicate something difficult had been resolved. Yes, there it was! Cynthia was actually starting to pick up her gestures.

"OK," said Cynthia, "but only on the understanding that I don't have to press your nose like a doorbell. And don't tell the others I am your special friend. That level of sissyness is just too difficult for me to deal with."

"OK, so long as you don't expect me to eat spiders."

With that they walked on, an awkward silence between them, Becky trying to work out how you could be friends with someone without giving them a hug. She was then distracted by what would once have been a grand marble fountain and pond. Now it looked very sorry for itself, with green water and rambling vegetation reclaiming the area in the manner of a long-forgotten Roman temple. Cynthia climbed up a partly toppled column, then stepped across to sit astride a stone angel. She then pointed to a great chestnut tree, with a rope hanging from one of the branches that spread over the downward slope of the hill.

"Flying lessons," she said, "are a most important part of becoming brave. It's the under twelves' swing, so it would not do for me to use it. For yourself..." she shrugged. "Show me something," she said.

Becky pointed beneath the flight path. "Brambles," she said.

"So you intend to let go!" exclaimed Cynthia in astonishment.

"No."

"Then what lies beneath your feet is not important, be it a 1,000-foot drop or a feather mattress. Bravery comes from understanding this."

"Sorry," said Becky, "but it's not something I've ever done. When the others came into the woods to play, I went to help Matron. To her, standing on a chair to reach the bandage cupboard was incredibly dangerous, taking flight over brambles beyond comprehension."

"What? Never! But all children are magnetically drawn towards swings."

"If we had some nice ones in the grounds perhaps, but not ropes. Matron would consider them to be nasty and dangerous."

Cynthia shook her head in disbelief. "I have made friends with an ultra-sissy," she mumbled. "It's even more embarrassing than being blackmailed by an eight-year-old. It needs sorting. Now follow, please."

"There are no ropes involved?"

Cynthia did not reply, just leapt from the angel to fly across the stagnant water, landing on the stone edge of the pond with two inches to spare.

Becky stared in astonishment. "You really cannot die!" she gasped.

"It's useful if the girls believe that," said Cynthia, "for who would argue with somebody who has no reason to fear death? But it's all an illusion. If I know I can jump ten feet, then jumping a gap of nine feet ten inches is not at all brave, just something I do. Trying to jump a gap of ten feet two inches is not brave either, just incredibly stupid. It's nothing to do with being brave, it's about assessing the situation correctly."

"But what about the first time, how did you know you could do it?"

"In your case, you could start by jumping over a small dandelion. When you are ready to jump over a really big dandelion, you will know."

Becky hated it when Cynthia said spiteful things to her. She hated it when the under tens threw potatoes. She hated being an appendage to Matron's apron strings. She so wanted to be like Cynthia.

Feeling quite dejected by her life, she followed Cynthia back to the path, then onwards to the other side, where the vegetation was more dense. Soon it was necessary to crawl on all fours. After hitting her head on a low branch, she made an exaggerated "Ouch!"

"I think you should know that I'm really not enjoying this," she said.

"I have brought you to this lawless place because you are still not accessing your situation correctly," said Cynthia.

She turned, and raised an eyebrow. "What hideous creatures could scamper about this woodland untroubled by overhanging branches?" she asked. "Our current difficulties are because we are giants. Could it be that what you consider unpleasant but safe is actually extremely dangerous?"

Becky laughed. "The under-tens zone is just a rumour," she said.

"No, it exists. Senior dorm never come here, they know better."

Then with the agility of a tiger, Cynthia leapt over a bush and disappeared to a place unknown. Becky looked around to realise she was quite lost.

"Miss Becky wets the bed," cried a squeaky voice behind her. Then the cry was taken up from three sides.

Instinctively, Becky crawled into the vegetated tunnel ahead, but this only led to more tunnels, or indistinct paths. They all looked the same, a maze of impossible complexity. The cries were more numerous now, like a flock of birds circling over an intruder. It jangled every nerve, causing her to cover her ears, which made it impossible to crawl away. And, all the time, the unseen enemy seemed to be getting closer, more hostile. Now the cry had modified to "Wet bed, wet bed."

Suddenly, she broke into the sunshine, stepping onto a narrow clump of turf that stuck a few feet over the bog.

Sticks started poking from the bushes, forcing her to balance precariously at the very edge of a slippery drop. They were actually going to do it, drive her into the swamp – to watch her die!

"Has anybody seen an under ten?" came Cynthia's voice, possibly from high in the tree tops. "Only I ate a load of spiders last night, and I'm full of spider gas waiting to explode. Such a waste without a face to sit on!"

There was a deathly silence. The sticks stopped poking. Then came a chorus of screams, fading into the distance.

"They were trying to kill me!" gasped Becky.

"Good," said the voice from above. "You are starting to assess your situation correctly. The question is, what are you going to do about it?"

"You," blurted Becky, before collapsing onto the turf in a heap of misery.

"How very interesting," said Cynthia.

But Cynthia did not elaborate, just sat on her branch, presumably looking down to watch her humiliation. Cynthia did not want to be her friend, nobody did.

*

The following morning, Becky was woken by a muffled scream. She was still trying to work out if it had been part of her nightmare about sinking into the bog, when her door opened.

"Get out of bed, sleepy head," said a voice. "There, how did I do? Is that the sort of thing I have to say to make Matron like me?"

Becky peeped out from beneath her pillow, where she

had spent most of the night crying. Slowly, the puffy image of Cynthia came into focus.

"No…Matron will never like you. Did I just hear a scream?"

"I can now imitate your walk. She only knew it was me when she looked up from her desk. I told her it was a beautiful day, and tried to give her some flowers I picked from the wood. But she did not want them, so you can have them instead."

Becky looked at the weeds sticking out of an old baked bean tin.

"I don't understand what you are doing here," she said. "Girls are not allowed in the staff quarters."

"How very sensible," said Cynthia.

She then got down on the floor to measure it with a one-foot wooden rule.

"Good," she said. "It will take the bunk bed I have in the attic, but it won't get out through the skylight, so we'll have to bring it down the old servants' stairs when Matron's not here. Do you have a screwdriver?"

"But you hate me. Yesterday…"

"But it was the best ultra-sissy lesson you ever gave me, all that howling and crying like a baby. I really think I am beginning to understand."

Cynthia sloped her shoulders, tilted her head, then clasped her hands across her chest.

"Isn't the weather dreadful?" she cried in a squeaky voice. "If a raindrop ever fell on my head, I would be certain to get pneumonia…and die!"

"I have never said that," gasped Becky.

"But it is the image you give, which is why the under tens know they can bully you. I haven't actually beaten up an

217

under ten for two years, but I give the image that I might. I am an unpredictable psychopath with no fear of death. Your image is rather more…"

Cynthia reached out to feel the dry bed.

"…Good girl," she observed. "Matron will be very pleased."

Becky stared into space. "I have never wet the bed," she sniffed. "Please, can't you make them stop saying that?"

"When you've completed my bravery course, you won't need me to do anything. That is the whole point of it."

Half an hour later, Becky allowed herself to be led to her place of execution. Standing atop the rocky outcrop of the senior swing, she stared into the abyss.

"Good," said Cynthia. "You now fear humiliation more than you fear death. We are making progress."

*

On Friday night, Mandy used a garden chair to climb through the surgery window, and headed directly to the bed. The following morning, Matron found her fast asleep and, having no idea how to react, went to get Becky. The two came scurrying back, just as Mandy was starting to stir.

"Mummy," she said, "have you missed me?"

"You are in big trouble…" said Matron. She could not think how to continue, because they were all in big trouble.

Mandy did not seem concerned, and merely swung herself out of bed to reveal she was wearing spotlessly clean clothes. The girl had been missing for three weeks, yet there was even some evidence to indicate her clothes had been recently ironed. How?

Becky knelt down to look directly into Mandy's eyes then,

applying self-assertiveness, got sufficiently close to block Matron from view.

"And did you enjoy the big wide world?" she asked.

"It was good."

"And David?"

"He was very good too. He kissed me, and I only had to tie him to a tree, in case somebody saw. And, because I rescued him from Cynthia, it means he has to marry me. He even gave me an engagement ring. Do you like it?"

Becky thought it looked like something a plumber might use.

"It's beautiful," she said. "And how is David? Is he hiding here?"

"No, Cynthia really frightened him. It's only me he wanted to kiss."

Mandy's face showed not a trace of hatred. Becky was very pleased for noticing this.

"So," she said, "if David is not here, he must be somewhere else."

"It's a secret," responded Mandy. "I promised never to tell, not even under torture."

"It's OK, we didn't tell Miss Buckley you had gone, so there will be no going to live with the nuns. Now, would you would like some breakfast?"

Mandy shook her head. "The lorry driver who brought me back gave me his sandwiches," she said.

"You got into a lorry by yourself!" exclaimed Matron.

"No, the lorry driver was there as well. I don't know how to drive."

"You know," said Becky, "the way grown-ups go into a huddle to talk about things they don't want children to hear and you have to listen through a keyhole? Well, there are some things that are not nice for your mummy to hear, and getting into lorries is certainly one of them."

Mandy screwed up her nose. "But he was a nice man," she whispered. "I think he came miles out of his way, and he followed me all through the woods to make sure I was OK. He was funny. He tried to get through the hole in the fence, but he was too big, and his ears got stuck."

"Never, ever go into the woods with a lorry driver," screeched Matron. "Didn't you think he might be a bad man?"

"Quick," said Becky, "go into a huddle. Now tell me as quietly as a mouse telling the others where the cheese is."

"Excuse me," said Matron, "I need to know if there is a bad man trying to get through the fence, and why didn't he take you to the gate?"

"This is very secret talk," said Becky to Matron. "Quiet, or we'll make you go outside and listen through the keyhole."

Then the two of them went into a complete huddle, whispering into each other's ears, a thing Matron found intensely annoying.

"Did you really?" said Becky presently. "Well, I don't think we should tell your mummy about that. But when would you like to see your future husband again, if your mummy gives us a very secret lift in her car?"

"Tomorrow, because I want to play with my friends today. Boys are very strange when it comes to that. I had to stop him making mud pies, and all he had was a rusty bucket that he found."

"But you don't have any friends, not since you won David."

"Do," said Mandy, "but not the under tens, they just run about like squeaky mice, being silly." She made her fingers scamper about as she twitched her nose. "My friends are all senior dorm."

"Well, I'm sort of senior dorm," responded Becky. "Do you think I could be your friend as well?"

Mandy tried hard to hide a smile, but not very well. Then she nodded.

"Oh good," said Becky, "but we must do things properly."

Becky, still on her knees, reached out to put a finger gently on Mandy's nose.

"Best-ever friends," she said. "There, it's official now."

Mandy went slightly cross-eyed, then shrugged, and returned the gesture. "Best-ever friends," she said.

"So now we can tell each other secrets," said Becky, "and never tell."

She gave Mandy a good hug, which made her feel all warm and contented.

Matron coughed. "You know what Miss Buckley thinks about physical contact, unless it's a medical matter," she said.

"But me and Mandy are best-ever friends," said Becky, "so it's OK. And I'm dying to know how the lorry driver got to the fence. I expect he was wearing enormous wellingtons, so as to get through all the brambles."

"Oh," said Mandy, "I never thought of that, I mean…er…I fell asleep in his cab, and he carried me up the hill. I expect he was wearing enormous wellingtons. I didn't wake up until we got to the fence."

This time, Matron actually left the floor as she shrieked out her protest.

"Didn't want my shoes to get muddy again," said Mandy. "See, by the bed, they are quite clean."

Becky put a finger to her lips. The important thing

was that Matron did not have time to think about the contradictions in Mandy's speech. Fortunately, Mandy seemed to understand that her fibs did not make sense, so walked away before she could be questioned further, closing the door as she left.

Becky resettled herself, sitting against the wall, her face a few inches from the keyhole.

"It's OK," she said, "she only snogged David...until he passed out with the joy of it."

"It's not at all OK!" shrieked Matron. "She thinks she's grown up, and can get into lorries...and that I'm really her mother!"

Becky stared incredulously at Matron. How could she have forgotten that Mandy considered a keyhole to be the way grown-ups told her stuff they might find embarrassing.

"You make a very good mummy," she said, pointing frantically at the keyhole. "Your daughter's made a very wise choice."

"It's OK," said the keyhole. "Miss Vera explained it to me."

"Is 'Miss Vera' anyone we need to know about?" asked Becky.

"She can see a long way into the future," said the keyhole. "One day my mummy will meet a man, then sign some papers so we can all live together."

Becky realised this conversation was too important to be conducted through a keyhole. She opened the door, and sat with one leg on either side of it.

"But we don't know any men," she said.

Mandy tried to hide a smile, then tiptoed backwards with a finger to her lips.

Becky felt totally comfortable operating in Mandy's world,

and mostly understood what was going on. Then she looked into the surgery.

"I do believe your daughter is the most sensible of us all," she said, "and I can't imagine kissing a boy is so bad. Whereas I couldn't even start my 'O' levels until I was sixteen, because of the daft old bat and her 'trouser problems.'"

Matron did not seem to hear, instead moving to sit on the surgery bed, possibly before she fainted.

"I expect I'll survive though," added Becky. "To be honest, I am more annoyed that I am still doing my 'O' levels at seventeen. And it was OK with the lorry driver, he couldn't come down the lane because it's too narrow."

But Matron still seemed to be thinking of something horrible, though Becky gave up trying to find out what it might be. A nice run-out in the country was what she needed, to find David. And who knows…a man?

*

Sunday saw the usual long column of boredom going into the assembly hall for a church service. Only Mandy was missing, on account of her sick note. Five minutes later she climbed into Matron's car with a great beaming smile on her face. "This is my mummy," she wanted to tell everybody, "and we are going for a family holiday." But the great masses were all doing God stuff, and there was only Becky to tell; but she knew already, so she kept quiet, and just grinned.

Becky was also grinning, partly because they were going for a nice day out, but also because this morning she had got up extra early to complete her final bravery exam. Even before it was light, she had stood in Bad Man Lane, closed her eyes, and counted to ten. No snakes coiled up legs. It was definite proof that her childhood fears had gone, and that she was now ready to do all sorts of brave things...wherever they were going.

Sadly, Cynthia had done less well with her studies; she had not even been able to answer a question about washing behind her ears correctly. "Every morning?" she had gasped on being told the answer. "That's, like, thirty times a month."

Becky was distracted from her thoughts by a breeze, bringing the scent of wild flowers through a little gap at the top of the car window. What was keeping Matron? At 10am she had gone up to the library to join the prayer meeting held for the mistresses, who preferred quiet whispering. But they only lasted for half an hour. It was almost as if Matron had asked for double rations, quite ignoring the wonderful weather God had already organised for their day out.

"Oh look," said Mandy, "Mummy thinks we are going to be playing hockey this afternoon."

Becky saw Matron walking around the corner of the building carrying a hockey stick. On opening her door, she reached over to put it on the back shelf, then got in, and looked at her passengers.

"And what are you two looking so pleased about?" she asked.

"Nothing," replied Becky and Mandy together. Then they both put a finger to their lips. There were some things you did not talk about in front of Matron.

"Before we start," said Matron to Becky, "I've brought something for you from the village. It's a present."

Becky looked at the card with three different types of hairband.

"Thank you," she said, putting it onto her lap. Then she

turned to Mandy on the back seat. "Now," she said, "we need to know your secret information. I'm authorised for level-three secrets."

"It's a level four," said Mandy.

"Then we are in a right pickle. I know, why don't you tell Pegatha, then she can tell me."

"I promised David I wouldn't see Pegatha anymore, if he would stop making mud pies. We are grown up now."

"Of course," said Becky, "you will need to make best-ever friends with your mummy, so you can tell her how to find David. Matron, you know what to do. Pressing a nose is like ringing a doorbell. It says, 'Please let me in.' A nose even looks like a doorbell – sort of."

Matron clenched the steering wheel with both hands.

"Oh well," said Becky, "it seems we will have to pay David a pretend visit." She started to bounce up and down on her seat. "Stop driving so fast," she said. "We are already on the big road at the back end of the woods…Oh, look at that boy and girl running from between the trees holding hands!"

"Huh," said Mandy.

"But I can see it in the boy's eyes. I know he wants to play kissing games because the girl is so pretty."

"Maybe," said Mandy. "Later."

"Stop!" said Matron. "OK, I give in."

Becky threw herself across to grab the steering wheel.

"Not while you're driving!" she screamed. "Stop the car first. Oh my giddy aunt, a lamp post."

She frantically ran her fingers over the wheel. "Hit the brakes!" she screamed.

Mandy laughed hysterically; this family holiday was going to be such good fun with her best friend, Miss Becky.

Nobody noticed that after the real journey began, Becky became very quiet. Car accidents were not something to joke about, if you lived at an orphanage. There were too many ghosts...

Though in truth, Matron was unaware of many things: the overnight luggage sneaked into the boot; the hairbands' disappearance down the back of the seat; or that Mandy knew precisely who her mummy and daddy were going to be.

SIX

Matron liked to drive with complete concentration on the road ahead, but today her eyes darted from left to right, all the time looking for a barn to which she could race with an armful of blankets. Sometimes, she looked for the sort of house where a bad man might live, and for this she had brought the hockey stick. After ten miles she stopped the car. It clearly wasn't possible for the children to have run any further.

"We must be lost," Matron said. "Could you describe where David is being held prisoner?"

Becky tried to cover the word 'prisoner' with a cough. "Are you sure this is the way you came?" she asked Mandy.

"No idea," said Mandy. "We just climbed into the back of a lorry with no windows. We got out when it stopped in a big car park."

"Young lady!" snapped Matron.

"We don't want to go the way we went before," continued Mandy, "because then we would have to swim across a river. I am trying to go backwards from the way the lorry driver brought me home. I was sitting in the front, so I could see everything. Just up here there's a field with an amazing white horse. After that, we turn to where he stopped to buy me a cup of coffee."

"You let a man buy you coffee!" gasped Matron.

"It's OK, I can drink coffee now…just so long as it doesn't have any rum in it."

Matron felt sick. Whatever had happened to this poor child throughout her missing days, had clearly caused great trauma. Really, she needed to telephone the police, but was already trapped in a web of deceit. To confess one thing, she must confess all, and that was now unthinkable.

Becky was now starting to look at the world through more curious eyes. Mandy was clearly telling fibs; the girls never went swimming, so Mandy could only have swum across an imaginary river. Also, it seemed unreasonable that later, when walking back to the home, she had simply climbed into a lorry with a big scary man – not without David, anyway. This lorry driver had more significance than she was letting on, but it was best not to talk about it in front of Matron.

"And were you in the lorry for a long time?" asked Becky.

"Ages, but it was ever such good fun. Sometimes he was doing sixty miles an hour, so everything just whizzed by."

Matron narrowed her eyes. She wanted to arrest the lorry driver for driving recklessly with a child, buying her coffee, and for generally being a bad man. Any normal person would have taken such a young girl to a police station, not delivered her halfway across England like a parcel. And, if he had been driving like a mad thing for ages, how long would it take her to travel sensibly in both directions? Increasingly this was a job for the police. Except they would immediately arrest her as an accessory to child-kidnapping.

After three hours, they had done over a hundred miles, leaving the main roads to travel down increasingly narrow lanes. Suddenly, Mandy started jumping up and down on her seat.

"I've found it!" she squealed. "It's over there, the sign to the village."

"It says 'quay'."

"Yes, it's a village made of boats."

Matron turned down a half-abandoned track, stopping immediately as she rounded a blind bend to find herself heading towards a river. Pleased by her careful driving, she allowed herself a smug smile, but only for an instant. Half a dozen sunken or neglected boats sat lopsided on the mudflats, and there was absolutely nothing suitable for living in. Still, so long as the boy had not picked up some terrible disease, she would try to remain calm. She got out of the car, and reached across to the back shelf for the hockey stick.

"Which boat is he on?" she asked.

Mandy pointed to a length of harbour wall, most of which had fallen into the mud.

"The boat that used to be there," she said.

"And what sort of boat was it?" asked Becky.

"An orange one," replied Mandy.

Mandy got out, and they watched her walk away, presumably out of embarrassment.

"Not too close to the edge!" shouted Matron. "Oh God, this is a disaster!"

After Mandy had gone about a hundred paces, she stopped, put her hands around her mouth, and shouted, "Mr Silver, are you there?"

Matron scurried after her, Becky following more slowly.

"Who are you shouting to?" asked Matron.

Mandy pointed to a yacht at anchor in the middle of the river.

"Mr Silver lives on that boat there," she said. "He'll know where the orange boat has gone."

"Wasn't the pirate in *Treasure Island* called Long John Silver?" asked Becky.

"That's him, but it's a secret. If anybody called, we had to say we didn't know him."

Just then, a man emerged from one of the sunken boats, that is to say a two-storey garden shed lashed to the top of it. The back of the boat had reduced to a skeleton of timbers poking out of the water, and it was only the sloping bank that allowed the front end to rise, the bows sitting proudly on the mud some thirty feet from the quay. Accordingly, the shed looked like the Leaning Tower of Pisa. Except it had a chimney, topped with an upside-down saucepan, complete with handle. Though why, given the shed's other misfortunes, the occupier should be worried by a bit of rain coming down the flue, was anybody's guess.

"Well, if it isn't my little Mandy," shouted the man. "And how are you, my precious?"

"You know that man!" exclaimed Matron.

"Yes, he's ever so funny. When his boat sank, he built a house on top of it."

"You mean a shed," said Matron.

"No, it's a proper house. I think he called it a chalet. He's really good at making people laugh."

"And he is called Captain Hook, I suppose," said Matron.

"No...George."

Becky studied George carefully. He was around forty,

and wearing the sort of cardigan only a 'George' would wear. Other than this, he had no distinguishing features; he was the sort of man who had been specially designed to go about his business completely unnoticed…at least until he did a funny sort of walk towards the bow of his sunken boat. Here he took hold of a rope that was tied to an overhanging branch.

"Trainee," he shouted as he swung over the mud to totter precariously on the quay.

Mandy laughed hysterically. "He means to shout 'Tarzan,'" she said, "but he shouts 'trainee' because sometimes he falls into the mud. See I told you he was funny!"

The man stopped his clown-like balance, and dropped the rope around a stake knocked into the ground. Becky then realised why his walk had been so odd: he was wearing carpet slippers, the hairy sort with two guinea-pig eyes at the front. She looked up to study his strange haircut, thinking how it might be improved. Anything was better than his present arrangement – a monk-like fringe making a complete circle, with a bald crown sticking out of the top. To her embarrassment, the man saw her looking, and tiptoed towards them finger-combing his head.

"Oh my lord!" he exclaimed. "The wind has blown away my wig again!"

Keeping a dead serious face, he stood on one leg, took a slipper from his foot, and placed it on his head. Mandy screeched with laughter, to which the man responded with a great caveman grin. Then Mandy raised her arms to indicate she wanted to be picked up, which he did. Becky stood in a state of shock; it seemed Mandy was being hugged, by a man!

The silence was broken by Mandy. "This is my mummy," she said, "and this is my best friend, Miss Becky."

George held out his free hand, which Matron refused to take, so Becky took it with her fingertips, and gave it a pathetic shake.

"Becky," he said, "David said you were the nicest grown-up in the whole universe. This calls for a celebration. Coffee at the chalet, I think?"

The man returned Mandy to the ground, and began to hop away with one hand holding the slipper on his head. Mandy ran after him, took off her shoe and, placing it on her head, hopped by his side. Becky wanted to laugh, but threw a cautionary glance towards Matron first. Her face was deathly white, and her fists clenched around the hockey stick so tight that her knuckles looked like marbles.

"It's OK," said Becky, "the man thinks you are her mummy. Good plan, because he'll be on his best behaviour for... whatever is about to happen."

On reaching the rope, Mandy immediately took flight to land neatly on the boat. George then took flight on a second rope to land beside her. Becky realised there were many ropes, which rather implied George was accustomed to receiving visitors.

"We need the police," whispered Matron.

"Why?" whispered Becky, in mock secrecy.

"Because of the man."

"Mandy's clearly been on the boat before," said Becky. "The under tens do not have the skills to use a rope swing so precisely on first acquaintance."

"Girls do not use rope swings at all!" snapped Matron.

Becky rested a hand gently on Matron's shoulder. "We need to talk," she said, "but later..."

Becky took two steps to look over the harbour wall.

"There are pools of water," she said, "with crabs trying to bury themselves in the mud to hide from my shadow, and seaweed…"

"It's just mud," said Matron.

"Assess the situation better," said Becky. "It means the tide has recently gone out. We are at the seaside, though I admit my childhood picture books did paint it as being a bit more yellow. However, I believe David found it sufficiently similar for him to get out his bucket and spade. Poor Mandy, to suffer so much for love."

Becky glanced at Matron. From her blank expression, it was clear the poor woman did not have the slightest comprehension of what was happening. Becky returned her thoughts to assessing the situation. The flight path to the sunken boat only just cleared the mud so, when the tide came in, any attempt to leave by rope would drop the user into the water. She walked a few paces further along the quay to look along the far side of the boat. Here, she discovered a little dinghy, just about floating in a ditch that drained water from the mudflats. Having established the escape route, she made her way back to the launch pad, and took hold of a rope.

"Now…" said George.

But she had no interest in anything he might be saying. After a great swashbuckling leap, she took flight, using her legs to exaggerate the swing as Cynthia had taught her. Oh dear!

George's astonished face was racing towards her at alarming speed. A moment later, they collided, to roll across the deck in a confusion of tangled limbs. George started laughing, quickly followed by Mandy.

Miss Buckley had a strict rule about giggling; such frivolity was not part of God's magnificent creation, and consequently, after the age of ten, it carried the same punishment as breaking wind. By the age of twelve the respectable girls had developed a reflex action that effectively controlled both ends. But here, Becky was struggling, and quickly looked away, just in case she needed to put the blame onto somebody else.

"At'a, girl," said George presently. "Half my visitors end up in the mud, even with me trying to catch them."

Becky turned back, and coolly raised an eyebrow. "How extraordinary," she said. "Why do you suppose they do that?"

"No idea," said George. "And do you know what? They always try to say it's my fault. Once, I wasn't even here, yet the lady telephoned me at work to say how much she hated me."

Mandy crawled across to sit on George's lap. "Me and David didn't fall in, did we?" she said.

"Oh," said George, "children never do, but it's the grown-ups. They forget how to do important things."

"Miss Becky is a secret double agent," said Mandy. "She's only a pretend grown-up. Really she's my best-ever friend."

"Ah," said George, "that would explain it. Now, shall we see if we can make your mummy remember what it's like to be young again?"

Matron stared in disbelief at what had suddenly become alien life forms. What was Becky thinking of, rolling about the deck with all its dirt and diseases? This entire place was a nightmare of madness. As for Mandy, she was eight, for Heaven's sake, and did not drink coffee. She doubted very much if the cups were clean, or the water boiled properly. Then she had the most awful thought: the only source of water was the river!

At the sounds of running feet, she looked around to discover two boys leaping wildly over the stones. "Mandy!" they shouted.

"Nicky!" squealed Mandy.

The first of the two children arrived. "Excuse me please, lady," he said.

Without hesitation, he took hold of a rope, and took flight across the mud. Then the other boy arrived, and did exactly the same thing. They did not even seem to be aware the mud was there. To them, it was just like running through the front door of a house. Once the three children were on the boat, they all started running about in excited circles, apparently in a game of tag.

At the other end of the quay, a woman was examining the green Morris Minor with a nursing sticker in the rear window. *Ah*, she thought, *the pretend mummy has arrived*. The flat tyre seemed to be a particularly good omen. They would be staying the night, which would give her a chance to work out if the boy needed to be found. After all, the circumstances of his arrival left a lot of questions unanswered. George had found him sitting in the mud, not wanting to stand up. He had been brought to her wrapped in a sail. "Stop flapping," she had told George. "Now get in your dinghy and fetch the hysterical girl from the far bank. She probably knows why he doesn't own any clothes." Two eyes had blinked at her from the mud. "Be a brave boy for Miss Vera," she had said. "After your bath everything will seem much better."

Miss Vera left her thoughts about Mummy's car to look along the quay. The lady holding the hockey stick was obviously the pretend mother. Not that she had told George about the pretend bit, for it would only confuse the poor fellow. The girl on his boat must be Miss Becky, but she wasn't important. Anybody who could cross that rope contraption could look after themselves. Vera reached inside the car for the ignition keys; sometimes fate needed a little help.

Matron saw the woman walking along the quay. She was dressed in flowing robes of vivid purple, and had lots of beads hanging everywhere.

"I'm sorry about my boys," said the woman. "Were you wanting to cross?"

"No…"

"Well, they should still have asked before pushing in. Guess they were excited to see Mandy again."

Matron felt her hand being lifted, and the 'purple lady' began a close examination of her palm.

"You'll have to excuse my little ways," said the purple lady. "I keep getting carried away with my work. I always find those without the gift fascinating, and I can't stop thinking it is my job to help them."

Vera studied the spotlessly clean hand with neatly trimmed nails. A glance down confirmed she was wearing shoes only a matron would wear. Looking up, she discovered the matron's eyes conveyed a sadness easily recognisable to those with the gift. This lady had found sanctuary in the orphanage after she had been betrayed…no, attacked. You did not go around carrying a hockey stick unless you expected it to happen again.

"I see two futures," said Vera. "In one, you are covered in mud, in the other you follow me. Come, please."

Matron looked towards the sunken boat for an escape route. The 'purple lady' was clearly more mad than George. But the children were nowhere to be seen, and Becky had turned away to look through the windows of the shed.

Only George seemed to be paying her any attention. Then he shrugged his shoulders.

"If you change your mind," he said, "just shout."

The next moment, Matron found herself being dragged along the quay sideways like a crab. George did not seem at all worried; being taken prisoner by the mad 'purple lady' probably happened to most of his visitors.

At the end of the quay, Matron turned to look where she was going. Realising the path went into the deep, dark woods, she put down her heels.

"Your daughter…" said Vera. Then she paused to let the sad lady interrupt.

"Ha!" said Matron. "Shows what you know."

"The gypsy sees many things, some of which fall from the future. Your daughter will be less confused, if we do not deny your shared destiny."

Matron wanted to protest, but merely forgot to keep her feet rooted to the ground, and let herself be dragged into the woods, where the 'witch' probably had a sacrificial altar. Suddenly, the nightmare got much worse: the path came to a sudden end above a steep bank, beyond which a mud-filled creek supported a narrow canal boat. The 'witch' vanished into the woods and, a moment later, leapt out from behind.

"Your daughter," she cackled, "will make this happen in a way you least expect: when you are signing the adoption papers. I see a man by your side."

This so disoriented Matron, that she stepped onto the gangplank, a place from where there was no escape. She found herself being shooed backwards like a hen. This inevitably led to the boat, followed by a descent of three steps into a room that was almost entirely occupied by an engine. Walking crab-wise around this took her to a door that opened into a kitchen. This seemed to be journey's end, because her captor put a kettle onto a stove, and lit the gas.

"Milk and sugar?" she asked.

Matron wanted to ask where the water came from. Then an even more horrible thought struck her: where did the toilet go, and if it went where she thought, did they still drink the water?

"I'm really not thirsty," she said.

"Of course you are. I expect you'll be wondering where the water comes from, that is all."

"No," said Matron.

Vera ignored the statement, instead looking out of the window to watch a sailing dinghy navigating accurately between the mudflats that lay across most of the estuary at low tide. In the dinghy, Mandy was gazing over the side, lost to another world as she trailed her hand in the water. Vera felt so proud of her boys for looking after a girl, who had not yet learned the ways of the world. And George was so kind to buy the sailing kit, when his own simple needs only required a set of oars.

After the dinghy had sailed from view, Vera reached across for the kettle of boiling water. "You take milk, but no sugar," she said.

"How did you know that?" Matron asked.

"The gypsy knows many things but, in this case, it was just a lucky guess. You are so thin, I doubt you would ever get within thirty yards of an unnecessary calorie. I expect you eat lettuce and stuff like that…but what interests me most is the way you keep fighting your destiny. You are stopping for tea, so we will talk about your daughter later. We are vegetarians

– I have some nut cutlets in the fridge. We eat in about an hour."

The mad purple woman had such an overpowering presence, that it gave her ridiculous ramblings some weird authority. Matron knew she must escape, before the madness got to her.

"I need to be going," she said, "to pick up Mandy."

"Oh, she won't be back for hours yet."

"If I have to go across the rope swing, then I will."

"But they are already on their way to the island to play pirates."

"Of course they're not, the boat's quite sunk."

"Oh hum," said Vera. "Why is it that you people won't accept anything without all the gizmos?" She went across to a cupboard and returned with a big crystal ball which she placed on the table. "I can see them clear as day," she said. "Oh look, isn't that cute, your daughter's trailing her fingers in the water."

"The boat…" said Matron, standing up and banging her head on the roof. She sat back down. "…It doesn't move."

The 'purple lady' peered deeper into the crystal ball.

"Look," she said, "you can see the sailing dinghy, and there is your daughter trailing her fingers, like I said."

"Sailing dinghy, what sailing dinghy?"

The mad purple woman made a humming noise, then began to sway from side to side. "Please be patient…ah, here we are. It's yellow with a white triangular sail."

"You can't possibly know that!" snapped Matron.

Vera went to the cupboard, and returned with a pair of binoculars that she handed to Matron.

"Some people prefer to use these," she said. "To the

untrained eye, they are easier to use, but they only work in straight lines. Go on deck..."

This was all Matron needed to hear. She had been given permission to escape. She grabbed the binoculars and ran all the way to the quay, without stopping. Here, she used the binoculars to scan the banks for the orange boat Mandy had told her about, where David was held prisoner.

The small dinghy was leaning over in a crosswind, the children sitting on the same side to stop it capsizing. They were so far out to sea that it was impossible to hear Mandy's screams for help. In complete panic, Matron ran back to the mad purple 'witch' who was still in the kitchen.

"They're out there," she gasped, "all alone!"

The purple lady glanced at the crystal ball.

"I do like watching the children play," she said.

"We've got to go after them!" yelled Matron.

"You new to motherhood?" said Vera. "I was the same when Nicky started going out on the boat by himself – butterflies everywhere. He was only six, but now he's been doing it for five years, he's a salty old seadog, and I don't worry at all. Mandy won't come to any harm with my lot."

"But they're children."

"You're clucking like an old mother hen. Just relax, breathe deeply if it helps. Now tell me about your daughter..."

"She's not my daughter!"

The mad purple woman smiled, then went to the sink to start washing the potatoes. "Cluck, cluck, cluck," she said, flapping her elbows.

"What's that supposed to mean?"

"You know what it means. It is in your heart. Only after you have faced the truth, can we have a sensible conversation."

Matron knew that she could never have a sensible conversation with the mad purple woman. She raced out of the cabin again. If saving Mandy meant speaking to Mad George, then she would do it.

Vera finished peeling the potato she was holding, then calmly reached into a cupboard to recover a radio microphone.

"Hello," she said, "it's me."

She could never get the hang of all that silly male banter. After a long pause, there was a crackled reply.

"Vera," it said, "I was expecting your call. Was that Mandy I saw sailing past my porthole?"

"Yes, the mummy has landed, but she's a bit hysterical at the moment, so you will need to organise her future."

After the radio call, Vera gave a great big shiver. Something was very wrong…and it was in her kitchen. She looked around to see the hockey stick propped up against the wall; it was bare wood. She got out a tin of purple paint, and contentedly restored the natural harmony of the world.

*

On first acquaintance, Becky had found the lower storey of George's shed to be something of a challenge. But on climbing the stairs to a trap door in the ceiling, she squealed with delight – not something of which she was particularly proud, given that many years had passed since her tenth birthday. But it was just so amazing.

The single open-plan room was about ten feet square; nearly four times that of her own accommodation. The walls, all highly polished oak panels, were dotted with brass candleholders, the flows of solidified wax suggesting they were frequently used; indeed, there seemed to be no sockets into which a light bulb could be screwed. Set into the wall facing the river was a stone fireplace, a railway sleeper beam above supporting the chimney breast. At the back of the hearth, a great tumble of logs were licked by yellow flames. These made the air smell rather nice, though perhaps a little hot for somebody wearing a jumper. The wall facing the estuary had a large window that gave a spectacular view of the sea. On the horizon, she could see the sails of a little boat racing across the water. How she wanted to be on that boat… and never return to the home again.

Becky turned away from the window to study a double bed, set against the wall facing the quay. Resting on top was a neatly patterned…well, she did not know what it was, but certainly nothing like the itchy grey blankets of the home. The thick cream carpet on the floor was so clean, she did not know if it was polite to walk upon it. George solved the dilemma by pointing to a box labelled 'muddy shoes', while also taking a towel to wipe the bottom of his slippers. He then went to close the little window above his bed.

"It's my 'speaking to the bank manager' window," he said. "You would not believe how personally he takes my overdraft. I only left it open to hear Mandy's return."

"You knew," gasped Becky, "that she was coming back?"

"Miss Vera saw it fall from the future, and she's normally right about such things, mainly because…well, to her the future is like Plasticine. She moulds it into shape and, only when it looks right, does she get out her crystal ball to do the mumbo-jumbo stuff. The other day, she said my cardigan was making the signal go cloudy, and that I needed to…not wear it."

"That's terrible," said Becky in mock surprise, "but if she says your future would be more predicable by not wearing it..."

She looked away, embarrassed at her personal comment about his outdated sense of clothing. But he did not seem to notice the comment.

"Tell me," he said, "I could not help noticing Mandy's mother was wearing sensible shoes. Is this normal?"

"Absolutely, not the slightest variation from one year to the next."

"Most satisfactory. It's what I always look for, sensible shoes. Ladies in high heels frighten me. I keep thinking they are going to topple over."

Becky thought it odd that a man should be frightened by a woman, and turned to face him. "High heels frighten you?" she asked.

"I don't understand them," he said. He pointed to his slippers. "These keep my feet warm, and make children laugh," he said, "so they have a purpose. What is the purpose of being all wobbly and falling over?"

Becky frowned. "Put that way," she said, "I have no idea. They are strictly banned where I come from. Miss Buckley likes it best if we clump about. I expect she is slightly deaf, and needs help locating us."

"Us?"

"Never mind. Now, tell me things I don't know, for instance why did Mandy ever return to us after finding this magical place?"

"It was after David spent the afternoon teaching her how to make mud pies. She brought the bucket, complete with contents, down on his head, and stomped back saying she wanted her mummy. Gave us quite a shock, since they had arrived claiming to be orphans. Anyway, Vera sorted it out. Apparently your visit is one of the things that fell from the future. Did Mandy pack the overnight bags?"

Becky was still unable to see how the need might arise, but nodded. She looked around the room. "Here?" she asked.

"Vera saw Mr Silver's yacht. She says my chalet makes her signal go cloudy. It is the only time I have ever heard her use the word 'unpredictable.'"

"Very unpredictable," confirmed Becky. "It is the sort of place where anything might happen…"

The conversation drifted easily this way and that until a noisy commotion outside distracted them. Becky knelt on the bed with the expectation of looking out of the window, but immediately felt herself sinking. She had no idea it was possible to get anything other than the metal-framed beds they used in hospitals, topped with three inches of semi-solid mattress. And how did it work, without sheets that could be tucked in? George's floaty sleeping invention certainly raised a lot of questions.

After a few moments, Becky returned her attention to the commotion that was taking place outside. After using the windowsill to pull herself up, she looked out to discover Matron was leaping about the quay in great excitement. Becky sensed the bed sink further, then George looking over her shoulder.

"Good heavens," he exclaimed, "discothèque dancing!"

"Don't think so. It's not something either of us would know how to do."

"It's where the lady shakes herself at a man. It's very frightening."

"Mandy's mum would never do such a thing. Her idea of fun is going to a tearoom."

"Most satisfactory," he said as he reached over her shoulder to open the window. "Do you want to come onboard for a cup of tea?" he shouted.

"No, I want…I want…I want to speak to Becky. Here, in private."

"A little girlie chat, I expect," said Becky. "It's what we do. May I say you like her?"

George shook his head, then opened his bedside locker from where he recovered a first aid box. From this, he produced two paper bags.

"If Miss Vera has been doing her act, she will probably prefer you to give her one of these to help her breathing," he said. "The second bag is for you because the quay is uphill. Your return journey will be on a lower flight path, and there's quite a knack in swinging your feet up at the end. I don't always totter on the edge just to make the children laugh. Sometimes not falling back into the mud is a bit of a battle."

Becky remembered Cynthia telling her things that made little sense at the time, one of which she called a 'spinny-out force'. On returning to the deck, she tried to look at the problem through Cynthia's eyes. She could do the 'spinny-out force' – not with the fancy trapeze acrobatics Cynthia would no doubt include – but the basic level looked possible. And what lay beneath her feet was not important unless she intended to let go of the rope. This problem was no harder than anything she had done during her flight training…

The next moment Becky was running across the deck, launching herself off the side, with all the determination of a fighter plane leaving an aircraft carrier. As the rope swung her around in a circle, she rose higher, bringing her back over the quay ten feet further along the bank. In that instant, she knew exactly what it felt like to be Cynthia: the exhilaration, the control, and the spectators who believed she could not die! She tried to convince herself it was nothing special, just something she did. But on seeing George's astonished face, a giggle escaped. Oh well, if her childhood was to begin here, in this new country, then the grown-ups would just have to get used to it.

*

Matron had been expecting to tell Becky about the children being all at sea, and about to die, but her mind had become distorted by the hallucination concerning her ability to fly. Only when the girl walked over, removing a brown paper bag from her sleeve, did Matron finally shake the hallucination free.

"Oh, two years at college," she snapped, "and you think you know all about panic attacks!"

"A little, yes, and you are having one. Come to the grass in case you faint…"

"I am not having a panic attack, I am…I am…merely hysterical because my daughter has been kidnapped by mad people!"

Becky raised her eyebrows. "Daughter?" she questioned. "Ah, you spent the afternoon with Miss Vera. George thought it might have some effect on you."

All of a sudden, their conversation was interrupted by the sound of footsteps. Becky turned around to find a man walking towards them in heavy boots. He wore overalls, and on his head, a flat cap. He lifted the hat, and waved it in a gesture of greeting.

"Good evening, ladies," he said. "Is that your Morris Minor back there?"

"What of it?" snapped Matron.

"Forgive my friend," said Becky. "She's just feeling a little emotional about something at the moment. Yes, it is our car."

"Do you know it's got a flat tyre?"

"No," said Matron, "it can't have."

She stomped up the quay, followed quickly by Becky. There they stared at the lopsided car.

"Those horrible boys must have let it down," said Matron. "I could see they were up to no good."

The man, who had wandered after them, stopped dead in his tracks. His previously friendly, or possibly bemused, face dropped to a stern, serious look. After a moment to recover, he walked to the offending wheel, and knelt down to feel about the tyre.

"A nail," he said. "People with half a brain leave their cars at the top of the track. You must be using the other half that doesn't work."

The man stood up, then walked away in long, deliberate strides. Becky did not think Matron knew about changing wheels. Their only hope was to stay close to the man in overalls. She abandoned Matron to give chase.

"I'm sorry," she said, "my friend's started to behave very strangely. She's not normally like this."

"Rude, you mean."

"Well…yes, there is no other word for it."

"Arrogant, that's a good word."

247

The man looked at her, but did not stop walking. "OK," he said, "for you I will change the wheel. But first we eat."

On reaching the end of the quay, she followed him along a little track to where an adorable little narrowboat awaited the incoming tide. Walking below decks, she discovered the back cabin was all to do with engine stuff, which meant her instinct had been right: the best way to change a wheel is to follow a man in overalls.

In the second cabin, she discovered a warm kitchen with lots of homely cooking smells. A rather bright 'purple lady' was laying the table with three plates, all of which had a mass of steaming potatoes on one side.

"My wife," said the man, "will tell you she's a fortune teller, though really she just heard two sets of footsteps coming across the gangplank."

"I am not a fortune teller," said the lady, "I merely see things others do not. Sometimes they fall from the future, that is all."

Becky realised that she was looking at Miss Vera, and gave a great big smile. She stepped forwards to offer her hand in friendship, but the woman gave her no regard. Instead, she peered into a crystal ball, nodding to herself and making satisfied hums.

"Becky," she said shortly, "I see you will be staying the night, so let us eat."

*

Matron stood by the car, feeling totally alone in the world. After half an hour, she began to wander aimlessly about, waiting for something to happen, but nothing did. Everybody had completely forgotten about her. Her only option was to get Mad George, to see if he could change a wheel. Becky had used that rope so easily it was silly to be nervous of it. All you had to do was hold on tight, and across you went. On the other side, she could find out about Mandy, and see if they could organise a rescue. There was the man they called Mr Silver, who had a boat that floated, and it looked like the sort to have an engine. They could go after her in that. Without thinking any more, she took the rope, closed her eyes, and walked off the quay. A moment later, she opened her eyes to see the mud racing beneath her, then the sunken boat a mere six feet away. But that was as close as it got, and the backwards swing did not return her to the quay. Her pendulum continued to decrease, until she was dangling in the middle. Then she did the only sensible thing she could think of. She screamed at the top of her voice. If she was going to die, she wanted people to know about it, not be sucked into a muddy grave, never to be seen again.

Becky came running onto the quay, and skidded to a halt. The sight of Matron hanging in such a position was not something she had ever expected to see. She could not stop herself from bursting into laughter, mixed only with the fear of what would happen when Matron dropped into the mud.

The couple from the narrowboat came up behind her.

"Ha," said the man, "that'll teach her."

"Already seen it," said Vera. She rested a gentle hand on Becky's shoulder. "Take my advice," she added, "stay friends with a gypsy woman, and never say bad things about her children."

Vera turned and walked back to her boat. She would

find no pleasure in seeing the sad, but ill-mannered woman covered in mud. The startled admiration in Becky's eyes was enough to return her to good humour.

George, this time wearing boots, walked solidly onto the deck of his sunken boat, then climbed over the side to sink up to his knees in mud. After a moment to get his balance, he sucked and squelched his way towards Matron. Once there, he turned around to present her with his back.

"Climb onboard," he said. "Sir Galahad is here."

Matron could think of nothing she wanted less, but Mad George bent his waist, and took a step backwards. Given his sunken position, he was just at the right height to part her legs, and pull her astride his back. Then, scooping his hands under her bottom, he stood up. In complete panic, she took a vice-like grip of the rope, so that when he squelched away, she started to rise in an arc, all the time falling backwards. George turned around so that her breasts were now squashed across the top of his head.

"Please," said George, "just let go of the rope. I can't see where I'm going."

The horrible man with whom she was wrestling seemed to have her at his mercy. She had no choice but to let go, and clasp his neck. George bounced her about until she slid down his back with his arms clasped underneath her legs.

"Good heavens," he exclaimed, "you weigh no more than a ray of sunshine!" The man took three steps towards the sunken boat, then stopped.

"Do you have a name?" he asked. "Only it wouldn't be proper to carry you over my threshold, if I don't know who you are."

"No, to you I do not have a name."

"But I can't keep calling you Mandy's mum. Go on, give us a clue, does it start with an 'A'?"

"No!"

"B?"

"It starts with nothing, now just put me down!"

"What, here?"

"No, on your shed thing."

"But if I don't know your name, that would not be proper."

"Look, it's Victoria. Are you happy now?"

"Lucky you said that. It takes a long time to get to V." The man took another two paces, and stopped. "Victoria Monnington," he said. "Yes, I like it, it's a nice name."

"I'm not called 'Monnington.'"

"But I am..."

Matron went stiff; she was on the back of a madman, surrounded by death. He walked on, to stop tantalisingly close to the sunken boat.

"And do you promise to stop having panic attacks?" he asked. "I was thinking you might like to relax over a nice cup of coffee, and tell me all about your troubles. And before you answer, I should warn you that the tide is coming in, and if we stand here arguing about it, the water will soon be lapping your ankles."

"You wouldn't dare. Now take me to your shed this minute!"

"He likes people to call it a chalet," shouted Becky, "and it's probably best if you don't upset him at the moment."

"Sensible girl, your Becky," said George. "Now would you like to come back to my chalet for a nice relaxing cup of coffee?"

"Yes, she would," shouted Becky.

"You know," said George, "I am beginning to like this conversation more all the time. Is there anything else you would like to tell me?"

"I'm sorry I called your chalet a shed," called Becky.

"Excellent."

George made the final two steps, and turned around to drop Victoria's bottom on the deck of the sunken boat.

"There you go, Victoria, my plum," he said. "Oh, I do like happy endings. For a moment back there I thought you wanted us to do mud wrestling."

George squelched back to the rope, which he then took to the quay.

"Why didn't you take me back to the side?" came a somewhat annoyed voice from behind him.

"Because you were obviously trying to get to my chalet, Victoria, my very special plum. Taking you back to where you started would have been silly."

Becky stared at him in amazement. She had known Matron for twelve years, but had never actually known her name. Everybody, absolutely everybody, just called her Matron. This man had known her for less than an hour and was already referring to her as 'plum'. Then she noticed Matron had turned to face the shed, her shoulders lowered, a slight shaking suggesting that she might start crying.

"It seems my friend found your rope a bit stressful," said Becky. "Perhaps you could see if the man who walked along the quay needs some help fixing the puncture?"

"You mean Garry," said George. "Doubt it, he's a tractor mechanic, but I can take a hint. If it helps, you can tell Victoria she's my number one bunny rabbit."

The thought of Matron being a 'number one bunny rabbit'

made Becky laugh. Matron was just 'Matron'; even calling her Victoria would seem odd.

Matron tensed as an arm went around her shoulder, but on realising it was Becky and not that awful man, she relaxed just a little. She found herself being guided into the lower storey of the shed, where she momentarily forgot her own misfortune.

"Oh my goodness," she gasped, "everything is screwed to the ceiling!"

"The tide comes in twice a day," said Becky, "so it makes perfect sense to have the legs going upwards. It just means the bottom of the table becomes the top. Though I should warn you, he calls this his kitchen, hence the gas stove is also hanging from the ceiling."

Matron stared at a flood-marker post by the door. By the side were a series of plaques, the top one informing her that on 7 January 1979 the water had reached three feet eight inches. It also informed her that the man was completely mad, and had been so for at least three years. Instinctively, she turned on the light switch, but the only thing to come from the lampshade was a spray of water which disappeared between the deckboards. Looking up, she discovered that where the bulb should be was a shower head.

"Do you think he's on drugs?" Matron asked. "You know, that LSD stuff."

"No," said Becky defensively. She turned off the 'light' and the water stopped running. "He calls it his 'bank manager trap'," she added, "just in case he makes it across the rope swing. He's forty-two by the way – not the bank manager, got no idea how old he is – George is forty-two."

Matron had never heard Becky talk this way. It was as if

she was catching whatever madness kept this place hidden from the civilised world.

"Why on Earth should I want to know that George is forty-two?" she asked.

"Because he called you his number one bunny rabbit!"

Matron, quite dumbfounded, looked at Becky, waiting for an apology. But the girl just smiled, and climbed the stairs. Not wishing to be left alone, Matron followed...

Matron knew she was hallucinating again, this time believing she saw Becky sitting in an armchair with her feet sticking out towards a fire. The hallucination spoke, using a nonsense language it was difficult to comprehend. According to this, George was really clever, and had built the fireplace himself using stones he had found along the bank, while the railway sleeper had come floating down the river. The hallucination then showed her a bed, from which she needed to jump away.

"Shoes..." said Becky.

Matron looked down to see a muddy footprint on what appeared to be an otherwise clean carpet. Then she looked at the bed again. It did not have sensible blankets that could be put on a sterilisation wash every month, but one of those modern French inventions, that George must throw aside every morning to reveal himself in pyjamas. In a situation like this, the most important thing was to keep close to Becky at all times, and it was only this that persuaded Matron to take off her shoes, and stand by the armchair. Then she took a step backwards; the chair would certainly have bugs, and all sorts of horrible diseases.

"Mandy's been kidnapped!" she gasped.

"Highly unlikely," responded Becky.

Then the footsteps began, first a series of dull thuds on the solid decking, these turning to lighter squeaks as they reached the stairs. To Matron's dread, Mad George was getting ever closer, until his hand rose into the room to fold its fingers around the hatch.

"I'm just taking a shower," he said.

Slowly the hatch closed, sealing the top room. Matron realised they had become prisoners in his den. If he slid bolts from underneath, there would be no chance of escape. They had been kidnapped, and now...

"There's a man down there without any clothes on!" gasped Matron.

"Yes, but now he's told us, you can't really go down to have a look by accident."

Matron stared at Becky. "Why is he taking a shower?" she demanded.

"Because his bottom half is covered in mud, I expect."

Becky had never sat in an armchair before; the home did not allow such things because they encouraged bad posture and general laziness. Now, she floated away in comfortable daydreams, while waggling her feet before the fire. Then she opened one eye to realise that the ankle sock with worn elastic had almost come off. She gave a guilty giggle, and reached down to remove it altogether, then the other sock also. Next, she picked up some sticks from the box by her side, and threw them onto the logs. They hissed and crackled before bursting into flames. A wayward wisp of smoke curled lazily upwards, missing the chimney to give a slight smell of bonfires. Giving a contented sigh, she leaned back, waggled her toes again, and closed her eyes to imagine George feeding her hot, buttered crumpets from a toasting fork.

Matron was rigid with fear. What if Mad George forgot to put his clothes back on? And what had happened to the nice, sensible Becky? She should be screaming the place down, not sitting in a chair, and giggling to herself. Just because she could cross that silly rope swing, did not mean she would be able to defend herself if the man became excited.

It seemed to Matron that many hours passed, before a tray of coffee and biscuits rose into the room, followed by George. He stepped across in his bare feet to present the tray to his visitors, then returned to study one of Matron's shoes.

"What remarkably sensible shoes," he said. "Size five as well – my favourite."

Matron stared at him; the madman had a shoe fetish, and Becky was encouraging him by laughing about it.

"So tell me, Victoria," said George eventually, "are you feeling better?"

Becky interrupted. "She is feeling quite better, thank you. Now dare I risk a biscuit? You mentioned Mandy baked them on her last visit."

"Mandy's been in your kitchen?" gasped Matron.

Becky hurriedly took a bite of the biscuit, and coughed. "They are a little hot," she said.

"I asked Mandy how much ginger we should use, and she upended the jar to pour it all in. 'About that much,' she said. It seems my cookery teaching needs some improvement," George said.

"You've been giving Mandy cookery lessons?" gasped Matron.

Becky thought Matron was doing an awful lot of gasping. However, her Human Biology course had not yet covered this topic. Possibly it meant the patient should be asked to sit down on the bed, while breathing into a paper bag. Ah, the bed; this, combined with the recent notion of her admirer taking a shower, presumably naked, had caused Matron to suffer extreme hormonal surges.

Becky realised the best way to cure this was to leave the happy couple alone to sort themselves out, in a situation where gasps could be expected. However, until this could be arranged, Becky passed the time by taking a more curious nibble of the biscuit.

"As a delicacy," she said, "I rather like them. It was just biting it in half where I went wrong."

"Pity poor Nicky then," said George. "Well, you know how children react to a plate of biscuits. He had to run to the sink screaming 'Arggghh,' then put his head under the tap. Such tears from Mandy, he had to eat six more saying, 'Yum yum,' before she would forgive him."

Becky held out the tray. "Matron," she said, "yum yum."

George let out a howl of laughter. Matron glared at him.

"Oh," he said, "surely you don't like being called 'Matron'?"

Matron frowned.

"What," said George, "like a spanking matron, with a hockey stick?"

Becky interrupted. "No, like a hospital matron."

"How very disappointing, but surely you do not call her Matron when she's off duty."

"Excuse me," said Matron, "I am still here, in the room!"

George turned to gaze at her, then gave a long sigh. "I know," he said. "I can hardly believe it, the centre of the universe here in my little chalet."

Matron looked frantically about the room. There was nowhere to hide, and now the bed seemed even bigger than before, the image of those awful pictures in the Swedish magazine imposed upon it. She must not drink the coffee, it was probably drugged.

Just then, a patter of footsteps climbed the stairs. Mandy, wearing a bright orange life jacket, rose into the room. She did not seem to be worried by anything.

"Are you having a nice time?" she asked.

"Best ever," said Becky. "How on Earth did you find this place?"

"This is the river we had to swim across."

"Quick," screamed Becky, "go into a huddle."

Given the bulk of the life jacket, this proved quite difficult, and Matron could just about hear what was being whispered.

"It's a very big river," said Becky.

"I know, David got halfway across, and was dragged under by your pullover. He came up ages later, without any clothes, and kept on swimming. George rescued him from the mud, then came to get me in his rowing boat, so you see, I was very sensible, I didn't get wet at all."

"Your mummy can't hear this," whispered Becky. "If she asks, George got you both in the boat...and there was no mud involved whatsoever. It will help her sleep better."

Mandy nodded, and Becky returned to the chair, where she took another bite of her biscuit.

"Oh," she said, "these are so delicious. Matron, you must try some."

"I baked them," said Mandy.

"Oh, such fibs," said Becky. "These have clearly been bought from a very expensive shop. Are they French?"

"No," said George, "Mandy baked them."

Becky stared at Mandy. "Remarkable," she said, "truly remarkable. And what is that orange thing you are wearing?"

"It's called a life jacket. George will not let me go out on the boat without it. It makes me float like a cork."

"And are you not frightened that you might float away on the tide?"

"Nicky knows how to rescue me. I form a line with the boys, and we swim like a crocodile, but the water's very cold at the moment, so we all went to the swimming baths. There was an awful argument with the attendant because we jumped in wearing clothes and life jackets, but Miss Vera used her magic to frighten him away. Later, we all jumped from the diving board, pretending it was a sinking ship."

Matron tried to find a gap in Mandy's excited babble to explain that nice people did not behave in such a way. But the girl did not pause for breath, and was now talking about the otters who lived on the island. Apparently, Nicky had almost tamed them, and they would get really close before running away to jump into the water.

"He's just passed his 11+," babbled Mandy. "He starts grammar school next year. If I pass the 11+, would you send me to grammar school, Mummy? Nicky would look after me, he would be…fifteen then, and you have to stay there until you're eighteen."

Matron was just about to begin many sentences, all of which began with the word 'no', when George cut in.

"We've got a water otter downstairs," he said.

Matron threw her hands across her mouth; this awful man had been giving Mandy cookery lessons with a slimy otter running about, probably sitting on the worktop waiting for them to get out the fish!

"Really?" said Becky. "How fascinating."

"It's just above the sink," said George. "Turn on the gas and it makes the water 'otter!"

Becky howled with laughter, made all the worse by George looking at her seriously, as if unable to understand why she found it funny. All of a sudden, she knew what it must be like to have a father, somebody like George, sitting there in his slightly embarrassing cardigan, and acting the fool. It made her feel all warm and safe. Unable to control herself, she leapt up to throw her arms about his neck, but stopped herself just in time. The last thing she wanted was a jealous matron thinking that she was trying to steal her admirer. So instead, she touched him on the shoulder.

"Thank you for making me laugh," she said.

Becky turned to discover Matron had a somewhat glazed expression on her face. It made her feel awkward, so she glanced at Mandy for support, but she had a strange look on her face, because she had just taken a bite from one of her biscuits.

Mandy folded her hand around the remainder of the biscuit, and held it behind her back. "Can we go and find David now?" she asked. "He needs to say sorry for making me play mud pies."

Matron realised that the little vixen had known where David was hiding all along. He probably had a den in the woods; of course, the orange ship did not make sense, it was just something she had invented to prolong her stay. Mad George seemed to understand this, because he picked up his guinea-pig slippers, but forgot to put them on his feet. Matron let the others race ahead, then went across to wipe his pawprints off her shoes with a tissue, which she threw into the fire. Things were beginning to improve; she had not sat down, drunk the coffee, and now they were all returning to dry land. All she had to do was follow Becky until they were back at the car.

On reaching the so-called 'kitchen', she stopped to stare at the water lapping through the open door. Then she imagined it rising up the flood-marker post, herself retreating up the stairs, getting ever closer to George's bedroom. Normal, sensible rules did not apply here. She tiptoed out of the door, then raced up the deck, chased by an imaginary wave.

When well clear of the water, she looked about to discover she was stranded on an island, but that still did not explain why Becky was sitting in the toy dinghy, used by the boys to do irresponsible things. Mandy was squashed into the triangular bit at the front, where there was too little space for a seat.

"Grown-ups," said Mandy, "sit side by side at the back, because it's very important to keep everything in balance.

"Grown-ups," said Matron, "do not sit in it at all, it will sink!"

"The seats act as buoyancy tanks," said George, "and by using oars, it's very stable…"

"…Even with a horse inside," continued Mandy.

"It is a horseboat," said George, "not like my chalet, which is a houseboat."

Becky found herself laughing, not necessarily at the joke, but at the way Mandy and George worked as a double act. He actually seemed to understand the world of children, so unlike Matron, who simply administered professional kindness to 156 girls in equal measure.

Matron looked at George, who was standing ankle deep in water on the sunken boat. Leaning across, he removed the mast and rigging from the dinghy, then took it across to his shed. On his return, he settled himself in the middle seat of the toy dinghy, dried his feet with a towel, and put on his slippers. Then he looked at Matron's wet shoes, and frowned.

"Victoria," he said, holding out the towel.

"Who's Victoria?" squeaked a small voice behind his back.

"It's your mummy's proper name, surely you knew that? Your mummy is called Victoria, in the same way I am called George."

Becky realised this was an opportunity to leave George and Victoria alone together, to sort themselves out and maybe even practise all the gasping they liked to do.

"Victoria thinks the boat might be unsafe with so many people inside," she said. "I think we should use the rope swing to go for a walk in the woods, while George and Victoria sort themselves out."

Strangely, this immediately caused Matron to crawl into the dinghy. George then looked over the side to watch the water level stabilise about three inches below the rim.

"Most acceptable," he said. "Victoria, my bunny rabbit, you are precisely ten stone four ounces – perfection."

"Ten stone two ounces," whispered Becky. "She is very particular about it."

"Oh dear," said George, patting his tummy. "I was quite forgetting the bowl of porridge I had this morning. This accounts for the extra weight. A ray of sunshine is always ten stone two ounces."

Matron sat rigid with fear, one hand grabbing Becky's shoulder, the other the side of the boat. George released the last mooring line, and pushed the dinghy away from the side with an oar. The following silence was broken by a tiny voice from behind his back.

"George," it said, "if you marry Victoria does that make you my mummy and daddy?"

"Yes," replied George.

Becky looked at Matron, who was white with fear, and seemed too petrified to start waving her arms about in another panic attack. Then she looked at George, who gave not the slightest clue as to what he might be thinking. His mind seemed entirely occupied by the rhythmic splash-splash of oars.

Then the voice squeaked from behind his back again. "I don't mind if you want to marry Mummy," it said. "I think it would be nice living here."

"Thank you," said George, "I will certainly give it some consideration."

Matron knew the nightmare was reaching its climax. Soon, she would wake up all hot and bothered beneath the nice warm blankets of her familiar bed. Then she realised they were heading away from the bank, and above them came the towering bows of a yacht.

"Are you ready?" said George. "All together now: 'Mr Silver, it's me, Gwendoline.'"

"He's very frightened of anybody not called Gwendoline," whispered Mandy.

"You must be very careful not to say any different," said George. "He thinks anybody not called Gwendoline might be a pirate, and there's no saying what he might do."

A man came out of the wheelhouse. "Ah, Gwendoline," he said, "how nice of you to visit."

"Hello," said Mandy, "this is Gwendoline my mummy, and this is Gwendoline my best-ever friend."

"Splendid," said the man. "I shall just drop the boarding ladder.

Matron realised the man had escaped from somewhere, and was now hiding on his boat in the middle of the river because the men in white coats were after him. She then had the misfortune to watch the others climb the ladder to the deck of the yacht. Why? She felt certain the plan had been to go to the shore, not be out here, where the water was hundreds of feet deep. Mr Silver then reached down for her hand.

"No," she gasped, "I'll wait in the boat."

"Yes," said Mr Silver, "it's nice watching the world go by, but don't get cold."

After the others had gone, Matron studied the oars. She knew they were supposed to go in the roundy things on the side of the boat but, besides that, it was all a mystery. She turned her attention to the tide racing over the mudflats, covering each one with alarming speed. Now, the river looked really wide, more part of the estuary. In the far distance, a lampshade flickered its purple light across the water, and finally she had to admit she was at sea, in a toy boat, after dark, and that her teeth were chattering with the cold. What had been a fantasy escape now became a realisation that only Mad George could get her back to land. Carefully she climbed the ladder. This time she would be firm. "George," she would say, "we need to be going...now!"

On reaching the wheelhouse, she discovered an open hatch in the floor, and down below everybody seemed to be laughing – at her probably. She descended the steps, feeling most out of place. Then, looking around she saw Becky sprawled casually across a couch, while Mandy was amusing herself by clipping brightly coloured clothes pegs to George's cardigan. Mr Silver poured coffee from a percolator into a mug, then carelessly added a splash of rum.

"You look cold," he said. "This will warm you up."

"It's scrumptious," said Becky. "Mr Silver got a keg of rum when he was in Jamaica. This yacht has been all over the world."

"We are looking for a boy," began Matron, "called…"

"…Gwendoline," interrupted Becky. "We are looking for a boy called Gwendoline."

Mr Silver momentarily raised an eyebrow, and was obviously impressed. However, he quickly regained his serious composure.

"Ah, yes," he said, "he has been found. There's a cross on the chart over there."

Matron looked at the chart. Her eyes were immediately drawn to the words 'Irish Sea'. There was a cross in the middle of it.

"No," she said, "the boy we are looking for will have a den in the woods, I expect."

"Don't know about him," said Mr Silver. "The boy I know is a brave little chap with green hair…"

"That's him," said Becky.

Mr Silver nodded. "When we get another sighting, we can add a second cross to see where they are heading," he said. "I suspect Dublin. If so, I will telephone the docks to tell them you are on your way."

Matron closed her eyes. This was no longer a job for the police; Interpol would have to be told. She would be going to prison for child trafficking! That was quite apart from the extra problem of being surrounded by completely mad people.

"Thank you," she said, trying very hard not to panic. "Perhaps you could take us back to the shore, George."

"Wah-ah!" screamed George. Then he jumped up to run about in circles.

Mr Silver dived under the table. Mandy let out shrieks of laughter, and Becky doubled up in giggles. Then Mandy started to run after George, trying to slow him down by pulling on his shirt-tails.

"Gwendoline," she shrieked, "come back here, she didn't mean it!"

Becky staggered to her feet to throw her arms about George's neck. "It's OK, Gwendoline," she shouted. "Gwendoline must have been having another one of her panic attacks."

Mr Silver came leaping from under the table. "Pirates," he yelled as he ran up the stairs. He came back a few seconds later with a loofah, with which he kept hitting George over the head.

"No, it's OK," shouted Becky, "he really is called Gwendoline. Gwendoline got it wrong, didn't you, Gwendoline?"

"Did you really, Gwendoline?" asked Mr Silver.

Matron just looked at him. She wanted to say they were all mad.

"Oh, come on, Gwendoline," said George, throwing himself on his knees before her. "Please tell them, 'cause the loofah's all wet and soggy. Gwendoline, go hit your mother with the loofah until she confesses. She gets terribly confused, honest, Mr Silver."

Mandy looked at the loofah.

"No," said Matron, "I'm sorry, Gwendoline, I don't know what came over me."

Mr Silver sat down. "OK," he said, "if you're certain."

Becky reached across for her coffee, and took two loving gulps.

"Ah, break out the grog," said George. "There be no pirates afloat tonight."

"We'd better be going," said Matron.

"Going?" said George. "To where?"

"Home."

"You're surely not going to drive all that way tonight?" said Mr Silver. "Gwendoline, show Gwendoline to her quarters."

"No," said Matron.

Mr Silver looked at her strangely, then changed his position to face Becky.

"You can have the forward cabin," he said. "It's the only one I have that's *en suite*."

"No it's not," said Mandy, "it doesn't have any sweets at all. I even looked under the bed."

George went into his Father Christmas belly laughs, imitated more weakly by Mr Silver. Becky saw Mandy giving a great tooth-missing grin – not something she ever did at the home. Full of rebellion, Becky reached out to give her a hug.

"Come," said Becky, "show me around while my next rum and coffee is prepared, if that is OK, Mr Silver?"

Mr Silver smiled his consent. Becky climbed the ladder without a care in the world.

Matron remained in a state of shock. It was obvious Mandy had been on this boat before, without sensible, grown-up supervision.

"I really can't stay here," she said quietly, "we need to get moving."

"Oh, that's fine," said George. "You can stay with me tonight."

"Naughty bunny rabbit," giggled Becky from the upper deck, a remark that she later supposed was something to do with the rum.

So the Devil had revealed himself. Now in complete panic, Matron raced up the steps, determined not to leave Becky's side until they escaped this evil place, inhabited by crazy men and a mad purple witch. Once on deck, she looked around to discover the others disappearing down a hatch at the front of the boat. She ran through the darkness, and reluctantly descended a ladder to stand in the cabin below. It was very cramped, with a double bed taking up most of the room. The so-called *en suite* turned out to be something the size of a broom cupboard at the pointy end of the boat. Sitting on the loo meant putting your feet in the shower tray.

"Mandy," said Becky, "do you realise lights-out in your dormitory was half an hour ago?"

"I know," said Mandy proudly. "I've got the world record for staying up late, but it's been the best day ever, so I could stay up until tomorrow."

"But you don't want to be falling asleep when we see David," replied Becky, "and I think Dublin is quite a long way, so to bed, young lady."

Mandy knelt down to pray, something all the girls had been taught to do and, by middle dormitory, had become routine.

"Dear God," she whispered, "thank you for sending me my mummy and my new daddy, and my best friend Miss

Becky and my best friend Nicky. And when we are all living here, please let me go to grammar school with my boyfriend, David. And please give Cynthia chickenpox. Amen."

Becky quickly knelt beside her.

"Everything that she just said," she whispered, "but without the chickenpox. Amen."

Mandy leaned across to whisper in Becky's ear. "But Mummy likes it better if I hate Cynthia," she said. "It's what she expects. David also wants me to hate Cynthia. It's easier to remember, if everybody hates her."

"But God does not understand hate. I bet he's already transferred your prayers to the other place."

"No," shouted Mandy seriously, "he would never do that!"

Mandy returned to her prayers, this time nicely and, for the first time, Becky realised the great gulf of age that had opened up between them. Mandy's parents still lived in Heaven, while Becky understood her own parents no longer existed. When she had almost been forced into the bog, it was not God who had intervened, but Cynthia, watching over her from above. And her enemies had been very much afraid, so fled in terror.

Becky's despondent thoughts were interrupted by a voice coming down the hatch. "Here," it said, "catch!"

A hot water bottle in a teddy bear outfit dropped into the cabin. Mandy caught it, and gave it a hug.

"Thank you, George," said Mandy.

"Wah-ha!" came a cry from the deck.

This was followed by a great clumping of feet, and George shouting that he really was called Gwendoline. Becky put her head through the hatchway, to discover George galloping around the front deck by himself. Realising that it might lead to another excuse to throw her arms about his comforting neck, she climbed the ladder.

"No!" she screamed. "Mr Silver, don't throw him overboard because the water's all wet!"

Becky thought what happened next might have something to do with the rum, because her collision with George was a little more disorganised than she had planned. After headbutting him in the chin, he was brought to a halt as her hands clasped his shoulders. As the dark moments passed by, she realised that his arms remained awkwardly by his sides. This man who cared for Mandy as a father, and Matron as a 'Lady Chatterley' person, had not the faintest idea of how to react to her unprovoked attack. Then she did the only sensible think she could thing of: she burst into tears. In response, George folded his comforting arms around her shoulders, making her feel even more confused since she quite liked the idea of nuzzling her face against his bare chest. And he smelt of carbolic soap, making him all squeaky clean after his shower.

Matron stared about the cabin, terrified about what might happen next. Instinctively, she threw her arms about Mandy, and held her close. "Shh," she said, stroking her hair. "It will be alright, you'll see."

"Will it really, Mummy?" she asked.

"Yes," replied Matron. "I'll make sure bad things never happen to you again."

Back on deck, Becky felt George fold a great caveman hand over hers, and lead her gently to the wheelhouse.

"Emergency," he shouted down the hatch, "drinking chocolate needed immediately!"

Becky went to the window, and pressed her nose against the cold glass. "It's weird," she said, "we have lost contact with the rest of the world. It could be 1820, with stagecoaches using the lane, and it would still look the same outside."

"True," said George, "but is that really what you want to talk about?"

"No, but it's difficult to explain…"

George remained silent, and obviously expected her to continue.

"Before," she said, "…a long time before…1969…the 4th of January. It was the day my parents were killed in a car accident. They tell me I was in the back seat holding an enormous teddy bear, though I really don't remember. But since that day I have only longed for the day when I would become a grown-up. I thought it was like that for all children. I had no idea what things were like on the other side of the fence. But now, I imagine growing up here, with somebody like you to watch over me, like you watched over David."

"We were very worried about him," said George. "Why was he wearing girl shoes, with green hair, and why was he so terrified of the cat-o'-nine-tails? The place he ran away from must be very cruel. He's got bruises all over his body."

Becky nodded. "David must never return there," she said, "and, quite honestly, I think Mandy would be better off down here as well."

"Her house does look like something out of a Gothic horror movie."

Without thinking how brave she was becoming, Becky went across to snuggle up to him.

"You're a lorry driver, aren't you?" she said. "I'm so glad it was you who brought her back. I know she was safe now."

Mr Silver climbed the steps into the wheelhouse. Becky took the drinking chocolate that was all frothy with whipped cream, and had a flake on the saucer. Never had she known such luxury; at the very least, it was equivalent to a year's supply of chocolate bars. And when she took a bite of the flake, she had to sit down with the pleasure of it. "Wow!" she said.

"George brings them back from Belgium," said Mr Silver. "It's a hundred per cent real chocolate. The stuff they sell in England is just pretend…Oh dear, I seem to have lost the 'Gwendoline' game."

"In which case," said George, "let me introduce you. This is Becky, and Mr Silver is Mr Silver, as far as anybody knows."

Mr Silver took her hand, then refused to let go. He moved around to look seriously into her eyes. Becky's heart missed a beat, then she remembered George was here to protect her, so everything must be alright really.

"What you said about David," said Mr Silver, "do you promise that he must never be returned to the home?"

"Of course."

"And if the authorities try to recapture him, you will somehow bring him back here? I have friends in the Med… but it would be a shame if he could not see Mandy from time to time."

"Yes, I promise all that, it has become my duty," said Becky.

"Duty, just the sort of word I was hoping to hear. David is on a boat lying at anchor at Caernarfon in Wales…or at least that is what you are to tell the others. When you get to Caernarfon, if things get awkward, you are to act stupid. If you think it is safe for the boy to be found, go to the Old Docks, and look at the forward masts of all the boats. One will carry three signal flags that spell out the first three letters of your name."

Mr Silver pointed to a box shelf with flags poking out of the end.

"B E C," he said. "Remember them well. Vera will telephone the information when she takes her children to school tomorrow morning. If we need to change our minds for any reason, the flags will not be flying."

"Mr Silver used to work for the Government," said George.

"I have retired," replied Mr Silver. "That is all Becky needs to know. Retired at fifty-five, I hasten to add."

Becky pretended not to be excited by meeting a real secret agent.

"Now," said Mr Silver, "about Mandy. Vera has seen her mother marrying George. If that happens, everything becomes much easier."

George shuffled about uneasily. "I don't think she likes me very much," he said. "She didn't even like my water 'otter joke."

"She's just shy," said Becky. "To the best of my knowledge, she's never had a boyfriend. I think your display of affection frightened her a little. If I got to the age of thirty without ever being kissed, I think I would be quite nervous. Even a hunk like you, George, would need to approach gently."

She looked up to find the men staring at her. Then Mr Silver scampered down the hatchway, and George began pacing the floor, coughing out a few words that she found difficult to catch.

"About Mandy's mother," said George eventually. "There is something your parents would have told you by now… about where…you are really not safe travelling all over the country without knowing…Oh dear. I'll just see if Mr Silver has any books…there is something you really need to know."

Becky managed to find a giggle from somewhere. "No," she said, "about Mandy's mother, there is something *you* need to know..."

SEVEN

Matron had not slept outside the home for thirteen years, and the double bed seemed hostile territory. Also, she always liked to sleep in a neatly ironed nightdress; wearing day clothes was the most unhygienic thing she could imagine. But with two drunken men on the prowl, and no hockey stick to defend herself, she could hardly sleep in just her underwear.

After many uncomfortable hours, footsteps came to the hatch, and Becky's shadowy figure stood before a backdrop of stars. She was obviously uncoordinated, and clumped into the cabin like a rhinoceros. She had probably stopped bothering with the coffee, and just put the bottle of rum to her mouth.

Matron had no intention of talking to the tramp who had just thrown herself at two men. She pretended to be asleep, and eventually felt the blankets lift as Becky got in beside her. Then the annoying background hum stopped, but only to give the wrong sort of silence. She could hear the water lapping against the side of the boat; any time now it would sink and, trapped inside this tiny hold, they would all be drowned. Then the blankets lifted again, and Mandy snuggled herself into the little space between herself and Becky. Miss Buckley would go mad if she ever found out about this level of intimacy; the job of a matron was to keep the children clean, healthy, and free of nits. This was as if Mandy really did believe she was her mother.

As the hours passed, Matron became increasingly aware that she needed a toilet visit. She tried to calculate how long she could delay the inevitable, and compared it to how many hours were likely to pass before she was able to visit a sensible, hygienic facility. But between the two locations, there was always George's toy rowing boat. If they got swept out to sea…?

Quietly, she left the bed, and reached inside the cubical to turn on the light. But however many times she clicked the switch everything remained pitch black. Then her hand found a cord, which she pulled, but still nothing. Finally, she took the candle from the bedroom and placed it in the soap dish. Now all she had to do was relax, and make certain not to make any embarrassing noises the others could hear.

Eventually nature took its course, and she was just attending to her hygiene arrangements, when that annoying background hum started again. A moment later there came a great whirring noise, and a powerful jet of freezing-cold water pinned her to the wall. Then the candle went out to leave her in a coffin-black prison, with water attacking her from a place unknown. Now she was having a panic attack.

A light came on outside, allowing her to locate the rim of the door. Finding the handle, she leapt clear, tripping inside her knickers to crash-land on the bed. She sensed Becky and

Mandy gazing down on her. A moment later, they burst out laughing.

Matron tried to force back the tears. "It's not funny," she said. "How am I supposed to go out like this? I'm soaked through."

She sat up to discover Becky pulling a suitcase from under the bed. It was identical to the one she kept under her bed at the home. Then Becky pointed to a toiletry bag on the locker. This was also identical to the one she kept in her own bathroom. Before she could remark on the coincidence, she became distracted by Mandy going into the toilet cubical. Here she pulled the ceiling cord, which seemed to stop the shower pump.

"Mr Silver said we mustn't waste water," she said, "because it's a bit of a nuisance for him to fill up the tanks."

She then operated the toilet hand pump to clear everything away. Matron thought nothing could be more humiliating than this. Then she looked down to see a length of toilet paper trapped inside her knickers trailing back to the cubical.

Becky could not understand how Matron had managed to sleep in her dayclothes. Yurk, all the dusty discomfort festering next to her skin. She liked wearing her familiar pyjamas which she took to the laundry room every third day. Fortunately, dear George had come to her rescue, rowing back to get everything from the car.

"Well," said Becky eventually, "shall we go and get breakfast while your mummy sorts herself out?"

"Stop!" screamed Matron. "You are still wearing your pyjamas!"

"It's OK," said Becky, "I think it's quite warm outside."

"But George...Mr Silver!"

"Oh yes, George said he's sorry he can't say goodbye, but he had to start work at 7am, and didn't think you'd be up in time."

"What do you mean work!" exclaimed Matron. "Who'd give him a job?"

"He's a lorry driver," said Becky. "He was the one who gave Mandy a lift home."

"George knows where I live?"

"Yes, but we'll have to visit him," interrupted Mandy, "because I didn't tell him about the other children. He thinks we live alone."

"And can you imagine how Miss Jones would react to hunky George walking about the grounds, asking for his 'bunny rabbit'?" said Becky. "Anyway, he's given me the telephone number of the depot where he's based. Said to leave a message before we visit him again, but he's mostly on long distance, so it's best to give him a week's notice. He's on his way to Italy at the moment, all alone in that big lorry of his, thinking about his Victoria. That's so romantic! And here's us driving all the way to Caernarfon to visit Mandy's future husband – that's even more romantic! And then there's me… just me, all alone in the world."

As soon as Matron was alone, she rolled off the bed to kneel on the floor.

"Dear Lord," she whispered, "please give me the courage to face the day ahead. Keep David safe from his evil kidnapper, and watch over those who hate me throughout these difficult times…"

Then came the confusion: what had Becky meant about driving to Caernarfon, and how was the girl wearing her pyjamas? Slowly, she lifted her eyes to the suitcase that had been recovered from beneath the bed.

A little later they all returned to shore in Mr Silver's tender, which had an engine and looked relatively respectable. Matron watched vaguely as her suitcase was passed up and carried to the car. Becky had said she didn't know how it had got under the bed either, only that she had stubbed her toe on it.

"Look!" cried Mandy. She pointed to a mountain of presents on the back seat. They were all neatly wrapped, complete with bows. She excitedly tore open an envelope addressed to her. "It's a birthday card," she said.

Becky laughed. "Last night," she said, "I had the most extraordinary conversation with Mr Silver. He thinks everybody should have their birthday on different days. I tried explaining that it would be much easier if everybody had their 'jelly and ice cream' day at the same time, but he seemed really upset by the idea."

Mandy opened her first present: a life jacket that she immediately put on. Then she found a book by Roald Dahl.

"Look," she screamed, "it says, 'love Nicky, John and Vera.'"

"I got a bag of real chocolate," said Becky, "and a swizzle stick to make the milk go all bubbly. And look at this, a whole box of Belgian flakes, and two spray cans of cream!"

Then she thought about Matron, who appeared to have nothing beyond the purple hockey stick, which had been returned to the back shelf. She reached out to touch her affectionately on the shoulder.

"Don't take it personally," she said. "This is a delayed children's birthday, I think. I expect George will do something special for you, when he comes back from Italy."

"No, look," said Mandy, "there's a note under the windscreen wiper addressed to my mummy."

"There," said Becky, "George is planning something after all. Do tell."

Matron grabbed the note, but slowly her eyes realised it was nothing to do with Mad George. It read:

Have changed your tyre – but next time lock the boot. Some stuck-up people think the kids around here are all thieves. Don't forget to get the puncture repaired.

Then Matron became aware of the others being silly on the back seat.

"It will be OK," whispered Becky, "if George wrote your mummy a love letter…"

Mandy giggled. "When we live down here," she whispered, "I want today to always be my birthday."

"In which case," whispered Becky, "let me see…it must be the 18th of March. I'll make a note in the diary that George has given me. Happy Birthday to you."

"And Happy Birthday to you!" replied Mandy.

*

Vera watched the Morris Minor turn into the lane, then trundle away at a speed that would have caused great alarm to the country folk of 1905. When the sounds of a crunchy gear change gave way to birdsong, she recovered a purple spanner from her robes, and crossed the road to remove the sign for 'quay', which Mandy had needed to find her way back. She then reached behind the hedge for the 'steep hill' sign that the Highways Agency preferred, and bolted it back to the post. Returning to the track, she closed the gate, to which were attached a wide selection of warning notices that Mr Silver had got from a disused army firing range. Once more, their little community disappeared from the twentieth century – a tranquil place where nobody bothered them very much, which is how they liked it to be.

*

After 120 miles, Becky became rather cross with the man who designed Morris Minor seats. He probably thought people would use the car to drive to the shops and back, not undertake epic journeys to faraway places. Also, she thought that Matron did not understand holidays very well; surely they should have stopped for refreshments by now.

"I know I don't have any money," Becky said, "but can we stop for a coffee? I promise to pay you back, as soon as the home starts paying me wages."

"No time for that!" snapped Matron.

She had not yet forgiven her passengers for telling Mr Silver of her toilet embarrassment. It was clearly not the least embarrassing way of explaining a wet mattress; anyway, it was the man's fault for starting the generator. She had certainly not forgiven Becky for sitting in his breakfast cabin, wearing her pyjamas while eating eggs and toast. What was he hiding from out there, in the middle of the river, a life of sexual deviation perhaps? Fancy having to call out 'Gwendoline' before he would let anybody onboard.

"I've got some money," said Mandy. "I'll buy you a coffee."

"Oh, would you? Except we are in a different country, and I don't think they accept chocolate bar currency in Wales."

Mandy reached into her carrier bag of clothes, and pulled out a £5 note, which she showed to Becky.

"That's what they are going to pay me a week when I've got all my 'O' levels!" exclaimed Becky. "I've never seen so much money all in the same place before."

"Mr Silver gave it to me," said Mandy.

Matron glanced back, and almost lost control of the car.

"You must never accept money from strange men!" she screamed.

"Mr Silver's not strange, he's my friend."

"Ah," responded Becky, "you do have to be careful of men who want to be your friend."

"I know all about those, they are called perverts, and want to look up your skirt. But Mr Silver doesn't want to look up my skirt."

"Of course he doesn't," said Becky. "I was just talking about strange men in general, and £5 is such a lot of money."

"It's because we're going to the seaside, and I need to buy ice creams, and go to the castle where Princess Diana is going to live. And George gave me £5 as well, but I'm saving that for my next holiday."

"We are not going to the seaside," hissed Matron.

"Well, actually," said Becky, "I rather think we are, but can we please stop for a break? It's such a long way."

"No. Now shut up and look for the signs to Caernarfon."

Becky thought Matron seemed really annoyed about something, though it was difficult to tell what. Then the awkward silence was broken by Mandy.

"Mummy," she squeaked, "I need a wee-wee."

"No you don't."

"We've been in the car for three hours," said Becky. "I

rather think she does. Mandy, shall we ask your mummy for a wee-wee together? Then she's got to stop."

"OK!" said Matron. "Next lay-by, but you'll have to go quickly behind a hedge."

"But Mummy, when the girls were out on their pervert patrol in the woods, they caught a man doing a wee-wee in the bushes. They managed to chase him away, but I don't want to go where the perverts go, they might want to watch."

Becky noticed Matron's hands shaking on the steering wheel. An experienced mother would know she was being controlled, but Matron didn't have a clue, which was OK, because Mandy had known exactly what to do.

Matron was overwhelmed by her own selfishness. How could she have forgotten that Mandy had come face to face with the monster who liked to fiddle with himself while reading the *Bunty*? And now the girl could not even request an innocent child wee in the bushes without seeing the dark images of Mr Tebbit towering over her. Oh, poor Mandy, to be troubled by such ideas when she was only eight. Full of remorse, Matron pulled into the car park of a service station, and immediately lost control of the situation as her captives ran towards the toilets, Mandy still annoyingly wearing her life jacket. Feeling most upset with the world, she followed them. *Five hours*, she thought. *I could have kept control of the bowel movement for that long, and did not have to use the stupid facility on the yacht at all.*

Once inside the toilets, Matron splashed some hygienic water over her face, then went to the canteen, where she found Mandy arguing with the staff. They would not put any rum in the coffee for her mother and grown-up friend.

"Sorry," said Mandy to Matron as she brought over a tray of coffee, "the man said you could not have any rum today."

Becky then came back from the telephone.

"I promised to tell Hilda when we found David," she said. "She's fine now, so there's no need to rush back, because she likes visiting the girls' home. She's made friends with...never mind. Then I telephoned George's depot, to thank him, and to say Victoria was missing him already."

"You what!" exclaimed Matron.

"The lady receptionist was really nice," continued Becky. "Wanted to know if Victoria had managed to cross the rope contraption. When I said she had managed the first half, she screeched with laughter. But she wishes you both well, and wants to be invited to the wedding."

Matron jumped up from her chair. "I am not going to marry George!" she shrieked.

Matron realised this proclamation had caused every man in the canteen to look in her direction. Unable to cope with all their lecherous thoughts, she scurried towards the exit, head bent in shame. On reaching the car she put her hands on the bonnet, and started to take deep breaths. For a moment, everything in the canteen had become very fuzzy. Mostly it was the shock of standing up so quickly, but she was also suffering from sleep deprivation and a lack of food. This morning, she had only sipped a little orange juice, before that nothing for twenty-four hours. She fumbled for her keys and managed to sit down in the driver's seat. Eventually, the world stopped spinning, and she saw her tormentors walking across the car park with three plastic cups.

"The man let us change to takeouts," said Becky. "Are you OK? You look a little white."

Matron felt unable to answer. *Just get to Caernarfon,*

she thought, *grab the boy, and go! Once back at the home, everything will return to good order.*

*

On the final approach to Caernarfon, Becky removed the wrapping from the chocolate bar that Mr Silver had given her, and studied the scratched map on the surface. She gave the necessary directions to Matron, until the car shuddered to a halt on a big car park overlooking the water. The final instruction said '*Eat me*', which she did with the help of Mandy.

Matron was still trying to calm down after her terrifying journey through all the busy traffic, when she saw Becky and Mandy walking away. She leapt out of the car to give chase.

"Stop!" she screamed. "Where are you going? And, Mandy, take off that life jacket this minute, you look ridiculous."

"But, Mummy," she called back, "how else will people know that we come from a boat?"

Becky walked on until she came to the Old Docks, now a marina full of expensive-looking yachts, their backs tied to pontoon walkways. Her eyes scanned the masts for the B E C signal flags.

"Oh my lord," she whispered when see saw it, "it's ginormous."

"Ginormous," repeated Mandy, savouring a new word that she thought meant something good.

Becky walked down a ramp, then along the pontoons, until she came to the back of the yacht in question. It had cream leather seats, polished wood, and brass trim. The bridge towered into the sky. A man in his mid-twenties,

285

dressed immaculately in a black suit, climbed the stairs from below. He was tall, very handsome and, with such broad shoulders, Becky found it very difficult not to step backwards as he approached.

"Edwards at your service," he said. "His Lordship is not to be disturbed while reading the newspaper."

"Lordship!" gasped Becky.

The man bent at the waist to get excitingly close to her ear.

"Our mutual friend works for the Government," he said, "and feels a certain degree of anonymity is required."

Becky began to nibble her fingers.

"I believe," said the man, "there is luggage?"

Becky nodded.

"In the Morris Minor?" he enquired.

Becky noticed the man had a slight curl to the side of his lips. She thought how silly she must look, and made a determined effort to speak soft and sexy, but it all went horribly wrong.

"There's a purple hockley stuck on the back window," she squeaked. "Victoria has a suitcase, I have a carrier bag."

Suddenly she had an awful vision of a worn pyjama sleeve hanging out, and possibly her spare knickers, the sort worn by the bigger girls – green, and designed to double as a PE kit. Then Mandy announced her presence, by pulling on the man's jacket.

"My mummy's scared to walk down the gangway," she said.

They all looked around to see Matron standing at the bottom of the ramp, nervously clasping her hands. Edwards walked along the pontoon to circle behind her. His chest was just about level with the top of her head, leaving Matron with no real choice but to step backwards. Becky ran to take her shoulders and, with some effort, guided her safely onboard the yacht. Here, Edwards and Becky advanced side by side, Matron retreating down the stairs to the lower cabin.

"Is there anything you require?" asked Edwards.

"I don't think so," said Becky.

The man bowed, then went to stand on the top deck. Becky fell into one of the great leather armchairs.

"Weee," she said. "I wish I had paid more attention to Miss Jones' etiquette lessons now. She'd be wet'n herself if she saw this."

Matron looked up the stairs, but only saw the back of the big, frightening man.

"Why have they taken us prisoner?" she asked.

Becky picked up the neatly folded *Daily Telegraph* from the coffee table.

"I am not to be disturbed while reading the newspaper," she said.

Then she happened to glance at a large mirror fixed to the opposite wall. It revealed that her hand-me-down jumper had obviously reached the end of its extended life while being worn by a girl of the middle dormitory. As a result, the hem had risen up her tummy to expose a circle of blouse, while the general shortage of material made it look as if she had two deformed dinner plates pushed down the top. All the darning had been done in black wool, whilst the general colour was obviously grey. What must Edwards think of her? No wonder he had wanted to laugh.

On hearing a door open, Becky looked up to see a lady in her early twenties. She was dressed in a maid's uniform, including a little white hat.

"Oh," she said, "Princess Mandy. But we were not expecting you to be so grown up. I shall lay another place at table. Would you like to help?"

Mandy seemed to think this quite normal behaviour. She ran to her side.

"And I can cook," she said. "I make ginger biscuits, toast, and egg sandwiches."

Mandy retreated with the maid towards the forward part of the yacht, while Becky made a determined effort to read the newspaper, though she had to admit that 'Mr Muscles' standing at the top of the stairs was rather more interesting.

After a few minutes, a door at the back of the reception cabin opened, and an elderly gentleman, wearing a black waistcoat, entered. He was followed by a well-dressed lady in a long yellow skirt. She was probably over forty, but her presentation gave the equal impression that she might be in her late twenties. Becky could appreciate that her apparently casual hairstyle took a lot of skill to achieve. The lady gave a perfect smile.

"Becky," she said, "how nice of you to visit."

Becky stood, then curtsied like Miss Jones had shown her.

"My dear," said His Lordship, "tut-tut, what will the maid think?"

He reached across to take her hand, and turned to Matron. "Did you have a pleasant journey?" he asked.

Matron managed a strangled "No."

"Oh dear," said His Lordship. He turned to the lady in the yellow skirt. "Did you hear that?" he said. "Victoria did not have a pleasant journey."

Matron felt completely disorientated. Until yesterday, the only person to know her name was the wages clerk; now the information had travelled to a different country. The lady advanced to take her hand.

"You poor thing," she said, "how dreadful, but your hand is quite frozen. Did the heater break down?"

"Morris Minors do not have heaters," said Becky, "at least not the old ones."

"How wonderful," said His Lordship. "We did the London to Brighton run three years back, in a 1904 Daimler, and that did not have a heater, but it was most bracing."

The lady rolled her eyes to the heavens. "Never again," she said. "I think you are so brave coming all this way in a vintage car."

"David," stammered Matron, "we are looking for a boy called David. I think we must have the wrong boat."

"Not at all," said the man.

Without any further explanation, he opened a door, and gestured for Becky to follow. Inside, she discovered a big oval table laid with more silver and china than she had ever imagined possible. Mandy was already sitting in one of the high-backed chairs, and did not seem at all worried that Miss Jones' etiquette lessons were limited to her tearoom experiences of the 1940s.

"About David," said Matron from the doorway. "Where is he?"

"With the captain. Now, please be seated."

"I believe he is a salty old seadog," said Becky.

"Indeed," said His Lordship, "joined the Merchant Navy on the convoy ships during the war. Sixty thousand men lost their lives to keep Britain fed. We owe a great debt of gratitude to his kind."

After refusing the offer of food, Matron went to sit

unhappily on the sofa. They did not seem any closer to finding David than when they had left the home twenty-four hours earlier; except she now felt increasingly dizzy from a lack of carbohydrates. This was the only problem of having a body mass index of twenty-three; there were no reserves for the times when the only food available was likely to be drugged or unhygienic.

Prior to this holiday, Becky could not remember having a meal outside the home, Cook providing her with two sandwiches to take to college, on account of Miss Buckley being a mean old bat. Now, sitting on the antique chair, she had no idea how to proceed, especially since the fish arrived on a silver tray, complete with head and tail. The upwards-facing eye looked at her accusingly. 'Murderer,' it seemed to say.

Mandy had no such inhibition and, on being told to tuck in, advanced with her knife and fork until the lady took her hands and showed her how to use the serving equipment. Most of it got onto her plate, and what fell on the tablecloth did not seem to worry them. Without stopping to blink, the lady then served Becky, while His Lordship took a bottle of wine from the chiller, and filled three crystal wine glasses. Mandy was given a tumbler of fresh orange juice.

"To the birthday girls," he said, holding up his glass.

Becky suddenly realised that this was part of Mr Silver's crusade to make everybody have their birthday on a different day. Then she took a nibble of fish, and questioned his eccentricity no more. To know what it felt like to be Princess Diana having lunch at Buckingham Palace was enough.

When the meal was over, the lady exclaimed that Mandy was wearing an engagement ring.

Mandy waggled her fingers. "I'm going to marry David," she said. "We've been engaged for ages."

His Lordship looked across the table. "By Jove," he said, "that's a very expensive ring. Copper plate over gold, if my eyes do not deceive me."

"I don't know," said Mandy. "George found it in his toolbox."

"It's where he keeps all his expensive things. Living on that shed, he has to bamboozle the burglars."

"You know George!" exclaimed Becky. "…His shed?"

"Of course! One day I was walking through the woods, when my partner said, 'Good heavens, somebody has put a shed on the old sunken boat.' And the next week, another shed appeared on top of that. Our barrister had never heard of such a thing, but George is such a solid young fellow, we decided to overlook it. That was ten years ago. I expect he must be middle- aged by now."

"Forty-two," said Becky.

"And he's going to marry my mummy," said Mandy, "and become my daddy. Miss Vera has seen it in my Disney."

Both the lord and lady laughed.

"Disney is where Mickey Mouse lives," said Becky.

"I know, but Miss Vera says a lot of strange things I don't understand."

The lord smiled. "We sold the woods to a consortium five years ago," he said. "They tolerate George well enough, but I shall speak to their MD just to make sure you are all left in peace. Miss Vera is the rather purple lady, I take it?"

"Yes," said Becky. "Is this how you met the captain on his orange boat – at the quay?"

"Boat?" said the man. "It's a great monster of a ship…"

"Ginormous," interrupted Mandy.

"Absolutely," continued His Lordship. "How he gets it up the estuary, I shall never know. Can't turn around of course, has to take it out backwards all the way to the sea."

"Astern," said Mandy. "Captain gets very cross if you say backwards."

"Quite right," said the lord. "I quite forgot. I expect you've had your crew training?"

"Yes, and Mr Silver took us out on his boat, and he let me steer it."

The lord looked puzzled.

"Our mutual friend, who lives on the yacht in the middle of the estuary," said Becky.

"Of course," he replied. "Since selling the woods, I've rather lost touch."

The maid arrived and started to clear the table, helped by Mandy. Matron remained on the sofa, feeling rather like a suitcase that was taken places, then dumped when no longer required. She was even more upset by Mandy telling everybody that she was going to marry George, making her guilty of madness by association. Idly, she glanced out of the porthole to realise the boat next door was moving...as was the pontoon!

She leapt up and ran outside to find they were in the middle of the dock, the boat manoeuvring around to face the exit. She looked up, to see the big, frightening man on the bridge, then ran back into the dining room.

"Where are you taking us?" she asked.

"To visit David," answered His Lordship.

This caused Mandy to jump up and down with excitement.

"Quiet," said Becky. "I don't suppose the nice man wants a

hole in the floor. Bounce, bounce, right to the bottom of the boat."

"It's fine," said the lord. "It's OK to be excited when you're off to see your future husband."

Becky relaxed; she supposed this nice couple had once had children of their own, albeit with the help of a nanny to do the messy things. She left the dining room, just in time to see the dock entrance passing by.

"This is the Menai Strait," said His Lordship. "The land across the water is the island of Anglesey. We could turn left or right, both ways take us to open sea. And now, my dear, this is most important: would you be so kind as to let me take hold of your arm? I'm not so steady on my feet as I used to be."

A few seconds later, the yacht swerved left with such vigour that it was only His Lordship's firm hold that stopped Becky flying off the deck. Matron was already clinging to a rail for dear life, and merely screamed. Mandy, who was on the bridge, threw her arms around Mr Muscles, and squealed with delight. Becky gave a troubled frown. She could easily have gone up to the bridge to take Mandy's part.

They were now travelling at such speed, the front of the boat appeared to be flying. The ancient town walls of Caernarfon vanished behind a spit of land and, when Becky looked ahead, she thought they were entering a massive lake. His Lordship pointed to a tiny gap in the sand dunes.

"That's the southern entrance to the Strait," he said. "See the fort on the Welsh side, guarding it?"

But everything was happening too fast for Becky to look at anything in particular. Then Mandy started shouting with excitement.

"The ship," she called, "and it's orange, just like I told you!"

By the time Becky recovered her bearings, the ship had become a towering wall of steel, streaked with rust, and supporting numerous dents, probably collected over a century of doing battle on the high seas. The back of the ship sat lower in the water, which seemed to make it their boarding place.

After the yacht had stopped, His Lordship took the controls, while Mr Muscles went below decks. Then the yacht began to crab sideways, closing the gap between the vessels, inch by inch.

"I am not going to argue with that," shouted His Lordship. "If I dented it, the captain would be mighty cross."

Becky laughed, at least until she saw Mr Muscles walking back along the deck with two carrier bags. She had been right about the worn pyjama sleeve and high-profile gym knickers. She tried to think how Cynthia would deal with such a disaster. Assess the situation…divert attention from the problem…oh, and give the impression she could not die!

Becky turned her attention to the side of the ship. At knee height there was a chunky steel shelf, which probably had something to do with stopping the main hull banging against harbour walls. A little higher was a hole that allowed water to drain off the deck, and above this, the wall that stopped people falling over the side. In the next instant, she was climbing, rolling over the top to land on the deck with relative neatness. Glancing back, she saw Mr Muscles staring at her open-mouthed. The diversion had worked; the pyjama sleeve and knickers were no longer relevant.

To save the annoyance of eating her fingers, Becky turned away to discover the ship was mostly cargo hold covered with tarpaulin. The wheelhouse towered above her but, besides this, there seemed nowhere to sleep. She looked at the hatch at the very back of the ship, but the two vent pipes either side trumpeted the sounds of an engine, suggesting it was where the generator lived. Then her thoughts were distracted by Mandy.

"I want to be like Miss Becky," she said.

Becky turned, to realise Mr Muscles was still staring at her – no, hypnotised, his brain far away.

"What?" he asked, without thinking.

Mandy tugged his jacket, and pointed to the side of the ship. "That way," she said.

After a moment to organise his senses, Mr Muscles picked her up and let her pretend-climb, until Becky reached down to lift her over the top. He then went to collect a set of steps, while Mandy slid back some bolts on the fence, and opened two gates. Their teamwork now made the ship relatively accessible. Becky then saw the maid guiding Matron along the deck. On reaching the steps, Mr Muscles helped her ascend in the nature of the Queen.

Rats! thought Becky. *Once again I seem to be in the wrong place.*

Matron staggered along the steel deck to sit on a bench in front of the wheelhouse. Here, she put her head between her knees, to take deep breaths. The maid then climbed the steps to take Matron's case to the wheelhouse, returning to the yacht, where Mr Muscles was now occupied by writing something on a card. He then looked up, to give Becky such a pleading gaze it made her gasp. Just in time, she remembered Cynthia's instructions to snatch in her tummy. To her it seemed quite silly, but it appeared to make Mr Muscles stop breathing. She supposed that when a man is actually looking up from below, some sort of health warning is required. Anyway, this being a medical matter allowed her to feel more confident. She reached down to place the back of her hand on his cheek, the external stimulation making him gasp for air, though his brain was still obviously starved of oxygen, for he seemed totally disorientated. Then he took hold of her hand, and placed something in the palm, which meant it was no longer a medical matter. She quickly withdrew from the intimate encounter, then opened her fingers to see a calling card. Within the fancy design work was the name 'Mr E. Morris', together with a telephone number. She flipped it over, and suddenly felt all peculiar. The message read:

His Lordship wants me to take the yacht to the Mediterranean sometime in April – please come as crew, or just phone. Where do you come from?

Mr Muscles gave no indication that a secret had passed between them and, not only that, but…the consequences were beyond her imagination. All of a sudden, she understood why Cynthia claimed that her sex lessons were far more important than knowing they mined zinc in Argentina, or that some French guy had invaded England in 1066. The ability to hypnotise men led to all sorts of exciting things. She then felt an ankle go all tingly and, looking down, realised Mr Muscles had reached out to pull up her sock with the worn elastic, but it was a lost cause, so he pulled down the other to match…

And Becky then knew for certain that the medical books were wrong. The ankles were connected to every nerve in the body, some areas more than others.

Mr Muscles stepped up to the ship, and lifted her hair to brush away imaginary specks of rust.

"I shall remember this moment for the rest of my life," he said. "I want everything to be totally perfect."

He knelt down to rearrange her socks to how they had been at the beginning, then tilted his head sideways.

"Any man who tries to improve your perfection is completely wasting his time," he said. "Such a thing is not possible."

Then he stood up, and bent at the waist so that...

Becky tried to stop eating her fingers, but failed. Mr Muscles appeared to register that her mouth was completely protected by her hands, and took a step backwards to change the gesture to a bow.

"Please telephone," he said. "Please come to the Mediterranean. Please let the rest of my life begin here...with you."

Then he descended to the yacht, His Lordship engaging the sideways propellers until the increasing gap made any meaningful eye contact impossible.

"I shall live in hope," he called.

I am absolutely certain he was going to kiss me, thought Becky. Then Matron's distant voice interrupted her dream-like thoughts.

"Where have they gone?" she asked. "How do we get off?"

"Uh," responded Becky. Then she gazed across the Menai Strait, beyond which white-capped mountains of Snowdonia stood proud against a clear blue sky. She closed her eyes, and turned to face the brilliant Spring sunshine. She could hear the gentle waves lapping against the sides of the ship. "Uh," she said again. Then she followed Mandy to the front of the wheelhouse, where the girl picked up a spanner that she used to tap a steel hatch cover.

"Captain," she called, "it's me, Mandy, are you home?"

Matron followed the other two, terrified of this dangerous place from which there was no escape. What if the so-called captain had some terrible fetish, and kept the boy chained in irons? Then a muffled voice came from below decks, and presently the hatch opened to reveal a huge hairy arm, followed by a bald head. After the hatch cover was secured upright on its supporting post, an old weather-worn face looked up.

"A ray of sunshine be right in me eyes," muttered the man to himself. "I'll have to go up and find the cause of it."

Matron looked into the dungeon, and listened for David's cries of help, or perhaps the rattle of chains, but all was quiet. The captain finished climbing the ladder to stand among them. Matron realised that he was wearing a string vest through which poked a forest of chest hair. It was not the sort of thing she wanted Mandy to see, but the man made no attempt to go back down to put on a proper shirt. Instead, his whole face contorted into a smile.

"Arrrr," he said, kneeling down to be at Mandy's height, "if it ain't me old shipmate, arrrr."

"Hello..." began Mandy.

"What be of the 'electrocution' lessons I be a teach'n thee?" asked the captain.

"Arrr," said Mandy, "if it ain't me old captain, arrr." Then she pulled Becky down to whisper in her ear. "He's not a very good pirate," she said, "he keeps forgetting, and talks much posher than Miss Jones."

"Me timbers be all of a shiver!" exclaimed the captain. "There be mutinous whispering, me thinks."

Mandy put her head into her hands to indicate her

embarrassment at his hopelessness, but Becky thought him quite wonderful, so far giving his full attention to Mandy.

"Arrr," said the captain to Mandy, "but what be this rainbow you have brought me?"

"Becky's my best-ever friend," said Mandy," and this is my mummy."

The captain gave Becky a smile, then examined Matron from head to toe.

"Thee be well put together," he said.

"George rather thought her a bunny rabbit," said Becky.

"That man might be a poet," said the captain. "I just know proper crumpet when I sees it!"

"Don't worry, Mummy," said Mandy, "crumpet is a nice word, it means he likes you." Then she turned to the captain. "Is David in?" she asked.

"He be hav'n a wee kip in the fo'c'sle." He gave Mandy his pocket compass. "What be the time?" he asked.

"What's the magnetic variation?" she asked.

The captain beamed with delight. "Eight degrees west," he said, quite forgetting he was a pirate.

Mandy gave her full concentration to the compass, and position of the sun.

"Three bells," she said.

"Shiver me timbers!" exclaimed the captain. "The lad been akip ten hours. 'appen he be wanting his breakfast."

Matron was trying to comprehend what the captain was saying. In the civilised world, her watch told her it was 1.05pm, and the horrible man had said…

"Are you trying to tell me David did not get to bed until 3.05 this morning?" she gasped.

"Ay, summ't like that."

Matron could not believe how anyone could be so irresponsible over bedtime.

"Little children," she began, "clean their teeth at 7.30…"

"But there be a right fearsome storm," said the captain. "We be need'n a full tide to get across Llanddwyn Bay."

Matron narrowed her mouth. The poor boy must be completely traumatised by his kidnap ordeal – the storm, no proper bedtime and, possibly, not even cleaning his teeth. Strangely, Mandy did not seem at all concerned. She set off along the narrow walkway, the canvas-covered hold on one side, a great frightening drop to the water on the other. On reaching the front of the ship, she took hold of a rope that trailed from a big brass bell and rang it three times.

"Remarkable," said Becky. "She is…grown up, like she told us."

"This be the old navy," said the captain. "Treat 'em sensible and there be no tell'n 'ow quick they learn. Me thinks Nelson sailed the Seven Seas as a nipper. Mandy now, she be a sensible lass to start with. There's some twice her age I would'na trust with a wire brush. The lad too, when George told me 'ow he swam across the river, I thought, there be a brave little boy. Then he told me 'ow the lad wriggled out of his pullover as he got dragged to the depths. No good being brave if thee ain't got a noggin o' sense."

"Dragged to the depths!" gasped Matron, who was still thinking about the storm.

"My proper jumper," moaned Becky. "Gone to the depths…forever."

Before either of them could consider the traumatic consequences of being dragged to the depths, a hatch cover set into the small front deck began to lift. Two little arms

300

came up behind it, then three tufts of green hair. When the hatch was secured on its restraining post, David looked up.

They live like moles, thought Becky.

"Mandy!" yelled David. He quickly climbed the ladder, and attempted to give her a clumsy hug but, since they were both wearing life jackets, it was an arm's length affair. Then Mandy leaned forwards to kiss him on the lips…and he did not fight back.

"Even more remarkable," said Becky. "He is a different boy."

"Grow up quick at sea," said the captain. "He be a right enough lad."

The captain walked to the foredeck, followed by Becky and, more reluctantly, by Matron. David saw them coming.

"Good morning, Captain," he said, "and Miss Becky, how nice of you to visit."

He looked curiously at Matron's head, then down to her wrist. There was not a hairband to be seen anywhere. Not knowing what to call her, he gave a bow.

"It is a pleasure to make your acquaintance," he said.

"How have you done it?" asked Becky. "Last time I saw him, he hardly spoke at all!"

"He's been 'avin' 'is crew training into becoming a captain, a most important part of which is a'charmin' the ladies. Go on, David, show Mandy what else thee been learnin'."

David looked awkwardly at his feet.

"I'm sorry about the mud pies," he mumbled.

"And," prompted the captain."

David shook his head.

"It be hard for a boy to talk about 'is feelings," said the captain, "but remember what I told thee: ladies like it best

301

when thee whisper into their lugholes, so there be no need for us to hear."

Nervously, David bent forwards to whisper something into Mandy's ear that made her squeal with delight.

"'appen there be many a sailor crossin' the Seven Seas for a smile like that!" beamed the captain.

Mandy held out her hand with the plumbing accessory on her finger, and waggled it about. David took the hand, and kissed it.

"Knee!" said the captain.

It was as if the voice of God had spoken, for David immediately dropped to one knee. Becky got the impression David did not understand why he was doing this, only that it was something Mandy seemed to like. And perhaps his time spent as a prisoner in the caretaker's cupboard meant he understood that life was generally easier, if he did what girls wanted.

Becky decided David needed some encouragement, and gave an excited whistle, even though she had never whistled before, and had no idea she could do so. Then she got down on her knees.

"Can you whisper it to me as well?" she asked.

David seemed more confident now. "I said she was very pretty," he admitted.

"Well," said the captain, "it be grand to see all the smiley faces."

"Indeed," said Becky, "if he comes to the girls' home now, he'll be the number one heart-throb."

"Uh," said Mandy.

"Ah," said Becky, "then I expect we'll have to visit him."

All of a sudden, Becky had this beautiful fantasy of coming

to see David and the boatpeople in their various locations. If she could persuade Matron to drive, they might even manage a Sunday afternoon every month.

Matron thought Becky had completely lost her mind. All that whistling, and now suggesting Mandy went to visit David at the boys' home. Quite apart from anything else, Mr Cranmore would never allow it. No, when Mandy was sixteen she could start to meet boys in respectable circumstances, like the tearoom. Perhaps their matron might know of a suitable boy to whom she could be introduced, though certainly not the type who had taken lessons in seduction from the horrible captain.

"Now," said the captain, "did anyone hear that thunder?"

Becky looked around the horizon for any storm clouds, but seeing nothing but blue sky, began to marvel at the captain's ability to sense a change in the weather.

"No," she said.

"It means his tummy is rumbling," said Mandy.

"Ay," said the captain, "'appen it be breakfast time. David me lad, egg sandwiches all round, if you please. Use a loaf and a dozen eggs, 'cause there's many a hungry mouth needs feed'n, me thinks."

"Right-o, Captain," said David.

David walked away, followed by Mandy holding onto his shoulder. Now he had said she was pretty, and sorry about the mud pies, she had no intention of letting him out of her sight.

Matron wondered why the captain had not gone off to make egg sandwiches, allowing her to speak to Becky in private about their escape plans. Then an awful thought came to her mind.

"The children," she said, "you are not expecting them to make egg sandwiches?"

"Don't worry," he replied, "they come out just fine."

Matron could not imagine how anyone thought it acceptable to use little children as galley slaves. She went to sprint after them, but with lightning speed the captain shot out his hands, and lifted her up by the armpits. Her legs kept on running in the air.

"Ship's medical officer," said the captain in a strict tone, "there will be no runnin' aboard my ship!"

"Put me down, you brute…you bully!"

"Thee be welcome to your opinions," said the captain calmly, "but I 'ave no likin' to be treat'n a smashed skull. Just suppos'n there be a rope across the deck? Now get those legs of yours still, and I'll set thee down."

David grinned. He had been right not to call the lady a 'matron' because those always had to wear a white hat, even in the bath. The lady was now a ship's medical officer.

Becky stared in amazement as Matron stopped kicking, to leave herself hovering in mid-air.

"There be no spare meat on thee," said the captain. "Can't weigh more than a sack of potatoes. George will like that. Me thinks 'e'll be waltzing thee up the aisle in no time."

Matron found her feet returned to the deck. Indignantly, she walked away, quite convinced that the horrible captain was looking at her bottom. On reaching the hatch down which the children had disappeared, she peered into the gloom beneath. There were no stairs, just a vertical iron-rung ladder descending to polished wooden floorboards perhaps fifteen feet below.

The terror of her descent did nothing to reduce the anger

she felt towards the captain for lifting her off the deck. Then, on reaching the bottom of the ladder, she turned around to witness the true horror of the situation. David was standing on an upturned milk crate in order to reach the gas stove. This allowed him to crack many eggs into a huge frying pan. On the next ring, a kettle was just starting to hiss steam. Mandy had squatted on the floor to gaze up at him, as if he were Superman.

"Don't panic," said Matron, "I'm here now."

But the boy waved a fish slice in her direction. "Don't distract me," he said. "Captain says accidents 'appen when the mind goes a'wanderin'."

Matron wanted to snatch him away from all the boiling liquids, but realised the resulting panic would be more dangerous than leaving him where he was. The boy splashed some boiling fat over the eggs, then stepped down from his crate, but only to slide it along the floor, where he once more stepped up to put coffee and powdered milk into five mugs.

"I'll put the water in," said Matron, using her best authoritative voice.

But the boy just told her not to distract him, because boiling water was dangerous. After filling the mugs, he placed them carefully into a steel bucket, then went to make the sandwiches which he stacked onto an enamel plate. After putting the plate on top of the mugs, he turned off the gas and walked to the bottom of the ladder. Here, he knotted a rope around the bucket handle, then, with the other end held in his mouth, climbed the ladder. When standing on deck, he hauled up the bucket.

"Breakfast is ready," he said.

By the time Matron found the courage to climb the

ladder, breakfast was already in progress, with everybody helping themselves from the bucket. She wanted to confront the captain over his dangerous activities with children, but decided the safest course of action was to hold her tongue… for now. After the others had finished eating, they could make their excuses, and leave.

She approached the gathering, and sat down carefully on the rope-tying thing. Here the bucket appeared before her face.

"Grub up, missus," said the captain.

She knew she would never be able to force the unhygienic food down her throat, and jumped up. Then everything began to spin around, and she held out a hand to steady herself against the anchor winch. Lack of sleep, lack of food, and the sudden standing up, all played their part in what she felt certain was going to be a faint. A moment later, a fuzzy captain appeared before her, his horrible rough hands once again holding her up by her armpits. Then nothing…

Matron came round with a thumping headache, which she found difficult to diagnose. She then realised her previous nightmare had been real, and the thumping was coming from the ship. The horrible man must have started the generator thing, though she could not imagine why. When they wanted a shower, she supposed they just stood on deck, and threw buckets of water over each other. Then she had this awful vision of David cleaning his teeth with seawater. She must rescue him, and quickly, before he got some terrible gum disease.

Standing in the narrow aisle, she discovered that her apparent faintness was due to the rocking of the floor. She steadied herself by holding onto the bunks at shoulder height. There were also two bunks at knee height, though how four people could sleep down here was a mystery, known only to seafaring folk of long ago. Then she realised the others must be waiting for her, so they could all go back home. She climbed the ladder to…

She shook her head, but the hallucination would not go away. Wherever she looked, there was nothing but sea. OK, it was not quite everywhere, in the far distance were some isolated bits of land, but they were much too far away to be of any practical use. She had been kidnapped, and wherever she might be now, it was not the same place as where she had passed out. Suddenly, everything got much worse. Looking to the wheelhouse, she saw Mandy's face peering out, and nobody else.

Matron made her way to the wheelhouse and looked inside, to discover Mandy standing on an upturned milk crate, hanging onto a wheel as tall as herself.

"Don't panic," cried Matron, "I'm here now!"

She climbed the four steps to the wheelhouse, where she noticed David sitting on the big bench along the back wall, apparently unconcerned by the situation.

"Carefully give me the wheel," said Matron.

"But, Mummy," said Mandy, "you wouldn't know what to do."

"Yes I would."

"We're holding a course of 348 degrees," said Mandy, "and Captain would be very annoyed if we lost it."

David picked up a broom, and banged the handle on the ceiling three times. The upside-down face of the captain appeared at the top of the window.

"Ah," came his voice, muffled by the glass, "and are thee feeling better?"

Then Becky's upside-down face appeared next to the captain's. "Come up," she said, "there's a ladder just by your side."

Matron remained firmly rooted to the spot.

"Don't distract me," said Mandy. "Captain says accidents 'appen when the mind goes a'wander'n. Look, I'm 349 degrees now."

Mandy gave the wheel a tug and, after it had moved a fraction, she peered into the big brass compass before her. Then she moved the wheel back, apparently satisfied by what had happened to the ship.

In a vague dream, Matron backed away from the door, and looked for the ladder.

"Where?" she gasped.

"Uh, there," said Becky.

Slowly, it dawned on Matron that Becky was referring to a line of metal hoops welded to the side of the wheelhouse. They were not wide enough to take both feet at the same time, and it was only the knowledge that her life was in the hands of an eight-year-old girl that gave her the superhuman strength to struggle upwards. At the top, she reached out for two lugs welded onto the roof, and slithered forwards on her tummy, until her body was folded over the edge with her legs still dangling in space. Unable to go forwards or backwards, it dawned on her that she was a victim of a cruel joke: there were obviously stairs at the other side of the wheelhouse. How else could Becky have got to where she was?

Her tormentor then reached out to drag her in, allowing her to crawl to the middle of the slightly rounded roof. There were no rails around the edge, and the swaying of the ship was greatly exaggerated by its height above the ocean.

"We thought about waking you up as we came under the Menai bridges," said Becky. "It was ever so impressive, but Captain reckoned you needed to sleep. It's why you passed out. Happens a lot with landlubbers apparently."

Finally, Matron found the courage to speak.

"Mandy's steering the ship!" she gasped.

"Certainly hope so," said the captain, "'cause I'm not."

"But what if she crashes?"

Becky laughed. "Into what?" she asked.

"Into anything that gets in the way," responded Matron.

Becky laughed again.

"Put thee mind at rest," said the captain. "We got twenty fathoms for a mile around. As for other boats, we can see them all the better from up here."

"But what if she goes off 300 whatever it was?" said Matron.

The captain checked his pocket compass. "Thee daughter's a grand lass," he said. "Nowt wrong with where she's going."

To Matron's horror, the captain lay down and closed his eyes, apparently sunbathing.

"You can't," stammered Matron. "Sit up!"

He opened one eye. "If anything dangerous 'appens," he said, "David knows he has to hit the ceiling with a broom handle three times."

Becky looked all about the horizon with a great big smile on her face. "This is truly wonderful, Captain," she said. "Thank you."

"Grand to have your company," he replied.

It all made Matron feel sick. What was Becky thinking of? Short of taking down her knickers, she could give him no more encouragement. Then her thoughts turned to the ship hitting a submerged rock and tipping over, so they all rolled off the roof into the sea. After all, the captain could not know there weren't any rocks; you could not see more than a couple of feet below the surface. And what if they ran out of fuel, or the engine blew up? Shouldn't there be somebody down in the engine room checking these things? Then Matron began crawling about, lying on her tummy to look over all the edges. There were no stairs.

After a long time, Becky spoke. "Big ship yonder," she said.

The captain sat up, and looked to where Becky was pointing. Without any explanation, he took on the form of a monkey and descended the loops. Matron slid across to Becky.

"Now you can tell me what you really think," said Matron.

"It's got two masts," Becky replied, "and seems to be coming this way, quite quickly."

"No! Not about the ship, about this...this...disaster!"

Becky laughed, then held out her hand to count along her fingers. "One," she said, "the horrible pervert from over the lane has been sent to prison. Two: Miss Buckley will do anything you say. Three: David has been found, and we are all together. Four: we are on holiday. Five: we are cruising on our own private ship in beautiful sunshine. At that, I run out of fingers, but it is enough. I would go through all my childhood at the orphanage again just to have another day like this at the end of it."

And finally, Matron understood the truth of the situation: the captain had given Becky drugs! Matron then had a hallucination in which Becky stood up, stepped backwards to the edge, and descended into the abyss. When her shoulders were level with the roof, she stopped and, holding onto the roof lugs, leaned outwards with her hair hanging free, drifting lazily on the breeze. Then she closed her eyes, and took deep breaths of salty air.

"Learn to assess your situation better," said Becky, "and stop worrying about trivial things." Then she took her hands from the lugs, and disappeared from view.

Matron lay down flat, and panicked. She had been kidnapped by a madman. How could that be trivial?

After half an hour or so, Matron found the courage to sit up, only to discover things were much worse. Now, they were beneath a towering cliff, so close that she could see people walking on the hillside above. She braced herself for a collision with submerged rocks, but it seemed the captain realised his mistake, for soon they drifted back out to sea, which had the unfortunate effect of making the land further away. Then she saw Becky, Mandy, and David doing stuff with the anchor winch at the front of the boat. By using great big handles, a heavy chain began to rattle through a hole in the deck. Matron could do nothing but crouch on the roof, while they lowered a boat or something. Yes, that's what would happen, like on Mr Silver's boat; he used a little dinghy to get back and forth. Soon they would all be ashore, and getting a bus back to the car. Then everything would return to normal...

Strangely, what actually happened was the captain walked to the tarpaulin and, after lifting a corner, descended into the hold. Then the others walked from the front of the boat to follow him. Every so often, the canvas pimpled, as if hit by something from below. Then she heard Becky excitedly shouting, "Goal!"...

*

Becky thought the football pitch was about twenty feet wide, and a hundred feet long, the goal posts having been painted on the steel walls at either end. The ribs welded to the sides made the ball bounce back and forth at all sorts of unexpected angles, making her feel quite dizzy. After the game was over, she sat directly on the wooden floor planks, from where she had scored the winning goal. She pointed to the steel ribs.

"I'm surprised all football pitches don't have those," she said. "They make the game much more fun. It's like playing inside a giant pinball machine."

"The captain likes you to use technical terms," said Mandy. "They are called 'football randomiser bouncy off-ers'."

The captain nodded, then told Becky about the old days, when the crew often came down here to play football, if no cargo was being carried. Meanwhile, the children climbed the ladder and disappeared to a place unknown. Then the lights went out, leaving them in total darkness.

"We are sitting on the bottom," said the captain. "In half an hour the water will disappear through the mud as the water table drops. There is no need to worry about the ship until the morning tide. The crew have turned off the generator, because the cooling-water intake will soon be sucking air."

Eventually, the crew returned and switched on a battery light. Becky did not want to appear stupid by asking what this meant; perhaps she would ask Mandy about it later, when they were on their own. Then her attention turned to the children, rolling out a mat. She realised they had changed into judo robes, and soon the captain was supervising their self-defence lesson, using his authoritative voice. It sounded really posh, probably because after the war, he had spent ten years working on a transatlantic cruise ship – a condition of service being that he took professional elocution lessons. It was so unlike Miss Jones, who only had a liking for old films, and screeched her way across the octaves.

Soon the children came to get her.

"No," she gasped, "I couldn't!"

The captain looked at her sternly. "It's most important for a lady to know how to defend herself," he said crossly. "Mandy, you are to take no nonsense from your pupil."

"Captain's got a black belt," said Mandy. "Me and David, working as a team, are pretty much the same thing, so you really don't want to upset us by being silly."

Becky's mind suddenly became alive with exciting possibilities; Cynthia was going to be so impressed when she got back! They were going to be such good friends.

*

Matron was overwhelmed with rage; the sun was nearly on the horizon, and she hated night driving. In fact it was something she never did. Now it would be pitch black by the time they got back to land, and Heaven knows how they were going to find a bus at this time of night. Slowly, she realised she had no choice but to confront her tormentors. She crawled towards the steel hoops but, looking over the side, her brain only registered a steel deck, beyond which lay the ocean.

Eventually, Becky climbed the loops to sit on the edge of the wheelhouse roof, with her legs dangling in space. Her bravery course had now taken on a life of its own, the captain showing her things Cynthia could only dream about. Even when everything had gone dark in the ship's hold, Becky had not felt the need to panic. As for the judo, well, that had dealt with her fear of physical contact with somebody who might want to throw you about. "Right," she would say to the under tens when she got back, "which one of you wants to be dangled out of the top-floor window?"

Matron returned to the middle of the roof, and sat with her arms outstretched to improve her stability. Desperately, she tried to think how to put her sensible ideas into words. Then the captain came up and, sitting beside her, began to talk about ridiculous things, the general theme being that he was sailing to Holyhead, where he had a Summer job on the cross-channel ferries to Ireland.

"They reckon I be too old for captain anymore," he continued, "but 'appen they let me potter about the deck. Keeps me active, and pays the rent."

"But, Captain," said Becky, "you don't have any rent."

"Me tub be a thirsty old girl to move around, so amounts to the same thing. But talk'n of me problem, Vera be coming to pick the lad up from Holyhead next week. But 'appen you could take David back to the quay, to save her driving all this way."

Matron narrowed her mouth; this awful man was treating David like a piece of property that he owned. For a few minutes, she listened to his horrible coarse voice. It was like having her eardrums rubbed with sandpaper. Then her long-suppressed rage got the better of her.

"He needs to go home!" she demanded.

"I thought he was an orphan?"

"Well, yes, but it's still his home!"

"I might 'ave it wrong," said the captain, "but I don't reckon he thought much of it. 'appen Vera looks after 'im, until George gets back from Italy?"

Matron felt her anger boil closer to the surface. "We can't always have the things we want!" she snapped.

The captain looked at her as if she was talking gibberish, then changed his position to focus on Becky.

"I'll miss the lad," he said, "but I'm on twelve-hour shifts, and can't leave 'im on the boat for so long by himself."

"Well," said Becky, "I could always look after David for you."

"That be a grand idea," replied the captain.

Becky gave a sigh. "Sadly," she said, "I was just daydreaming. I have to get back to work."

"David reckons thee be a nurse."

"And general assistant, yes, at the girls' home."

"But ferries do that sort of stuff, thee could be a nurse there. The two of us could easily sort something out for the lad."

"Don't you need to have hundreds of papers?" asked Becky.

"Two weeks at naval college before they let you on board, then it's train as you go. Starting pay's not much, but you're welcome to kip in the fo'c'sle with David for free. Can't promise anything, but you're a bright lass. They'd be mad not to offer you something."

"Starting pay?" said Becky. "You mean they actually pay you wages?"

"Sixty quid a week or something, but they sort out your training and pay for college."

Becky's eyes glazed over. £60 a week was an absolute fortune; she could go places, and buy a proper grown-up jumper.

"If thee don't mind telling a wee fib," said the captain, "you could claim to be my daughter, which would make me right proud. I don't reckon to 'ave any kids, but there's no saying I haven't. David says thee grew up in an orphanage, so up you pops. They'd be certain to offer my nice, reliable daughter a job. I'll explain you got a lik'n for ships on account of you now liv'n here."

Matron disappeared into a nightmare of her own. How dare the awful man say such things. First, admitting he was a lecherous beast – which she knew all along – but second, making Becky promises he could never keep. £60 a week was ridiculous; it was what the home paid *her*, after all her years of experience. The idea that a seventeen-year-old girl would get the same was clearly nonsense. Besides, what sort of life was that, going back and forth on the ferries, with all the drunks and people being sick everywhere. No, Becky would be much better off at the home, where everything was safe and reliable. When she got her 'O' levels, she could start a proper nurses' course, not something cobbled together by a ferry company. Then the captain's voice broke into her troubled thoughts.

"Mind you," he said, "thee would 'ave to be trained in surgery and deliver'n babies, so it's not for the squeamish. But you get to study tropical diseases, and me thinks you can transfer to a land hospital later on."

Becky found her head spinning. She could imagine herself working on a cruise liner in the South Pacific, and saving somebody's life by taking out an appendix, in her own surgery, even though sixty seconds before it was not something that had remotely crossed her mind. Then she was distracted by the children climbing the ladder to stand on the now crowded roof.

"We have finished our PE lesson," said David. "What time do you want us for Trigonometry?"

"When the stars be out, me old shipmate. 'appen we figure out where we are in the world?"

Becky looked at the captain. "Can I come too?" she asked. "It sounds like the sort of thing I need to know."

"With your brain, and my looks, 'appen we'll get it down to a pinhead."

"Anything you want us to do in the meantime, Captain?" asked David.

"Everything be in fine order. Can you think of anything, Becky?"

In truth, Becky had been totally preoccupied by £60 a week, and sailing the high seas diagnosing obscure tropical diseases. She looked at the children standing to attention.

"Would you like us to cook tea?" asked David.

"Grub up," said the captain, "and what's on the menu?"

Up to now, Matron's fear of being attacked had kept her mostly silent, but the children needed protecting from this wicked old man, who wanted to take them away from all things civilised. Her coiled-up rage could take no more.

"You wicked old man!" she screamed. "You can't go around using children as your galley slaves! You evil child abuser. I'm going to the police, see how you like going to jail. Yes, that's what happened to the last pervert who tried to interfere with the children!"

Becky stared in astonishment. Then her face turned stony white.

"If you ever do anything to stop the children going to the seaside," she said in the most menacing voice she could manage, "I'll hate you for the rest of my life!"

The captain's face had also lost its friendly appearance, possibly when Matron had called him a child abuser.

317

"I must say," he said, "any mother who does not try to get her daughter to the seaside by the age of eight is slightly odd. Sadly, there is nothing I can do, but David is a different matter. I believe you, Becky, would have an equal say in such things."

Mandy responded with an ear-piercing whine.

"She's not my mummy," she sobbed, "nobody is!" Then she threw her arms around Becky. "Please don't let them take me back to the home," she wailed, "I hate it!"

"There," said Becky to Matron, "you have your way. You no longer have a daughter."

David had remained silent throughout this. Then with great big tears in his eyes, he turned to embrace Mandy's back.

"Don't worry," he said, "we'll run away together again, and again, until they let us go."

"Sadly," said Becky, "David is right. Matron might not be Mandy's mother, but she is still her guardian, and has the right to treat the children as she wishes – until they run away. However, I wish to play no part in this cruelty."

"Well," said the captain, "the matter is settled. Becky, you will stay with me, until you go away to naval college."

"I'm staying with Miss Becky," sniffed Mandy, "and if you try to fight me away, I will bite!"

"And I'm staying with Mandy," sniffed David.

"It seems you have a fan club," said the captain to Becky, "but, in any event, there is nothing to be done at the moment, since we are lying on mudflats. The tide will float us in the morning, and we can get off in the tender two hours either side of high water..."

Matron shut her ears to whatever the captain said next. Instead, her eyes darted about; the water had gone away to

318

leave them in the middle of a vast expanse of mud, across which there was no possible escape. Then her tormentors filed down the hoops. She crawled to the edge, just in time to see them all descending into the captain's dungeon. Not once did they look up, or even acknowledge her existence.

Shaking with rage, Matron returned to the middle of the roof. When the captain had got angry, he had forgotten to use his pretend voice. He had spoken as if he were the captain of the *Queen Mary*. Who was he? A captain dismissed for child abuse, or a pirate hiding from a life of rape and wickedness? Either way, he was a dirty old man, who wanted to get inside Becky's knickers; and what a tramp she was turning out to be. But the children, she must protect them. How were they supposed to realise how dangerous this was? He was proposing to sail across the ocean to Holyhead, yet had crashed into mud, and had Becky complained? No, she had gone down to play a silly game.

Soon darkness fell, and the surrounding mudflats began to glisten under the light of the stars. Seabirds of all kinds were walking about, pecking for shellfish, while others made soulful cries in search of a mate. In the distance, a solitary lighthouse flashed a lonely signal. This was the sort of darkness she had never known, presumably because she had never been to sea before. Though technically, she supposed, she was still on land, just not the sort you could walk on.

Eventually the cold became intense and the breeze stronger. Matron began to ponder Becky's strange words. 'Assess your situation better'. What had she meant? She was about to die of exposure. How could that be assessed? Then reality dawned. There was no chance of surviving up here in her dayclothes; exposure would come and, in the morning,

319

her frozen body would be found, presumably to be thrown overboard to sink without trace.

Having assessed her situation, she realised that only by doing the unthinkable would she have any chance of still being alive by morning. Shivering intensely, she crawled to the edge, but could only see a vague outline of the first hoop. Then she remembered Becky showing off by going down backwards... except Matron now realised that going down forwards was impossible. And so, the hours of crawling to the edge began, sometimes with one foot hovering in space, other times trying various lying-down techniques of her own devising. And all the time, the exposure was getting worse. Gasping with fear, she eventually began a blind descent and, to her complete astonishment, by using Becky's method, reached the deck safely. From there, she scurried to the crew quarters where she had slept earlier. It was not really a hiding place, but it was out of the wind, and had four sets of blankets. If the captain came down, expecting to do honeymoon things...No, he would go to Becky first, for not only was she a tramp, but also quite pretty, in a young sort of way. Most likely, he would send the children back, while she stayed in his cabin.

Matron thought about her own time as a student nurse. She had been like Becky then, always willing to make a new friend. It had never crossed her mind that a respectable doctor over sixty would be interested in a teenager; want to force himself inside her most private part; and find pleasure in all the blood of lost virginity. Becky was merely the victim of the same innocence, knowing nothing about how cruel men could be.

Suddenly, Matron's dark thoughts were interrupted by the captain's face peering down the hatch. He began to descend the ladder. Terror caused an instinctive cry of "No!" as she retreated to huddle in the dark corner of the bunk. The belief that this time she would fight back faded with the reality that he had more strength in one hand than she had in her entire body. Now all that mattered was staying alive…and in so doing, save the others. Slowly, she straightened her knees until her legs were flat on the bed. She knew her face would be ash white with terror, and he would like the feeling of absolute power this gave him.

"There's no need to do it with Becky," she said.

But the captain seemed to be ignoring her. He got down on his knees and reached under the bunk, to recover a suitcase identical to the one in the Morris Minor. Then he climbed back up the ladder, one-handed.

"There's enough water to get away in the tender," he said.

Matron began to shake from head to toe. She had really thought he was coming for her; he could have. How could she have been so stupid to get herself into this vulnerable position? Without doubt, it was only Becky who saved her; all that loose hair letting the captain know she was the easier option. Well, let the tramp have it her way. Matron had to get off this mad place, and back to the home, where she would be safe from the dangers that lurked beyond the fence. She crawled from the bunk and climbed the ladder. On reaching the deck, she discovered the captain had already lowered the boat. It looked antique, but at least was quite large.

"Where are the children?" she asked.

"Hiding in my cabin hoping you don't go down," he replied.

She looked over the side to where a rope ladder was hanging. She was too tired to argue and, after a clumsy descent, staggered across the tender to sit in the middle of the back seat, like Mandy had once said, to keep everything in balance. The captain came down like a monkey and, without any apparent effort, settled himself on the middle seat, to take up the oars. They moved away in silence. Only when she realised they were not heading to the shore did she find the courage to speak.

"Where are you taking me?" she asked.

"West beach," he said. "If you walk into town from there you'll find a railway station."

He stowed an oar, and reached into his top pocket.

"Here's £10," he said. "I'll not have you saying I abandon my passengers in the middle of nowhere."

"I'm OK, I've got my purse."

"Take it, you are in no position to argue."

She realised that if he threw her over the side, nobody would ever know. She took the money and kept it clasped in her hand. "Thank you," she said.

"If you want to call the police," said the captain, "the children have agreed to wait on Llandudno Pier, between the hours of six and seven this evening. If you do not show, Becky will become their guardian, and they are welcome to stay with me for the Summer."

Matron sat quietly, until the breaking waves lifted the tender and surfed them to a sandy beach. As the water slid back, the captain stepped out. Her weight at the back lifted the front end, so he could pull the boat further in. Here, the captain took the suitcase from beneath a seat, and dropped it onto the sand. Then he stood in silence, waiting for her to do something. She clambered out, whereupon he pushed the boat into the waves, and jumped onboard. He quickly unfurled a sail from the mast and, taking hold of the rudder, skimmed effortlessly back out to sea.

Matron stood on the sand, feeling totally disorientated by her rapid change of surroundings. She had escaped... was free...and was now totally alone. She imagined them on the orange ship, all cheering when they heard the news. Overwhelmed by a heavy sadness, she fell to the beach to lie in a crumpled heap of misery.

How long passed in this fashion, she could not say but, when she looked up, the ship had gone. Then her attention turned to the case. She opened it to stare at all her belongings, including her neatly ironed nightdress and unopened toiletry bag.

*

Matron discovered nearby Llandudno to be a large town, built on a thin strip of land with the sea on both sides. A second beach was more commercial, the wide promenade overlooked by a grand sweep of Victorian hotels. To her left, a long pier had a few low buildings at the far end. Lying at anchor, about half a mile from the shore, was the orange ship. Looking around the curve of the bay, her gaze came to a tender, sitting on the beach. The children were playing at the water's edge, while Becky sat to watch. After a little while, Matron saw the captain walking towards them with ice creams.

Matron felt the world beginning to spin in a series of confused images...and then the awful truth dawned on her. She did not even have the strength to get to the railway station, let alone drive a car. She turned towards the nearest hotel entrance. It looked expensive, but all she could think about was lying down to sleep. For the cost of a week's pay, she was shown to a tiny room at the back. A few minutes later she fainted onto the bed.

When Matron opened her eyes, the clock on the wall told her it was half past five. She lay dazed and confused...until reaching a very bold decision.

She would go to tell the children that it was OK for them to go to Holyhead. Also, she would try to pull Becky to one side, to tell her what the captain meant by 'free accommodation'. It made her shiver to think of the awful old man forcing himself inside her. "I've got you a job," he would say. "Now..."

Oh, it was too awful the way men spoke, even when they were doctors. Tears began to run from Matron's eyes, both for what had passed, and for what was about to happen to Becky...

As soon as Matron walked onto the wooden boards of the pier, she began to feel peculiar. Through the cracks she could see waves crashing against the supporting ironwork, and presently the rise and fall of the swell.

When some distance from land, she looked up to see a commotion taking place at the far end: the awful captain was removing his clothes! When stripped to his long johns, he climbed over the rail, and disappeared from view. Becky and Mandy had been leaning over the rail, but, letting go, now came racing towards her. Becky arrived first.

"If you want to take David prisoner," she screamed, "you go and get him!"

Mandy arrived and, without warning, sank her teeth deep into Matron's arm, tearing at the flesh like a crazed animal.

"I hate you forever!" she screamed, only letting go to race after Becky.

Matron, unable to believe what had happened, stared at the blood running down her arm. Then she looked along the pier for David, but he was nowhere to be seen. There were just two rather large ladies leaning over the rail to point, probably at the captain showing off. Well, if he was going to be that irresponsible, she would do as Becky had said, and go to get David.

An amusement arcade at the end of the pier had an out-of-season feel to it. Unable to see David, she went to talk to the ladies.

"Have you seen a boy?" she asked. "He's got green hair."

"Gone," said one. "One moment he was looking down the pier, the next he jumped over the side. His granddad's gone in after him."

"Might have been his father," said the other. "He's built like that wrestler on the telly."

Matron forced herself to look over the side, and immediately felt sick.

"Not down there," said a lady. "The current took them, they're long gone. The two girls have run to get help."

Matron ran to a tourist telescope, and fed it coins. Scanning the vast ocean, she eventually found a tiny speck of life bobbing up and down on the swell. The captain swam alongside, making no effort to rescue the boy, but seemingly keeping pace while forcing him away from land.

Looking outside the telescope, Matron realised the combination of swimming and tide were taking them diagonally towards the ship. She followed them on the telescope, until a wall of orange steel appeared. The captain directed David to the rope ladder where, to her horror, the boy rose from the water wearing just his underpants. The perverted captain watched him climb, then compounded his recklessness by swimming away.

Matron watched David walk along the dangerous ship, all by himself. Only after he had disappeared down the front crew quarters did she look outside the telescope to see a tender rolling chaotically over the swell. It was totally out of control, with Becky leaning over the side, trying to recover the lost oars. The current had them and, looking further along the bay, Matron saw they were being taken towards a sheer cliff that bulged outwards to form a rocky headland. Waves crashed over isolated boulders at the bottom. It was obvious the antique boat would be smashed to pieces, the occupants drowned.

The captain was now wading out of the water and, after crossing the narrow beach, began to run pervertedly along the promenade in his long johns. Just before the cliffs, he returned to the beach, where his cowardice revealed itself. He was ahead of the tender but, instead of swimming out to help, he just stood to watch the unfolding disaster.

Matron moved the telescope back to the tender, to discover Mandy setting the sail, then sitting down to take the rudder. The boat seemed to get some purpose and was soon fighting the current to make slow progress away from the cliffs. The captain walked along the adjacent promenade and, when he thought it safe, swam out to clamber onboard. He made no effort to help Mandy, rather he behaved as if he had just flagged a taxi.

Matron watched the white sail getting ever closer, until it swung around, and the tender turned to dock with the ship. She was expecting lifeboats, helicopters, and all sorts of things to be happening; but no, the three of them just climbed the rope ladder, and set about doing stuff. The captain's dangerous activities with children made her feel faint, and she sat on the boards, where she noticed her arm was still oozing gooey blood. Unable to stand, she did her best to close the wound with a handkerchief. Meanwhile, the two ladies came to take control of the telescope, and began to make 'cooing' noises.

"He could wrestle me any day," said one. "Just look at the way he's lifting that anchor!"

"You'd have to fight me to get to him," said the other. "But that can't be right, those girls seem to be driving the ship."

Matron gave up with the handkerchief and looked critically at the wound. Mandy's frenzied attack had left the last of her milk teeth embedded near her radial artery. She hoped the hotel had a good first aid kit. Incoherently, she staggered a few paces, but the shore seemed to be getting further away, and she collapsed onto a bench, to feel the darkness surrounding her. She knew that after the two ladies left, it might be hours before the drunken men came this way with their beer cans.

"Excuse me," she called out, "I think I need your help."

EIGHT

On eventually returning home, Victoria carefully made her way to her normal parking space behind the building. The morning lessons were still in progress, allowing her to reach the surgery without being seen. Once safely inside her own private space, she closed the door and relaxed; with the exception of making some explanation to Miss Buckley, the nightmare was over.

"Hello," said a voice, "did you have a nice holiday?"

Matron spun around to discover Cynthia sitting in *her* chair reading *Anatomy and Physiology for Nurses*.

"What are you doing here?" she gasped.

"I've been excused lessons. I am doing what Miss Becky did, at least while she's away. Is Miss Becky with you?"

"No. Does Miss Buckley know about this?"

"Her brain is on holiday at the moment. Hilda said it was OK."

"Do you mean Matron?"

"Yes, when I am over there I have to call her Matron, but over here, I call her Hilda, because having two matrons would be too confusing."

"Over there? You don't mean she has let you into the boys' home?"

"I wanted to see what her surgery looked like. It's not so nice as yours. Anyway, I have kept the accident book up to date."

"You are not trying to tell me you have been looking after the children?"

"If anything serious happens, I have to get Hilda, but she has shown me how to clean wounds, and I particularly like using iodine."

Cynthia stood up and casually went to switch on the electric kettle. Matron, unable to cope with this new information, staggered to the chair and slumped down. Looking across to the book, she was amazed to find it open on a page regarding the digestive system. She was only distracted from her hallucinogenic trance by a cup of tea... and a plate of biscuits.

"You didn't tell me," said Cynthia, "did you have a nice holiday?"

"It wasn't a holiday," said Matron.

"Oh, Hilda said it was."

"What would she know?"

"Becky telephoned her, said you were going to the seaside. Hilda reckons the way Mr Cranmore and Miss Buckley are behaving, you two can do pretty much anything you want. I only had to ask Miss Buckley why the man wanted me to touch the sausage he was holding between his legs, and she came over all peculiar. That's when she agreed to let me be your new second assistant. Is your tea OK?"

"No, it's not OK," snapped Matron.

"Sorry, is there too much milk or something?"

"I mean, you can't be my assistant, you are thirteen!"

"Estimated. I came without paperwork. Miss Buckley said I can go to night school when I am fifteen, like Miss Becky."

"Miss Becky was sixteen."

"Ah, but if you mention sausages, you get a better deal. It's because Miss Buckley thinks we are all traumatised by what happened, and that it's all her fault. I'm going to take 'O' level Human Biology…"

"You can fool Miss Buckley, but you can't fool me. You only got the nurses' book for the sex bits."

"In the beginning, of course, then I started reading the rest, and it seemed interesting, especially the vitamins. B6 is my favourite."

"And what about The Three Musketeers, aren't you something to do with that?"

"That was just a children's game. When is Miss Becky coming back?"

"Soon, I expect."

"Not too soon, I hope. This morning I've missed double Geography, boring or what. It doesn't even help you become a nurse. I've just been reading about the bile duct. Funny to think we've got all that working away inside of us."

"And does Miss Buckley know you've got the book?"

"Heavens no! She seemed nervous about me taking Biology when I become fifteen. It was only when I mentioned the sausages that she agreed. To get rid of me, I expect. Are you going to tell me about your holiday? It sounded really good."

"No, I just want you to go away."

"OK, shall I go and tell Hilda you're back?"

"No, you can't just walk into the boys' home."

"It's fine, I've got Becky's keys for our gate. Hilda likes me talking to her."

"Only because she doesn't know what you are like. I bet all the boys buzz around you like a honey pot."

"You would think so – with me being a nurse and everything – but not a single boy has come forward to have his penis examined."

"I forbid it!"

Cynthia scratched her head. "But it's the most basic boy psychology there is."

"Stop. You should not be talking like this at your age."

"But isn't this how all nurses talk?"

"Not exactly."

"You mean they still call it a 'dick' when there are no patients around?"

"I mean you are not a nurse."

"But Miss Becky's a nurse, and I want to be like her."

"Miss Becky is older than you."

"She is still only taking her 'O' level Human Biology, like me. I have read half the book already. Go on, ask me a question about vitamins."

"I'm too tired."

"Ah, lack of iron, or vitamin C that helps the body convert it. Try some oranges, and if you're no better in the morning, come back and see me again. There, how did I do?"

"Stop, you are giving me a headache."

"Are you allergic to aspirin?"

"No."

Presently, Matron felt two aspirins being pressed into her hand.

"But this is the sort of headache you get, when people won't stop talking to you," she said.

"OK. Can I go and talk to Hilda then?"

"If you want to be sent to live with the nuns, then yes, just go!"

Cynthia took a white coat from the hook, put a stethoscope around her neck, then picked up the big first aid box with a cross on the side.

"What on Earth are you doing?" asked Matron.

"Illusion. The masters find it difficult to register a girl walking up the drive, because it never happens. This simple disguise is quite sufficient to make the girl bit become invisible, except for Mr Cranmore, who has a panic attack on seeing anything in a white coat. At least I think he's the man I have seen running away, but it's difficult to tell from 1,000 yards."

Cynthia slid the surgery notepaper across the desk and wrote out an urgent request for a bottle of aspirin. Matron was determined not to sign it, but it did not matter, because Cynthia did it for her.

"It is my job to help you," said Cynthia, "including your secretarial requirements. I've been practising your signature from the chocolate bar IOU you gave me for the condoms. Good eh?"

Cynthia walked towards the door, the white coat sweeping the floor behind. Matron tried to shout "Come back," but her brain refused to let her issue such a foolish command.

Matron spent the rest of the day hiding in her room. She slept a little, had three cups of tea, and then worked out her plan. She decided to say nothing to Miss Buckley because, as Cynthia had said, her brain was on holiday. Then she became aware of a noise outside. Realising it was Wednesday, the day the clean clothes were handed out, she opened the door to find a line of children all queuing up.

"Hello," said one of the girls, "did you have a nice holiday?"

Matron ignored the question. "I'll be with you in two minutes," she said.

"No need, Cynthia's doing the clothes. She's organised Angela Kent to cover the junior baths. I hear you had your holidays on a boat. I am so jealous."

"How did you know about that?"

"Miss Becky telephoned Matron from over the lane. Strange the way Cynthia got the job as your assistant so quickly. Not that I mind, but I absolutely refuse to call her Miss Cynthia, because she's a year younger than me."

"Estimated," shouted Cynthia from the clothes room.

Matron withdrew, closed the door, and tried to do deep-breathing exercises. When she finally found the courage to come out, there were only two girls left, and Cynthia was ticking down the column in the clothes book. Matron knew she must protest, but could not think how. After the last girl left, Cynthia took a few seconds to complete the records, then snapped the book shut.

"All done," she said. "I am just going to take over from Angela in the bathhouse. Numbers six, eighteen, and 127 need to start wearing a bra. I've made a note. You'll know who they are, because they've got great big smiles on their faces."

By the time Matron thought of anything remotely sensible to say, Cynthia had gone. She decided to let her do the baths just for tonight. It seemed easier, and a hundred screaming children would only make her headache worse.

*

The following morning, Matron awoke in her nice familiar bed. Had it all been a horrible dream? Would she step into the surgery to find nice, sensible Becky, her hair all neatly held within a band? She rolled over to look at the alarm clock, and was horrified to discover it was 10am. She jumped out of bed and, forgoing the normal bathroom routine, dressed quickly. On reaching the surgery, she found Cynthia making two cups of tea.

"You've been asleep for a whole fourteen hours," she said. "Your holiday must have been really exciting to cause such tiredness."

Matron slumped into her chair; even the Cynthia nightmare was real. Then tea and biscuits appeared before her eyes, causing a dreadful flashback to the egg sandwiches in a bucket. But she no longer had the energy to leap up, so she put them on the desk.

"I've done the morning surgery," said Cynthia. Then she picked up the telephone, something the girls were strictly forbidden from doing, both on the grounds of cost, and the possibility of a 'trouser problem' answering.

"Hi," said Cynthia into the receiver, "it's me, I'll be free in half an hour…OK, an hour, I'll meet you at the gate…not yet, she's been having a lie-in, but it'll be fine."

Cynthia put down the receiver. "Now," she said, "is there anything you want me to do before I go?"

Matron knew any conversation with Cynthia about her not going to wherever it was, would end up with the girl talking about unfortunate things. At this time in the morning, she just could not bear it.

"Fine," she said.

There, thought Matron, *a single word and the problem has gone away…*

But it was even better than that; she did not see Cynthia for two days!

*

The following Thursday night, Matron lay in bed to worry about things. The home had paid for Becky's college fees, so Miss Buckley would consider an assistant had been provided for the remainder of the year. A new assistant could not be obtained until the petty cash allowed, and that was not likely to happen until next year. Then she heard a beautiful sound: footsteps in the passage. Becky's door opened, and a little later she heard the bathroom being used. The consequences were almost unimaginable; Becky was back, the nightmare was over!

Next morning, Matron awoke and immediately began to plan how her first meeting with Becky should be conducted. The girl would obviously feel guilty, and be terribly embarrassed by her acceptance of the captain's false promises. But she was back, that was the main thing.

This gave Matron the motivation to get up and begin her normal half-hour hygiene routine. Leaving the bathroom, she dressed in her nice starched blouse and freshly pressed dress. Doing up the laces of her sensible shoes, she once again felt like a proper matron.

Having missed breakfast, she made herself a nice cup of tea and dipped into the box of biscuits she had bought (after Cynthia had used up her chocolate bar allowance). Then she walked along the corridor to tap Becky's door. There was no reply, so she took the notebook from her top pocket, and wrote '*Welcome back*'. There, that should alleviate any embarrassment from their first meeting. She opened the door and...

335

How long she stared into the room she could not say. Where Becky's bed should be there was a double bunk. Then, slowly, it made sense; the top bunk must be for Mandy. What awful things had the captain made her do, and was the pretend mummy game still going to run? Eventually, she left the note on the lower bunk, and retreated.

Throughout the day she saw nothing of Becky, who was presumably hiding, out of embarrassment. At 7pm she went to check on the junior dormitory, only to find Mandy's bed unoccupied. On returning to the surgery, she heard giggles coming from Becky's room. How was this going to work? Mandy should be asleep by now. Deciding to let the rule drop just for tonight, she made two cups of tea and poured a glass of orange juice. She arrived at Becky's door with a tray that included a plate of biscuits. She knocked, and a muffled voice shouted for her to come in.

Cynthia was on the bottom bunk.

"But, Matron," she said with exaggerated alarm, "I am your assistant, you should not be doing such things. And I already feel so guilty for going away for so long, but it was not until I found the 'welcome back' note that I realised how much you would miss me."

Beryl climbed down from the top bunk, and took the shaking tray from Matron. She carefully placed it on the bedside locker.

"I hope you don't mind me sharing Cynthia's room," she said. "I'm going to be a stay-over, teaching History to the under tens. Cynthia sorted it out with Miss Buckley."

"It was nothing," said Cynthia. "You are the sort of person she likes. Common sense really."

"When Becky comes back…" stammered Matron.

The two girls looked at each other.

"Oh," said Beryl, "I've just remembered there's something I must do."

She grabbed a handful of biscuits, and left carrying the orange juice.

"You'll miss a lot of exciting positions if you put on too much weight," shouted Cynthia.

Beryl let out a girlie giggle and scurried away.

"Ah, bless," said Cynthia. Then she looked up at Matron. "Victoria," she said, "we both know Becky's not coming back."

"Yes she is," stammered Matron, "she's just taking a little holiday..."

"No she's not," said Cynthia. "She waved Hilda and myself goodbye from the orange ship yesterday, and I know Becky was taking the children to the beach for the afternoon. She starts naval college next week."

"No, that can't be true! I heard her last night."

"Must have been a dream." Cynthia gently touched Matron's bandaged arm. "I'm sorry," she said. "If it's any consolation, when I first walked onboard, Mandy somehow took me down to the deck, giving David time to lock himself in the crew quarters. Fortunately, Hilda took one look at the captain emerging from the hatch in his string vest and floated into a different universe, the sort where even me lying flat on the deck went unnoticed."

Very slowly, Matron backed away. As she reached the surgery, a darkness began to fill the corridor. Her tormentor was closing in. Then she remembered nothing, until coming around on the surgery floor, with a pillow under her head. Dazed and bewildered, she looked up, to see Cynthia sitting in her chair. Around her neck was a stethoscope.

"There's nothing to worry about," she said. "I've taken your blood pressure – 92, 62, pulse of 60. Passing out was to be expected. Only problem is, Becky said it happened before on the ship. Apparently you never eat. I think you've got salt deprivation. Now, when you feel able, just pop yourself on the scales as I need to weigh you."

*

It took Matron four days to recover from the shock of regaining consciousness on the surgery floor, to see Cynthia, pretending to be a nurse. Indeed, it was not until the following Sunday prayer meeting that she found the strength to deal with the traumatic experience. "Right," she would say to Cynthia, "I am the matron, and this is how it's going to be."

On returning to the surgery, Matron tapped Cynthia's door…Becky's door…Cynthia and Beryl's door…Oh, it was all so confusing. Anyway, she tapped the door, and using her best authoritative voice, called for Cynthia to come through to the surgery, "Now!"

When Cynthia came into the surgery, Matron looked up from the note she had been pretending to write.

"Right," she said, "first, I have decided that a boys' home is no place for a girl. Do you understand how sensible that sounds?"

"Don't you think it's important for a nurse to get experience at dealing with both sexes?" responded Cynthia. "I mean, boys are more confusing to help."

"Look, I am not Miss Buckley. I know you only go over there to check them out."

Cynthia laughed. "But they are just boys," she said.

"And you are just a girl."

"Honestly, Matron, I have no intention of doing it in a wood, up to my arse in stinging nettles. And now I have seen the book, I want my first time to be in a bedroom, with candles, and all the trimmings. Also, I feel my breasts need to develop a little more, not that they are small for my age, but a man might find them so…"

"Stop!" gasped Matron. "That is no way to talk. I have just been to church!"

"Anyway," continued Cynthia undeterred, "I am starting to think love is important. Even before I put my hand down his pants, I will expect chocolates, a Valentine's card, and flowers sent Interflora to the nurses' college. I think I am pretty enough to expect that."

"Stop!"

"OK, I was just assuring you that I have no intention of doing it with anyone who can't provide a bedroom. So your second point is?"

"What?"

"You said the boy stuff was your first point, which rather implies there is a second."

Matron's rehearsed speech had turned into a complete mental block. She needed to improvise…

"And what if a boy does…like Mr Tebbit…jump out of a bush…naked," she stammered.

"The full naked body thing is more for middle-aged men. A boy will only wave his penis about, or give me a rule to measure it."

"You are talking like a prostitute."

"Not really, though I do remember, at the brothel, there was a special ruler, 1.2 inches to the inch. It made the customers believe a professional service gave them a better erection, which is something their brains are pre-programmed to believe."

Matron slumped into a chair feeling utterly defeated. If Cynthia seemed uncontrollable as the leader of The Three Musketeers, the adult world into which she had crashed seemed even less able to defend itself.

NINE

Matron's daily routine was so well established, that she had stopped thinking about the future...until now. In three years' time, Cynthia would reach the age when she would leave the orphanage forever...

From this magical thought, Matron found herself drawn into a fantasy, in which she saw herself sneaking into the records office, to recover Cynthia's file. As the girl had said, her age had been estimated, so it was quite easy to amend. A few other changes here and there, plus the odd creative medical note, and Cynthia would miraculously become fourteen.

And so, three years would became two. Praise the Lord!

But Matron did not practise deceit, unless it was entirely to benefit others and, even then, she tried to keep it to the shaking of her head, when a nod would have been more appropriate.

A more serious issue occupying Matron's mind was that the boat nightmare had reawakened her past fears. Now, she often saw haunting images of rape, so long repressed. In these, the doctor and the captain became a single dark force of terror. How would Becky cope with the captain's sexual demands? At first, Matron had assumed the girl would come running 'home', ashamed and in tears. Now she was not so certain. Given Becky's recent behaviour, it was quite possible she would just lie down, and let him 'do it'. After all, at his age, this could not happen…very often. Such a submission might even prevent the physical injury she herself had suffered, then and later during her first months living within the seclusion of the orphanage.

When the surgery door opened, Matron took a few seconds to leave her tormented thoughts.

"This arrived for you," said a voice. "Miss Williams said I should bring it to you straight away."

Matron saw Jackie Smith limping towards her, carrying a parcel. Matron could not imagine who would be sending her anything; in any event, it was not likely to be important.

"Tell me," said Matron, "Miss Williams thought she saw you walking in the copse last week, seems to think you only limp when people are watching."

Jackie shook her head.

"Well," said Matron, "I still think we should send you to the hospital to get you checked out. There are some new drugs that might help. While you are still growing is the best time to try."

"I just brought you the parcel," said Jackie. "Can I go now?"

"Perhaps, when you explain why you are going red, and chewing your pullover. Limping is nothing to be ashamed of."

Jackie stared out of the window. "Cynthia's told you, hasn't she?" she said. "I made her promise not to tell. It's all so embarrassing."

Matron thought the time had come to practise deceit. She nodded.

Jackie walked to the bed and sat down.

"It's a miracle!" exclaimed Matron.

"I don't think Miss Buckley is going to believe that," said Jackie. "It's much easier if I pretend to limp. Anyway, it still hurts a little, and I can't run or anything, so I'm really not ready for games...well, except the sort that Cynthia teaches."

"Of course," said Matron vaguely. "Do continue."

"It's the way she talks about all the rose petals floating in the air," said Jackie, "and what the boy might be doing. It makes me forget the pain. I know 'the swan' is easy for Cynthia, but...er...getting my legs into that position seems to have sorted everything out." Jackie began to back away to the door. "I find this very embarrassing," she said. "Please can I go now?"

"Stop!" said Matron. "I shall tell Miss Williams I have been giving you physiotherapy. I don't want to see you limping again. But have you ever thought about what will happen, if a boy gets too excited and tries to force himself on you?"

"But I could never do it with a boy watching," said Jackie, "it would be much too embarrassing, it's just pretend. The advanced classes are more serious. They can now do real tantric sex in front of a real imaginary boy without laughing. Though for me, I just wish Miss Becky had given her a good book on hairdressing, and not the *Kama Sutra*."

"You have seen this er..."

"Only the advanced class get to see it," said Jackie. "Apparently some of the positions are quite dangerous."

It was difficult for Matron to extract any more information, without admitting she hadn't a clue what they were talking about. However, it was reasonable to assume all the talk about positions meant it was something to do with sex.

After Jackie left the surgery, Matron remembered the parcel, and cut away the wrapping paper to find…

What she was looking at made no sense whatsoever. Inside the box were a couple of things that she supposed were meant to go on the feet. But they only conformed to the loosest definition of footwear, for they had bright rubber bottoms, and all around the sides were flashes of vivid pink and yellow. In short, they were the sort of things a clown might wear to make people laugh. She turned her attention to a note, which read:

Something for the next time you visit – which I hope will be soon.
    Love George.

Matron spent a little while trying to comprehend all the madness that existed beyond the fence. Then came the terror of George taking a shower while she was trapped in his bedroom. From this, her thoughts turned to the inappropriate book that, according to Jackie, Becky had sent from Wales. Well, that would have to be confiscated, before it did any more damage.

Matron marched directly to Cynthia's room, and opened the door of the bedside locker. But the book was not there, and the following more general search, under the mattress, found nothing remotely illicit. Then she realised Cynthia must have a hiding place. How else could the magazines and condoms not have been kept secret?

She pondered. The caretaker's cupboard!

At last, Matron realised she was starting to understand how the world within the home worked. On her last visit, the boy had demanded all her attention; there could have been a box in the corner, and she would not have noticed.

Matron walked to the bathhouse corridor, just in time to see a girl scamper ahead, scratching her nails over the outer door as she walked by. Before, the gesture would have gone unnoticed, but now she realised it was a warning signal. Self-consciously she entered the cupboard, and stared at the back wall. There were secret bolts for which you needed a specialist tool, but it was a lot easier to play dirty.

"Cynthia said I could read the book," she shouted.

Silence.

"I know you're in there," she shouted. "Please, there is something I really need to check."

This time she heard giggling, and soon the sound of bolts being slid back. The wall opened to reveal three girls with jumpers pulled over their heads. They scurried by, their giggles bursting into laughter as they raced down the corridor.

The needlework book they had left on the chair was clearly a decoy, so Matron went around stamping the floorboards and tapping the walls, but nothing seemed hollow. Utterly defeated, she turned to leave, but the wall would not reopen. She began her search for secret catches…then Becky's words came to her: 'the wall will not open until the outer door is closed'.

Matron sat down with the needlework book on her lap. Calling for help would be too embarrassing, besides, this secret cupboard had been passed down through the generations. If she brought it to Miss Buckley's attention, the girls would hate her forever. And if the police ever found out it had been used to imprison a boy, the consequences would be unthinkable.

Then Matron began to wonder how she was going to cope without Becky. She understood the strange ways of the inmates who, in reality, made no sense whatsoever. And who was going to do the haircuts? Indeed, how could she cope without a proper assistant, especially during the holidays when there were no lessons? Then came another problem: how was she going to explain to the girls that she had been so desperate to read a needlework book?

Idly, she tried to flip the pages, but the cover would not open. Shaking the book, then holding it upside down did nothing to reveal the secrets of needlework. Next she pulled the little bookmarker, and miraculously the front cover released. She flipped to chapter one, but it was just needlework, and not particularly interesting. Then she was distracted when the wall opened, to find a girl staring at her. Suddenly the girl turned on her heels and fled. Matron jumped up and tried to claw the wall, but once again it seemed the outer door had been left open. She gave a heavy sigh. But, when she turned to see the needlework book lying on the floor, it had now opened to reveal a void stuffed with tissue paper. Overwhelmed by the sense that something really bad was about to happen, she sat down to steady her legs, then lifted out the inner package. After removing the tissue paper, she went into a hallucinogenic trance… It was not the *Calming Sultan*, or whatever Jackie had said, but something much worse…

The trance was broken by a cough, and she looked up to see Cynthia had entered the room. The girl prised *The Joy of Sex* from her fingers, and placed it back in the needlework book.

"We will talk about this later," said Cynthia sternly, "but I've got gym class now."

It took a few moments for Matron to realise that Cynthia had left, fortunately this time closing the outer door, allowing her to give chase. On reaching the next corridor, she skidded to a halt. Twenty yards ahead, Cynthia was talking to Miss Buckley. The woman had a look of panic in her eyes, the sort that said *'I'll do anything you want, if only you'll go away'*.

Cynthia turned to Matron. "Ah," she said, "one of the girls has tripped and grazed her knee. I came to say you are wanted in surgery. I've cleaned the wound with iodine, but she started to cry because her skin went a funny colour, and I didn't know what to do next."

Miss Buckley used the interruption to escape. Cynthia walked on, still carrying the needlework book. Matron tried to follow, but a tug on her sleeve caused her to look down. Little Maisie gazed up at her with big tearful eyes.

"I don't like it when Cynthia uses iodine," she said. "It's like she's washing cars with a sponge and bucket. And I heard the big girls saying it made the leg died."

With some difficulty, Matron managed to reassure the simple child that 'died' did not mean the leg would fall off. Then she looked up to notice Cynthia was nowhere to be seen. There were just a lot of other faces peeping out of doorways, disappearing whenever she looked in their direction.

Matron found the surgery to be deserted, nor was there any evidence of iodine being used. She made herself a cup of tea, then sat down to worry about how impossible her situation had become. By now, every girl in the home would be giggling about her sitting in the caretaker's cupboard, reading Cynthia's book.

Eventually Cynthia walked into the surgery, and sat down on the bed.

"Sorry I couldn't invite you to gym class," she said. "Today we were practising getting from the 'foot yoke' to the 'sky foot number two'. The girls would have been too self-conscious with an adult watching."

"It's a disaster," said Matron.

"Hardly, the girls are getting really fit. Next time Miss Williams gets out the vaulting horse, she's in for a terrible shock."

Matron felt very vulnerable at the terrible thing that had been unleashed.

"What did the girls tell you," she asked, "about what they think they saw in the caretaker's cupboard?"

"All sorted. I just told them you were looking for a new position to try on your boyfriend. They were ever so impressed."

Matron could only manage a speechless stare.

"Surely you did not want them to think you were just looking at the pictures?" continued Cynthia. "Your position here would have become impossible. This way you are a mysterious heroine." Cynthia reached across to lift a trainer from its crinkly wrapping paper. "A rich boyfriend," she added, "who sends you nice presents."

Matron grabbed the embarrassing item, and hid it behind her back. "He's not my boyfriend," she gasped.

Cynthia raised an eyebrow to question the statement, then casually took the note from the box. "Love George?" she said. "Is this the George who lives on a boat?"

"Lives in a garden shed, actually."

"Becky called it a chalet. Apparently, it's got a really nice bed…and downstairs, a shower…"

Cynthia left the statement to hang in the air, thereby giving Matron time to consider her response. However, the woman merely leapt from her chair, and ran to her room.

How very curious, thought Cynthia. Then she remembered that her next awayday with Hilda was to be at the boat village. Only after meeting George would she decide what needed to be done regarding Matron. As for the trainers? Well, at some time in the future, she felt certain they would come in useful. Carefully, she returned them to their box, then took them to her room for safe keeping.

Inside her room, Matron lay on the bed, her head underneath the pillow. The fantasy of changing Cynthia's records now seemed rather more real.

The week after the unfortunate incident in the caretaker's cupboard, Matron was sitting in her room, when she heard Cynthia run into the surgery.

"Alison's been pushed off her chair," she shouted down the corridor, "and split her head open on the corner of a desk. She's leaking blood everywhere!"

Matron rushed into the surgery to find Alison slumped across Cynthia's shoulder. Matron threw a pad over the wound and held it in place with a quick bandage. Then she lifted Alison into her arms, and started backing out of the door.

"This one's for the hospital," she said. "Get my car keys, they're in my bag on the dressing table."

By the time Matron was walking down the corridor, Cynthia was scurrying ahead. She held open the main doors, then rushed to the car. How what happened next, happened, Matron could not say; Cynthia was just there. Even in the little hospital casualty room, the girl had acquired a gown and mask to watch the stitching taking place. Only when Cynthia asked to have a go with the needle, was she told to be quiet, which she did; except for offering cotton wool, tweezers, or anything else that she thought might be useful for an operation.

When the work was done, the nurse went to the next patient.

"I wonder if you should take Alison to the ice cream parlour, when she comes round?" said Cynthia. "I am fairly sure it's what a parent would do."

Matron was too busy trying to comprehend what she was looking at to register the question. According to this vision, Cynthia had subconsciously lifted Alison's hand, and now held it gently in her own.

"I'd buy the ice cream if I had any money," continued Cynthia, "but all I have is a stash of chocolate bars. These won't help because they've got the wrong sort of vitamins to cure a bump on the head. Ice cream's OK though, especially if we have the one with lots of fruit."

Matron turned her attention to what Cynthia was saying. Then she looked into her purse to count out the change.

"All I have is £2.80," she said.

"OK then, knickerbocker glory, they are £2.02. Alison's never been to an ice cream parlour, you see. It will help the anaesthetic go away quicker."

Half an hour later, Matron and Cynthia were sitting on a bench to watch Alison sitting outside the ice cream parlour across the road. Cynthia licked a 35p cone they had bought from the newsagent, while Matron sipped a lukewarm cup of coffee from the hospital vending machine.

"I don't understand," said Matron, "how you knew a knickerbocker glory was £2.02."

"Hilda sometimes takes me to the ice cream parlour," replied Cynthia. "I am quite experienced at knickerbocker glories by now."

"That doesn't make sense," responded Matron. "Why would she buy you ice creams?"

"It might be something to do with not having grandchildren. Her husband was killed in the Korean War thirty years ago, just after she became an SRN. Dedicated herself to the boys' orphanage ever since. Anyway, she likes buying ice creams, and I like eating them. We work as a team."

Matron gazed at the cardboard cup of coffee. How reminiscent of her student days before... Why had she ever dropped out of her course halfway through? Miss Buckley had the philosophy that half qualified meant half-pay, and there was very little she could do about it. She wondered how much Hilda earned, and if she sometimes got left with only 18p in her purse. In that instant, she imagined Cynthia going to college, then holding a patient's hand as they came around from anaesthetic, and never having to worry about only having 18p in her purse...

*

With Miss Buckley showing all the symptoms of becoming a mad woman who lived in an attic, a logical person might reasonably expect to see chaos and disorder spreading across the kingdom over which she had previously reigned. However, Matron thought the opposite seemed to be true. It was almost as if some mysterious unseen force had filled the power vacuum, resulting in a harmony never before witnessed within the orphanage.

Another curious fact was that mistresses started coming to the surgery, asking for headache pills, then hovering awkwardly by the door on their way out. "I wonder," they would say, "if I could have a little word with Cynthia while I'm here?" Sometimes they asked for Beryl, or Becky.

Becky was obvious; it meant the mistress wanted their hair cut without the traumatic experience of going outside the fence. Matron resolved this problem by buying a book on hairdressing, and giving it to Beryl. After practising on a few nervous girls, Beryl seemed to acquire a tremendous power, which, of course, she did. "Do as I say," went the implied threat, "or I shall cut your hair using a pudding bowl!" However, why the mistresses wanted to speak to Cynthia remained a mystery.

Even more spectacular than the home's increased discipline, was the improvement in girls' health. Those who had spots now had fewer spots, which Matron thought was something to do with Cynthia's boy studies – the section on vitamins. It was not, given the home's catering budget, possible for girls to become fat. But now, even the slightly podgy ones reduced their body mass index to 22.5. More confusing, the really skinny girls increased their weight to this ideal number. And it wasn't just the girls who had transformations; the Games mistress began to walk around in a cloud of happiness. Apparently, some of her girls could now stand on tiptoe, while the other leg made pretty patterns in the air.

"It's like they're training to become famous ballet dancers," she was heard to say.

Matron dare not ask Cynthia about it, for it was obviously something to do with her 'boy studies'. However, she once found the courage to enquire about the complete lack of catfights within the orphanage.

"When we invade the boys' home," she had replied, "we need to work as a team. In the meantime, any disagreements are sorted out in my judo lessons. Whoever wins is right. Much the same as before, but judo doesn't involve scratches or bite marks, for when they all meet the boys."

Matron found it quite comforting to know that the girls could still inhabit a childhood fantasy land. Cynthia just had a wilder imagination than most.

TEN

At the beginning of September, Matron led Cynthia into the college building to organise her 'O' level courses in English and Biology. Ordinarily they would not take a girl who was so obviously of school age. Matron shivered at the very thought of it; you could not have fourteen-year-old girls mixing with boys, who probably came to college on motorbikes. Yet she must, since the home had no facility to cater for qualifications, certainly not Biology with all the rude bits left in.

At the reception counter, the clerk looked quizzically over the glasses balanced on her nose. Even standing on tiptoe, Cynthia looked unusually short.

"What a lovely hairstyle," said Cynthia. "Now I am seventeen, do you think I should be going to one of those expensive salons?"

"Aw," said the clerk, "it's only the one in the high street."

"Really?" said Cynthia. "How do they get it so shiny? Mine always looks so dull."

Eventually, Matron found herself with nothing to do but hand over the cheque. If the clerk noticed the date of birth on the application, she did not say anything, as she was too busy playing with her hair.

On reaching the foyer, Cynthia sat down to rest her feet. "And now," she said, "it is my turn to help you, like I promised, and to show you the result of all my hard work."

Matron watched Cynthia lean down to re-do her shoe buckle, even though it seemed to be in no need of adjustment. A few seconds later, Matron felt a presence.

"Hello, Cynthia," said a voice.

"Oh, Uncle George," said Cynthia, "what a lovely surprise. Are you enrolling on something too?"

"No, but I thought I would come to see how my favourite niece is progressing. This is a very big building, are you sure it's not a university?"

"Almost, but let me introduce you to my boss, my supporter, and my altogether best friend. Victoria, this is my Uncle George."

"Good Heavens," said George. "What a delight!"

"You know each other?" asked Cynthia.

George gulped, his confidence apparently beginning to falter.

"I know," said Cynthia soothingly, "why don't we all go to the zoo for the afternoon?"

"What a splendid idea," said George.

Without saying another word, George and Cynthia walked out of the main doors. Matron tried to comprehend the situation; the girl she was supposed to be looking after had just walked off with a man who lived in a garden shed. She gave chase and, on reaching the car park, heard the toot of a horn. Cynthia and George were already in a car, the back door of which was open.

"Get out of there this minute!" yelled Matron.

Cynthia responded by retrieving a piece of paper from the bag she had been clutching all morning.

"A present for you," she said, "just to say thank you for sorting out my college – guess I won't be needing it anymore."

Cynthia put her tongue on the paper, then stuck it to the window on her side. There, for all the world to see, was the IOU for the condoms. Any moment, Mad George could turn around and see it too. In a mad panic, Matron threw herself across the back seat, Cynthia diving the other way to pull in her feet, and close the door.

"Uncle George," she said, "to the zoo, if you please."

Matron shoved the IOU in her tunic pocket and was just about to leap from the car, when Cynthia pushed something totally horrendous beneath her nose.

"I've brought your trainers," she said, "the ones you really liked. They are much better for walking around the zoo."

Looking at the clown shoes caused Matron's brain to go blank. By the time she had recovered, the car was speeding along some bypass or other.

"I don't want to go to the zoo," she said quietly.

"OK," said Cynthia, "well, thank you very much for sorting out my college, I'll see you back at the home later. Uncle George, when you give me a lift home, would you mind explaining to Miss Buckley who you are, otherwise she'll think I'm the sort of girl to go wandering off with strange men. Not that you are strange, but Miss Buckley seems to have a problem with anyone designed to wear zip trousers. Once she knows that you are my uncle, she will be OK, and will let you visit me whenever you want."

"But if Victoria really doesn't want to go to the zoo?" responded George.

"What is there not to want about going to the zoo?" said Cynthia. "Ah, I see, we have a bad case of brain-mouth dysfunctional syndrome. What your brain is clearly thinking about is how you really want to spend the afternoon telling Victoria how perfect she is. This is why I am here as your date manager, to correct such things."

Victoria watched in horrified astonishment as Cynthia somersaulted onto the front seat. Horrified because her legs had been clearly visible; astonished because, compared to the Cynthia she had known, it was remarkably graceful.

"What Victoria meant to say," said Cynthia to George, "is that she really wants you to take her to the tearoom. But I have heard about those places. You have to eat cake with a fork, and hold out your little finger when you pick up a teacup. And if anything astonishing happens – say an old man loses his false teeth in a rock bun – we have to say 'Oh my goodness.' It is a war zone of etiquette, a place you can never take Victoria without being her proper gentleman friend, practically engaged. Honestly, George, the zoo is a much better place, because if you can't think of anything to say, you can talk about the animals."

Matron looked out of the window. It seemed as if George was following Cynthia's instructions, and had totally forgotten about his offer of not going to the zoo.

"Now," said Cynthia, "as your date manager, I am requesting no kissing today. Only later, when Victoria is a mere whisper of longing, is the first explosive, atomic snog to take place!"

But George did not smile at her chatter. Rather, he seemed

to be in a trance. "You are so perfect," he breathed. "…Oh, I said that out loud, didn't I?"

"Yes," said Cynthia, "we have brain and mouth resynchronisation. My work here is done."

Cynthia backflipped into the rear seat. "Hello," she said. "George is quite cured, he thinks you are so perfect…"

Cynthia's voice trailed off. Victoria's face was deathly white; her body shrivelled as she bunched herself up against the door. Cynthia supposed it must be really frightening to get a first boyfriend when you are so old. Virginity was meant to be lost when you were overwhelmed by the hormones of puberty.

Cynthia began to think about her own panic attack all those years ago, when a customer had come into her gloomy room expecting a full service. She had been right to poke him in the eye, then jump out of the window. And she had been right to emerge from the woods six months later, with a different name. The orphanage had served her well; even Miss Buckley, the daft old bat, could now even be viewed with some affection. And now came this amazing day at the end: college, the zoo and, in all probability, ice cream. She reached out to touch Victoria's elbow as a gesture of sympathy.

"George can never tell lies," she said, "so if he says you are perfect, then it is what he believes. Now, your nice trainers, let's see them on your feet. However pretty you think they look, they can't stay on your ornament shelf forever."

Victoria stared at the things that had come to haunt her. "I can't wear them today," she said, "they would not go with my uniform."

"Umm," said Cynthia, "I suppose you do look a bit grey. I agree, it would make your nice trainers look very odd. Oh,

Uncle George, what is to be done? This is a disaster, and it's all my fault."

"Oh, I expect something will turn up," said George. "It usually does."

Cynthia leaned forwards to look at George's face, then nodded her approval. Sitting back, she recovered an A4 writing pad from her bag of student things, and started to make notes, stopping occasionally to chew her pen, deep in thought.

Eventually, George parked the car, and jumped out to hold the door open for Matron.

"I'll have to get out your side," said Cynthia, "my door doesn't work."

"Yes it does," protested George.

Cynthia gave a deep sigh, then gave Victoria a push. "But this saves time," she said. "Go on, Victoria, they feed the penguins at two, and I want to watch."

Matron reluctantly let herself be pushed out. "This is not the zoo car park," she said.

"It's close enough," said George. "It's only a short walk around the corner from here."

After they had walked a hundred yards, Cynthia linked her arm into Matron's, and swung her around so as to walk through a wide doorway. Matron looked in horror at the shop, with all the people rushing about to buy things. She sensed the panic rising – fear of crowded places, they called it, but it was only recently, since the boat nightmare, that it had really started to take effect. And, both times, George had been there; it was obviously all his fault.

Cynthia looked around the large clothes store for the assistant who best suited her purpose. Identifying a confident young woman, she rushed off to explain what was required. They returned together.

"My friend," said Cynthia to the assistant, "has been held prisoner for the past ten years in a big castle, where you are only allowed to wear grey. But she has just escaped, and wants something to go with these."

Cynthia gave the assistant the trainers.

"Well," said the assistant, "I see a pink and yellow pattern for the dress. Come this way, madam, if you please."

With the assistant on one arm, and Cynthia on the other, Matron found herself involuntarily taken to a rack of dresses.

"How about this one, madam?" asked the assistant.

Matron looked at the dress, which was even more vivid than the clown shoes. She shook her head.

"Perhaps a smaller pattern," said Cynthia. "What about this yellow one with little pink flowers?"

Matron looked at George. It would cost money, something men who lived in garden sheds did not have. When he started to run away from the tills, all she had to do was follow.

"Don't understand clothes shopping," said George. He turned to the assistant. "You're the expert," he added.

The assistant seemed to go weak at the knees. Then she reached across to touch him on the arm, as if he were a god.

"Oh, madam," she said, looking entirely at George, "it's perfect. You must try it on."

"There," said George, "it's perfect."

Matron took the dress, not because she would ever wear it, but because it would allow her to sit quietly in the changing room while she worked out how to escape. If she climbed out of the window where would she go? How could she get back home, without Mad George and his car?

Back in the main shop, Cynthia turned to George. "I've left something in your car," she said. "Can I borrow your keys for five minutes?"

George handed her the keys, but Cynthia made no effort to go anywhere. Instead, she stood back to look at him.

"I'm sorry," she said, "but that cardigan's got to go."

"But it's my favourite, my best, I wore it especially for Victoria."

"It looks like something from the war," said Cynthia. "And the corduroy trousers...what can I say."

"Your little friend is right," said the assistant. "Against your 'friend's' new dress, you will look...Oh, I can't bear it, sir, come this way, please. Let us see what is to be done."

"I trust you will be kind but firm," said Cynthia. "It seems this is his first visit to a clothes shop for thirty years!"

Matron sat in a cubical, waiting for five minutes to pass, after which she would be legally allowed to tell the assistant that she did not like the dress. Then the curtain twitched.

"Are you OK in there?" said a voice. "May I come in?"

"No," said Matron.

But the curtain opened anyway, and the horrible assistant peered in. "Your little friend explained that you have Grey-Munchausen Syndrome," she said, "but this is the worst case I have ever seen. Never mind, I am specially trained to deal with such disorders. Now, madam, put the dress on, and look in the mirror, that is all I ask. I shall be waiting outside, and will not let you leave until I have witnessed the transformation."

Matron sensed the whole world was ganging up on her. What had Cynthia said to make the evil guard so ruthless?

"I must say," called the guard from the other side of the

curtain, "you are very lucky to have a gentleman friend who likes clothes shopping. I bet all your friends are dead jealous."

"He is not my gentleman friend."

"But your date manager seems to think he is. How does that work exactly? Your date manager locates a man, who owns a chalet by the river, has his own sailing boat, and brings you clothes shopping? Most of my mates get drunk and see what they find in bed the following morning. It makes me think I need a date manager…"

Victoria peeped through a little gap in the curtain, to discover the guard was reading from a sheet of A4 paper. She obviously considered herself to be an actress in a play.

"Right," said the guard after she had delivered her soliloquy, "have you changed yet, because I am opening the curtain in three seconds."

"No, give me another moment…I'm changing now."

Matron realised that what her tormentor had actually given her was a nightdress. It was certainly not the sort of thing she wanted to wear in the main changing room, without having a dressing gown on top. Nervously, she opened the curtain. "There," she said, "are you happy now?"

The guard started flapping her arms in a panic.

"No, no, it's all wrong," she wailed. "The shoes, the shoes. Oh, I can't bear to look! Put the trainers on."

"If I put them on," said Matron, "will you promise to leave me alone?"

"Oh this Grey-Munchausen Syndrome, it's so horrible! Is that why you have been living in the grey prison your little friend told me about?"

"Huh," said Matron. Then she bent down to put on

the clown shoes, after which the guard took her arm, and marched her to the full-length mirror.

"Success," said the guard. "You look wonderful! Oh, I am so happy. Are you cured? Please say you are, I couldn't bear it if you wasn't."

"I am cured, now can I put my proper clothes back on?"

"Let me savour the moment. Oh yes, it is all so truly wonderful."

Matron noticed the guard was actually looking over her shoulder.

"Please wait," she said, "…a moment longer…almost… Ah."

Then, to Matron's astonishment, the guard just left. The nightmare was over, allowing Matron to scurry back to her changing cubical. Then she tried the next cubical, and the one after that. With a rising panic, she realised that her proper clothes had been stolen.

A long time passed, before she nervously made her way to the main door, and peered around the crack. Everybody had totally forgotten about her. She felt naked, the light fabric seemingly made of air. Surely people could see her knickers and bra because the little dress barely covered her knees. And when she had looked in the mirror the shadow between the top of her breasts was clearly visible. She was wearing a prostitute's dress, clown shoes, and was miles from home.

Standing in the doorway, she waved frantically at the assistant and, on attracting her attention, explained that her normal clothes had been stolen.

"Fear not," said the assistant, "your date manager has taken your work clothes back to the car. Enjoy the rest of your day."

"And where is she now? I need to kill her."

"I wouldn't advise that, madam, she is in the male changing room, trying to persuade your boyfriend to come out."

"But she's a girl!"

"You try and stop her then. She reckons it's nothing she hasn't seen before."

Then the door to the men's changing room opened, and George came sliding out across the polished floor. Cynthia appeared to be pushing. George was wearing a yellow short-sleeved shirt, open at the neck, and a pair of red trousers. There was no sign of the cardigan. Then George saw Victoria, and went all limp. Cynthia led him the rest of the way, without difficulty.

"I'm sorry," said George, "I couldn't help it. She has stolen my proper clothes and locked them in the car."

Matron wanted to laugh, but could only blink at all the bright colours.

"Now," said Cynthia, "please can we go to the zoo?"

Once out in the sunshine, the clothes shone even brighter. Victoria played with the hem of her dress, trying to pull it down, but this only exposed more cleavage. George fiddled with his shirt.

"Other men will think I fancy them." he moaned.

"Easily sorted," said Cynthia. She took his arm, and interlinked it with Matron's. "Now people will know you fancy Victoria," she said. "Stay close, and if a man approaches, introduce her as your wife. Call it a practice run for what Vera has seen falling from the future."

George untangled his arm. "I'm sorry," he said, "but this is something Victoria needs to decide for herself. To walk in her shadow is enough."

"But Becky told me that Victoria has already been draped

over your head, after you rescued her from death," said Cynthia. "Apparently you couldn't see where you were going. So what is wrong with a little arm-linking? Be brave, George, don't panic, I am here to supervise such things." Cynthia re-linked their arms, and this time George did not have the strength to fight back.

Matron realised that the awful incident in the mud had happened when she had been wearing proper clothes, which protected her from knowing too much about what was happening in the outside world. Now they were forcing her to wear a nightdress, so George's presence was more obvious. The dress didn't even have any sleeves, allowing his great hairy arm to become welded to her own. Why did he have such hard skin? Very probably he used a Brillo pad in the shower, which she rather hoped he had taken this morning – or at least sometime this week.

Victoria awoke from her nightmare to find herself in the entrance compound of the zoo. Cynthia walked ahead to examine her carefully. Then she looked at George, before stepping back to admire them both together, almost as if they were a single item.

Cynthia nodded. "Well," she said, "you should be OK on your own now. I'll see you back here in three hours."

Then she ran off, and Victoria found herself at the mercy of George's armlock. She had no idea of what to say, or where to go.

"Well," said George presently, "how about going to see the elephants?"

"Or, we could go back to your car to get our proper clothes?" she replied.

George went a little red and shuffled his feet. Then he played nervously with his shirt. "Cynthia has stolen my car keys," he said. "She was just everywhere, I didn't know what was happening."

"Well, couldn't you just take them back?"

"Not really, she has put them down her bra."

Matron let out a horrified laugh. "Well, in that case," she said, "I suppose we'd better go and look at the elephants."

Three hours later, Cynthia was standing by the exit to watch the families walking this way and that. She thought George would make a good dad, though not for a child already hardened by the ways of an orphanage; he was too gentle to take any meaningful control over such a situation. And, according to Becky, even after she had explained the reason for Victoria's shyness, he had merely commented that twenty years ago many women remained virgins until they married. And he still took her clothes shopping…

And Victoria had not even thanked him for the nice dress. If she was not careful, he would be lost to the receptionist at his depot, whom he had only rejected because of the rude word she had used after inexplicably diving head first into the mud. Eureka! Victoria was scared of the rope swing; no matron could reasonably be expected to deal with so much mud. Even Hilda had commented on it, and only truly relaxed at the boat village when the tide was in. Cynthia decided that all Victoria needed was some proper rope-swinging lessons to remember what grown-ups somehow forget. Getting her to the chalet was the difficult bit; the final few steps to George's bed would be a trivial detail.

Cynthia was distracted from her thoughts by two bright splashes of colour coming towards her. Their arms were not interlinked anymore, but neither did they seem to be at war. She supposed they might pass for a shy couple who had just met.

"Did you have a nice time?" she asked.

"Yes," said George, "and thank you very much for organising it."

"Victoria, your views, please."

"Leave the poor girl alone," said George. "She did not dislike it, and that is progress, is it not?"

"I did like it," said Matron quietly.

"And does this mean we are going to stop at the ice cream parlour on the way home, Uncle George?"

"Only if you stop calling me 'uncle'."

"Only if you stop wearing your 'uncley' cardigan!"

"That's blackmail!" protested George.

"She's very good at that," said Matron. "I expect it's how I come to be standing in a zoo car park wearing a nightdress. Today was meant to be about college, and we end up...well, I don't really know what happened."

Cynthia smiled. "The uncle cardigan had to go," she said, "and now you don't look at all 'uncley'." Cynthia stepped back, curtsied, then demurely held out the back of her hand. "Hello, George," she said, "I'm Cynthia. I very much hope we will be friends."

George took her hand to shake it. "Nothing could be more certain," he said, "unless, of course, you have actually thrown the cardigan into a bin."

"Ah," said Cynthia, "we need to talk about that. Miss Vera said its very existence kept interfering with her signal!"

*

At the ice cream parlour, George sat with Victoria on the back bench, while Cynthia plonked herself on an opposite stool to observe her students with pride. Not only was her little project surviving the opening moves, but there was ice cream and lemonade between them. Next time, she would organise their date at a picture house, like Becky had told her about. She had never seen a moving photograph, and the notion of it intrigued her.

Victoria had not liked the way George had accepted Cynthia's hand at the zoo exit. It didn't look right…and now, he had bought her an ice cream. Not just any old ice cream, but a fancy knickerbocker glory. Cynthia had virtually admitted throwing his cardigan in the bin, yet he still behaved like a man who wanted to be her friend. Slowly, everything began to make sense. She remembered Cynthia doing gymnastics over his car seat. "You are so perfect," he had breathed. Only he was not talking about herself; he had just seen Cynthia's legs…

This is how bad men worked: latch onto an adult, then target their children. She was only dragged along as excess baggage, to make it look respectable. Really, it was Cynthia he had taken to the zoo, and now he would find it a lot easier to get her into bed. Yes, that was it; he was behaving differently today, as if his mad perversions had cooled. He had stopped trying to get her into isolated settings, and the 'bunny rabbit' language had ceased. He was not wearing a yellow shirt to impress her, but because Cynthia had suggested it. Victoria froze; Cynthia had gone into the male changing room; he must think her so eager to give him satisfaction in return for ice creams.

"I'm surprised you think taking Cynthia to the zoo is so interesting," Matron said.

"Why? She is a delightful girl."

"And do you really not know what she did to David?"

"No!" screamed Cynthia. "Please, I was different then, and yes, I am ashamed!"

"You mean the chair?" said George. "Mandy mentioned it when she told me about David locking himself down the crew quarters of the captain's ship, after you walked onboard the ship."

"Ah-ha," said Victoria, as if this made some very important point.

Cynthia noted the strange tone in Matron's voice, but it was obvious George did not.

"Anyway," continued George, "David later told me he likes Cynthia, but can't say, because it would upset Mandy. And Mandy told me that she only threw you across the deck because…"

"No," screamed Cynthia, "shut up, George…she sneaked up on me, and how was I to know Captain had been giving her judo lessons?"

Matron screamed. "The captain has been picking up little girls to throw them around?"

"I would be very grateful if you would both stop screaming," said George. "The captain learnt his judo from a Japanese crew member, so is quite able to teach it safely. As to Mandy throwing you across the deck, it's just her way of showing David she will protect him from anything frightening that comes his way. If anybody ties him to a chair again, they will find themselves flying out of a window."

Cynthia turned to look directly at George. "You know all about this," she said quietly, "and you still like me?"

Instinctively, she reached out to put her hand over his.

"Though just sometimes," she added, "it's best not to let on you know things. Becky is not very good at editing facts."

"Becky only told me what I needed to know to understand things. I expect where you came from, seeing naked men tied to chairs was quite normal, when you were little. Anyway, before you gave David sanctuary he was having the worst possible childhood, so entertaining a lot of girls was still a great improvement on what had gone before. And then you let him escape, so to him you are an angel in human form."

Matron stared at Cynthia's tiny hand resting over George's. Why could nobody else see why George was so enthusiastic about buying her ice creams? He had almost admitted to finding pleasure in the idea of Cynthia tying him naked to a chair. But when she had confronted the child abuser on the ship, it had all gone so wrong, and now the captain could throw Mandy about whenever he wanted, and pretend he was playing judo. No, this time she must get George to confess, by pretending what he wanted to do was acceptable.

"So why are you treating me differently today?" she asked.

"When I first saw you, I thought you were Mandy's mum. Mandy never talked about her dad, and you weren't wearing a wedding ring, so I thought, why not be a little naughty? And now I've seen you in your dress, I realise you're only a fraction over twenty, and I feel quite ashamed of the way I behaved."

"Reality check!" said Cynthia. "You also look ten years younger since you, er…lost your cardigan. I think it's very much in order for you to be Victoria's boyfriend."

George shook his head. "I am truly sorry for being so forward on your first visit," he said. "Your first boy…"

"Stop!" screamed Cynthia so loudly that George recovered his hand so he could protect both ears.

"I think it is fairly inevitable," continued Cynthia, "that

unless you learn to tell fibs, and quickly, I am going to require ten pence."

"I was only going to say…" began George.

"Ten pence," said Cynthia, "or I shall scream again, even louder!"

George gave her ten pence, which she clasped in her hand.

"You were talking about Becky," she continued. "Where did you say she took the children last Saturday?"

"No," said George, "I was saying that I might have had something to offer Victoria and Mandy as a package deal, but as her first boyfriend, it's like Becky said, the first time needs to be magical. I am neither young nor good looking, I don't even do dancing or go into pubs. Today only worked because you were here to make it a family day out at the zoo."

Cynthia looked at Matron's horrified face, and knew a situation like this required backup. She raced to the telephone, fed in the ten pence, and dialled.

"Hello," she said, "it's grown-ups being silly again…"

Having called for backup, Cynthia confined herself to looking around the corner, observing Matron's stony face, and the pleading George, who was undoubtedly digging himself into a deeper hole. Then she looked at her ice cream and, realising it was melting, went to rejoin her students.

"…But it's OK," George was saying, "I am a virgin also."

"You shouldn't say that," said Cynthia, "it makes it sound as if you are looking to be cured. It needs to be qualified: 'I am a virgin because I am a monk,' for instance, though in your case, I think it is more to do with the rope swing!"

"No," said George, "it's something that needs to wait until you are very much in love."

"Yes," said Cynthia, "we talked about it earlier, until Victoria is no more than a mere whisper of longing…"

Victoria wanted to scream out the words, "I was raped!", but the dark images had been so long repressed, that she could never let her tormented thoughts escape now, not even when it meant the others having a good laugh about her supposed virginity. So she just sat, ridged with fear, terrified that the slightest movement would bring her back into the conversation.

"…But it's OK for me and Becky to talk about our virginity," Cynthia was saying. "It's what friends do, though not necessarily so truthfully as you seem to like. But I am fourteen, and Becky seventeen. Doesn't it get embarrassing when you're…a bit older?"

"It's simply the way life has turned out," said George. "Better this than accidentally spending the rest of your life with somebody you don't really like."

Victoria tried hard to concentrate on the fact that at least things could not get any worse. Then Cynthia turned to the family on the next table.

"I'm their date manager," she said. "Do you think George should marry Victoria?"

"He's very fashionable," said the lady.

"And he owns a chalet by the riverbank," said Cynthia.

Victoria realised that, since all the screaming, the whole parlour had gone silent to better hear their conversation. She bowed her head in shame. Cynthia, meanwhile, had started to get everybody organised. How did she do it? Soon, everyone in the parlour had an opinion on whether George should marry Victoria, and the merits of a chalet by a river. But at least now Victoria knew, with absolute certainty, that it could never get any worse than this. Then she sensed a shadow, and something very heavy landed on the bench beside her.

"Well, hello!" said Hilda's voice. "Victoria, don't you look nice, and who is this dashing man? How amazing, is that really you inside that yellow shirt, George? Oh, I must take the weight off my feet. Cynthia, be a luv and get us a coffee. No sugar, because I'm on a diet."

Hilda might be on a diet, but that still left Victoria with eighteen stone of woman squashed against her side. George was on the other, his great hairy arm pressing into her own flesh. She was completely trapped between two mad people, and herself wearing nothing more than a nightdress. Any moment now, George would move his arm across her shoulders, then slide his fingers down her top. And this prostitute's dress gave her no protection at either end. Anyone kneeling on the floor to pick up some change could see right up her legs. And all the time George was playing out his fantasies about doing it with somebody who had no previous experience. He would probably give her a sex manual, and suggest they started at page one, or perhaps he would want Cynthia to watch, and shout out instructions.

"And where have you two been?" asked Hilda. "I must say you look the perfect couple. Do you realise your clothes match? Yellow and red, very bright and cheerful. I hope Cynthia has been behaving herself, she is such a handful, but what would we do without her?"

"I do not believe you arrived here by accident," said Victoria quietly.

"But of course, I often come here with Cynthia. Not to eat ice creams anymore, but their coffee is quite delightful. Did I tell you about my diet? I'm going for a stone a month. Next year I will be able to wear the sort of dress you're wearing, Victoria. Where did you get it? Oh, I'm so jealous! What do you think the captain would say if I walked onto his ship like that?"

George thought the captain was very lucky to have found such a woman – well, a complete family of women really – plus one boy. He managed a smile. "Honestly, Hilda," he said, "do you really want to know?"

"But of course, George, my little fashion hero."

"He says he likes a woman with a bit of meat on her. I wouldn't get too carried away with your diet."

"Now, there's a thing. What do you think he would like best?"

"Stay as you are," said George.

Victoria felt a bead of perspiration drip from her chin. Her body was starting to let her down; in stressful situations, the bladder muscles often relaxed of their own accord. How could she cope with the result of it spreading across the plastic bench? It would become a stream running in both directions; perverted George might even get some pleasure out of it. Her heart began to race and her breathing impossible to keep stable. All that mattered now was escaping a situation over which she had no control. She leapt over the table and ran towards the exit. On reaching the pavement, she sprinted away like a schoolgirl on a demented cross-country run. After all, she was wearing bouncy clown shoes, and a dress so light it seemed not to be there.

Cynthia saw the flash of yellow streaking across the ice cream parlour, and looked around just in time to see Victoria dashing through the doorway. She scurried across with Hilda's coffee.

"What happened?" she asked.

"I really don't know," replied Hilda. "One moment she was sitting between us, the next she was leaping across the table."

Cynthia looked at George. "Did you say anything?" she asked.

"I didn't let him get a word in," said Hilda. "I was just talking about nice things, and whoosh, her bottom seemed to catch fire!"

George looked very unhappy. "Shouldn't we go after her?" he asked.

"No point," said Hilda. "The speed she was moving we'd never catch her."

"It was me, wasn't it," said George. "She thinks I'm horrible."

"I've got no idea what's going on in her mind," said Hilda, "and at this moment I don't really care. George, did you say the captain liked a woman who was not terribly thin?"

"Yes."

"In which case I'm going to grab me an ice cream. Cynthia, do you want seconds?"

Cynthia shook her head. "Bath night," she said. "I've got to be back at six to hand out the clean clothes."

"I'll give you a lift back," said Hilda. "If we're late, it will only be a few minutes. Anyway my coffee needs to cool."

Cynthia frowned. "But, Hilda," she said, "you've always been so punctual. If this is what love does to you, I think I'd rather avoid it."

George found himself relaxing; this was the Cynthia he liked. With Victoria she was much too bossy, but with Hilda she was a genuine friend.

*

Matron covered the half-mile to the college in a few minutes, and quickly threw herself into the car. Then she did her first ever wheel spin to career along the main road, until she reached the country lanes. But she could not go up the drive yet; the children would be everywhere, all running across to gaze at her, and probably wondering if a prostitute's dress helped you get a man. She swung the steering wheel hard to divert into an abandoned farm track on her left, but miscalculated how fast she had been going. The car skidded onwards, crashing into a boulder, then veering sideways until it came to a halt between two rusty tractors. Panic changed to general nervousness, and eventually she found the courage to restart the engine. She tried to drive away, but the car made an awful racket, and stalled. Getting out, she discovered the front wheel had a flat tyre, together with a buckled rim. There was nothing to be done; her spare still had a puncture, and all the garages would be closed for the night. She opened the rear door, and lay down on the back seat, to hide from the outside world, until she could sneak into the home after everybody had gone to bed.

*

Cynthia arrived back at the home to find a short queue, and no Matron. Halfway through handing out the clothes, number forty-six stood before her, obviously suffering from the start of a cold. Cynthia looked in the clothes book to discover her name.

"Tracy," she said, "do you want to spend the night in sickbay to save spreading your germs?"

"Wouldn't mind," replied Tracy.

"Well, go and sit down, I'll see you as soon as I can."

The two girls behind considered this to be excellent news, both announcing their colds were much worse than Tracy's. Cynthia sent them to sickbay, and carried on with her work. After all the clothes were distributed she went to see her patients. She was carrying a big bottle of cod liver oil, and three coffee cups.

"I'm sorry about your colds," she said, "but this will cure you in no time. I'll give you two cups now, followed by another in the morning. It's all the vitamins, you see, Matron swears by it."

"Well, actually," said number eighty-five, "I feel a lot better after my sit down. I think I will have my bath, and see how I feel."

"Erm, I was only here to keep her company," said the other. "I'm off!"

Tracy just looked miserable, with a red nose, and streaming eyes.

"That's the worst cold I've ever seen," said Cynthia. "I don't think cod liver oil's going to work for you. How would you fancy a glass of lemon drink, and perhaps some blackcurrant lozenges to be left by your bedside?"

"Thank you," said Tracy.

Cynthia sorted out the junior baths, then returned to her patient. By 9pm everything was done, with Tracy tucked up in bed. There was still no sign of Matron, so Cynthia settled down to read about some interesting diseases. At 10pm she looked up, and wondered if she should telephone Hilda, but it seemed too late; so deciding not to leave Tracy on her own, she crawled into the other bed to listen to her patient's troubled breathing. Then she thought about college, the zoo, and ice creams, soon dropping off to sleep to live it all again in her dreams.

It had been dark many hours before Matron thought it safe to creep quietly up the drive and into the building. She made it to her room without disturbing anyone, and locked the door. She was shivering intensely. How prostitutes could work the streets in such flimsy clothes she had no idea; they must always be catching colds. She took off the awful dress and threw it to the floor in disgust. Tomorrow, she would parcel it up with the clown shoes, and go down to the incinerator. With a bit of surgical spirit, it would make a nice blaze, and she could warm her hands as a symbol that this awful day was going up in smoke.

She lay in bed for a long time before she stopped shivering. Only then could her mind dwell on all the problems that had fallen into her life. The car needed to be sorted out. She did not want anyone from the home to know she had crashed into a curb; it would only give them something else to laugh about. She would have to find a garage, and let them do whatever was necessary, which she felt certain would take a lot of running about, since the spare wheel needed to be repaired first. But it was probably going to be more complicated than that. Her collision with the boulder had been quite severe, and the garage was bound to say that she had broken a big end. At least she thought that was what they called the thing that held the steering in place. In any event, it was bound to be expensive.

As the night wore on, Matron became overwhelmed by the greater misfortunes of her life. She could imagine everybody packed onto the purple boat, all discussing her private life. Every so often, they would laugh as Cynthia said something else to humiliate her. Could anything be worse than this? Then she realised Mad George had stolen her clothes, in the top pocket of which he would find her IOU for the condoms. Now he would be thinking about all the stuff in that awful book – the wild positions that Cynthia told the girls she got into! Thank goodness the children had not seen her in the prostitute's dress.

Eventually, Matron realised that she would never sleep, and climbed out of bed to get a bin liner into which she threw the prostitute's dress and clown shoes. This made her feel better, so she went to have a nice hot bath, after which she got dressed in her spare set of proper clothes. Then she had a true Eureka moment: when Cynthia had started blackmailing her, the girl had nothing to lose; now, the blackmail was the same, but the outcomes reversed. A few orphanages would still take an unqualified matron at reduced wages, so she would be no worse off. In fact, working at a place where the girls did not think she was a love goddess would be an improvement. But there was no way Cynthia could continue her college studies if the truth came out. The girl would not risk it; her reign of terror had come to an end.

Matron scurried down the corridor to Cynthia's room, and entered without knocking. The bed had not been slept in; the tramp had realised her mistake and gone back to the dormitory of her own accord – peace and tranquillity at last. Matron opened the locker to discover her study books; how tame *Anatomy and Physiology for Nurses* seemed now. She pulled out the three books at the bottom. *The Joy of Sex...* well, that could go in the incinerator. But what was this? *Lady Chatterley's Lover*. After her heartbeat had stabilised, she sat on the bed to look inside. On the title page was a handwritten library grid which showed it had been issued sixteen times since April. If the girls read it in groups of three…Oh, it was too awful! Becky would be in so much trouble, if she ever dared show her face again. In a moment of inspiration, Matron recovered *The Joy of Sex* and looked at the price. Proof: the two books came to a total of £9.98, the amount of the receipt for the psychology book – a hefty volume indeed. She had been funding pornography and vice! Finally, Matron opened the *Kama Sutra* – just to check the library grid – but all the title page said was '*Happy Birthday from Wales. Your best-ever friend*'.

Matron put the sex manuals into a bin liner but, when it came to *Lady Chatterley,* her hand began to hover. Perhaps she should inspect that, just to find out how much the girls had been corrupted. After all, it was written a long time ago when people only went to bed together in the dark. Perhaps it just contained the sort of 'trouser problems' Miss Buckley would find distasteful. She decided to worry about *Lady Chatterley* later, but the sex manuals and prostitute's dress needed immediate action. She felt the radiator and, finding it cold, knew the caretaker was not yet in the boiler house. Anyway, the heating did not go on until the outside temperature dropped to 10°, and that did not normally happen until late October. She picked up the sack and, taking a bottle of surgical spirit from the shelf, hurried along the corridors to the back door. From there, she made the fleeting dash across the lawns to the boiler house. After walking down the stone steps, she found herself in a gloomy cellar with a hillside of coke going up to the delivery hatch. It all made her quite nervous, not only the industrial-looking stuff, but also the caretaker's general existence. For a brief moment, she felt overwhelmed by

Cynthia's bravery, to come down here and risk an encounter with such a person in the fire-breathing dungeon.

The present caretaker was the result of Miss Buckley's nationwide prayer for a female who knew about caretaker things, thus keeping all men where they belonged – outside the gates. God answered her prayer by making this woman read the advertisement in a copy of *Woodworkers' Weekly*. She had brought Miss Buckley great delight ever since: fixing the plumbing, rewiring the kitchens, and doing a wonderful bricklaying job for the new outhouse at the bottom of the drive. It had a place for the postman to leave mail, the bin men to pick up rubbish, and an alcove for any visiting nuns to shelter from the rain while they telephoned for an escort. A telephone system that had, of course, been installed by the caretaker. More importantly, the caretaker had promised Miss Buckley that on no account would she ever bring a man onto the premises. As far as anybody knew, she had kept strictly to this rule, though possibly only because she was likely to terrify any man who set eyes on her. She never wore anything but overalls and, throughout the Winter, usually a cloth cap. To upset the caretaker often resulted in a little visit. For this, she would wear old boots – the ones from which the leather had worn away at the front to reveal the steel toecaps beneath. Just to have her standing in front of you with a sledgehammer over her shoulder, was enough to make any sensible person drop to their knees and plead forgiveness. It was said that nobody had dropped a single piece of litter after the 'sweet wrapper incident of 1975'.

Looking about the caretaker's dungeon, Matron saw a big iron door set into the brickwork of the far wall. She pulled it open and peered inside. It had cinders at the bottom and a chimney at the top. Matron laughed at her own silliness. How difficult could it be to burn a bit of rubbish? She threw in the sack, poured on the spirit, then stood back to throw in a lighted match. There was a great whoosh of flames, some of which leapt into the cellar. She quickly closed the door, making everything roar up the chimney. Holding out her hands, she felt the warmth of all the horrible prostitute things going up in smoke. A smile spread across her face; she could manage without Becky just fine.

The caretaker seemed to appear from nowhere, and rushed straight to the wall to spin some valves around. "Stupid cow," she shouted, "you've got a cloud of black smoke blowing across the grounds, smells like burning rubber!"

Matron scampered backwards until she trod on something round, and her feet shot skywards. The next moment she was sprawled like a sacrifice on a hillside of coke. She had been mad to come down here on her own. If the caretaker put her into the furnace and shovelled a load of coke on top, nobody would ever know.

"Just contaminated clothes," she said weakly.

The caretaker pulled a leaver and an electric motor began to hum.

"I know what burning rubber smells like," she said. "I wouldn't be surprised to see a fire engine racing up the drive, and you know what that would mean: a lot of men running about, with Miss Buckley having another one of her funny turns. It would be chaos, all the girls asking to be rescued on their shoulders."

Matron froze in fear; the caretaker was stepping across to attack her. Though, as it turned out, she merely reached out to lift her from the coke, and set her upright on the floor. An action that seemed to require no more effort than picking up a piece of balsa wood.

"I only burnt one bin bag," said Matron weakly.

The caretaker gave a condescending sniff. "The boiler will explode if there's no circulation," she said.

Matron looked down at her feet, ashamed and very frightened. Why wouldn't the caretaker go away to let her watch the furnace in peace? She needed to look inside, just to make sure everything had turned to ash. If the books had not burned properly, she needed to poke about, and pour on the last of the surgical spirit to blacken what remained beyond recognition.

"Is there anything else?" asked the caretaker. "Only you seem to be hovering."

"Er," said Matron, "I was just worried about all the ash, just in case any germs survived."

"I clear everything out before the beginning of Winter, and give the ash to Miss Buckley to spread on her bit of garden. She suffers terrible from acidic soil. Any bugs will not survive long, once her roses get to work."

All of a sudden, Matron knew that bits of the book would survive. Glossy paper never burned that well, especially when well pressed together. She would have to come back tonight, recover the evidence, and throw it all into the boating lake.

"I'm sorry I used your furnace without asking," she offered.

The caretaker seemed to soften. "If you like," she said, "I'll show you how to use it properly, in Winter, when I have to shovel in the coke. Hot, sweaty work, really clears out the pores, so I can jump in a cold bath afterwards. There's really nothing like it for making the skin tingle. I'm Alex, by the way, and you are?"

"Everybody just calls me Matron."

"OK then, Matron, until we meet again. Though I think you'd better leave now, the girls might wonder what you've been doing in here all this time."

Matron scurried up the steps, and back into the open air, still singed with the smell of burning rubber. She was now more convinced than ever that the pictures had survived, and were waiting for whoever opened the furnace door next. This must be herself, even if it was at two in the morning.

*

Cynthia awoke to the sound of footsteps walking along the passageway. She jumped from the couch and opened the door, just in time to see Matron going into her room.

"Matron," she said, "I'm so glad you're back. I was quite worried about you."

Matron stared at the cause of all her problems. "Won't you ever leave me alone?" she snapped.

Cynthia could sense the wave of hostility. "Have I done something to upset you?" she asked.

Matron thought about the total humiliation and fear she had just suffered when lying on the coke. It was all Cynthia's fault for forcing her to wear a prostitute's clothes; but, more than this, she now realised not even Cynthia was foolish enough to go into the caretaker's den.

"I don't believe you burned the Swedish magazines," Matron said.

"Of course not," replied Cynthia. "Apart from anything else, where would I get the matches?"

Before Cynthia could add that the magazines were thrown

into the lake, she saw Victoria's hand flying towards her face. It was weak and uncoordinated, but what lay behind it was obviously a psychopathic tantrum. Cynthia easily ducked then stepped to one side.

"Is this because of what we talked about yesterday?" she asked. "I know Becky said I should never talk about your virginity, but George is so honest, the moment just got the better of me…"

"You are banned from my surgery forever!" screamed Matron. "Do you understand? Forever! If you get ill, go to see you friend over the lane. I'm sure you will have loads to talk about."

Cynthia did not understand what was happening, other than it was something to do with grown-ups being silly. Making a strategic withdrawal, she edged around the wall to the surgery, where she grabbed a white coat and stethoscope, before leaping out of the window. This was how everyone, who had no intention of coming back, left the surgery.

The front door of Hilda's surgery opened directly onto the veranda that went around the central parade ground. This was difficult territory for Cynthia, but a climb-through window overlooking the back yard allowed her to gain access. It was by this route that she generally visited, on this occasion without difficulty.

Hilda listened carefully to Cynthia's account of the morning, that could not, for various reasons, include the bit about the magazines.

"It has started then," said Hilda, "the descent into madness."

"But Victoria is my friend, I can't let that happen."

"Too late. All the women who stay over there eventually

end up becoming like Miss Buckley. But you have more serious problems to worry about. You do realise that you have been put into quarantine?"

She gave Hilda a questioning look.

"You have made it to the outside world," said Hilda. "This is why you have your own room, with Matron watching over you. Miss Buckley will not allow you to return to the dormitory, because your knowledge can infect the other girls. Once she finds out what has happened, you will be sent to live with the nuns."

"Never!" said Cynthia.

"In which case there is only one thing for it: take all your lessons at college, live a twilight existence, and hope Miss Buckley doesn't actually know what is going on. Very much as it is now, I expect."

"I think I am too young to be a full-time student," said Cynthia.

"Then become a part-time student twice."

"But how am I to pay?"

"Uhmm…difficult. George would want to pay, as would my kind, generous captain. But this would upset Mr Silver, who thinks you need a birthday present every year. So, to make things easier, I am going to be very selfish and take all the pleasure myself."

Hilda squeezed her eyes shut with pure delight. "My very own college girl!" she exclaimed. "But we must act quickly, in case Matron makes it bad for you with Miss Buckley. I'll have to corner the daft old goose, while you've still got a halo around your head."

After Hilda had left, Cynthia made herself a cup of coffee, then sat to ponder the important details of her new life.

Eventually, she decided that, as well as the under tens, the Art master was crucial to the whole operation, because his teaching room had direct line of sight to Matron's window.

The under tens believed her to be a space alien, at first a thing of terror, but more recently a creature of interest. This, together with her skilful interrogation, allowed them to tell her about secret things. Cynthia's knowledge of what she now understood to be typical of 'special brothel customers' – who kept their brains in their pants – allowed her to fill in the bits they did not understand. Well, she reasoned, those men like the Art master, who found pleasure in rubbing their trouser bulge against children, would naturally gravitate towards a boys' home, with brothels charging more for those with 'special' needs. It was thus that, last week, when the Art master had caught her climbing through the surgery window, she had immediately dropped back to the ground next to him to take control of the situation.

A few days later, when she had almost come face to face with a horrible-looking master, she had run into the art room class and hid under a tablecloth with a plant pot on her head. The under tens seemed to think it was a really good game and, as soon as it was safe, they all rushed forwards to show her their pictures. All the Art master could do was look on helpless, perhaps knowing that, in the surprise of the moment, he had enabled her to become invisible. He had kept quiet like a powerless bystander, and now the girl was controlling him and the room. He bowed his head, ashamed of his deviant behaviour which, thirty years before had led to his daughter and now ex-wife threatening to call the police, unless he disappeared immediately from the world of civilised men.

Having got the Art master – her first man on the inside – under control, Cynthia thought the time had come to begin work on Hilda's general assistants. These were boys who had come to view the other side of the fence with absolute terror. Hilda took them on as laundry staff, or more generally, as free domestic labour. Given their terror of girls, they always went into hiding during her visits, even though two of them had now reached the age of nineteen. At the moment there were five in total, though Mr Cranmore believed it to be the regulatory two. Anyway, Cynthia was now ready to begin sorting out their psychological disorders; a complete cure being part of her more general project to get the boys' home running sensibly. She got up and went to a side door, behind which she knew the boys were hiding.

"Don't panic," she said, "I'm coming in."

*

Hilda found the girls' home to be something of a madhouse. Miss Buckley asked three times what the corridors were like, and twice looked out of the window to say it was all very worrying. The rest of the conversation made even less sense, and she seemed to confuse Cynthia going to college with Mr Tebbit going to prison. However, since Mr Tebbit was where he was, it seemed reasonable that Cynthia was also where she needed to be.

Hilda felt great relief in returning to her surgery. It was the sort of homely place where she could bring her captain, except he would want to…

At first, she had been really embarrassed when he had got on his knees to wash her feet. The gentle massaging of the soles, then around to the ankles, had sent electric shocks up her legs. She had wanted to blow out the candles so he could not see all the fat that had made her take the mirror from her bathroom wall ten years before. But he had ignored her requests, and merely put his tongue between her toes.

And Cynthia had brought all this happiness into her life, the little angel, and she was now about to spread her delight into the big wide world.

On returning to her surgery, Hilda heard a lot of furniture being moved about in the side room. Five minutes later, Cynthia emerged, dragging a boy behind her.

"This brave boy is almost cured," she said. "By the end of the week, he should be ready for the ice cream parlour."

She pointed to the door through which she had just come.

"The ones hiding behind the furniture in the corner will take more effort," she said. Then she turned to her prisoner.

"Bet you've never had a knickerbocker glory," she said. "It's an ice cream with fruit and biscuity bits."

The boy had not yet found the courage to speak, but was able to shake his head.

*

Hilda had recently bought a brand new car, asking the man in the showroom for something that would get her to Holyhead in two hours. Now, on the way to college, Cynthia sat in the comfortable passenger seat, feeling quite nervous at all the speed.

"You do realise," said Hilda, "that colleges do 'O' levels in ten months?"

"Not a problem," said Cynthia happily. "I expect it's because students don't mess about in class, and always do their homework."

"I'm not sure about the homework," said Hilda, "but yes, mess about and they will simply ask you to leave."

"There you go then," said Cynthia. "I'm sure it'll be fine."

"You seem to know everything in the nurses' book already, so I'll put you down for Human Biology. That leaves English Literature, which overlaps with your general English course."

Cynthia wondered if this would mean she would get *Lady Chatterley* to read, which would give her yet another advantage. She decided not to ask Hilda about it, even though it was quite obvious she was given to lustful thoughts over the captain in his string vest!

"And have you thought what you are going to do then?" asked Hilda.

"Become a nurse, I told you."

"But five 'O' levels at your age is a bit special. I expect the college will want you to stay for your 'A' levels. Then you can go to university, and become a doctor or a surgeon."

"Slow down," said Cynthia. "I'm quite happy to be a nurse."

"But I want to watch you progress. If I had children I would want them all to be like you."

"And a husband like the captain, I suppose?"

"Oh yes. I bet you think I am a silly old woman."

"Not at all, I simply diagnose 'teenageritus'. It is a complaint that can strike at any age. I expect you have irresistible urges to go clothes shopping, and I'm sure you are going to explode if you don't talk about your boyfriend soon."

"He keeps wanting to wash my feet!" gasped Hilda.

"Well, I hope he uses scented water, with rose petals floating on the surface."

Hilda turned her face away, looking out of the side window, which Cynthia thought to be rather dangerous while she was driving. Such a situation required shock therapy.

"These feet embrace the Earth," she said. "These feet carry you through the world. These feet are beautiful, I honour them."

Matron slammed on the brakes, and skidded to a halt. "That's just what he says," she said, "but I can't find the poem anywhere in the library, and I'm too embarrassed to ask the English master."

"Mallanaga Vatsyayana, a third-century Hindu sage," responded Cynthia calmly. "It's one of the sixty-two arts of love in the *Kama Sutra*."

"What must you think of me!" exclaimed Hilda.

"I think your captain is one hot grandpops. We need to talk about him, and what you are going to do to make him consider me as his granddaughter. In the meantime, perhaps you could practise your next emergency stop outside the ice cream parlour."

*

Victoria was sitting at her desk and having nightmares about the caretaker. At this very minute, she could be looking inside the furnace to see all those horrid photographs laid out before her eyes. At other times, Victoria thought about her car. A mechanic could not walk up the drive to collect the keys, which meant she would have to go to the outside again. Occasionally, she thought about Mad George finding the condom IOU in the clothes he had stolen.

After spending the morning in such torment, she became aware of a presence. She looked around to find the worst of her nightmares had just come true. The caretaker was standing in the doorway, eyes looking about the surgery as if she expected to find rude books on the shelves. It could only mean one thing: she had opened the furnace to find the evidence.

The caretaker was wearing blue overalls and paint-spattered boots, with the shiny steel toecaps poking through holes in the leather. She walked across the surgery to stand with her heels touching, but toes apart. Swinging the sledgehammer from her shoulder, she tapped the steel toecaps together with a click.

"Hi," she said, "just thought I'd pay you a little visit."

Matron leapt back and tried to say something, but only managed a squeak.

The caretaker walked to the electric kettle and started to boil some water. "How do you like your coffee, Matron?" she asked.

So this was how blackmailers worked: discuss terms over a cup of coffee. "Whatever is easiest for you," said Matron.

"Makes no odds to me," said the caretaker. "Milk, sugar, or a marshmallow floating on the top, I can manage it all."

"White, no sugar, please," said Matron.

Matron watched the fearsome woman tip the coffee powder into the lid and, when it looked about right, empty the lid into the cups. It was obviously going to be undrinkable.

"You've never visited me before," whispered Matron.

"You never visited my boiler house before," replied the caretaker.

Matron backed away to the window, and lifted the catch.

"Oh," said the caretaker, "stop being so nervous. You obviously think I've looked inside the furnace."

"No…no…why should I think that?"

"Because you jumped like a startled rabbit when I walked in. Fancy burning your sex manuals at six in the morning. Just raking out the ashes, and there's a fanny winking at me. I was very shocked!"

"It wasn't mine."

"Of course it wasn't. You're not the type to let Becky go down there with grooming scissors. My guess is you go furry, am I right?"

Matron gasped. Not even Cynthia had gone that far; this was blackmail with generous helpings of humiliation.

"The book," gasped Matron, "belonged to the girls. They kept it in a secret room next to the bath-house. It was so disgusting, I had to get rid of it before they were corrupted any more."

"If you say so."

"You don't believe me?"

"Not in the slightest."

"But I can show you the cupboard. The back wall opens. The previous caretaker built it, so he could watch the girls."

"Matron, calm down, I'm not going to tell anyone your secrets. I take it you've given up on the sex toys as well?"

"What!"

"The rubber you weren't burning. A clean break, out with the books, out with the dildos?"

"They were just shoes."

The caretaker laughed. "That needed burning at six in the morning?" she said. "Take my advice, when you're in a hole, stop digging."

The caretaker took a screwdriver from her pocket to stir the coffee, then handed Matron a mug.

"You dark horse," she said. "Now just relax. Do you want to come down the pub tonight?"

Matron felt herself starting to cry, but would not let the caretaker see how easy it was going to be to blackmail her, which was surely the only reason for asking her down to the pub. She would be expected to buy the drinks, then food, and finally anything else this fearsome woman desired.

"I don't go into pubs," said Matron, "it wouldn't look right."

"Oh, I go to a special one, a long way away. Nobody would recognise us there. What do you say?"

"No, I really can't, I've got somebody in sickbay at the moment, I have to be here."

"Another time then, but tell me, what do you do, if you don't go into pubs?"

"I don't know…time seems to pass."

"Sounds a bit dull, stuck here with just your sex toys for company." The caretaker took advantage of being six feet tall, to reach behind the books on the shelf to recover *Lady Chatterley's Lover*. Idly, she flipped through the pages.

"You like this stuff?" she asked.

"No," said Matron, "it belongs to the girls, it's horrible, I don't want it. I should have burned it this morning."

The caretaker showed her tobacco-stained teeth in a coarse laugh. "Sorry," she said, "it's just the image of you running across the lawn, this book in one hand, your dildo in the other. I can see why you chose 6am! Anyway, do you feel any better, now that you have seen the light?"

"You won't tell anybody?" gasped Matron.

"Your secret will go with me to the grave."

It occurred to Matron that the caretaker wasn't trying to blackmail her, but thought her a lonely lady who needed a friend. She gasped out loud. Lonely because of the book, and the belief she used sex toys. Oh, it was too awful! To hide her shame, she turned to gaze out of the window.

After a long silence, the caretaker broke into her thoughts. "Anything wrong?" she asked.

At first, Matron could not think how to answer, but then it crossed her mind that, compared to the caretaker's present imaginings, the car wasn't very embarrassing at all.

"Just problems," she said, "…with my car, but you'll think I'm silly."

"You ran out of petrol?"

"No, I've got a flat tyre, and the spare's flat as well, and it's all abandoned on a farm track, half a mile up the lane."

"Hardly a problem. I'll sort it out in my lunch break."

"What? You really know how to change wheels?"

"Can't everyone? Give me the keys, and I'll bring it back this afternoon."

Matron could not believe that such kindness existed in the world. This woman might save her yet. She let out a sob of gratitude, but this only opened the floodgates to everything else that had gone wrong in her life. Strangely, she felt herself being turned from the window, then two gorilla arms closing around her back. Even stranger than the huge bulk of the caretaker were her pendulous breasts coming to rest on Matron's tummy, a curious formation when squashed into overalls.

"There, there," said the caretaker, "it's only a flat tyre."

But the caretaker's kindness overpowered any words.

Matron could not stop crying, partly from gratitude, but mainly because here was a woman who understood.

"I was supposed to take Cynthia for college enrolment," she sobbed, "but she fixed me up with this horrible man, who lives in a garden shed. And then they made me wear a prostitute's dress, and Matron from over the lane pushed me into him. Why are men so horrible?"

The caretaker began stroking her hair. "They just are," she said, "making us shave our fannies so we look like little girls. I ask you."

All of a sudden, Matron heard something fall to the floor. Looking under the caretaker's armpit, she saw Tracy standing in the doorway, with her mouth wide open. A box of tissues had landed at her feet.

"It's OK," said Matron, "I'm just having a silly moment, but I feel better now."

"Better," stammered Tracy, "yes that's it, better. I feel better now. I must be going back to my lessons."

With that, Tracy turned on her heels, and ran down the passage.

"Little vixen," said Matron. "I found her in the sickbay this morning. Heaven knows how she got there, but she clearly wasn't ill."

The caretaker stepped back and removed her cap to give her head a good scratch.

"Unfortunate," she said. "It's probably best if I get straight off. Give us your keys, and I'll have the car sorted in no time."

"Yes," said Matron, "of course. If I give you £20 will that be OK?"

"We'll sort it later. Might only be a couple of quid to repair a puncture."

"You make it sound so easy. I really do feel better now."

"And a little hug always helps, just so long as it's not with that horrible man they tried to fix you up with."

"Yes," said Matron, "the horrible man who lived in a garden shed. If he tries any more sneaky tricks, I'll kick him in the shins."

"Good for you. Do you want to borrow my boots?"

Matron laughed, happy that she had at last found a friend who understood her problems.

After the caretaker had gone, Matron went to have another nice, relaxing bath. Life seemed so much better now the car was being sorted. It was odd to think that her tormentor had turned out to be her saviour. After her bath, she made her way to the dining room for lunch. When she entered the hall, all the girls stopped eating, their knives and forks remaining perfectly still in mid-air. She walked on towards the counter, feeling quite bemused by all the strange things that must go on in the minds of young girls nowadays.

Feeling nicely clean and well fed, Matron left the dining room to take a gentle walk around the grounds. When she saw her Morris Minor coming up the drive at about three miles per hour, she raced to her appointed parking space.

"Oh, thank you," Matron cried.

The caretaker got out. "Don't thank me yet," she said, "the crawl up the drive was because your wheel mountings are knackered. You need a new track rod end, shock absorber, and some other bits as well. I've made a list, but you'll need to be sitting down before you see it."

"Oh dear," said Matron, "and do you think the garage will charge a lot?"

"A fortune. You'd be better to scrap it and get something

else. Even if I get the bits at trade, it's going to cost £100, and we'd still have to sort out a new spare wheel. Though I could get one of those from the scrapyard for a tenner, complete with tyre."

"And what would you charge for labour?"

"Matron, you insult me. A friend in need is not to be abandoned without transport. But, whatever you do, don't try to drive it until it's fixed. I'd say your front wheel's about ready to fall off."

"And could you fix it? Really, I'd be ever so grateful."

"It's an old motor, might be time for a change…"

"Oh no, please make her better. I've had her since I was a student nurse, she's become part of my life."

"OK, I'll get the bits ordered. You got £100 lying about?"

Matron was overwhelmed with joy; her car would be made better, and all because of this wonderful person. She could not stop herself from returning this morning's hug.

"Oh, thank you," she said again. "I'll go to the bank first thing tomorrow."

"OK," said the caretaker, "but you'd better leave now, all the girls on the hockey pitch have stopped to watch us."

Matron thought the caretaker had a strange fixation about people watching her. Nevertheless, she agreed to the request, and walked away smiling. Then she realised going to the bank would involve going to the outside – on her own! She wondered if Cook could organise such things – probably, because half the staff had not been beyond the fence for years. Then she thought about the college receipts in her bag; she had paid for the course fees with her own cheque, and the study books in cash. On locating the receipts, she was surprised to discover it all added up to £150. How perfect;

she would go to see the secretary now. Then she would give the money to the caretaker and, if there was any change, she was welcome to keep it.

The secretary looked at the receipts and frowned. "I don't keep that much in petty cash," she said, "and I would have to clear it with Miss Buckley first."

"She already knows. Cynthia helped me throughout the Summer to pay for it."

"That was before this morning. Miss Buckley seems to think Hilda has sorted out a sponsorship deal of some kind. I'll have to ask, just in case she misunderstood."

Matron wondered what on Earth it had to do with Hilda. That woman just couldn't help poking her nose into things that did not concern her. Presently, Miss Buckley came out of the office. "It's good news," she said, "it's all sorted!"

"What?" asked Matron.

"The nice matron from over the lane has booked Cynthia into a special girls' college, so we don't have to pay for anything."

"That can't be right, I got everything sorted yesterday."

"Tut-tut, I am very disappointed that you did not think about the special girls' college. Cynthia will find it much nicer there."

"And what about Beryl's 'O' level History? I paid for that as well."

"Wicked, wicked man," mumbled Miss Buckley. "Henry XI, he had eight wives you know!"

After Miss Buckley had shuffled away, the secretary stood up to lean over the desk.

"Those who have problems," she whispered, "tend to go to the surgery. You might want to talk to Cynthia."

Bursting with rage, Matron stomped down the stairs, fuming at the daft old bat who had been conned into thinking that a special girls' college existed outside of her own warped imagination.

*

Hilda sat in her surgery, to give Cynthia a full report on the masters. Using a group photograph for mugshots, she pointed them out, then gave a detailed report on their routines and attitudes. Two were full-blown versions of Mr Tebbit, believing all children needed plenty of caning to turn them into righteous adults. Three were open to new ideas, and one even said "Good morning" to her! Mr Cranmore didn't know what was going on, and would do whatever made his life easiest until he retired in two years' time. Then Hilda's finger hovered over the Art master as she tried to find the right words.

"He's harmless enough," said Cynthia. "Now, tell me about the one who says 'good morning' to you."

"The English master," said Hilda. "On his days off, he goes to the outside."

"What's his first name?" asked Cynthia.

"Andrew, but it's only me who knows this."

"Good," said Cynthia. "It will really confuse him when I say 'hello' for the first time."

Suddenly, the door crashed open, and Victoria burst in. Her face was red with fury, and her arms waving about incoherently. "How dare you!" she yelled.

"How dare I what?" replied Hilda.

"Interfere, you nosy old bat!"

"Interfere in what?" asked Hilda.

"You are not denying that you went to see Miss Buckley this morning?"

"I went to see her," said Hilda, "though may I ask what you went to see her about?"

"None of your business! Miss Buckley thinks you're sending Cynthia to a special girls' college."

"What I actually said was that Cynthia is a very special girl, which is entirely true. I cannot be held responsible for Miss Buckley misunderstanding things."

"You have the nerve, the audacity, to sit there so smug, and laugh at me. Well, I tell you who's laughing, me at you, because ever since you let that dirty old man inside your knickers, you're behaving like a clown!"

Hilda stood up, and took the pose she used to control the naughty children, generally without the need for words. But this was obviously far more serious.

"How dare you call my kind, generous captain evil," she said. "If you want to spend the rest of your life playing with yourself, don't let me stop you, but if you ever again insult the man who has brought so much happiness into my life, I'll take the cane to you!"

Cynthia had not previously known what it felt like to be shocked, but now she sat with her mouth open, yet quite unable to speak. In the next instant, she watched Victoria charge across the room, with her hands reaching for Hilda's throat. Hilda sidestepped and gave Victoria a hip bump as she passed. Victoria crashed onto the couch, and immediately Hilda sat on top of her. Victoria tried to struggle free but, flat on her tummy with sixteen stone sitting on her bottom, she found it impossible to move.

"Are you going to leave quietly?" asked Hilda. "Or shall I get some prefects to throw you out?"

Cynthia suddenly came to her senses, and jumped up from the chair.

"Victoria," she said, "please don't make this any worse for yourself, just go, please. I promise I will never bother you again. Hilda, please stand up. Victoria surely knows she could never beat you in a fight."

Hilda stood up, and carefully watched to see what Victoria would do next. But Victoria merely remained lying down, gasping for breath.

"Go!" said Hilda. "I am banning you from my surgery. A spiteful cow such as yourself has no place here."

Victoria got a little energy back, but no enthusiasm to use it. Tears dripped from her eyes onto the bed. She felt Cynthia take her arm, and she was pulled upright. Then she was led outside to the veranda.

"Please don't say any more bad things about Hilda," begged Cynthia.

Victoria heard the door close, and looked up to find herself alone. In that instant, she knew that everybody hated her, even sluts like Cynthia, and a boy who had been cowering behind the desk.

Back in the surgery, the boy emerged from his hiding place. "A captain," he asked, "like in *Treasure Island*?"

"He's Matron's boyfriend," said Cynthia. "A real hunk."

The boy giggled, then ran off to hide in the side room.

"Enough sympathy," said Hilda, "I feel quite recovered. Cynthia, you'll have to stay here tonight, I'll make up a bed in sickbay. Don't know how I'm going to sort it with the head, but I will."

"I won't say anything," called the boy from the next room, "and if Cynthia left by the back window – as normal – he would never know."

All of a sudden, Hilda let out a fearsome cry. "My captain," she wailed, "how do I get to see my captain, if Victoria won't cover my holidays? I could never go on working here, if my holidays were taken away."

"Simple," said Cynthia, "there's me, John, and five boys in various degrees of hiding."

"No, it would never work, you are nowhere near ready to look after my boys yet!"

"I was going to add Becky," said Cynthia. "I'm sure she'd like to come and visit for a few days, while you are away on your little adventures."

"But she's still not a matron."

"Really? She's worked in a ship's medical bay for the Summer, and I'm sure she's got some sort of qualification for that."

"The head would never agree to it."

Cynthia raised her eyebrows. "But you said he doesn't know what's going on, and I can't think of anything I need to tell him. And I could look after the under tens. As far as they are concerned, I'm an interesting space alien."

"Ah," said Matron, "I was going to talk to you about that. From what I overheard, it seems some boys have forgotten the 'space alien' bit. If you still want to be called Miss Cynthia, I'd stick with the under nines."

"But the under tens are taller," said Cynthia. "If I drop to all fours, I can use them as cover. The only question is, could you cope with living on the ship, if Becky came back here? I mean, both Mandy and David go to school. You would be totally alone with the captain, with nobody to supervise your daytime activities."

"Sold!" said Hilda. "I mean, if Becky came here, I would have to go down to look after the children, wouldn't I?"

"So you would," said Cynthia. "I shall write to Becky this evening."

Hilda seemed hesitant.

"Some little detail I've missed?" asked Cynthia.

"No," said Hilda, "but I wonder if you could take me to the place where Victoria got her dress, and do you think they would have my size?"

ELEVEN

The unthinkable happened. Victoria began to miss Cynthia. Then came the guilt. Cynthia was just a child; how could she be expected to know that a man, who lived in a garden shed, was totally out of place in a world of sensible grown-ups?

At the beginning of October, Victoria made her way to the college, where she hoped to speak to Cynthia, in private. Pretending to be a student, she entered the canteen, and joined the queue for the subsidised meal. This proved to be a lot better than the food she got at the home, but that came as part of her wages, and was free, so any visit to the college canteen was still a relative extravagance.

As she ate, she looked around for Cynthia, determined to apologise, and ask if she wanted to come back. But Cynthia did not come, filling her mind with even more guilt; the girl had clearly been unable to continue her studies.

Victoria left the building…only to jump sideways to hide behind a pillar. She could see Cynthia sitting on a low wall, eating sandwiches from a sheet of newspaper. Victoria gulped. Of course, how could Cynthia afford to eat in the canteen? And how small she looked, compared to everyone else. It gave Victoria an almost irresistible urge to run across to give her a big hug; but, after what had happened in the surgery, the girl would think she was under attack. Then Victoria noticed the way Cynthia's clothes made her fade into the background, as a splosh of grey. All the other females were wearing bright colours. Oh no! Some wore the sort of clothes she had been given, except their skirts tended to be even shorter. Half the students also wore clown shoes. Matron ran back into the building, then along corridors to a side exit, now overwhelmed with shame; it had not been a prostitute's dress, just the sort of thing females in the outside world had started to wear.

Victoria began to wish she had not argued with Hilda. From that time, everybody had agreed to her request of being left alone. Even Mad George had crawled quietly away, albeit with a set of her clothes. It was just the caretaker calling in for coffee, and asking when she was free to go down the pub. This made her feel guilty – all the work she had done on the car – but pubs! She just could not face all that smoke, drunkenness, and fights.

Victoria decided that she must find out how Cynthia was coping at college, where she was sleeping, and if she was eating properly. Once back at the home, she made a half-hearted approach towards Beryl, but the girl legged it across the grounds before she even got within shouting distance. Strangely, all the other girls also seemed to be running away. There was nothing else for it but to face Hilda, and perhaps even make some sort of apology for calling her an interfering old bat. You could not have matrons not talking to each other; even before the new idea of holidays, it was understood that they covered for each other in an emergency. Shaking with fear, she tapped the door of Hilda's surgery.

"It's not locked," came a muffled voice.

Victoria opened it just a fraction, and spoke through the gap. "I've come to apologise," she said.

"Is that Matron?" asked a strangely familiar voice.

"Yes, is Matron there?"

"How very confusing," came the reply.

Victoria peeped around the door. "Becky!" she gasped. "What are you doing here?"

"Just visiting."

"Why did you not come to see me?"

"I would never go where I was not wanted."

Victoria retreated, then stood outside the slightly open door, wondering what to do next.

"It was unfortunate," she said presently, "what happened."

"Not what I want to hear," said Becky.

Victoria realised the Becky she had once known was no more. This was a grown-up version, who had the confidence to stamp on anyone who tried to argue with her. She supposed it was something to do with working at sea, with all the hundreds of drunken passengers fighting each other. Heaven knows what injuries she would have seen – people with broken bottles sticking out from the top of their head, probably.

Victoria returned to the crack in the door. "Where's Matron?" she asked.

"Just popped out," came the reply, "though after calling the love of her life a dirty old man, I feel you should be gone by the time she gets back."

"So you don't like me either?"

"You tried to stop the children going to the seaside."

Victoria waited for Becky to finish her speech but, after a minute of silence, she realised there was nothing else she wished to add. Becky had stated her fact, and now considered the matter closed. Full of shame and humiliation, Victoria walked away.

That night Victoria was unable to sleep; everybody hated her, and mostly for good reason. What on Earth had made her try to stop the children going to the seaside? It was evil. How could she have banned Cynthia from the surgery? That was stupid!

The following morning, nobody came to see her. Fourteen days without a patient; it was as if the children knew how horrible she was; as if she was personally responsible for stopping them all going to the seaside. She supposed at least half of them had never seen the waves rolling up a beach. How could she have become such a wicked matron?

At 11am the caretaker popped in for a coffee. This was her only friend in the world, the person who had fixed her car, and understood about horrible George. Perhaps the time had come to make the best of what was on offer – a night down the pub with this nice person, who had not told anyone about the horrible books, or the alleged burning of the sex toys. And so it was that she made two very bold decisions. Firstly, she agreed to go to the pub that evening; and secondly, she decided to write a letter of apology to Hilda. At midday she walked across to the boys' home, and stood nervously to watch the surgery door. It did not have a letterbox, but she could push the letter underneath, then walk briskly away before anybody came to shout at her.

Bending down at the door, she heard a muffled voice that sounded very much like Becky. Why was she still here? Who was looking after Mandy and David? There were so many things she needed to know. She tapped the door, and stepped inside.

"Who is looking after the children?" she asked.

Becky cut short the telephone call. "Much better question," she said. "The children are well cared for at all times, thank you for asking. Is that a letter in your hand?"

"It's a letter of apology for Matron," said Victoria.

"Good," said Becky. "I'll make sure she gets it."

"If I had known you were here, I would have written one to you as well."

"No need."

"You didn't tell me who was looking after the children."

"They have learned to speak Welsh, and it is a community that looks after its own. Child-minding is never a problem."

"So they are well?"

"That is what I was waiting to hear, though really it should have been your first, and most important question. Perhaps I should make you coffee, and I will give you a full report."

"You would, really, tell me everything?"

"Not sure about 'everything'. Also, in return, I want an undertaking that you will never refer to our captain as 'dirty' again."

Becky got up and opened the window.

"If you do," she said, "you're leaving that way – head first!"

Matron backed away to the door.

"Do not be alarmed, we have all promised the captain never to use his self-defence lessons in anger. I only threatened to throw you out of the window to emphasise that the children are well protected by a circle of adult friends, and any attempt to treat them cruelly might well result in injury to yourself. It is because of this pledge, Cynthia only used minimum force when you tried to attack her in the surgery. Captain's a black belt, and Cynthia's a willing student, whenever she comes to visit."

Becky took the letter from Matron's trembling hand, and read it. After taking it to the desk, she scribbled some notes, while crossing out other things.

"Rewrite it like that," she said, "it emphasises the advantages to Hilda of having a business arrangement. I have only been able to cover this week because it's virtually the end of the season."

"Covering…you…I don't understand…Matron has just popped out."

"To Holyhead, yes, I expect her back on Friday. But if anyone we don't trust asks, we don't add to Holyhead, because Mr Cranmore doesn't exactly know."

"So you are a matron…looking after…on your own?"

"More a medical officer. Command and control of the under tens is entirely down to Cynthia…"

"Back at the home," interrupted Victoria, "there is very little command or control of anything. Miss Buckley is permanently confined to the top floor, and last week I got hit on the head by a potato, covered in gravy."

"Most of the staff have a quiet word with Cynthia, if there's something they need to sort out with the girls. She and Beryl can resolve most things."

"Beryl keeps running away whenever she sees me. Gone back to the dormitory, so I am completely on my own now."

Matron accepted her coffee mug, then looked down at the couch.

"Is this where Cynthia sleeps?" she asked.

"Not certain."

"But you must know."

"Where she sleeps is no concern of yours. She gets by…a twilight existence of ducking and diving. It is much harder on the other girls. Cynthia convinced them that they could make something of their lives, other than working for the canning factory or becoming chambermaids. Now, it seems going to college means being attacked by Matron, and effectively being expelled for knowing too much. Throwing potatoes at your head is just the start of… You do realise that Cynthia has been giving the girls proper self-defence lessons? There's not a single fourteen-year-old who could not floor The Teapot, if he came back now. It's the captain. He believes all females should be able to defend themselves from any man…"

Becky let her voice trail away to silence. Matron had burst into tears, and run out of the door.

*

Cynthia returned from college to find her under-tens fan club waiting in the back yard. Having dealt with the various traumas of childhood, she climbed through the window and slumped in the chair. She did not think it possible to feel so tired, or so hungry, but nothing about the new regimes in the homes tied in with her own schedule. Only at weekends could she eat all her meals at the girls' home.

Presently, Becky returned from her walk around the grounds, wearing the uniform Hilda had kept in her wardrobe, from a time when she was a thin young woman.

"It worked," she said. "One of the masters definitely pretended not to see me."

411

"They think a matron has to be female by law," replied Cynthia. "Pretending you don't exist is their way of coping. All they see is the uniform, which makes them nervous. Anyway, more importantly, we have our second man on the inside – Andrew, solid guy, thirty-something, teaches English. I happened to see him going to the village shop, so ran into the lane, you know, the narrow bit by the blacksmith's forge. When his car turned from the main road, I was sitting against the wall with my legs across the lane. Had he tried to run over my feet I would have let him pass, but he stopped to ask why I was crying. I sobbed that nobody would tell me what a 'dangling participle' was. Totally threw him! He took me to the tearoom to explain it, so I was learning 'O' level English at the same time. When he dropped me off at the gates, I let him see me change into my medical disguise, and walk up the drive. I put a finger to my lips. He will not betray me. Too busy dangling from the hook of curiosity! In fact, I fully expect him to pay us a little visit this evening. His name is Andrew. Remember that, it will disorientate him. Anyway, when the 'new order' comes, he is to be spared, but it won't happen yet. To take over the boys' home, I needed you to be working on the inside. Your move to the high seas has delayed things."

Becky gave a patient smile. "You and Beryl might control the girls' home," she said, "but you don't realise just how horrible things are over here. The prefects are all trained psychopaths!"

"Handpicked to worship The Teapot," said Cynthia, "but, with their leader gone, the system is becoming increasingly unstable. Faced with 150 girls charging up the drive, there is no saying how the prefects would react. Except for the one called Morris, he's instinctively evil. The under tens live in terror of his sexual perversions. But my existence over here is too precarious to deal with him just yet. If we are destined to meet, it will be when I am stronger, and his followers are more like normal boys."

"You might be too busy for all of that," said Becky. "Victoria was asking for you earlier. She wants you back over there."

Cynthia shook her head. "I was really horrible to her," she said.

"What, horrible recently, or horrible as in The Three Musketeers?"

"Worse. You know I tried to fix her up with George, and she had to jump over the table to escape…but I really didn't know, not then."

"Know what?"

"About Victoria…being a lesbian."

Becky gave an instinctive laugh. "Just because she's never had a boyfriend doesn't mean…"

"It means Tracy caught her full-frontal snogging the caretaker in the surgery," interrupted Cynthia.

"Oh my God!" exclaimed Becky. "I shared a bed with her on Mr Silver's yacht! Thank heavens Mandy got between us, before the wandering-hand service started!"

"And I tried to give her sex lessons about men," said Cynthia. "She had to lock herself in her bedroom to escape."

"She's dead," said Becky presently, "as surely as the old caretaker took a flying lesson from the roof. Ah, that explains the potato!"

The conversation was interrupted by a knock on the door. A thirty-something man entered and looked curiously about the surgery. Becky jumped up, and circled behind him to prevent any escape.

"Andrew," she said, "how nice of you to visit."

Cynthia also jumped up then firmly shook his hand.

"What sort of biscuits would you like with your coffee?" she asked.

Later, Cynthia walked into the surgery of the girls' home, to be greeted by a suffocating hug. The grown-up breasts pushed into her face and sent her tumbling backwards into the dark pit of childhood memories – men drooling over the sweaty bodies of two women with a little girl trapped between them. She had been told it was a pretend game, something that only very special customers liked to watch. But this was different: Victoria was a real lesbian! Cynthia thought about the caretaker coming in for her full-frontal snog, and it made her feel a little sick, causing her to wriggle free, then stumble back to the far wall.

"I don't do hugging," she said, "it's weird!"

"But it's OK with me," said Victoria, "it's just the boys you need to worry about. I suppose you know they all want to get you pregnant?"

But Cynthia's mind was fixated by the caretaker. As far as she could tell, the woman never wore a bra, so her breasts rested on top of her enormous tummy. How Victoria could enjoy giving the fearsome woman oral sex was a mystery; she must be crawling with diseases, given the number of women who came to stay at her caravan. Keeping Victoria safe from the girls was going to be the hardest thing she had ever done.

"I suppose I'd better go and do my rounds," said Cynthia, "let the others know I am back, and willing to help, or make their lives a misery, if that is what I choose. Becky told me I must threaten them with haircuts, whatever that means."

"Yes, of course, but I won't be here when you get back. I'm going for a drink with the caretaker."

Cynthia gulped. "I hope you are not leaving at the same time," she said.

"Strange, the caretaker said much the same thing. I'm meeting her in the lay-by up the lane. The walk will do me good, don't you think?"

"Do not underestimate the girls," said Cynthia. "Since Miss Buckley redirected her telescope on Mr Cranmore's bedroom window, their out-of-bounds has increased considerably. They have eyes everywhere."

"Can't see in the pub," said Matron. She bent down to kiss Cynthia on the forehead.

It took Cynthia all her strength to hide the revulsion she felt at the other things those lips would be doing later on!

*

Victoria always considered herself to be sensible about clothes. She had her best uniform that she would wear for the dentist, or going to the respectable tearooms in the village. Eventually, these became her working clothes, until they were downgraded to her messing-about clothes, after which they were thrown in the bin. At the moment, she only had two sets, the one in the middle having been stolen by Mad George. What should she wear to go to a pub? One seemed much too respectable, yet the other had worn fabric. In the end, she chose her best uniform, and loaded her bag with ten handkerchiefs, in order to wipe away any unpleasant substances she encountered.

On reaching the caretaker's car, she looked in, and was

surprised to see her companion in overalls and a cloth cap. She thought fashion was something she would never understand. The caretaker threw her downmarket newspaper onto the back seat, then gave a nicotine smile.

Victoria was always nervous about getting into other people's cars. They drove so fast; she was certain Mad George had been doing over 40mph on the way to the zoo. The caretaker proved no exception. Trees whizzed by, then a village, followed by fields. It seemed an awfully long way to go to a pub because, after fifteen miles, the caretaker was still pretending to be a racing driver. Then came a town with grimy streets, and finally an industrial area comprised of factories and discount warehouses. After they had pulled into a big car park, Victoria looked up to see a massive three-storey building. It was covered in white emulsion, and had a big, garish sign above the entrance. It told her that this particular drinking house was called 'The Flag'.

"Is it a hotel?" asked Victoria.

"The rooms above do basic bed and breakfast, but it hasn't got a restaurant or anything."

"Do they have many fights?"

"If anything unpleasant comes our way, I promise to give it a good kick. You'll be fine with me."

The caretaker reached into the back of her car and recovered a sledgehammer.

"What are you doing with that?" gasped Matron.

"What are you doing with a handbag?" responded the caretaker.

"It's a shoulder bag, it's where I keep my things."

"Exactly," said the caretaker. She then swung the sledgehammer onto her shoulder. "Happy now?" she asked.

Victoria walked across the car park with her head bent in shame and, once inside, maintained a close study of her feet. At the bar, the caretaker swung the sledgehammer onto the sides of her old boots, the steel toe caps clicking together.

"A pint of bitter," said the caretaker, "and whatever the lady wants, if you please, barman."

"Oh," said Victoria, "but I must pay. I'll have a Coca-Cola, please."

Both the barman and the caretaker laughed.

"She means a rum and Coke," said the caretaker, "and don't take her money, unless you want a punch in the throat."

Surprisingly, the barman seemed to accept this statement in a good-natured way. Presently, the caretaker led the way to a corner table, where she put the sledgehammer next to the shoulder bag. In order to cover the first awkward silence, Victoria took a sip of her drink, and coughed. It had been fifteen years since she had tasted alcohol, and the rum was overpowering. The barman was probably frightened of getting a punch in the throat, and had let his hand slip. However, she wasn't going to argue with the caretaker, who, she reminded herself, had fixed her car. Anyway, it was now 8.20pm; in two hours ten minutes it would all be over. That's assuming the caretaker wanted to stay until 10.30, which she probably would not.

All of a sudden, Victoria heard two excited squeals heading in her direction. "Matron," came a voice, "what a wonderful surprise!"

The next thing she knew, two girls had gathered about her, both bending down to kiss her on the cheek. One of the girls then did an excited sort of stamping dance.

"I really can't believe it's you!" she said.

Matron looked up and, to her horror, realised she was being greeted by former pupils. They had left two years before, one being called Janet, the other…Anna, that was it. They had been close friends at the home, she remembered.

"Janet and Anna," she said, overwhelmed with embarrassment.

"You remember us!" said Anna excitedly. "But this is wonderful! What are you drinking?"

"Rum and Coke," said the caretaker.

"And yourself?"

"Get us another pint, if you like."

Matron was going to protest, but Anna was already skipping away to the bar, and Janet had sat beside her to clasp her hands.

"What's your name?" asked Janet. "I mean, when you are away from the home?"

"She still likes to be called Matron," said the caretaker.

"Kinky, I can't wait to tell my friends about this!"

"Not too many friends," said the caretaker.

"In fact no one," said Victoria, gulping back her rum and Coke.

Immediately, another drink appeared, then Anna sat down.

"She still likes to be called Matron," said Janet, "even when she's out!"

"Matron and the caretaker," said Anna, "has a sort of ring to it."

"I'm still Alex," said the caretaker, "though I've got my bag of tools in the car, if you want me to pay you a caretaker sort of visit?"

"No, our plumbing's fine, thank you, and before you ask,

so is our washing machine, or any other domestic appliance you can think of."

Victoria felt glad to lean back, and let the nonsense chatter continue without her involvement. Now, there was only one hour fifty-six minutes to closing time. For reasons that she couldn't understand, however much she seemed to drink, the glass always remained full. The last time she looked at the clock, there was only one hour thirty-four minutes to go. Then she finally got the hang of going down the pub. You got drunk, and nothing seemed to matter anymore! What happened after 9.30pm did not stick in her brain, except for a vague notion that she had been dancing around a sledgehammer in the middle of a dance floor.

*

Victoria became aware of a headache. Everything in the universe was made of this, a big bang of headaches that only slowly formed into other things. The first thing she registered was a tangled confusion of limbs. Then came the horror: she was naked, and not all the limbs belonged to her! Opening one eye, she saw a foot in front of her face, and thought it might be another foot behind her head. Something was forcing her legs apart; Mad George had drugged her to do this thing. No…the underneaths pushing into each other were all wrong for a George!

After a few moments of terror, Matron decided the thing along her back was definitely a leg. She remained lying on her side, but her muscle tension must have changed, for the attacker withdrew its tongue from between her toes.

"I thought that would wake you up," came a voice from the bottom of the bed.

The horrible legs withdrew from their scissor arrangement and, the next thing Matron knew, a bare bottom sat astride her hips.

"Shame you didn't bring your sex toys," said the voice. "I'd have soon got you screaming the place down."

From somewhere in the distance came two little squeals. The faces of Janet and Anna appeared from over the back of a settee.

"Sorry," said the caretaker, "I quite forgot you were there. The sex toys is a secret, right!"

"Right!" said the girls.

Matron watched Janet and Anna walk around the settee, and come to sit on the double bed. They seemed completely unconcerned that they were naked. They clutched Matron's hands.

"Oh, we're so glad you're normal," said Anna. "At the home we never guessed a thing. We must have a proper coming-out party for you!"

"Well," said the caretaker hoarsely, "we could begin with you two getting into bed with us."

"Control yourself," said Janet, "you know we have been completely faithful to each other from the age of fourteen."

"Forever," said Anna, "unless there's something you haven't told me about?"

"Forever," said Janet.

"But it's driving me insane," said the caretaker. "Can't we even have a group hug?"

"With the steam coming out of your ears, we could turn off the central heating," said Anna, "which is very flattering, but quite wasted on us."

"Oh fuck!" said the caretaker, jumping up and rushing to

put her hand against the window. "Fuck!" she said. "The girls will be freezing their tits off. I've got to get the heating on! I'll have to take a quick shower, and be off."

"Don't you have to give Matron a lift back?" asked Anna.

"Yeah, but don't join me in the shower, Matron, you know how I get distracted. You take it five minutes after me."

The caretaker stomped into a side room and, a moment later, a shower began to run.

"I think you've made Alex very happy," said Janet, "but you must control yourself at the home. I don't understand why, but even the young ones use the term 'queer', though how they think having a willy poking about inside you is normal, I have no idea. We kept our love secret, still do. Even at The Flag you have to be careful. Some of the men only pretend to be gay, then offer £10 to watch."

"And don't tell anyone you go to The Flag," said Janet. "It's amazing how many people know it stands for 'For Lesbians and Gays.'"

Victoria watched her two former girls stand up, then walk hand in hand to the settee. After a long passionate kiss, they fell from view. Victoria broke from her petrified fear, and started to shiver. It was a shiver of disgust. Within these smelly, sweaty sheets, the caretaker had been all over her. And the girls had seen the depravity of the caretaker taking her pleasures! A caretaker who would, in a few minutes' time, expect her to get into the same car.

Victoria slipped quietly out of bed and pulled on her clothes any way she could. With shoes in one hand, purse in the other, she crept to the door. A moment later, she emerged into a long passageway, only to realise she had absolutely no idea where she was. For all she knew, there were guards who would stop her leaving, until she passed some test of whatever was happening here. She put on her shoes, and hurried to the left. On reaching the landing, she froze with fear. Two men were coming down the stairs from the upper floor.

"Hiya, Matron," said one cheerily. "Alex obviously gave you a good ride last night, or whatever it is you do. Are you joining us for breakfast?"

Victoria managed to shake her head.

The men smiled at reach other, then started kissing. Victoria, in the hope of finding an escape route that did not involve getting past the guards, turned on her heels, and followed the signs for the fire exit. This took her to a door with a bar, which she pushed. Looking out, she discovered an iron balcony with a ladder descending to a prison exercise yard, twenty feet below. After descending the ladder, she ran to a wobbly stack of beer barrels which allowed her to reach the top of a high wall. Overwhelmed by the fear that, at any moment, an alarm might scream out to warn of her escape, she rolled from the top and sprinted away. Only after finding a shop doorway in the next street did reality return: she did not know which town she was in, or have any idea of how to get home.

At the orphanage, three girls peered through the Victorian gates to smell the outside air of freedom. Their mouths opened in surprise; a taxi had pulled up, and Matron rose up from the back seat. She got out, unlocked the gate, then scurried up the drive. Five minutes later, the same girls jumped behind the trees as the caretaker's car screeched to a halt, the occupant running up the drive to the boiler house. The girls' anger began to rise; having a lesbian matron was bad enough, but their night away had meant them shivering through breakfast, and that was even worse. Slowly but surely, plans would be drawn against them. Having a lesbian caretaker was no longer funny, not if it meant that she couldn't attend to the central heating.

*

Victoria was lying in her bath, pouring in disinfectant in the hope of making the smell of the caretaker go away. When her skin developed a rash, she got out, and went to brush her hair. Then she put the contaminated clothes into a bin liner, added her shoes, and tied the bag with a firm knot. Next, she rubbed disinfectant into the carpet where her clothes had been, after which she got back into a lukewarm bath. There she stayed for the remainder of the morning, changing the water as often as the immersion heater allowed.

When her body had been washed in the manner of heavily soiled clothes, requiring five cycles, she left the final rinse to crawl into bed. Here, she threw the blankets over her head, and spent the afternoon having tormented nightmares.

Presently, there was a knock on the door. "Are you OK?" called Cynthia's voice.

She froze; how could she ever face Cynthia again? With horror, she remembered the girl's concern at the night out with the caretaker, suggesting they left at different times… telling her that the girls had eyes everywhere! Though they did not need to be everywhere, because this morning, in broad daylight, she had got out of a taxi feeling like a prostitute who had spent all night on the streets. That was it, she was a prostitute; the caretaker had fixed her car, and had now taken her payment by indulging her pleasures. And the

423

former pupils had seen it all, and concluded she was one of them!

"Are you in there?" repeated Cynthia's voice.

Victoria pulled herself tight into the foetal position, with hands over ears. Time passed, yet the voice did not return. Finally, darkness fell, and she realised muffled voices were now coming from the surgery. She must know what they were talking about – herself probably, and how disgusting she was. Crouching with her ear to the keyhole, she could just make out the words. She recognised Becky's voice, and listened even harder. For Becky to be called across from the boys' home something really serious must have happened.

"…Well," Becky was saying, "I've obviously been trained to diagnose appendicitis, but I've not yet come across a positive case. It nearly always turns out to be peritonitis."

"I don't care what it is," said a girl, "just make the pain go away!"

"Well, let's have a little look," said Becky. "Alison, lie on your back please. Does that hurt, and that, or that…?"

There were various cries of "Yes!", "No!" and "Argggghhh!"

"Well," said Becky, "I'm as sure as I can be that it's not appendicitis, but this really needs Matron."

"No, please, I'm sure you're right."

"The problem is," said Cynthia, "that you've eaten exactly the same food as the other girls, and none of them have tummy troubles. When was the last time you opened your bowels?"

"Tuesday, I think," said Alison.

"Really?" said Becky. "Some people get confused about such things."

"OK, Saturday, but I couldn't come to the surgery before because…"

"Five days, that's serious. I think I'd better take you to the hospital in my car," said Becky. "I know it's what Matron would do."

"Matron's only here so she can watch us take baths," said the girl, "you're a proper doctor."

"It's like this," said Cynthia. "For some unknown reason, you've got a blockage. Your digestive juices are still being produced but, because nothing's moving, they are burning away your intestines. It can be as serious as appendicitis. If we're going to fix you, we would have to go in from the bottom end, and this really goes beyond what we can do."

"Please, not Matron, I don't want her poking about down there, she might start licking my fanny."

"But she can do that with the caretaker whenever she wants, so I really don't think she would be interested in you."

"She might. Anyway, can you imagine what the other girls would say, if they found out Matron had been playing with me? Honestly, they all want you to be the proper matron. I'll even call you Nurse Cynthia, if you want?"

"But this needs her experience to diagnose why everything has stopped working."

"What if I had eaten differently to the others, then would you make the pain go away?"

"But you haven't."

"Well," said Alison, "if I tell, will you promise not to shout at me. Oh, anything's better than having a 'lesbo' look up me fanny! You know your emergency stock of chocolate bars?"

"Ummm…"

"Well, it's not there anymore. I didn't meant to, honest, just one, I thought, and for the first day, it worked…but they were just so lovely, the second day I cracked. After eight bars,

I thought I may as well have the last two, just to save me coming back."

"That makes things a lot clearer," said Becky. "They have formed a plug, and everything else has backed up behind. To put it bluntly, you have become like a full cement mixer that has been left standing for a week!"

"And my insides are burning away. Look, I'm lying on my tummy. Just do what you have to do. I promise not to tell anybody, ever!"

Becky gave a cough. "It would look rather good on my CV," she said. "It would make my entire time here seem more important."

"OK," said Cynthia, "Nurse Cynthia is prepared to make a deal. She will take over anything that involves removing underwear, and in return, you will try to stop the girls attacking Matron. Nurse Cynthia is not interested in what plans you have for the caretaker."

"Yes…yes…"

Cough.

"Yes, yes, Nurse Cynthia," added Alison.

A long time passed before the voices came back. "Well," said Cynthia, "that's done. It will start to work in about ten minutes. I suggest you go and sit on the toilet."

Victoria heard footsteps, then somebody tried the toilet door.

"It's locked!" shouted Alison.

"Go through my room at the end," called Cynthia.

Victoria froze in panic. All the doors were bolted from the inside. The confrontation was more than she could bear. She looked about her prison. She owned virtually nothing but the old set of clothes she was wearing. Quickly, she stood up, threw on her coat, and emptied the contents of her document drawer into her shoulder bag. Then she opened the narrow window, to throw the sack of contaminated clothes outside. There was a lot of trying doors now, then came the dreaded cry, asking if she was in there. A conversation began into the puzzle of how all the doors had become bolted on the inside.

"Argghhh," shouted Alison, "it's all starting to work!"

"Quick," shouted Cynthia, "the litter bin in the surgery. We won't come in!"

Victoria could not let the girl suffer. She opened the door, turned, and immediately ran to the window through which she jumped. It saved the others having to look at her. Also, for reasons she could not explain, it just seemed the right thing to do.

Once outside, she picked up the sack of contaminated clothes; it was not for others to deal with her filth. She was driving away before two figures appeared against the light in the front doorway. But peritonitis was a sensible diagnosis, so they had done the right thing. Their careers in nursing were just beginning, just as hers was coming to an end. She could never return to this place, where the girls would rather risk death than have her look between their legs.

At the bottom of the drive, she threw the bag of filth into the bin, then drove away to her new life – whatever that might be.

TWELVE

Becky walked along the quay, thinking how lucky she was to live in Holyhead, a busy town built around the docks from where ferries sail to Ireland from the island of Anglesey. For the children it meant long Summer evenings spent wandering on the foreshore, or weekends on the large hill that had strangely acquired the title of Holyhead Mountain. According to David, he was the first explorer ever to reach the cliffs that dropped down to the sea. At such times, Mandy just accepted that she had a strange boyfriend, and went off to play with the numerous horses who lived on the lower slopes, slowly infiltrating the families who might let her ride them.

Becky was distracted from her thoughts by the children coming towards her – not running, because the captain said they mustn't in places where there might be ropes lying about. Instead, they were holding hands, a thing David no longer seemed to find embarrassing, even when they set off for school.

"*Maen amser rhyfeddol,*" said Mandy, "*Modryb Hilda wedi mynd â ni i'r zoo. Fe oedd yn ardderchog.*"

The children called this game 'Welsh-speaking Friday'. It was, they said, to help her, so they spent the whole day talking in Welsh.

"It's been a long drive back," she said. "Please can't we forget it's Friday, just for tonight?"

The children looked at each other, then scratched their heads in confusion.

"*Mae hi wedi mynd yn rhyfedd,*" said Mandy.

"*Yn hollol,*" said David.

"It's OK for you," said Becky, "you go to a Welsh-speaking school, and have spongey brains for new words."

But the children were clearly not going to accept this. After some thought, Becky managed to come up with "*Hir gyrru cysgu.*"

Saying she was tired after a long car journey seemed to satisfy them. They snuggled themselves against her hips, and she responded by putting her arms around their shoulders. All of a sudden, her eyes opened wide.

"*Modryb Hilda?*" she asked.

"*Modryb Hilda, Capten, a ti,*" said Mandy, "*r'yn ni teulu nawr.*"

Becky sighed contentedly. Yes, she was part of a family now, albeit a mad one! But Becky could only guess at what wild things had been going on with the captain to make Hilda suddenly become 'Aunty Hilda'.

*

The following morning, Becky awoke to discover the children had already left the crew quarters, which was a shame, because she always liked to start Saturdays by saying, "Good

429

morning," in well-pronounced English. Presently, she got out of the bunk, to be surrounded by cold air. Dressing quickly, she climbed the ladder and scurried along the deck to the captain's quarters. The children were huddled around the wood-burning stove, gazing at the flames through the open door.

"Good morning," said Becky.

"It is that," said the captain. "What do you reckon to jumping on a ferry to Dublin?"

"Yes please," said Mandy.

"That OK with you, David?" asked Becky.

"I've learned not to argue with Mandy," he replied.

"But we need to have a talk first," added the captain.

"This wouldn't be anything to do with Aunty Hilda?" asked Becky.

"Aunty Hilda's just fine being Aunty Hilda," said the captain. "No, this is about us four."

Becky often worried that her perfect life could not last beyond a few months.

"I hope there's nothing wrong," she said nervously. "Surely everything's going so well."

"Wonderful," said the captain. "Your Welsh nattering last night was a joy to me old ears."

"Do you mean I have passed whatever test I was expected to pass? Really, it is over?"

"You are making reasonable progress," said the captain. "So what language do you want to learn next, Italian or Spanish?"

"I was rather hoping to have a go at English."

"What, you who are destined to sail all the Seven Seas? There's a lot of men who don't reckon much to lady officers.

They need to be hiding in corners having the screaming abdabs, 'cause you are so much better than them. With your radio operator's licence you'll be a godsend, steaming down the coast of South America."

"You speak as if it's actually going to happen, though I don't actually have a radio operator's licence."

"Yet," said the captain. "You do not have a radio operator's licence yet, but the matter be in hand. You have not sailed down the coast of South America yet, but you will. Don't go wishing your life away. I was nineteen before I first saw the Pacific, and it never did me any harm. So what language do you want to learn next?"

Becky sniffed, to indicate that she was not very impressed with this conversation. "What do you suggest?" she asked.

"Spanish got blown far across the oceans in the days of sail," he said, "while Italian is the language of love."

"Italian," said Mandy, "then I can say love things to David that only we will understand."

"What language do they speak along the Amazon?" asked David.

"Native, but you might get away with Spanish here and there."

"Spanish then," said David.

"Ah," said the captain, "it seems you have the casting vote, Becky."

"Oh, please say Italian," said Mandy, "then you can say love things to your boyfriends."

"Spanish," said David, "then you can come with me when I explore the Amazon in my canoe."

"What's a ship called in Italian?" asked Becky.

"*Nave*," answered the captain.

"And in Spanish?"

"*Barco*," he added.

"What an exceptionally silly word," said Becky. "Sounds like something a dog would say to a postman! So if I am forced to choose under threat of exile, I will say…Italian."

"Now," said the captain, "your last sailing of the season is on Friday, so we will go on Sunday."

"Go? Go where?" asked Becky.

"Italy of course. Now, kids, you will have to get your brains working overtime, because I know the schoolmistress there, and you're not to embarrass me by saying I'm your grandma or something! In fact, we will have our first Italian-speaking Thursday in three weeks, just to see how we get on."

"Excuse me," said Becky, "I think I must have missed something. You mentioned something about Italy."

"You said it was where you wanted to go," said the captain.

Unconcerned by her exaggerated expression of confusion, he focused on the children.

"We anchor in an old pirates' cove," he said, "so you will need to have your own rowing boat and two bicycles to get to school."

"Does Hilda know about this?" asked Becky.

"Nothing for her to worry about. I met the Italian lass just after the war, me not long out of short trousers, she living on a bombsite. Lots of things went on then that the Pope didn't know about. Kids, don't be telling your classmates that. She's a posh bird now, been married for thirty years. She and Hilda will get on just fine."

"Hilda's coming?"

"Fretted on missing the boys too much, so she's driving to wherever we end up, for a holiday visit."

"This is Hilda we are talking about?" said Becky. "The furthest she has ever driven is up here."

"If I have captured her heart, she will come," said the captain. "Mandy, *se io avere la amore mio signora volontà venire.*"

"Oooh," said Mandy, "doesn't that sound romantic, Becky? You'll soon get a boyfriend over there."

Becky was accustomed to getting out of the crew quarters, and seeing the island of Anglesey across the bay. What the captain was proposing to do would surely leave her confused.

"How long have you been planning this trip for?" she asked.

"Migrated with the birds for the past five Winters, I told you."

"Ages ago, when we were in Llandudno, but, for some strange reason, I didn't connect it to anything that would happen to me."

"But this is your home. Surely you did not think I would dump you on the quayside? And you need your crew training. By the time we get to the Mediterranean, I'll be sunning myself on the roof, and you can take us the rest of the way. Then I'll have a word with my mate on the African ferries. I know you are set on being a medical officer, but any shipping company will expect you to have a steering ticket, if you want some stripes."

Becky felt her thoughts swimming around in confused circles.

"You'll have to excuse me," she said, "but six months ago, I was an unpaid assistant taking an 'O' level in Human Biology."

"Then the children brought you here, where you belong," said the captain, "and your life has moved on. Don't spend your days dreaming of what has passed. Now, children, Ship, Dublin, depart – *Nave, Dublin, partenza!*"

Becky could only suppose that the captain knew things about the world that she did not and, that by using his logic, his mad idea of going to Italy would actually work. Though, with regards to his idea of Hilda driving all that way for a visit, he was probably wrong.

*

Matron awoke to the intense convulsions caused by hypothermia. Then the awfulness of everything that had happened came flooding back. When the uncontrolled jerking of her limbs reduced to a general shiver, she sat up to stare out of the car window. What was supposed to happen now? Unable to think of anything, she lay back down. Previously, her entire life had included sleeping under nice warm blankets, awaking to find everything in good order, with a nice vase of flowers on the dressing table. Today, her eyes had opened to see the back of a car seat. Yesterday, they had opened to find the caretaker taking her pleasures. Where had all this depravity come from, and why had Becky and Cynthia not rushed to her defence when Alison had said those terrible things? Instead, they had both seemed to accept that there were certain jobs somebody like herself could no longer do.

When the cold became unbearable, she sat back up, until a feeling of hopelessness made her fall back down. In this way, she passed the morning, the fear of the outside only slowly giving way to the demands of her bladder. Eventually, she opened the door, to be greeted by a blast of icy air. She immediately got out, and walked briskly to the far end of the lay-by, where a path wandered into the woods on her left. Disappearing behind a hedge, she had an awful flashback to something that had happened on the way to Holyhead. She had been so cruel to Mandy, refusing to let her go to the toilet properly. Yet the girl had still called her Mummy, and Becky had also wanted to be her friend, until she tried to stop the children going to the seaside. How had she turned into this horrible person, someone so hated that she had now been reduced to sleeping in the back of her car?

On leaving her improvised toilet, she wandered deeper into the woods, until she found a stream. Here, she knelt down to cup her hands into the water and splash it across her face. But she still felt dirty and, thinking of the awful things the caretaker had done, she rolled on the grass to cry. Then she got up to wander some more, and so passed her Friday.

Saturday was worse. She had given all her money to the taxi driver who had brought her home from the pub. Now the banks were closed until Monday, so all she had was the woodland stream for water, and perhaps the hope of finding some blackberries. But how she longed to rush to the nearest café to eat, and sit by the radiator. Not even her shameful dirt mattered, now that her insides felt so empty.

On Sunday, the hunger became starvation and, with some difficulty, she forced herself to drive to a bed and breakfast. The landlady looked at her suspiciously, and obviously wanted to turn her away. Victoria said she would leave her car on the drive, and give them the keys for safe-keeping. That night, she had a bath, an evening meal, and a warm bed. But her sleep was restless. What her bank balance might be, she had no idea, but it could not sensibly afford this.

On Monday, she was waiting for the bank to open and, without asking for a balance, took out £50. First, she scurried to the café for a second breakfast, then returned to the B&B landlady to pay for her stay. She collected her car keys and drove back to the lay-by to think. As far as she could remember, her bank balance had been £800. However, she had not been able to recover Cynthia's college expenses, and there had been the bits for the car repair. All of a sudden, she froze; there was all the money she had spent on the boat nightmare: the petrol, another hotel at Llandudno and a meal on the way home. Throughout the Summer, her expenses had been far greater than the home had been transferring into her bank. Of the £50 she had just taken out, only £28 remained. Money just vanished when you did not have full board and lodgings provided by an employer. She looked at the petrol dial. It was almost on empty, so her next stop would be the garage, and then the £28 would also be gone.

At 3pm she returned to the bank. This time she got the courage to ask for a balance, only to discover her fears had been justified. The total sum of her wealth stood at £388.56, and there was so much she needed. She took out £88.56, and hoped very much that she did not have to come back before the end of the week.

That afternoon, she bought a toothbrush, paste, soap, and a towel. Next, she went to the camping shop to buy a sleeping bag, and then to a supermarket to get a pillow. While there, she ate in the café, and realised there was something else she needed. Her shoes, though comfortable in the wards, were completely useless for her current circumstances. Her feet had become so cold and blistered that she was finding it difficult to walk. After her meal, she did the unthinkable:

she went to the sports shop to buy a pair of clown shoes! To her astonishment, the sort Mad George had bought were top of the range, and had cost…No, it was too awful to even think about, and she had thrown them into the furnace! Eventually, she bought a much cheaper pair in dark grey. She then purchased some nice warm socks, and realised that tomorrow she would have to return to the bank. In the space of a day, she had spent a third of her entire wealth.

After the nightmare expenditure of Monday, things began to settle down. The sleeping bag was quite warm and she discovered that if you went to the swimming pool, there was a little room where you could have a private bath for 40p. Sometimes you had to queue, and there was one horrible tramp who went inside for ages. She had complained about him, but the attendant just said that he used the bath water to wash his spare set of clothes. The attendant then sniffed and walked away. Victoria was so embarrassed that she left the building, and went to the bank to withdraw another £50. With this, she purchased a spare set of clothes, though, unlike the tramp, spent the afternoon in the launderette, where she discovered you could warm your back on the drying machines for free.

Victoria only had one plan of action: to survive another day. But, come November, even this became difficult. The cold rainy days meant going outside was generally more unpleasant than staying curled up on the back seat of her car. How she longed for a heater; the lack of one was causing her joints to ache as she limped along with arthritic twinges in her left knee, and her back bending with the pain of rheumatic ligaments.

When the night-time darkness increased to fifteen hours, the sleeping bag struggled to keep her warm, and she often woke up shivering in the middle of the night. She thought it must be December, which meant the car tax had expired, as had the MOT. Anyway, she couldn't afford the petrol to go anywhere, so the lay-by was where she stayed – two miles from the swimming baths, where she learned to wash her clothes, drying them on the radiator while she went into their cafeteria for a cup of coffee.

One morning, Victoria awoke to find herself surrounded by an eerie greyness. Still in her sleeping bag, she sat up to discover the car windows had become white panels, through which nothing could be seen. She realised that she must be under a blanket of snow, and that opening the door would let in an icy blast. But the insulated car was not so cold as it had been a few days before. Then she had gone to her stream in the woods to find it frozen, and had not managed to get warm for the rest of the day.

As she huddled in her sleeping bag, her mind began to wander this way and that, until finally reaching some conclusions. First, she realised the horror of the caretaker had become a dark part of her past. Now, she only felt dirty because of her clothes and infrequency of baths, not because of the smell the caretaker had ground into her skin. Second, she realised that her worthless existence was the result of foolish pride; the belief that she was a matron, who could only earn money for doing respectable jobs. Today, if she had the chance, she would be grateful to clean the public toilets in return for a little food. This was the problem of her life now – hunger, and the fact that all the money in the bank had gone. In desperation, she began searching down the back of the seats for any loose change. Then her fingers found something: a card with three hairbands. She stared at it incomprehensibly, then burst into tears. How carelessly she had parted with £1.49 for those hairbands. She had never considered that one day it would mean the difference between eating or starving.

Eventually, she got the courage to struggle from her sleeping bag, then to push her way out of the dome of snow that covered the car. She stopped to smooth down her clothes, hoping the dampness would turn to ice, thereby insulating the outer layers against the wind. Then she set out on her new plan; people never starved to death in England, there must be some way of getting food that she did not know about.

She walked into the high street, where she knew a woman was often to be found sitting on the pavement, with her lower body in a sleeping bag. Victoria looked into the box by her feet which contained a handful of coins.

"I'm sorry to bother you," she said, "but I wonder if you can tell me how to get food if you have no money? Surely in England it is not possible to starve to death."

The woman looked up to regard her suspiciously. "You can nick food," she said. "Even if you get caught, the coppers will take you off to the cells, and give you some grub."

"No," said Victoria, "I could never do that."

The woman shrugged her shoulders. "Well, you're not going to earn much on the streets, unless you tart yourself up. Anyway, you need to start the game when you're fourteen. A pimp would never take you on at your age."

"Oh no, I could never do that either."

"Fussy bugger, aren't you," she said. "Guess you're not hungry enough yet?"

"No…no, it's just that I'd rather die first."

"It happens. You got a place to sleep?"

Victoria bowed her head in shame. "A car," she mumbled.

"Well, you're not going to die of cold. Look, go to the greengrocer's at the end of the high street. He always cuts the leaves from his cauliflowers. They'll keep you going for a day or two. But if you're going to be so fussy, next time make your Giro last."

"Giro?" said Victoria. "What's that?"

"What the social give you…don't tell me you haven't registered?"

"I tried – some time ago – but they said I wasn't eligible, because I left my last job of my own accord."

"And you accepted that? What a prat, you really don't have a clue, do you."

"But they told me to go away."

The woman laughed. "OK," she said presently, "this is what you do. Get yourself down the social with your sleeping bag, and lie across the front seats. The smellier you are the better. They'll soon get the message. You will get an emergency payment this afternoon, but don't settle for less than a fiver. After that, you will be able to pick up a Giro every Friday. There is a higher payment for being homeless. You got kids?"

"No."

"I've got a mate who can lend you one, though that makes it a lot more complicated. You're best to stick with single homeless, then they won't bother you for a lot of details. Rub some snow on your cheeks. You want to look as if you're about to die in front of them, that'll speed things up."

The woman reached in her box for a 20p coin, which she held up. "Tell 'em this is all you have," she said, "and beg the clerk for another 5p to work the coffee machine. If you say you've got absolutely nothing, they won't believe you. The clerk won't give you 5p, but it makes you look proper.

And remember, you want the social, not the unemployment, office."

That afternoon, driven by starvation, Victoria did everything the woman had told her. And so it was, that after two hours of complete humiliation, she emerged with a Giro for £5. As darkness fell, she was walking down the street, stuffing herself with chips, and feeling quite overwhelmed by her success. In three days' time, she could pick up a Giro for £33.25 and, with that, sort herself out to look for a job.

"It worked then?" said an unexpected voice by her side.

Victoria looked around to see the woman she had met that morning. For the first time, she looked directly at her face, and was shocked to realise how young she was. Two years before, she could have been a girl at the orphanage, leaving that protected society, only to find herself unable to cope in the outside world. She had now acquired two small children, though for what purpose Victoria had no idea. Surely the social had closed ages ago?

"It worked," said Victoria. "You have truly saved me from starvation!"

"You hear that, kids?" said the woman. "That's how posh people talk. If the Queen ever comes to visit me, you must say 'truly grateful', not 'tar miss's'."

"I'd be truly grateful for a chip," laughed one of the children.

Victoria gave her the bag. "They are yours," she said, "because your friend helped me a great deal this morning."

"In which case," said the woman, "can you hang onto these two for three minutes, while I get warm?"

With that, the woman snatched her hands away from the children, and disappeared into the night. Victoria looked in horror at what she had left behind. The children were not much more than toddlers, but they did not seem to be at all concerned.

"You gonna buy me chips as well?" asked the girl.

"When you friend comes back," said Victoria, "but we can't go now, because she will wonder where you are."

"They make Mummy stay in the pub," said the boy. "She wants to come back, but never does."

"No, that is not possible, I am sure she will be back soon."

"Want chips," wailed the girl.

"Give me the money," said the boy. "I'll go, then you can see that Mummy does not come back."

"But you're too small to go off on your own."

"No I'm not. Give us £2, and I'll get fish and chips that we can all share."

Victoria looked about, but their mother was nowhere to be seen. To keep the children occupied, she gave the boy £2, and he ran off in the direction of the fish shop.

"Can I have 50p for some pop?" said the girl. "When Mummy does not come back, there is nobody to fetch the water."

It was the greatest horror Victoria had ever known. She gave the girl her last £1 note. A moment later she darted away, and was lost to the night. Victoria stood in a state of shock. Their mother would be furious that she had lost the children so quickly. Then she nearly jumped out of her skin, for their mother emerged from the shadows.

"Wise up," she said, "or get yourself off the streets, 'cause you're the sort who'll end up dead!"

"But the children, I've lost them!"

The woman shook her head, apparently in disbelief. Then she walked away. Victoria gave chase.

"But I don't understand," she said. "Shall I help you look for the children?"

The woman gave a sudden sprint...and was gone. Victoria began to cry, not for herself, but for the children she had just met. And for Cynthia, who, aged five, had once lived the same twilight existence. Then her icy fingers reached into her pockets, and managed to gather 87p. It was just about enough to buy some more chips.

THIRTEEN

Anna was relaxing in front of the television, when Janet came home from work, and rushed across to turn off Anna's favourite programme.

"Disaster has struck!" she cried.

"You forgot to pay the TV licence?"

"No, serious disaster. I've just been browsing about a garage, and do you know what I found?"

Janet had passed her driving test three weeks before and, since that time, had devoted much of her life to finding a suitable car. Sometimes, she thought a yellow MGB would be nice to complement Anna's red one; at other times, she wanted an estate to deal with the supermarket run.

"You've found a car you really like," said Anna, "but can't afford. Now please can I have my programme back?"

"But this is a really old Morris Minor with two careful lady owners, and a nursing sticker in the back window. At first I thought I was being silly..."

"Buying a Morris Minor is very silly."

"I mean, thinking it was Matron's, but I could just see it

parked outside the building, then I remembered the number plate – VIC 8. Such things are part of our childhood, like Matron herself."

"So you want to buy Matron's car…just don't expect me to sit in the passenger seat in daylight."

"I don't want to buy it, but I asked the man where Matron was living. You remember, we promised to ask her round to dinner?"

"At last, you are making sense. So where did she disappear to?"

"Well, the man was very shifty. I knew there was something he wasn't telling me…"

"He's a car salesman, there was probably quite a lot he wasn't telling you, like the gearbox fell out."

"No, after a lot of nagging, he told me. The lady he bought it from had been living in it. She only sold it when the police threatened to take it away for having no tax."

"Well, that couldn't be Matron. I expect she gave it to some tramp after the gearbox fell out."

"No, it seems the salesman had a heart somewhere, because he was quite worried about her, said she didn't look the sort to be living rough. He only bought the car because she looked hungry. Apparently he had to spend a fortune getting it through the MOT."

"I have a problem with that statement: for a start, the number plate VIC 8 is worth a few thousand, with or without, the gearbox."

"Will you stop going on about the gearbox."

"Well, it must have something missing, otherwise Matron would never have sold it."

"Suppose…? Anyway, the salesman told me the awfulness

of everything he had seen. He thought the lady was average height, in her fifties, and blonde. If she had been living rough, that could easily be a thirty-something."

Anna looked thoughtful. "I don't understand why anybody would be living in a car with such a number plate," she said. "Unless, of course, they had been in isolation since number plates were just number plates…Ah."

"So," said Janet, "is this sounding more like Matron we know? And Alex had no idea where she went, after the home. Matron needs our help, like we once needed hers."

"Depends how much the salesman gave her for the number plate. She's probably gone to live in the Caribbean or something."

"I can hardly bear to tell you…" replied Janet. "Anyway, he's given me a map to where she had been living. It was only three weeks ago, and she can't have gone far without a car. She might even be in the adjacent woods. We could ask some local walkers, if they had seen anybody."

"Or," said Anna, "you could phone the dole office to see when the homeless pick up their Giros."

*

The following Friday, Anna came home from work, to find Janet in tears.

"Oh, it was awful," sobbed Janet, "I haven't been able to go to work this afternoon."

"You found her?"

"I found what I thought was an old woman shuffling into the dole office. Then I recognised the remains of her uniform, just rags now. I didn't think she'd want to see me in the dole office. Besides, it made more sense to let her pick up her Giro first. When she came out, I followed, not knowing what to do. The first café she went into threw her out. Then she went to the chip shop and came out with food and a bottle of Coke. Only after she had finished did I have the courage to approach. But she just kept turning away, and wouldn't even speak to me. Fortunately, she kept looking down, so didn't realise I kept following. She was walking ever so slowly. She is dying, I know it! One day, she will collapse, and they will find her in the morning, all cold and stiff. So I kept a long way behind, until she wandered into the woods by the lay-by. She didn't look back. I'm not even certain if she knows what is happening beyond what she sees around her own feet. Anyway, halfway down a footpath, she pushed her way through some bushes. I didn't follow her after that, I couldn't, not on my own. Oh, we must go tomorrow, first thing!"

"Well, I don't expect you're going to get any sleep tonight. I'll get my coat and let's go now."

Thirty minutes later, Anna parked the MG in the lay-by, and the two girls walked along the path by torchlight. When they reached the bushes into which Matron had disappeared, they turned off the light, and whispered nervously to each other about what to do next.

*

Victoria lay curled up in her sleeping bag, worrying about the day's confrontation. If Janet had found her, was not the caretaker also likely to come? Whether or not they wanted to laugh at her, or get her to do lesbian things again, she had no idea. Then she heard whispering, and became rigid with fear. Nobody had found her little tent in the middle of the bushes, and the fact they had done so today made her suspect the lesbians. Besides, it was dark, and the walkers would have left the woods some time ago.

"Hello," came a voice, "it's me, Janet."

How on Earth had she been found, unless she had been trailed? She should have looked behind on her way back from town. Tomorrow she would find somewhere else to camp. All she had to do was keep her away for tonight.

"And me, Anna," came another voice. "Please come out."

Victoria put her fingers into her mouth, to disguise her voice.

"I don't know who you are," she said, "leave me alone."

"But, Matron, surely you remember us – Janet and Anna – we met you at the pub five months ago."

"I'm not Matron. I'm not anyone you need to worry about. Please just go away."

"Now, Matron," said Anna, "I'm going to open the tent flap, just to see how you are."

The idea filled Matron with horror. These girls had seen her first humiliation when the caretaker was doing horrible things to her, and now they wanted to see her second humiliation too. They had once been at her home, and still called her Matron. They must never see her like this.

"You can't make me come out," she said, "this is my tent, and my privacy."

"I'm still going to open the tent flap."

"No, please. Is the caretaker with you?"

"Sorry, we haven't seen Alex for ages. Perhaps you don't know, she's on the run from the police. It was an awful scandal.

Somehow she found out about the caretaker's cupboard, and…you don't want to know about that."

For the first time in many months, Victoria *did* want to know about something other than her own misfortune.

"What happened?" she asked.

"The girls screwed up the secret door while she was inside. At first, there was an awful fuss because nobody lit the boilers, so Miss Buckley and some of the girls tried. The safety valve blew its top, turning the boiler house into a sauna. While this was happening it is assumed Alex realised the girls were never going to let her out, until she died of dehydration. So she wrenched a pipe off the wall to have a drink, we imagine. Anyway, this sent a flood of water running down the corridors, so a plumber had to be called, for this and the boiler house. Miss Buckley was providing a walking guard to the plumber when they came across the caretaker cupboard. The girls had stuck a sign on the back wall saying '*Beware of the Lesbian!*' Then they found Alex all locked up. Of course, the plumber blabbed to everyone."

"The girls knew about the caretaker?" asked Matron. You know, what she liked to do."

"Made it pretty obvious, though she never tried anything on with the girls when we were there. Even after she caught us in the woods, she never asked anything of us until we left, and then saw us in The Flag. But this is not helping you. All we can offer is food, warmth, and clean clothes. I'm afraid we have no kind words for your partner. Spying on young girls is sick, at least when you're as old as the caretaker. According to the newspapers, she was forty-six."

Victoria turned things over in her mind. Anna and Janet did not seem intent on doing her any harm. Indeed, weren't they supposed to be faithful to each other? Why would they fancy her, when she was only eleven years younger than the caretaker?

"Can I see you tomorrow," she said, "when I've got cleaned up, at the swimming pool cafeteria, perhaps?"

Yes, thought Victoria, *that was the right thing to say.* Tomorrow she could go to another town to avoid seeing them. Perhaps she could steal a supermarket trolley to carry her stuff; you sometimes saw these being pushed down roads a long way from any shops. Then she realised the tent flap was being opened, and though hiding in her sleeping bag, she could sense two faces looking at her.

"You looked after us for thirteen years," said Anna. "Now it is our turn to look after you. Get yourself out of that bag and come with us. We refuse to take no for an answer."

Victoria felt too weak to argue, and there was the possibility of food and warmth. Even if it only lasted an hour it would be nice. She crawled from her sleeping bag, then out of the tent.

"I've got a bar of soap somewhere," she said. "I do try to keep clean, but it's expensive, you know. And I've got a comb. At least let me wash myself in the stream."

"Matron, the water's freezing. Please put yourself into our care, like we put ourselves into yours, then we will all get along just fine."

Victoria shielded her eyes from the sudden torchlight. "No," she said, "please don't look at me!"

"I'm just trying to find my way out of here," said Anna. "If you lead, we will follow, without a torch if you like."

It went dark, and Victoria tried to stand up, but couldn't. The ligaments in her right leg were paralysed by rheumatism, while her calf muscles were so weak from the lack of food, the strain put upon them produced only pain.

"I'm getting cold standing around," moaned Anna. "Do you want the torch?"

Matron used a branch to pull herself into a stooping position. Her right leg was not much use but, by using a stick, it could be dragged along as she shuffled forwards on the other. She pushed her way through a weakness in the bushes to reach the path.

"Where are we going?" she asked.

"To the lay-by, the place where…well, we hear you spent the Winter in your Morris Minor. How did you survive the cold nights?"

"How did you know about that?"

"Janet saw it up for sale. The guy eventually told us how he conned you."

"No he didn't. The police were going to take it away, so I sold it to him as a piece of metal that couldn't go anywhere. He gave me enough money to buy a tent and a little camping stove. A car without petrol was of no use to me."

"The scoundrel!" said Janet.

"Leave it," said Anna. "Matron needs to concentrate on getting better, not beating up a dodgy car salesman."

On reaching the lay-by, Victoria saw a car door being opened, and was guided down to a low passenger seat.

"See," said Janet, "I said we should get an estate. I'll walk to the town and get the bus back."

Victoria thought this must be a secret code for how repulsive she was, but, looking about, realised she was in a tiny, two-seater, open-top sports car. Anna got in, and a moment later they were pulling out of the lay-by. For the next fifteen minutes, Victoria forgot all about her problems. Anna was pretending to be a racing driver, doing things with the gear stick to get around bends. Matron realised her pathetic existence was going to end in a crumpled heap of metal.

Surprisingly, the car stopped safely in a courtyard. After the door was opened, Victoria crawled onto the tarmac, then used the back of the car to pull herself up. Only pride allowed her to overcome the terrible pain required to shuffle after Anna. On reaching a block of flats, they took a lift to the fifth floor. Here, the doors opened to reveal a wide public space. The stairs only went downwards, indicating this was the top floor. Around the space were six doors, and Anna went to the door marked 5A. Anna did not give a guided tour, but took her straight to the bathroom.

"There you go." she said. "Get yourself into a nice warm bath, while I sort out some clean clothes. Help yourself to anything you need from the cabinet."

Victoria could only blink at the bright light shining off the white tiles. She felt totally ashamed that she had been seen under fluorescent tubes. Then Anna left, and Matron realised the door did not have an internal bolt. If Anna walked back in, it would be so embarrassing; a lesbian was about to supervise her bath! She looked in the cabinet to find some bubblebath and, having made a camouflage of froth, undressed quickly to get in. As the warmth surrounded her body, she realised embarrassment was a small price to pay. At the public baths, the attendant measured six inches of near-boiling water into the tub. It was left to the customer to decide whether to add sufficient cold water to have hot water covering your legs, or warm water halfway up your body. Without a key, you could not put the hot tap back on, which ultimately meant washing your clothes in nearly cold water. Here, all the water was hot, and the bubbles reached her nose.

Presently, there was a knock on the door, and Anna walked in. She draped some clean clothes over the back of the chair, then looked down at the pile on the floor.

"Can I throw these in the bin?" she asked.

Victoria now had a better instinct for survival. It did not pay to throw anything away; besides she had no money to replace them.

"I'll take them to the launderette tomorrow," she said, "though I don't know how I am going to get your clothes back to you."

Anna looked puzzled. Then using her fingertips she picked up the dirty clothes. "I'll put them in our washing machine," she said.

After Anna had gone, Victoria wondered if this was actually a nightmare – to be naked, a long way from home, and without access to her clothes. Two minutes later, Anna returned, this time without knocking. She was carrying a pair of clothes tongs and made no effort to hide her disgust as she picked up the trainers – a smelly mess of canvas, held together with safety pins and a bit of bailer twine. She dropped them into a bin liner.

"Now, these are going down the waste chute," she said. "I don't know how your feet have survived in these."

"But how do I get home?" asked Victoria.

"Home? This is your home for the time being, surely you realise that?"

"No, I can't imagine you want me here. I expect to go back to the tent as soon as...after you've fed me?"

"What a silly idea! Dinner will be ready in half an hour,

then you can sleep in our spare room. Our house rules are quite simple: if you bring any women back, be discreet. Our neighbours think we are two career girls on a flat share. If they had any more information, it would only complicate things. Also, Janet has a rule about no toenail clippings being left anywhere she might find them. Also, I have just invented a new rule of no going back to tents. Is that clear?"

"But you'll soon get fed up with me."

"Doubt it. But for the time being, let us say you looked after us for thirteen years, so we shall look after you for thirteen weeks."

Anna left, and Victoria began to wonder on the impossible situation in which she found herself. Now she was in a hot bath, the idea of going back to the cold, damp tent filled her with horror. But to stay here would mean pretending to be a lesbian…one of the sisterhood! Henceforth, her secret would be that she did not fancy other women. She would have to tell them, but tomorrow, when she could get back into her recently washed clothes, and once more walk away to her solitude. But how, without footwear? Mad George floated into her mind. In future she would try to think of him as Shoe George, though he was still mad for spending all his money on her.

Eventually, Victoria got out of the bath, and quickly wrapped a towel around herself. Then she looked at the clothes on the back of the chair. There was a T-shirt – something she had never worn in her life – and a little pleated skirt. It was even shorter than the one Shoe George had bought her. Even more embarrassing were the knickers, made from light cotton, and apparently missing some material at the sides. She had only ever worn sensible grey knickers not these strange things. Clearly, people were expected to see them, otherwise they would not have bothered with the floral pattern.

Realising they were special lesbian knickers, she returned them to the chair. Then she happened to catch sight of herself in the full-length mirror…and gasped in horror. Looking back was an old, grey woman she did not recognise. Bones stuck out from stretched skin and, where her joints had been pressed against the hard ground on which she slept, were great bruises. A bramble cut on her leg was surrounded by gangrenous flesh. She let the towel drop, to reveal wrinkled folds of skin where her breasts had once been. At that, she fell to the floor and began to sob. Then she heard the door open, and Anna gasp.

"I'm calling the doctor," she said. "It's OK, she's one of us, and very understanding."

Victoria knew she must escape, but how? They had stolen her shoes. Of course, they would be in the waste chute, still on top of the rubbish at the bottom. She staggered up, and began to run…

Anna found her a few moments later, slumped before the washing machine, a hand clasped around the handle, as if to recover the few rags swirling around inside, but the door was locked for the duration.

Matron returned to consciousness to find herself in a bed, gazing up at a strange woman in a green and black camouflage jacket. She tried to roll away, but the bed was against the wall, preventing any escape.

"Sorry about the dress," said the terrifying woman. "I was on my way to dinner, when Anna telephoned. Doctor Kirsty at your service!"

The woman removed a huge camouflaged rucksack, from which she extracted a black doctor's bag.

"Your friends tell me you have not been looking after yourself," she said.

"No...I'm OK, really."

The woman tried to pull down the duvet, which Matron clasped to her chin. The woman, totally unconcerned, pulled up the duvet from the bottom end, and started feeling her legs. Victoria tried to curl up into a foetal position, but was very weak, and could do nothing against the lesbian who was pretending to be a doctor.

"You are clearly suffering from starvation," said the woman, "and probably a handful of diseases you picked up from Alex. I am prescribing antibiotics, even before I get the results of your smear test..."

"No..."

All of a sudden, the woman became very severe.

"Your girlfriend's genitals were a biological weapon," she said. "I wouldn't go near them without full protective clothing! As to spying on little girls in the bath, don't expect any sympathy from me. This consultation is over!"

At that, the door burst open.

"No," squealed Anna, "Matron never spied on the little girls, I am certain of it!"

"And she is nearly dying," pleaded Janet.

"I know," said Kirsty, "even an anorexia clinic would treat her as a severe case. Had you not found her, she would have been dead within ten days. But I detect no gratitude. Let the hospital sort it out."

"No," begged Janet, "the men doctors wouldn't understand. Please, Kirsty, do something!"

"Then you do as I say," said Kirsty. "Medicine, food, exercise...whatever I prescribe."

"Yes," said Anna, "anything. We won't let her leave!"

Matron looked up to find herself imprisoned by a circle of lesbians. Then she felt a needle going into her leg, followed by...nothing.

*

Matron came round to find her arm connected to a drip. Her eyes darted about the room; this was not a hospital, she was still in the secret prison. Anna was guarding her by sitting in a chair to read a book. She looked up.

"Doctor Kirsty said I am to take no nonsense," she said, "so you are having a high-energy drink for breakfast."

Matron looked at the catheter in her arm.

"GPs can't set up drips in people's homes," she protested.

"Kirsty ran a field hospital in some war zone or other," replied Anna, "but she's a GP now, so we have registered you as a patient."

Anna put down her book and sat on the bed to hold hands.

"You'll have to excuse Kirsty's outburst," she said. "Alex gave her former girlfriend a dose of something, so it's a bit of a sensitive subject."

Matron looked at the hand resting over her own, and was surprised to see it looked quite ordinary. You wouldn't actually know it belonged to a lesbian.

"Aren't you scared you might catch something?" asked Matron.

"Not in the slightest, the only thing I am likely to catch from you is a bad case of antibiotics." Anna pointed to the needle in her arm. "You are not to take that out," she said. "Kirsty wants immediate access to your bloodstream."

Matron managed a slight whimper, but decided not to fight anymore. Now fear of going back to the cold, damp tent was greater.

Eight days later, Matron got out of bed to do her physiotherapy exercises, and, for the first time, found she was able to bend over to touch her toes. The girls were at work, so she went to the kitchen to make herself a cup of tea and prepare an egg sandwich. Then she noticed a booklet by the side of the kettle. On the cover was the image of a rainbow-coloured flag, though to which country it belonged, she had no idea. Underneath were the words, '*Sexual Health*'. Stoically, she opened a random page to find...

She staggered back, then slumped to the floor. The girls thought she had done that, and the caretaker actually did!

"Oh, George," she said out loud, as if to surround herself in a protective coat, "if only I had not jumped over the table!"

"Oh God," she moaned, "how will I ever convince Cynthia that I do not do these things?"

*

The following Monday, Victoria somehow managed to catch a bus to Cynthia's college, to check the recent disruption had not affected her studies. Eventually, she located the lecturer for Human Biology, and made enquiries regarding Cynthia's progress. He replied that she had not turned up for the past four weeks, which, he added, was a great shame, because she was his star pupil. He also mentioned there seemed to be some problem with her examination fees...

Victoria stormed down to the accounts office, furious

with Hilda for not finishing what she had started. She would tell the secretary that she would pay herself…somehow.

"No," said the secretary, "you don't understand. I have a cheque from 'The Captain', posted in Italy."

Victoria looked at the cheque. It was indeed printed *The Captain*.

"And a cheque from a Mr George Monnington, that arrived with a German stamp," continued the secretary. "Also a cheque from a Mr Silver, again with no return address. What I want to know is, which one am I to bank?"

"George," said Victoria without thinking.

After leaving the college, Victoria caught a bus to the village, from where she walked to the girls' home. Here, she stared at the entrance. From each of the two gate pillars, a high security fence ran back either side of the drive for about fifty feet. Strands of barbed wire overhead made a tunnel, through which the determined visitor could walk to a second set of gates more suited to the entrance of a top-security jail. They had huge padlocks, and generally looked able to withstand a dynamite blast. Adjacent to the 'passport control' was a caravan, to which had been stuck a bright yellow sticker stating *Site Security. No Male Visitors.* Nearby was a floodlight, probably relocated from the tennis courts, but now fixed to a rotating base, supported by pram wheels.

Victoria had no idea how to get up the drive without reporting to whoever was in the caravan. She walked back to the boys' home, where it was still possible to enter without difficulty. Here, she would apologise to Hilda, then try to get some information about what was happening with the girls. She knocked on the door to the surgery, and was told to come in. She opened the door just a fraction.

"It's me, Victoria," she said. "I have come to apologise."

"Who is Victoria, and what are you apologising for?"

Victoria opened the door, to see a lady she did not recognise.

"I'm a friend of Hilda's," said Victoria. "It's a personal matter."

The woman looked her up and down. "Have you been ill?" she asked.

"A little, but it wasn't contagious. Do you know where Hilda is?"

"Italy."

"That cannot be possible, she is always here – at least for the last thirty years, I think."

"So I heard, but she's in Italy now. She was meant to drive down for a holiday after Christmas, but never came back. Can I ask who you are?"

"A friend...I can't believe Hilda has left for good."

"All Mr Cranmore got was a postcard of an olive grove, and on the other side, her words of resignation. She must be quite something, because she's landed a millionaire with a yacht. I reckon he must be a famous Hollywood actor, because the boat's even got a football pitch. And here's me, stuck in a draughty old prefab, last decorated in 1950. As soon as they get a replacement, I'm off!"

"What about Cynthia? I've heard she has stopped going to college."

"After all the fuss with the lesbian caretaker, they tightened security. Girls don't get in or out without the new headmistress's say so."

"What happened to Miss Buckley?"

"Finding the lesbian just about finished her off. The men in white coats came for her."

Victoria left the rambling matron, who clearly wasn't the slightest bit interested in looking after the boys. They needed Hilda, just as the girls needed herself. Victoria let out a cry of anguish; if she went back now, they would push her into the cupboard, and put that awful sign on the door.

On returning to the flat, Victoria explained the events of the day to her friends. Then she added something of the history that made Cynthia's escape so important.

Janet and Anna looked at each other, then, as if talking telepathically, both nodded at exactly the same time.

"We don't know this Cynthia," explained Anna, "but we gather you consider her to be your daughter?"

"I need to protect her from whatever is going on behind those awful gates."

"Well, you know the law, men in wigs going bla-bla-bla. The last time one of our sisters tried to adopt officially, they actually used the term 'kidnap'. But in the real world we are much more civilised. You offer, she accepts, and we all have a party. We will give your daughter somewhere to live, but she'll have to share your room. Did you say you paid for her enrolment fees?"

"Yes, together with Hilda."

"And the home paid for nothing?"

"No."

"Good, so they will have no record of what college she is at…"

"Miss Buckley thought it was a special girls' college."

Anna turned to touch Janet's arm. "Like you are special," she said, "because you are the only perfect person in the whole world!"

The next moment, the two girls were lost to a world of passionate kisses.

"Sorry," Janet called back as they made their way to the bedroom, "we'll have to talk about Cynthia later…"

Victoria wondered how she could bring Cynthia to this place of perversion. How could she not? Only Anna and Janet were sufficiently well established to provide a home. And so, the lies would have to continue because…because she was pathetic and, if they threw her out, all she could offer Cynthia was a tent.

The following day, Victoria found herself able to consume large amounts of food; she must get strong to protect Cynthia. That evening, the bathroom scales hovered on seven stone. At 11pm the girls returned home, and sat on the settee holding hands.

"It was awful," said Janet. "What they have done at the home shouldn't be allowed."

"Cynthia – did you see her?" Victoria asked.

"Couldn't get that close. Whoever runs that place has a fantasy about playing prison camps. Every so often, a woman wearing a nun's robe emerged from the caravan with a great snarling Alsatian. The dog knew we were there and barked like crazy, drooling slime and everything. The place is completely isolated from the rest of England, except for the entrance, which appears to be the passport control.

Victoria started to cry. "So it is hopeless then," she sobbed. "Cynthia can't finish her college."

Both girls ran across to comfort her. "Of course it's not hopeless," they said. "The nuns have only done what is necessary to stop the girls escaping by their own efforts. They are not expecting the sisterhood to attack from the outside. Tomorrow, we are down The Flag to organise an escape committee!"

*

It was a slightly damp Sunday morning, and the long column of boredom was making its way to the church – a practice introduced by the nuns, who thought God should have the final say in such things. Halfway through the march, the girls in the middle heard a short whistle, as did the Alsatian dogs, who pulled on their chains, snarling in the hope it might lead to the taste of human flesh. Instinctively, the nuns guarding the column swished their canes, but were too busy keeping back the dogs to pay any attention to what was happening in the wider world.

Cynthia looked up from her feet, to see a lady standing between the trees. As soon as their eyes met, the woman turned away, then disappeared into the woods. For a brief moment, the piece of paper stuck to her back had been clearly visible. It stated: *'Gwendoline, your friends are waiting for you.'* Also stuck to the sign was a patch of silver paper.

Cynthia tried not to show her confused frown. The woman must have been there for some purpose. Then she remembered the secret code they used at the boat village: 'Gwendoline' meant you were an authorised visitor. Anyway, Mr Silver and the silver paper were too much of a coincidence. She cast her eyes left and right, but saw nothing to indicate that any friends were waiting. Then her spirits soared; her friends would only be waiting, if they intended to take her away from this misery. For the first time in many weeks, she became alert to anything that might be happening outside her own misfortune.

Nothing else happened on the way to church and, once inside, she looked around to see if there were any adults brave enough to be sitting in the pews. But the locals knew to avoid this service, and no strangers had unwittingly entered the world of bored children.

After the prefects had put the screens along the centre aisle, the girls heard the boys being marched into the opposite pews. Cynthia knew this to be a recent concession to the monks – twenty boys drawn by lots from a hat, and generally supervised by Mr Cranmore. Presently, the vicar entered, but Cynthia did not think he was an undercover agent either. Then began the normal rituals of standing, kneeling, and occasionally sitting. It was like a PE lesson, combined with a Religious Studies course, with some singing practice thrown in for good measure.

About halfway through the service, the vicar was droning on about something or other, when Cynthia heard the boys starting to break out in giggle fits. The vicar pressed on regardless; to him, it was all in a day's work. Cynthia's eyes darted this way and that, all the time trying to look for something unusual. Then she noticed that the organist had a finger and thumb clenched tightly over his nostrils. A moment later, one of the girls let out a gasp, and clutched a handkerchief to her face. All the boys were now in uproar, so that not even the vicar could be heard. Then the overpowering smell of a stink bomb washed over Cynthia. Well, not one stink bomb, probably half a dozen.

Suddenly, the organist cracked. He leapt from his stool, rushed down the aisle, and threw open the doors. It was the signal the boys had been waiting for. Their stampede was immediately joined by the girls. In the doorway there was a lot of intermingling, with some boys trying to cower away; others, whom Cynthia had been able to normalise, being more disorientated.

The children exploded onto the grass outside the church. Immediately, the commandant began a hysterical rant at

Mr Cranmore for letting the boys sneak stink bombs into the house of God. Then she slapped him across the face so hard that his false teeth flew out. The combination of stink bombs and false teeth was too much for the infant boys, who doubled up with laugher. The junior boys looked bewildered; girls were supposed to be sissy, so how did they survive the prison camp guards? The two senior boys wandered about in a daze; back there, in the scrum, it had been really nice, with 'tingles' happening in ways they did not understand.

Cynthia looked at the frenzied dogs, but quickly established their biting zone extended only ten feet from the gates to which their chains were fixed. Quietly, she made her way to the edge of the scrum, but, unlike the others, looked away from the sprawling masses. A woman, standing on the far side of the church wall, was staring at the scene in total astonishment. Then she seemed to jump to her senses, and quickly turned around. On her back was a piece of paper, with an arrow pointing to the right. The woman returned to look at the chaos, then gave Cynthia a nod.

Cynthia idly wandered around the outside of the crowd, and, with a quick jump, managed to get behind a supporting buttress of the church. Keeping close to the building, she crept to the graveyard at the rear. Here, a woman was bending down, and sobbing.

"My dear," she said, "my eyesight's not what it used to be, can you tell me if I've got the right grave? Does it say Gwendoline?"

"I believe it does," said Cynthia.

"I'm so glad," said the woman, "and do you think Gwendoline would rather be here, or going back to college?"

"College."

The woman reached into a bunch of flowers she was holding, and pulled out a compass.

"Here," she said, "you will need this. Go out of the back gate and keep walking along the path. After 500 yards, you will see a half-eaten apple lying on the ground. Turn right into the trees, and keep heading north west until you are told to stop. There is no need to run. If anybody comes looking for you, I shall say I saw a girl running across the field. But don't dawdle either. As soon as they find all the stink bombs that have been pushed through the vestry letterbox, I expect they'll do a head count."

Cynthia followed the directions, until a woman appeared from behind a tree. "This way," she said.

"Who are you," asked Cynthia, "and why are you helping me?"

"I am a member of the Cynthia Liberation Front," she said. "I am not at liberty to tell you any more."

After a short distance, they came to the edge of the wood.

"Don't break cover," said the woman. "I am going to the Austin Maxi over there to take a good look around. If the police have been called, they are likely to be coming this way. Only after I have opened the back door, and taken off my headscarf, are you to dive onto the rear seat and hide underneath the blanket."

Cynthia did as she was told and was soon lying across the back seat.

"Stay down," said the woman. "I don't want anybody to see me driving with a girl in the back until we are well clear. Underneath the blanket, you will find some new clothes. Get changed, and put your uniform into the bin bag. I will dispose of these as soon as possible. You will not be needing them again. At the other end of the journey, you will no longer be a schoolgirl."

"There is also a wig," said Cynthia.

"You are blonde and short, the wig is florescent red with long curls. Need I explain more? You should also find some sunglasses."

Cynthia again did as she was told, then waited under the blanket.

"Have we got far to go?" she asked presently.

"A safehouse, twenty miles from your prison, and fifteen miles from your college. I think we have just about crossed the border to safety. If you are now a redhead, you may sit up."

Cynthia sat up, and for the first time in her life saw what the world looked like through sunglasses. "Where are we?" she asked.

"I cannot remember where I picked you up, and am highly unlikely to remember where I set you down. Your are just a hitch-hiker who jumped into my car, and I am afraid we are quite lost."

Cynthia looked out of the window, and soon realised they were turning into a car park.

"This is where I drop you off," said the woman. "You might want to walk to the block of flats over there. Then get the lift to the fifth floor, and knock on the door marked 5A."

Cynthia got out of the car and said thank you. Then, wearing her fashion outfit, she walked towards the quite respectable block of flats. To make sure she was going the right way, she looked back to the woman, but the car had already gone. Cynthia realised she had just been magically transported from being a bored schoolgirl in a church, to a young woman in sexy clothes somewhere in the middle of a city.

Cynthia emerged from the lift and walked across to a door marked 5A, where she rang a bell. It was answered by a woman she did not recognise.

"Ah, Cynthia," she said, "please come in…"

Victoria was sitting on the sofa rehearsing her speech, and hoping a teenager would find it rather cool. As the living room door opened, she looked up, but only managed a strangled cry of horror. A strange woman was standing there, which, given the nature of this flat, meant a lesbian. Her outrageous red hair was in the style of Madam Whiplash!

Anna reached across to lift up the wig, and the lady removed her sunglasses to reveal Cynthia.

Cynthia bravely stood her ground as Victoria ran across to do the hugging stuff.

"Victoria!" she exclaimed. "You are so thin, what happened to you?"

"Your mother has not been looking after herself," said the woman.

"Mother?" asked Cynthia.

"She is taking care of you, therefore, as far as our nosy neighbours are concerned, she is your mother. It stops a lot of awkward questions."

Cynthia looked at the woman, then at the other one, who had just walked in with a tray of biscuits. The idea of Victoria living as a threesome made her want to laugh, but she thought it might be inappropriate.

"We used to go to your home too," explained the girl with the biscuits, "but you'd have been in middle dormitory when we left, so I don't suppose you remember us."

Victoria had taken up with two former girls!

"Excuse me," said Cynthia, "I just need to stand in your kitchen for a little while; my brain is struggling to keep up with my vicissitudes." (This was a long word she had learned to send the English mistress floating away with happy dreams of Victorian literature.)

"I'll come with you," said Victoria.

"No," said Cynthia, "you three stay here. This is something I need to work out for myself."

To prove she wasn't frightened, she took two biscuits from the tray, picked up what she assumed was her coffee mug, and walked quietly away.

"You gave us the impression she was a child," said Janet. "Seems quite grown up to me."

"I suppose she's changed since going to college," said Victoria. "I just never noticed before, but you do like her?"

"Time will tell," replied both girls together.

A few minutes later, Cynthia returned. "Right," she said, "I have adapted."

"That was quick," said Anna.

"Adapting is something I am rather good at," replied Cynthia, "and this seems a great improvement on my previous circumstance."

Cynthia slowly opened her hands to reveal a mass of scabs. It caused Janet and Anna to throw themselves into a hug.

"Mother Superior rather likes caning," said Cynthia. "It helps drive out the Devil, apparently."

"We need the police!" shrieked Matron.

"No we don't," said Cynthia, "there would be a herd of social workers armed with clipboards surrounding the flat. A kid living with three...I'd be taken back into care."

469

Janet peered forwards. "Dare I ask what crime you committed?" she asked. "Are we all to be murdered in our beds?"

"Perhaps I forgot to mention Matron wasn't around. Hilda was on hand, if something difficult came up. When she did a runner to Italy, I expect I should have said something, but, by then, the girls had accepted me as Matron, so it seemed easier to keep quiet. Of course, Miss Buckley was totally doolally after all the fuss with the caretaker, and didn't have a clue what was going on. With the girls taking control, it soon became Heaven on Earth, at least until a group of nuns turned up to find two girls sunbathing in just their knickers, and another sitting on the entrance steps, reading *The Joy of Sex*! The nuns who did not actually pass out, quickly realised the Devil had taken over the institution, hence their search for the most fearsome nun in the whole world. The following week, men in white coats arrived to take Miss Buckley away, and the commandant marched up the drive, followed by a load of fearsome nuns, all swishing their canes through the air. Anyway, it did not take long for them to realise why Matron wasn't attending staff meetings. First, they caned me for being disobedient, then for not telling them when or where Matron had gone. I was kept in the cellar, and brought on stage every morning assembly. No more than six strokes, but every day I committed a new crime by keeping silent. For some reason, they were obsessed with finding out about Matron. If I had cried, my credibility with the girls would have been lost. As it happened, I increasingly became a challenge to their authority. They had to break me, on stage, with the others watching. Equally, I had to break them, to show the girls the nuns did not have absolute control. And so, day by day, the skin slices got deeper, into the tendons, breaking the scabs of the day before. At the beginning of the third week, they cut through something important, and my hands started squirting blood everywhere. A few girls passed out. The new matron is the commandant's sister, I think. Anyway, she didn't have a clue about medical stuff, so I had to run around getting the girls into the recovery position. Then the others got the hang of it, and passed out also. It was chaos, but, more than this, it showed the nuns the power 150 girls have, if they all act together. Just as they fell down, they could rise up. Anyway, after I sorted them out, I went back up on stage, looked directly into the commandant's eyes, and held out my hand, dripping blood everywhere. She blinked. The cane did not come, nor was I sent back to the cellar. I won, and have now escaped, to become their leader-in-exile. After I finish my 'O' levels, I will see what can be done."

"I'm so sorry I wasn't there to protect you," said Victoria.

"You didn't have any choice, after Tracy caught you snogging the caretaker in the surgery..."

"What!"

"But, it's OK now," continued Cynthia. "As I pointed out, the more lesbians there are in the world, the more boys are left over for us. If you went back now, they would be much more understanding, so long as..."

"So long as...?" prompted Anna.

Cynthia was very aware that her audience were also her landlords, whom she did not fully understand.

"Well," she continued cautiously, "some of the girls are squeamish about oral sex, even with a boy..."

"Yurk," said Anna and Janet together.

"But, as I explained in my sex lessons," continued Cynthia,

"if they want men to buy them chocolates, they need to get used to it, because men just love snuffling about down there. Then the girls find out Victoria's doing it with the caretaker. It's why they kept running away…they all think you might find it hard to control your desires."

Anna went to the sideboard and recovered a book.

"This," she said, "is about normal sex. It might interest you. Then perhaps your lessons could be more balanced. You will see that the male urinary organ is not at all necessary."

Very quietly, Victoria stood up, and walked into her room, closing the door behind her. There, she spent the afternoon lying on her bed, staring up at the ceiling. Outside, three girls were talking about doing perverted things in a way that would have made the nuns at her convent school spontaneously combust. She could not even defend herself, because she did not like using their words.

Eventually, Victoria crawled to the bedroom door, and opened it just a fraction, to peep out. There were now seven women sitting in a circle, all gazing at Cynthia, and hanging on her every word. How could Cynthia not be terrified, they could pounce at any moment! Victoria listened to what Cynthia was saying; it was a story about living in the brothel, the pretend-lesbian show, and all the men getting out their male urinary organs.

"So," continued Cynthia, "I know how deceitful men can be, all the time growing up in the orphanage, thinking that one of those customers could be my father. I hated it!" Cynthia held the stunned silence for two seconds. "Then I met George," she said, "my pretend dad…he can't be my real dad, because he is much too kind and gentle to ever visit a brothel, so pretend will just have to do!"

Victoria listened to Cynthia telling the story of the boat village, but in a way she found difficult to follow. George seemed like a superhero, crossing rope swings, buying clothes, and being completely honest in the ice cream parlour.

"And the tragedy of it all," concluded Cynthia, "is that George really likes Victoria."

There was a hushed silence, then all eyes turned to Victoria.

"Bastard," said one presently. "Just because he bought you a dress, thinking he could sit next to you – pervert!"

"On the other hand," said another, "just imagine what he would have done to look at our tits – buy us a house probably."

Cynthia was on her feet in an instant, her hostile body language filling the room.

"My superdad needs a superwoman," she said. "I suddenly feel the need to throw you out of the window, to see how well you fly!"

Victoria stared in astonishment; the lesbians were actually cowering away. How did Cynthia do it? It was like at the ice cream parlour; she had total control of the room. Then a girl of about eighteen threw herself on the floor, and rested the side of her face on Cynthia's shoes.

"If only you were normal," she said, "I could so worship the ground on which you walk! Have you thought about electric-shock treatment? I believe that works sometimes."

But Cynthia paid no attention, rather she stared into space, her eyes becoming moist as she began to tell her silent audience all about George. Only when she mentioned that he drove a great big lorry, did one of the girls interrupt.

"I would really like to meet your dad," she said. "At school, the careers officer told me that girls did not do lorry driving…I hate my office job. I want to go all over Europe, and get paid for it."

"If you were like my superdad," said Cynthia, "you'd buy your own tractor cab. That way you earn a squillion quid an hour for taking other people's trailers here and there…and yes, I'm sure he would tell you about it."

Victoria stared into space. If George earned a squillion quid an hour, why did he live in a garden shed…overlooking the river…with a log fire…and a clean duvet on the bed?

The following day, Victoria and Cynthia walked into the bank, where Anna had opened an account for them, apparently depositing £100. While in the queue, a man waved at them from the other side of the glass. He seemed to be pointing to a door at the far end of the counter. A minute later, it opened, and the man signalled for them to step into the small private room. Victoria wanted to run; it was a trap, it was nonsense to believe the girls had opened an account on a Sunday. But Cynthia led the way and, once in the small office, sat down.

"We need to be going," hissed Victoria from the doorway.

Cynthia pulled her inside, and shut the door. "Mr Bank Manager," she said, "I hope we are to leave with our shirts?"

The man laughed. "Of course," he said, "but there is something I don't understand. How could the orphanage not know Victoria left?"

Matron had never seen this man before; this could only be one of those mad setups. Cynthia took a more pragmatic approach, and studied his hands. There was just a flicker of pink nail polish on his thumb.

"Like I was telling the girls yesterday," she said, "the orphanage couldn't know Victoria left, because I didn't tell

474

them. Only when Mother Superior arrived, with her fearsome regiment of nuns, all swishing their canes, did it become an issue."

The man smiled. "So the question becomes," he said, "what have they done with Victoria's wage packets?"

"Didn't think about that," said Cynthia. "Wages are something grown-ups get."

Victoria became aware that both the strange man and Cynthia were looking at her.

"Oh," she said, "I haven't seen a wage packet for years, I'm paid by direct credit."

Cynthia turned to the man. "So this explains why the nuns were desperate to learn when Victoria had left," she said. "So what happens now?"

"As far as the orphanage is concerned," he replied, "it might be wise if Victoria disappeared." He waved a hand at the wall, the other side of which were the tills. "If you closed your old account…" he added. "Just a suggestion."

Once out on the pavement, Victoria looked back into the bank.

"Who was he?" she whispered. "Has he escaped from somewhere?"

"You know him better as Twiglet," said Cynthia. "But stop dawdling, which bank do we go to?"

Eventually, Cynthia managed to get Victoria to focus on the practical things in life, which meant recovering her identification documents from the tent. After a bus ride, they both stood in the lay-by where Victoria had once lived.

"You wait here," she said, "I'll go into the woods alone."

But Cynthia followed anyway. In a little clearing, Victoria looked down on the small tent. For the first time, she admitted that she had been through a nervous breakdown and, now the depression was lifting, had no idea how she had ever stayed here. She watched in horror as Cynthia crawled inside the tent to recover her bag.

"I am so ashamed," said Victoria.

"Why?" asked Cynthia.

Victoria pointed to the cheap tent, now sagging in the middle.

"No shame in being poor," said Cynthia, "though I have no idea why you did not go to stay in George's chalet. It's OK, Becky's told him you're a lesbian, so he understands why you jumped over the table."

"What!"

But Cynthia was already walking back down the path.

"Bank…" she called back.

For the remainder of the morning, Victoria got the impression she was being taken places to make certain things happen, but had no understanding why it might be so. When she asked Cynthia to explain, all the girl said was, "I have adapted."

At 2pm, for the second time that day, Victoria found herself leaving the bank where the strange man lived. Somehow, she now had £300 in her account, while Cynthia had a student account with a £200 credit balance. In her shoulder bag was a further £200 in crisp £10 notes.

"Now what?" asked Victoria.

Cynthia shrugged. "In old money," she said, "you are worth 50,000 chocolate bars! I cannot imagine such a fortune. Perhaps a cup of coffee in that posh place over the road might help me adapt further?"

On returning home, they found Doctor Kirsty having an

improvised meal in the kitchen with the girls. It was probably a social occasion, because she was wearing her camouflage suit.

"The lady at the church!" gasped Cynthia.

"And what fun that was, haven't laughed so much for months. But your friends asked me to look at your hands."

"They're fine," said Cynthia. "At my age, the tendons will mend themselves."

But the lady came over to inspect them anyway. Cynthia passed the time looking at the camouflage suit. She never felt comfortable wearing the ultra-sissy clothes the girls had given her, but could imagine herself walking down the street in that. They were the sort of clothes that said 'don't mess with me' – young, but grown up at the same time. Her feminine side could come from the pink and yellow trainers that Victoria had bought her after the coffee. Kirsty's black leather combat boots looked a bit too lesbian – certainly if she was living in this household.

Two weeks later, Anna came home from work to tell Victoria that it was all sorted.

"Nurse Rosie, at the hospital, has managed to find your old records," she continued. "Your two years as a student nurse has been reactivated. A ward sister will take you on as an auxiliary and, if all goes well, you can start third-year college in September. You've got an interview at 10am tomorrow. Doctor Kirsty has given you a reference, so they won't be contacting the orphanage."

Victoria felt a moment of terror at the thought of going to work in a hospital, with all those important people, and eighteen-year-old student nurses following doctors around, hanging on their every word as if they were God. She had been like that once – the bastard! It was with some relief that she realised the girls were playing a practical joke; hospitals loved form-filling procedures.

"It doesn't work like that," she said. "You have to go through personnel."

"Oh, I expect you'll be on bedpan duties for a little while," said Anna, "but as soon as you've proved yourself, Rosie will make sure you're fast-tracked to where you belong. It's OK, you'll be fine, she's one of us."

Later that evening, Cynthia came home smiling from ear to ear. "Best day ever," she said. "Thanks for the introduction. Rosie took me to the premature baby unit. It's so…emotional. Me, who would have thought it?"

Victoria looked up from the *Nursing Times* she had rushed out to buy.

"Then," continued Cynthia, "she introduced me to Doctor Thomas. He's an absolute dreamboat!"

"No!" screamed Victoria. "You mustn't, you don't know what they are like."

"Victoria, sit down," said Anna. "Cynthia's disability is quite incurable, she'll just have to cope with it the best she can. Though perhaps, Cynthia, you should not call men 'dreamboats' in front of your mother."

"But to a peculiar person like myself," said Cynthia, "that's what Doctor Thomas is. He let me watch a colostomy operation."

"That, I do not believe," said Victoria.

"But medical students watch operations all the time," said Cynthia, "and the patient was already comatose level three. Made no difference to him if the United Nations were watching."

"But you are not a medical student," said Victoria.

"Yes I am," said Cynthia, "I'm taking 'O' level Human Biology and was already robed up when Doctor Thomas met me and Rosie coming out of the baby unit. I was not going to let a chance like that walk by. Wearing my cap and mask, my alluring eyes did not betray my age, merely conveyed that he was an absolute…I expect Rosie's quite a 'dreamboat' too!"

The two girls howled with laughter.

"She's much too mumsy for that," said Janet.

"Doctor Thomas likes her," said Cynthia. "I could see it in his eyes."

"Everybody likes her," said Janet, "but I expect he was thinking more about her home baking that she brings in for the patients. Nobody wants to die, if there's a chance of another cream horn next Friday."

Cynthia grinned. "I was just eating one in Rosie's little alcove, when Doctor Thomas came to see a patient," she said. "It made him laugh. He reckons students fall into two categories: those who pass out on seeing a colostomy, those who manage to stay upright, and there's me – just me – who comes back to eat a cream horn! He reckons I will make an excellent surgeon when I leave university. Then he coughed, and walked away laughing to himself. Of course, I followed, asking questions, and since I would not leave his side, he ended up buying me supper…"

"No," screamed Victoria, "I forbid it!"

Cynthia waved the objection aside. "Relax," she said, "I was on a table with three other consultants, and I was still wearing my gown. There were a hundred eyes upon us, all wondering who the new surgeon might be, and I will not disappoint them, even though it will be four years before I actually hold a scalpel."

"You cannot be a surgeon when you are eighteen," said Victoria.

Cynthia recovered *Gray's Anatomy* from her rucksack, then slouched across the sofa to read it.

"Wanna bet," she mumbled.

*

Lower-ranked nurses were expected to muck in, and nobody noticed Victoria was restricted to the most menial of duties. And all the time, Rosie seemed to be watching her. At the start of the second week, the terrifying woman approached.

"You're doing OK," she said. "Stop being so nervous. From tomorrow, you can start doing blood pressure and saturation tests."

"Really?" said Victoria, more pleased that Rosie had not been thinking lesbian thoughts. Then she realised the impossible had happened: her career would soon be at the point where it had been abandoned all those years ago.

With money in the bank, Victoria decided the time had come to get some transport, so caught a bus to the garage, where Janet had said her faithful Morris Minor was parked on the forecourt. It proved to be a run-down place with a large caravan for an office. The garage owner came across.

"Two nice lady owners, that," he said.

"I know," she replied, "I was one of them, and I bought it from the vicar's wife a long time back."

"That's not possible, the lady I bought it from...well, she wasn't like you."

"You mean she was living in it. That was me, and thank

you very much for the £50 you gave me to buy a tent, it probably saved my life. Anyway, I would like my car back now, please."

The man looked at her awkwardly. "It's £495," he said.

"Like the sign in the windscreen says," said Victoria. "But I don't like the new number plates – too plastic, I prefer the old metal ones. Besides, VIC 8 sort of spells my name…I remember the vicar's wife thought it quite amusing."

The man gulped. "Given your disposition," he said, "I have something rather special around the back."

Victoria followed him around the building to find herself looking at a large van with side windows. Inside were two narrow beds, a little sink, gas stove, and what might possibly be a large cupboard or shower cubical.

"It's not really for sale," said the man. "The 1950s Dormobile's going up in value all the time – two grand now, ten grand by the end of the century, I reckon."

"I haven't got £2,000," said Matron, "and I rather like the Morris Minor. We have been together since I was a student nurse."

She looked at the man, to discover he had become very shifty. There was something he wasn't telling her. Of course, the van was pointing towards the workshop; there was something wrong with it. Something like this needed a confident man, who knew about mechanical things."

"When my boyfriend comes…" she began.

The word 'boyfriend' had made the man step back, and she did not want to let it rest. Then she realised how it must look to him, a lady living in her car; her boyfriend was likely to be a wild outlaw with a sawn-off shotgun.

"…Out of prison," she added. "He gets parole next week.

481

He would have to check everything over, and it's probably best if you're not here…"

Victoria had no idea where that statement had come from. It was almost as if she had learned Cynthia's technique for getting things done.

"Prison!" gasped the man. "What for?"

"Only armed robbery…but what's he going to find when he looks over the Dormobile? I am curious, that is all."

"It's a bit difficult to find top gear sometimes," he said.

"Is that the one that makes it go downhill?"

"Yes."

"Then I would be conning you. I have never used the downhill gear in my life, makes it go much too fast! But, as it happens, I was just testing, I much prefer my Morris. Get the old number plates screwed back on, and I'll be here tomorrow with the cash."

The man began shifting his feet. "Go on then," he said, "you twisted my arm, you can have the Dormobile for a thousand."

Victoria pondered her situation; both her home and job were subject to a conspiracy of lesbians. Her life could so easily go wrong. How different things would have been, if she had left the orphanage driving a Dormobile. No, those problems were caused by her nervous breakdown; the Morris Minor was just a victim of her misfortune.

The man rested his arm against the Dormobile, and leaned against it, as if to show how solid it was.

"Thing is," said the man, "you can live in something like this, if your boyfriend ever gets violent."

"George could never get violent!"

Victoria threw her hand to her mouth. What had made her say that? Then the awful truth dawned in her: her mind had subconsciously mixed up the words 'boyfriend' and 'George'.

"...Except, of course," she continued, "to protect me. That's why he shot the burglar. Couldn't claim self-defence because the intruder was trying to climb out of the window, when both barrels went into his pants. It's why I was living in the car. The police wanted to ask me about the incident. But now my boyfriend's coming out, we can drive to Spain in my Morris Minor. Nobody thinks you might be a drug dealer, if you drive one of those."

The man clearly thought she was insane, and her boyfriend a general menace to society.

"Go on," he said, "make me a silly offer for the Dormobile."

But Victoria was so pleased by her 'Cynthia moment' that she decided to quit while ahead. All she wanted was her Morris Minor back. She took a £20 note from her purse.

"Well," she said, "you did ask for a silly offer...now kindly screw the proper number plates onto my car and I'll..."

Her voice trailed off. The man had taken the £20 from her fingers, and was walking to his shabby office. When she joined him, he handed her some keys.

"To the Dormobile," he said. "I just want you to sign that I have bought your Morris, VIC 8, for £2,000. It's for tax purposes. The Dormobile's £1,980, sold as seen. Finish. You have robbed me blind!"

Later, Victoria stood on the car park beneath the flats, to stare at what she had bought. How had it happened? She had behaved exactly like Cynthia, even got the salesman stepping backwards in terror. And yet, here she was looking at a Dormobile, painted orange with psychedelic yellow blobs – obviously using household gloss! It was clearly worth less than her immaculate Morris Minor. It was no good, she would have to take it back, admit she had made a mistake, and beg forgiveness. All she wanted was her old Morris Minor, how difficult could that be? Then her thoughts were distracted by two visiting lesbians running across the car park, one of whom looked through the windows to observe the beds.

"Are we all going to a pop festival?" she asked.

"No," said the other lesbian, "I see a quiet field somewhere, with the scent of wild flowers drifting through a slightly open window, and Victoria waking up in my arms all safe and warm."

*

And Victoria knew the salesman had been right, this did better suit her circumstances. It was an escape capsule that could be left on the car park at all times, pointing towards the exit, with a tank full of petrol, and all the necessary survival provisions.

FOURTEEN

It was late Summer, and Beryl was returning from college, thinking about food. For lunch, the orphanage had provided her with a solitary cheese sandwich, dusted with a slight trace of green mould, and now, as the bus bounced its way around the narrow lanes, it was fermenting inside her tummy. Then she thought about the evening meal, which was always boiled potatoes, congealed gravy, and something that looked vaguely like cabbage.

On stepping from the bus, her mind turned to the two-mile trudge down the lane to the isolated prison camp, where her various misfortunes were based. After the nice Miss Tucker had left in floods of tears, she had been asked to take over as the History mistress. Why? At the time she did not even have an 'O' level to her name. She only accepted because the girls had begged her not to leave, for, if she did, another fearsome nun was sure to arrive.

When Beryl walked around the corner of the blacksmith's forge, she discovered a woman, sitting against the wall with her legs across the lane. A ridiculous amount of red hair tumbled over her army uniform which seemed several sizes too big. Beryl realised the woman's desire to terrify pedestrians must be something to do with wanting money, using her legs as a toll gate to stop anyone getting past until a suitable fee was paid. This caused Beryl a problem, since the home did not like money, believing it to be the root of all evil. All she had in her bag was college books and a used bus ticket.

"Excuse me," said the woman, "I was wondering if this is the way to the girls' home?"

Beryl thought the woman might have abandoned a baby at the orphanage, presumably being too drunk to remember exactly where it was. However, the home believed all babies found outside the gates had been given to them by God, so could never be returned to their original owner. Beryl, unable to tell lies, thought the best thing to do was walk backwards, then find a place to hide. But the woman seemed determined to spread her terror throughout the universe. She jumped up, then circled around to prevent the escape.

"You live around these parts?" she asked.

"Erm..."

Then the lady lifted up her red hair, and removed the sunglasses.

"Hi," she said, "just testing. If you don't recognise me, the nuns never will!"

After a moment to recover, Beryl leapt forward to do that hugging stuff, but Cynthia defended herself by holding out a box of Belgian chocolates.

"Happy Birthday," she said. "They're from Becky. Don't know why, it's just her thing. She said they will blow your socks off!"

Beryl stared at the expensive-looking box.

"I thought Becky was in Italy," she said.

"Working the Harwich–Zeebrugge route for the Summer. These chocolates came from a little shop in Belgium. But come, let us walk."

Cynthia returned the wig and sunglasses to their previous location, then walked briskly down the lane. Beryl gave pursuit; Cynthia was still holding the chocolates. On reaching the boys' home, Cynthia slowed to a more normal pace.

"You wait here," she said. "I'm going ahead to see if the coast is clear."

Beryl watched Cynthia walk away, throwing a casual glance towards the gates of the girls' home as she passed. On reaching the depths of Bad Man Lane, she stopped, turned, then gestured for Beryl to follow.

Beryl thought about the snakes, the boiled potatoes and cabbage for tea, and finally, the chocolates. After a few minutes, she bravely joined Cynthia further down the lane.

"Where are we going," she asked, "and why are you still holding the chocolates?"

But Cynthia did not seem to hear, and walked further into the depths of snake valley. Beryl now thought it safer to follow than to be abandoned.

On reaching the bottom of the lane, Cynthia opened the box of chocolates, and handed one to Beryl. She then jumped over a stile, and walked along the sort of path only a circus performer would use.

Beryl looked at the disappointingly small chocolate in her hand, then at Cynthia, who, having reached the start of the boys' hillside, had turned around to wave.

"How do I get over there?" called Beryl.

"Eat the chocolate!" Cynthia shouted back.

Beryl thought Cynthia was not making much sense, but ate the chocolate anyway. She ended the experience with a long, mournful moan for the chocolate, now dissolving in her tummy.

From the far side of the path, Cynthia shook the box of chocolates, as if calling chickens with a bucket of corn. Beryl thought the sheer drop into the quarry no longer looked quite so severe. Shaking with terror, she arrived where Cynthia was standing.

"G'me, g'me," she said, "I need stabilising!"

After the box was half gone, Cynthia returned it to her rucksack.

"My present," gasped Beryl. "They belong to me!"

"All in good time," said Cynthia. "Now follow."

Beryl did as she was told: the God of Chocolates was ahead.

Eventually, the lakeside walk came to an end near the beginning of the dam. To the left of this, woodland rose up the hillside to the boys' fence. Cynthia got down on all fours to push her way through a little gap in the vegetation, standing up in a secluded clearing after a couple of feet. When Beryl arrived, slightly cross at getting her knees dirty, Cynthia removed her rucksack, and fished about inside.

"Here's a birthday card for you," she said. "There's more writing inside, using invisible ink. Hold it over a flame, and you will get the telephone number of my flat, plus details of a special taxi company given to helping damsels in distress... but, I really need you on the inside."

Cynthia then recovered a walkie-talkie and gave it to Beryl.

"To contact me," she said, "press this button here, and say 'C', nothing else. Remember, anybody with a walkie-talkie can hear you, and I've got no idea what the birdwatchers get up to. For this reason, I will contact you by saying 'B'; the hippopotamus snoggers are to be called HS..."

"Hippopotamus snoggers?" interrupted Beryl.

"The collective noun for the nuns. It identifies them as a common enemy, who are so ugly, only another hippopotamus would consider giving them a snog. However, on the radio, always use the term HS, because anyone who has seen them will know who we are talking about. If you wish to identify Mother Superior, refer to her as 'the commandant'. Set up your command centre in the attic. The radio reception will be better, and there is plenty of room to spread out all the maps, which I shall give you nearer the time. The radio will reach me in the boys' home, but not much further."

"But you're a girl!"

"So everybody keeps telling me. Now stay here and don't follow."

Beryl knew the path could go nowhere, so understood Cynthia had become shy about 'spending a penny'. Suddenly, she leapt back with a scream. The thing in her hand had just said 'B'.

"I heard that scream from here," said the walkie-talkie. "Are there any birdwatchers rushing to see who is being raped?"

"No."

"Then we are alone. Follow the apples."

"What?"

"Return to radio silence."

Beryl wondered what to do, then decided that, since she was alone on the boys' hillside, her only option was to follow the chocolates. After fifty feet, she found an apple, and so it went on, descending into the V-shaped gorge that, she guessed, was somewhere beneath the dam. Then she almost jumped out of her skin as Cynthia dropped from a tree a few feet to her right.

"Well," she said, "you can obviously manage the apple signposts, but I could hear you a mile off. Learn to move as silently as the shadows. Most important of all, don't scream if I talk to you on the radio."

"But I don't understand what is happening," protested Beryl. "For instance, why am I standing by a stream, when the other side is like the Grand Canyon, only covered in brambles, and why are you giving me a pair of wellingtons?"

"Because we are civilised young ladies."

Cynthia seemed to think the statement was so obvious it needed no further explanation.

"I'd leave your shoes there," she said, pointing to a grassy bank, "also your college bag, just in case…"

Cynthia then took the radio she was holding, and walked up the shallow stream, without explaining what 'just in case' meant.

"I still don't understand what is happening," called Beryl.

Getting no reply, she put on the wellingtons, and reluctantly followed Cynthia to a place unknown, which turned out to be the bottom of a dam. Looking up, she saw that Cynthia was magically climbing up this. On reaching the huge pipes near the top, she crawled inside, then made herself comfortable, with her bottom on one side, feet against the other, the water passing beneath her legs.

Beryl looked at the rough stonework of the dam. It was inclined at about forty-five degrees and, since she was standing in the stream at the lowest point, it looked massively high.

"You are not expecting me to get up there?" called Beryl.

Cynthia recovered the half-box of chocolates from her rucksack.

"Keep to the main watercourse," she said. "The sides are covered with slippery algae."

When Beryl arrived at the pipe, Cynthia edged back to give her room.

"See how much I care about you," she said. "My bum has even warmed your sitting place!"

Beryl was pleased to be handed the entire box of chocolates. It could only mean there was nothing difficult left to do.

"I am putting you in charge of the escape committee," said Cynthia. "You are to appoint three generals, one from each dormitory. Can't do much for the babies, they'll make too much noise, but you need to start collecting their nappies for chemical warfare. Put them in a bin, or something. You will find some wartime gas masks in the attic…"

"Woah, slow down. First, I don't have the key to the gates, and they only let me out for college. The out-of-bounds fence now has coils of razor wire in front of it, so the only way to escape is by digging a tunnel."

"Exactly," said Cynthia. "When the time comes, it will be waiting for you. Those who dig it will leave a trail of apples to the entrance across the games field. Bit more complicated than today. A bite mark will indicate the direction to the next one. It will be a moonless night, and you cannot use torches."

"…Second, why would I want to bring the girls through an imaginary tunnel and into the woods, where we would surely die of starvation?"

"Don't know," said Cynthia. "You will have to explain it to me later."

Cynthia then crawled to the far end of the pipe.

"Coast is clear," she called back. "If you do this in daylight, make sure there's nobody on the boys' side who can see you. Anyway, don't dawdle."

Beryl reluctantly crawled through the pipe and, looking out, saw Cynthia step onto a big stone block nearby...then into the lake...on top of the lake. Looking down, Beryl realised there was a cobbled path about one foot below the surface, the angle of reflection keeping it hidden, except when viewed from above.

"It's the old packhorse route!" she gasped. "I was reading about it in the library."

"The girls do not want a history lesson," responded Cynthia, "they want miracles. Now, take off your coat, and carry it!"

Beryl thought getting her coat wet a minor inconvenience compared to her other troubles – being abandoned inside a wastepipe, with no sensible way of getting back down – and, all the time, Cynthia kept walking further away. Only when the splashing of her wellingtons faded into the distance, did Beryl feel able to rationalise her problems more precisely. It all came down to the fact that she was a History teacher, and not a member of an elite daredevil army unit!

When well inside the inlet on the girls' side, Cynthia stopped and turned around, apparently standing on water. She seemed confused to find herself alone. Then she pointed to her wellingtons, before making flappy movements with her hands, possibly to imitate the feet of a waggling duck.

Beryl stared down at the cobbled track that was just wide enough to take a packhorse. Then she looked back into the pipe, the circle of light at the far end representing the first of many ways to die. The only thing to do was follow Cynthia, who must have a secret plan to get back safely. She stepped onto the block, then into a world where no History teacher should ever have to go.

On reaching Cynthia, she grabbed her shoulder for support. "Is it deep," she gasped, "if I fall in?"

"Same depth as if you don't fall in, I should imagine," responded Cynthia. "But yes, if you miss the turn to the pipes, the causeway ends at some steps that go down to… well, I don't know exactly, but down is the only information you need. Trip head first down those, and you will die, unless you have been trained to take off a coat underwater. Mr Silver paid for me to go on a survival-at-sea course with Becky, and even I found it quite hard. The instructor had to drag me back up a couple of times before I got the hang of it, and that was without wearing wellingtons."

Beryl realised that ignoring anything Cynthia might say was extremely dangerous, so took off her coat, then followed her leader, until the cobbles disappeared beneath a sandy beach. Here, Cynthia dropped to all fours, and crawled through a low gap in the surrounding dense vegetation. Beryl realised that asking if she was expected to follow would be pointless. The only way out of this desperate situation was to keep by Cynthia's side until…? Maybe she would recover a rope ladder to get back down the dam.

After crawling through the tunnel, Beryl found herself able to stand in a little clearing. She realised another miracle had just taken place: she had arrived in a land that the rest of the world had forgotten without using a boat. Even more amazing, her socks were still dry.

"Tell me about the girls," asked Cynthia. "Are they still a well-disciplined bunch?"

"What…oh yes, it's like a military camp."

"Excellent. On the night, precision will be vital. The girls need to walk in a perfect straight line, like you just followed me, one hand on the shoulder of the girl in front. Only you will have the knowledge to lead them."

"Excuse me, I am their History teacher. I should be spending my days in the library or museums."

"Excellent cover, nobody will suspect a thing. Now, tell me about the hippopotamus snoggers, how many and where?"

"Er…the commandant, the secretary, Matron, her assistant, the caretaker, and the Geography teacher. They all try to out-do each other in being the most horrible."

"Horrible is good," said Cynthia. "It will make the girls more single-minded about escape."

Beryl shook her head. "Even if they escape, the social workers will bring them back. The hippopotamus snoggers would be all sweetness and light for the handover."

"Good," said Cynthia. "You understand the situation correctly. Our mistake before was not to consider how grown-ups see the world. Unless we can demonstrate discipline, getting rid of the hippopotamus snoggers is pointless. The nuns will simply get some more, or the social workers will scatter the girls far and wide to various foster homes. The girls must live in absolute terror of these facts. I need all 150 girls acting as a single military force, loyal to you. I am their leader-in-exile. It is for you to bring them to the 'promised land'. Now, this is most important: the enemy must never find out about the secret crossing, so you must keep this information confidential, even from the generals. When the time comes, we must have the hippopotamus snoggers running into the lane, and not scattering into the woods where we cannot predict their exact location."

Beryl looked a bit vague. "You keep saying something about 'when the time comes'?" she asked.

Cynthia nodded. "There are things we need to do first," she said. "Now, I'm just going to inspect the fence. I won't be back 'til well after dark, so I'll see you next week after college."

Then Cynthia disappeared between the trees.

"Hello?" called Beryl. "How do I get back? Hello?"

*

For the following week, Beryl was all topsy-turvy. She could not decide if she hated Cynthia for abandoning her in the woods, or liked her for bringing a different sort of terror into her life. Then there was the question of who she should hate; last week, on her return to the prison camp, the caretaker had been so furious at being disturbed from her caravan at nine o'clock, that she kept her locked between the two gates for half an hour. Was this Cynthia's fault? The humiliation of wetting herself had three possible culprits: the caretaker, Cynthia, and the snarling Alsatian that been allowed to prowl around the wire cage in which she was trapped.

By the time college came around again, Beryl found it completely impossible to concentrate on her studies. Even throughout her 'A' level History class, all she could think about was Cynthia and if she would be waiting by the blacksmith's shed. Secretly, a little devil inside told her that it was something she very much wanted to happen.

On leaving the college building, she was surprised to find a woman of about forty-five stepping into her path. She was wearing the same sort of outfit as Cynthia – except for the trainers. This lady was wearing great big army boots.

"Agent K," said the lady. "I am here to give you a lift."

Beryl had never been in a car, and had absolutely no intention of doing so now, especially with such a scary person.

"Ah," said the woman, "Cynthia said I might need to show you some identification."

The lady produced a box of Belgian chocolates from her rucksack.

"I am putting these on the back seat of the Austin Maxi over there," she said.

Eventually, Beryl found the courage to peer through the back window of the car. The chocolates were there, but sadly so was the woman, sitting in the driver's seat. Then Beryl decided that saving the half-hour wait for the bus would see her back to the prison camp early. This would please the caretaker, and the chocolates would mean she could miss the potatoes and cabbage for tea. She got into the car.

"How did you know it was me?" she asked as she set about demolishing the chocolates.

"You are quite easy to identify," said the woman.

Beryl was pleased to get the whole box of chocolates; it meant there was nothing dangerous left to do. She began to relax and, looking out of the window, felt the need to wave at people, like the Queen, who also went places in the back of a car. She decided Cynthia was nice, and hoped to find her waiting by the blacksmith's forge so she could tell her about all the incredibly brave things she had done to get back to the prison camp, after being abandoned the previous week.

On reaching the village, she told the woman where she lived, and warned her that Cynthia might be sitting with her legs across the lane around the corner. But the woman did not seem to hear, instead continuing along the main street.

"Back there," said Beryl. "I live two miles down the lane."

"Cynthia thinks you need to know something of the surrounding countryside," said the lady. "We are now following the lane around the back of the boys' home. Please remember as many of the landmarks as you can. It might be useful when the time comes."

"Why do people keep telling me about when the time comes?" asked Beryl.

"Because we do not know exactly when it will be. Notice that barn? It could easily hide 150 girls, if things go wrong. It is one mile from the village."

OK, thought Beryl, *I've got into a car, with a mad person, who is clearly on drugs.* The feeling of being trapped was so overwhelming, she hardly noticed the turn onto a dual carriageway. Then, after a mile or so, the car stopped in a lay-by, just before a concrete bridge. Here the frightening lady got out, and gestured for her to follow. Then the woman pointed up the hill.

"You can just see the dam," she said. "Beyond that is the lake you already know. The path to the right of the stream is well used by birdwatchers, and quite easy to follow. Don't think about going back the way we came, it's six miles to the village." The woman then got back in the car and drove off.

Beryl stared after the disappearing vehicle. She had been abandoned again. After taking five minutes to consider how much she hated Cynthia, Beryl crossed the dual carriageway, and began the long, slow plod into the high mountains.

Beryl was nearing a line of trees that came up from the river gorge, when something prodded her in the back. She jumped around, hoping whatever had attacked her would run away because of all the screaming she was doing.

"You are still not paying attention to what is going on around you," said Cynthia. "I've been close behind you for the last quarter mile."

After Beryl's recovery from the shock, came the complete astonishment at Cynthia's appearance. She was wearing a short pleated skirt, and a neat white blouse.

"You have a wardrobe?" she gasped.

"Of course, it's only this place that thinks a single coat hook is all a lady requires. This outfit is to impress old men of my respectability, but it only needs a little twirl to show my knickers!"

Cynthia recovered a walkie-talkie from her rucksack, and pressed a button.

"K," she said.

"C," came the reply. "B left 20.14."

"Out," said Cynthia.

Cynthia looked at her watch. "Twenty-eight minutes," she said. "Definitely room for improvement. Agent K ran the same route wearing full army kit in less than seven minutes. Now, if you can get to the command centre at four o'clock tomorrow afternoon, without arousing suspicion, call me. It's just to test the communications work, so keep words to a minimum, the batteries are too important for idle gossip."

She dropped the walkie-talkie in Beryl's bag, then rearranged the books on top.

"Sorry I couldn't give it to you before," she said. "Becky's only borrowed them from the shipping company, and would be in awful trouble if it got wet."

"If I fell in the lake, you mean, after you abandoned me in the woods."

"That sort of thing."

"I hate you!" said Beryl.

"You must never hate anyone," said Cynthia, "it makes you do irrational things. Like last week, when you were locked in the prison camp entrance. You did not think, 'I hate this person,' rather you decided to turn the situation to your advantage. The puddle of urine on the floor was complete genius. It actually made the caretaker laugh. You have put yourself completely beyond suspicion. And well done for not falling into the lake."

"I hate you even more now," said Beryl.

"Becky said much the same when she started her bravery lessons. It will pass. Come, let's see if I can show you how much progress has been made this side of the lake."

Beryl followed Cynthia through what turned out to be a narrow line of trees. On the far side, Cynthia stopped, to take a good look around. Finding the coast clear, she took hold of Beryl's arm and dragged her onwards.

"It's the boys' home," gasped Beryl. "We mustn't get too close."

Cynthia appeared to have gone deaf, for soon they were standing a few inches from the fence. Here, Cynthia gave a complicated whistle. The young boys playing football on the other side immediately abandoned their game.

"It's Miss Cynthia!" they cried, running across to look at her through the wires, like caged animals in the zoo.

"And this lady by my side is a very special agent," said

Cynthia, "so secret she does not even have a name. Just call her 'The One.'"

The boys looked at The One, then at Cynthia climbing the fence, jumping down from the top.

"And have you all been naughty boys?" she asked. "I do hope so."

They all tried to tell her of their adventures, which did not seem very naughty at all.

"Now," said Cynthia, "I've got a really good game lined up, but it's very secret, so you must promise not to breathe a word to the masters."

Just then, she noticed a boy of about twelve making his way sheepishly towards her. He clearly considered the hand behind his back was holding something really important and, for the time being, very secret.

The boy stopped just beyond touching distance, then turned to look at a group of boys loitering by the trees. Their hand signals seemed to give him some reassurance, because he turned back, and took the final step into a zone from where he could be captured. He then reached out and poked her on the shoulder. After withdrawing his hand, he looked at the finger that had done the poking, and gave it a good sniff.

"You're a girl," he said, apparently not quite certain of his facts.

"And you, I presume, are middle dormitory," said Cynthia. "Yet another piece of the jigsaw that needs to be sorted."

The boy was clearly confused, but presumably felt the time for retreat had passed, because he took his other hand from behind his back, to reveal it was holding a dead rat by the tail. Cynthia looked at the rat, then directly at the boy, who was trying to shake the animal to make it appear alive. She gave him a great big smile.

"Is it a present," she asked, "for me? Really, you like me that much?"

The boy gave a nervous twitch, as if about to run.

"And such a nice long tail," continued Cynthia. "The other girls will be so jealous. Tonight, as a dare, I shall sneak out of the dormitory and tie it to the door handle of the headmistress's study. Is that what you do with them, or do you drop them in the soup when the cook's got her back turned?"

The boy's expression changed to one of absolute panic. "Girls are frightened of mice!" he gasped.

"It's how the grown-ups expect us to behave. When Cook picks up the dead rat on her soup ladle, we all run away screaming. It is such fun!"

"Pretend," said the boy, "but you're sissy. All my friends say you play with dolls and like having your hair cut."

"Sissy!" she gasped. "One of your friends called me that? Who?"

"It's a well-known fact."

Before the boy knew what was happening, he found himself knocked flat on his back and, looking up, he saw that the girl had picked up the rat by the tail and was swinging it over his face. With each swing, it was getting just a little bit closer to his nose. He tried kicking his legs, but the girl had her horrible great knees poking into his shoulders, and there was no way he could escape from somebody so much older.

"Tell me," said the girl, "who would you rather kiss, me or the rat? Now think very carefully before you answer because you are going to be in so much trouble if you get it wrong."

Cynthia noticed her under-tens club were gazing down in great admiration. Behind, a circle of taller boys was starting to gather.

"Me or the rat?" said Cynthia. "Who ya going to kiss?"

The intermediate boys began to chant, "Do it to the rat!"

The whiskers were almost brushing the boy's face, and, cross-eyed with fear, he frantically tried to make his neck more flexible. Realising he was on the verge of crying, Cynthia took the chant to be his response also.

"Right answer," she said. "Kissing is so sissy!"

Aware that her audience now included senior boys, she looked directly at them, hoping her alluring eyes would make their minds travel to a place of which they had no understanding (confusion being a well-established military tactic). Then she noticed Morris standing by the trees. So the time had come – their first meeting – and only one of them could leave this field of battle with any self-respect.

Morris knew that after he had organised the beating-up of Scrag, his position had become invincible. Mr Tebbit had even invited him back to his room to show him a cat-o'-nine-tails. Then it had all gone wrong…

After Mr Cranmore had been attacked at church, he became officially weird, and was frequently seen talking to his flowers. More recently, things had improved a little. The new matron did not know what was going on, and was so feeble, he could piss through her open window to drench the papers on her desk. As for fighting, he was now only three weeks off his sixteenth birthday, so the fact Mr Tebbit was no longer there to protect him was less important. He could beat up who he wanted, truly a top dog in a world of smaller boys…

And now, without warning, he had come across this girl trying to take over his position. His whole reputation depended on beating her up, but how? One good smack in the mouth and she would be snivelling on the ground, or running to Matron, because she had lost a few teeth. Given all this, why had his cock turned into a broom handle, and why did he have a strong desire to drag her into the bushes to do the stuff he had read about in the English master's books? Well, perhaps later, first he would have to show her who was boss, and that tormenting the boys required his permission.

He rushed forwards, pushed her to the ground, and gave her a gentle kick. Then he picked up the rat, dropped it over the boy's face, and squashed it in with his shoe. Some of its guts slid down the boy's cheeks, though much of it went into his mouth.

"You're just a sissy girl," Morris said. "Now clear off and leave us boys to our fun."

Cynthia looked about the audience: the under tens were expecting her to do something magic; the intermediate boys seemed to be pleading with her to make it stop; and the older boys were looking up her skirt with great interest. Slowly, she stood up, then took off her jumper in a way that accidentally lifted her blouse.

Cynthia knew it would be the first time the boys had seen a real bra. She gave the older ones time to absorb the new information, which she knew would make Morris something of an irrelevance. Then she looked directly at Morris. His bulging eyes told her his brain had descended into his pants, which is where it needed to be. She threw her jumper to the crowd and raised her fists. This was only done in the way a magician uses sleight of hand, to divert attention from the real action. In this instance, Cynthia's mind was focused entirely on the judo lessons she had received from the captain. If the attacker rushed towards her at full speed, his own body weight would be enough to send him flying over her shoulder.

Morris looked at the girl in total bewilderment. Not ten seconds before, he had been staring at her knickers, trying to get their shape in order to imagine where his cock had to go. Then he had seen the breasts packed neatly into a black bra. Not being able to think of what to do, he stamped harder on the boy's face, sending bits of rat squirting out at the sides. That should show the girl how strong he was.

Cynthia responded by dropping her fists, undoing the bottom buttons of her blouse, then flapping the material over her tummy, as if she was overheating.

"Oh God," breathed Morris, his knees almost buckling due to his raging hormones. He frantically looked around for the nearest hole in the fence, through which she could be dragged. Then he had a better idea: this year, he had won every dick-measuring competition by at least half an inch, and now it was even bigger. He unbuttoned his trousers, pushed down his underpants, and thrust his entire, enormous manhood into the air.

Cynthia faked a laugh. "Sorry," she added, "but I've seen a bigger winkle on a hamster!"

Morris had never known such anger. He charged at the girl – a completely uncoordinated attack, with one fist ready to punch her face, the other hand going down to rip off her knickers. Then both hands decided they wanted to grab her breasts, all of this complicated by the fact that he needed to pull up his pants so his legs could work properly. Suddenly though, nothing seemed to make sense. Why was he looking at the sky, and what was causing this feeling of flying? Then his back hit the ground, sliding to a halt after a few feet. When he looked up, he saw the girl hovering above him. A moment later, her knees, and all her body weight, crashed into his rib cage. With this came more pain than he ever thought possible.

Cynthia knew that broken ribs would totally incapacitate a person, but also that a knee drop could kill a person by stopping the heart, or puncturing the lung. She stood up and looked down to make certain Morris was not coughing up blood or turning blue. Deciding he was not about to die, she went around kicking him. Politically, she needed tears; his old followers must see him cry. Soon, he was curled into a ball and howling like a baby.

"What a sissy cry baby you are," she said. "Not going to play with you anymore, it might be catching." She picked up his feet and dragged him to the trees. "Oh, stop whining," she moaned. "I'm using your winkle as a sledge runner. If I was pulling you from the other end, you might have something to cry about." On reaching the trees, she stopped. "You fell out of a tree," she said. "Just a suggestion to stop the police laughing at you for getting beaten up by a girl you were trying to rape!"

Cynthia looked at the audience who had followed, and now stood open-mouthed to watch. She turned Morris onto his back, thereby displaying his recent erectile dysfunction. Then she stood on his tummy.

"Right," she said, "who wants to be in my gang?"

*

Beryl had been clinging to the chain-link fence for support, first because of the dead rat, then because of all the blood…

and the other thing she had just seen. Now, she only saw Cynthia standing on the boy, in the pose of liberty, her blouse flapping in the breeze.

"If this is war…" Beryl breathed "…bring it on!"

*

The new matron thought she was finally getting the hang of looking after 150 boys. Their idea of hygiene was nil, and their tolerance of injury somewhat better than the adult patients she had dealt with as a volunteer for the St John Ambulance Brigade. And now, still in her early thirties, she had her own surgery, and everybody called her Matron, even though Mr Cranmore knew her only qualification was a basic first aid certificate. Of course, she only got the job because the pay wasn't very good, but they provided her with board and lodgings, and it was better than staying with her boyfriend, whom she had caught in bed with the slut from next door.

When the door to her surgery opened, she looked up, only to gasp with horror. There was a boy, but where his face should be was just a mass of blood and gore. Really, he should be dead, or perhaps he was a ghost come to haunt her for not telling Mr Cranmore she had a history of passing out, if things got too bad. Holding the boy's hand was a girl, and they both walked into her surgery, without explaining why she was there, or how the boy was still standing. Then came a mass of spectators, all crowding in, and making an awful noise. The girl put up her hand.

"Quiet, please!" she said.

Matron witnessed her first true miracle, because the boys immediately fell silent. But she was just on the verge of fainting, so could do nothing but remain in her chair, with her head between her knees.

"Ambulance," she mumbled, "we need an ambulance."

"Do not alarm yourself," said the girl. "He is a boy, he does not need such sissy things."

Matron came out of her blackness to find herself lying on something soft. She opened her eyes to find a mass of fuzzy faces all looking down at her with great interest. Then she noticed the back of the girl bending over a boy on the opposite bed. Matron closed her eyes; this must be a horrible nightmare, like she had sometimes, though generally she was in a war zone and unable to cope. Never before had a girl been involved. When she opened her eyes again, she saw the girl looking down on her.

"Are you feeling better?" asked the girl.

"No...who are you? Oh God, I'm going to get the sack!"

"Shh..." said the girl, "don't say such things, the boys like you."

"But the one with the missing face...I should have called an ambulance."

"So you said, but he is lying opposite, quite mended, so there was no need. You see, most of the blood and gore was a dead rat that Morris stamped into his face. The worst injury was where the rodent's teeth went through his cheek, but I have sterilised the wounds, and now the boy only awaits his antibiotics and tetanus injection, which I will give shortly."

A bandaged face on the other side of the room gave a slight whimper.

Matron sat up. "Morris did this to one of my boys?" she said. "I might be getting the sack, but I'll make sure that great oaf gets kicked out at the same time, if it's the last thing I do."

"Calm yourself," said the girl. "Morris is currently lying on the top playing field with three broken ribs. You only have to telephone for an ambulance, and he will be gone."

"How? I don't understand."

The girl put a finger to her lips. "In this place," she said, "there are some things it is better not to know."

With that, Cynthia went to the refrigerator to recover a phial of anti-tetanus serum. Drawing the fluid into a syringe, she tapped away the bubbles and gave a little squirt like she had seen Rosie do. She advanced on the boy.

"No...!" he began.

She put her finger across his lips. "We must not appear sissy," she said. She wiped his forearm with antiseptic and, a moment later, the deed was taking place. Dr Cynthia had landed.

*

Mr Cranmore sat in his office, blissfully unaware that the sounds of an ambulance were anything to do with him. Indeed, these days he was aware of very little besides the awful woman who had attacked him, with all the boys watching. On hearing a knock on the door, he looked up.

"Enter," he said.

"You're a girl!" he exclaimed, as if such a thing had never previously existed.

Cynthia paid no attention to this somewhat obvious statement, and went to look out of the window.

"Nice chrysanthemums," she said. "Whoever looks after them clearly has great wisdom."

"This is the boys' home," babbled Mr Cranmore.

"Exactly," said Cynthia. "Thank you for letting me live here. Over the lane has gone absolutely dreadful since the commandant took over. She is so rude, and the way she attacked you after she broke wind in church was unforgivable. You are such a sweet man."

"It was stink bombs in the vestry."

"So she claims, but why she can't just own up to her flatulence problem, I have no idea. Anyway you will be pleased to hear all my 'O' levels went well, and that I start my 'A' levels in September. So my success, dear sweet man, I owe entirely to you."

"You do?"

"Of course. I could never have gone to college without your support. Anyway, to say thank you, I have come to offer my services for the Summer, looking after the under tens, like I did last year."

"No, I'm sure that cannot be right."

"I understand, so if we meet in the corridor, you are still going to pretend not to see me?"

All of a sudden, Mr Cranmore's subconscious brain alerted him to the images of a dwarf matron in a white coat... No, this hallucination was different; it was casting a shadow on his carpet. What had just walked through his door was real.

"Go away," he spluttered. "You live over the lane!"

"What a very silly idea," replied Cynthia. "You run this place much better. But now I have a flat and officially go to college, do you still need to pretend I'm not here, helping Imogen with the under tens, like I did last year for Hilda?"

"No, that can't be right. It's your age, you see, female staff have to be over thirty."

"How very sensible."

Cynthia reached across to shake his hand, then bent down to kiss his forehead. "Thank you again for everything," she said, heading for the door. She turned. "Oh," she said, "under your rules, I am now also the number one prefect, 'cause I just beat up Morris. See you next week!" Then she was gone.

For a few moments, Mr Cranmore stared into space. Then he leapt from his chair. The governors must never find out he had let a girl live in the boys' home; they would think he was going senile. He raced to the door, only to see a long column of boys marching along the veranda, following the girl, as if she was the Pied Piper.

Ever since the new English master had arrived with his inappropriate books, the under tens had been suffering silly ideas about needing a mother. What senior dormitory got to read, he had no idea, but it had obviously caused some sort of collective mental breakdown. But middle dormitory, they would surely find girls embarrassing? However, the line of boys following the girl had no gaps in the height range; she had taken control of their minds, and in all probability was now leading them to a spaceship parked on the top playing field.

*

The following week, Beryl was walking down the lane with watery eyes. Cynthia had not been waiting for her near the blacksmith's forge, like she had hoped. Why had she been so horrible to her last week? "I hate you even more now," she had said.

Suddenly, boys began falling from the tree branches overhanging the lane. Like a well-trained unit of paratroopers, they quickly regrouped to form a circular wall, three deep, with herself trapped in the middle. A moment later, Cynthia's upside-down face appeared, her knees presumably hooked over a branch.

"Good," said Cynthia. "You are now acting together as one very efficient army unit. Your next task is to escort The One to the top playing field, then back to Matron's bunker, completely unseen. She will pretend she doesn't want to come, but it's all part of her amazing act to test how good you are on active service. There will be lemonade and cakes waiting for you in the prefab."

At that moment, purely on a temporary basis, Beryl hated Cynthia very much indeed.

FIFTEEN

The commandant was lying in bed, almost, but not quite, smiling. Beryl was surely the most successful History teacher of all time; the girls actually saluted her! As for Beryl's punishment regime, a girl caught talking in class was put on nappy-changing duty for a month, and sometimes she would punish the whole class by frogmarching them to the gym, and making them climb up and down the frames. But last Sunday had been spectacular. On the way to church, one of the girls had giggled, so she had made them all walk with one hand on the shoulder of the girl in front, herself rushing back and forth to flick their legs with a cane if they moved even slightly out of line. It seemed so right – the great march forwards, to praise the Lord, in a perfect straight line, allowing no deviation the Devil could exploit. All of this, yet the silly cow was still happy to work for her college fees, which meant her actual wage packet could be used for better things.

Presently, the commandant got out of bed to begin the highly skilled task of applying make-up in a way that spread the maximum amount of terror to those who saw her.

Suddenly, there was frantic banging on her door.

"Oh, disaster," wailed a voice from the other side. "Miss Hodson, please come quickly."

The girls could not work out why she was called Miss Hodson, most believing that her real name was Miss Frog Face, which better suited her appearance.

The commandant opened the door, to discover Miss Hooper standing in the passageway. She was one of the original mistresses, whose nervous personality made her panic at the slightest change to her daily routine.

"Something awful has happened," cried Miss Hooper. "It's the children...they have all turned into boys."

"What gibberish are you speaking," snarled the commandant.

"No, honestly, I have just gone to wake up senior dormitory, and the girls all threw back their blankets – except they weren't girls anymore, they are boys!"

Miss Hooper slumped to the floor and began to do breathing exercises.

"Show me your hallucination," snapped the commandant, "then, perhaps we will see about changing your medication."

The commandant grabbed Miss Hooper's collar and dragged her along the corridors towards the senior dormitory. Then she realised that coming the other way was a boy of about fifteen. Behind him trailed three others who were a bit younger.

"Good morning, Miss Hodson," they all said as they filed by. "Good morning, Miss Hooper," they added as they stepped over the body she was dragging.

The commandant was so confused by the encounter, that her only response was to stare in disbelief. Then she heard a terrible scream, followed by a thump. It seemed to have come from the ground floor, so she marched down the nearest stairs to see who had just been murdered. Outside the junior dormitory, she found Miss Jones slumped on the floor. The commandant stormed into the dormitory, only to stagger back, tripping over Miss Jones to crash-land on the floorboards. In a slight daze, she looked up to see a lot of horrible little boys all looking down, apparently studying photographs.

"Good morning, Miss Hodson and Miss Jones," they said presently.

Those who had been queuing up behind, all repeated the chant as they sneaked by.

Soon Miss Bevan came walking briskly towards them. She was a fearsome mistress, related to the commandant.

"Miss Hodson," she said, "what are you doing down there?"

"Boys," said the commandant, "hundreds of horrible boys!"

"Yes, it is the same for the middle dormitory. What have you done, and why didn't you warn us?"

The commandant sat up. "I haven't done anything," she said. "I only know what I have seen: all the girls have changed into boys!"

Cook and her assistant were waiting behind the serving table, and speculating on the various screams coming from the dormitories. They both hoped Miss Hodson had been murdered, but neither liked to say anything. Then Cook dropped the porridge ladle. A long column of boys was walking towards her.

"Good morning," said the lead boy. "May I have some of your finest porridge, please?" He had been learning his lines all week. "I hear it is so much nicer over here, so we are all very excited to try it."

"Well, bless my soul!" said Cook.

"I have been told you are a nice person," said the boy, "so if you would like to serve us, we will not cause you any bother."

Then Cook looked at her assistant, who was now sitting down and fanning herself. One of the boys left the ranks, and picked up the milk jug.

"Reporting for porridge duty," he said. "Perhaps we should start, the troops will not appreciate cold porridge."

"Does Miss Hodson know about this?" asked Cook.

"Of course," said the boy. "She has gone to have a little lie down on the floorboards."

*

At the boys' home, the masters had no idea of how to deal with so many girls, who had now congregated in the dining hall. The girls, meanwhile, knew exactly what they were doing: they were in a play, like the one they did at Christmas – only better! Finally, Mr Kent decided the time had come to restore order. He stood up and banged a spoon on the table. Immediately, three girls came running across.

"Oh, Mr Kent," screamed the first, "you are going to take us for our History lesson, we are so excited!"

"I am certainly not going to take you for a History lesson," he replied.

The girl let out a horrible high-pitched whine, which was quickly joined by the other two, both at a slightly different pitch so as to create the most horrible discord imaginable. Cynthia had been told that their choir practice had needed to take place in a cupboard, and, even then, the guard outside had requested cotton wool in her ears. Now, at full concert-performance volume, it made Mr Kent stagger backwards, clutching his ears to reduce the pain. A girl in camouflage uniform came running across.

"My dears," she shouted, "what on Earth is the matter?"

A girl, who was not part of the terrifying chorus, shouted across what had been said.

Cynthia got right up close to Mr Kent's ear. "How could you be so cruel!" she yelled.

But Mr Kent could stand the noise no longer, and ran to the exit.

"There, there," shouted Cynthia, "the horrible man has gone away now. Shall we find someone who likes you better? How about Mr Hill for Geography?"

The whine slowly died down. "But he might not like us either," said the lead actress.

"Oh, but I'm sure he does. Go and ask him nicely if he will take you for Geography."

"Really, do you think so?"

"Well, unless you ask, we will never know," replied Cynthia.

Three girls came running across and began to pull on Mr Hill's jacket. "Oh, please take us for Geography," they squealed.

In the next instant, Mr Hill found himself surrounded by thirty girls, all begging to be taught Geography. The fear that they all had lungs like the first three Wagnerian opera singers, made his legs buckle.

"I suppose I could," he said.

All the girls fell silent, but for one. "Can we have a double

Geography lesson?" she asked. "We have heard they are such fun."

Mr Hill had been teaching for ten years, and this was the first time he had ever been asked for a double lesson. Perhaps it was just boys who were not interested in the wider world.

"Do you like them that much," asked Cynthia, "to take them for double Geography? Of course you do. Now, girls, follow him quietly, and no talking in class. Now what do you say?"

"Thank you, Mr Hill," came the chorus.

Mr Brown came striding across. "There will be no Geography lesson," he said, "double or otherwise."

Cynthia stood on a chair to stare directly into his eyes, then began to hum in a way she had copied from Miss Vera. It made Mr Brown wish he had remained quietly in the background.

Cynthia detected his insecurity, and gave an almost imperceptible finger sign to Little Maisie, who stepped forward and pulled on his sleeve.

"Please, sir," she said, "would you tell us about Schrödinger's Wave Equation?"

Panic overwhelmed him. A little girl had asked a question he could not answer, and it seemed the whole world was watching. His heart began to beat faster and, all the time, the girl on the chair was staring at him without blinking.

A few weeks earlier, Cynthia had asked her college lecturer to tell her the hardest thing he knew, and he had replied that Schrödinger's Wave Equation was really only understood by a handful of professors. Now, she looked down at Maisie, ready to give it a practical application in the real world.

"You do realise, Schrödinger's Wave Equation is an

implicit function, concerning the distribution of quantum particles?" she said.

"What's that?"

"Perhaps Mr Brown could explain it better than me?" responded Cynthia.

Mr Brown felt the perspiration run down his forehead. He had once heard the phrase 'implicit function', but it was not something he had ever needed to teach, and now desperately he tried to recall some detail of it.

Cynthia, using Miss Vera's psychological analysis, was surprised to discover that Mr Brown had panicked at the mention of implicit functions. Were it not for this place, with its low educational expectations, there was no way he could ever be a Maths teacher. Cynthia had, under the Miss Vera principle of changing a situation to match a desired outcome, just a few minutes to remould his future into something more agreeable. She gave the hand signal that told the junior dormitory to unleash the full terror of pre-teenage girls. They surged forwards to hang from his jacket.

"Oh, please please tell us about Schrödinger's Wave Equation!" they squealed.

Imogen, that is to say Matron, was surprised to see that Cynthia's plans actually seemed to be working. It made her less nervous about using the new weapon Cynthia had given her. Apparently, it was supposed to lift and separate, but looking down, all she saw were two cones that made her go slightly cross-eyed. She advanced on Mr Brown from behind and rested her head on his shoulder. "Ohh…" she whispered in his ear.

Cynthia had said this was akin to launching a nuclear attack, but did not bother to explain why it might be so.

Mr Brown realised that any escape would involve reversing into an unknown woman, pushing away a teenager on a chair, or fighting his way sideways, through a crowd of teenyboppers. Then, slowly, he found himself floating into a different universe, one in which the mathematics were very strange. πr...πr...his brain repeated this many times, but it could not even cope with the basic formula for a cone. Then the events that had brought him to this place ten years before, started to fade from his memory...and with one, final hormonal surge, the geometry pushing into his back filled his mind with beautiful things.

Cynthia spoke in the style of Miss Vera. "The dark clouds have gone," she said. "Mr Brown is saved."

She looked down at the swarming crowd of teenyboppers.

"If I tell you all about Schrödinger's Wave Equation tonight," she said, "will you now go nicely with Mr Brown to learn your simultaneous equations?"

Mr Brown looked at the mathematical goddess who had saved him.

"The girls are going to take you to the Mathematics room," said Cynthia. "You will feel safe there."

Mr Brown found himself nodding, and was led away without resistance.

The English master came over. "I can't help thinking I got away lightly with dangling participles," he said. "Perhaps you can explain what is going on later, though for now, I expect you want me to take an English lesson?"

"Not necessarily," replied Cynthia. "Just be yourself, and let the girls see you as their male role model. But yes, take them somewhere safe where the hippopotamus snoggers can't get to them."

"I know just who you mean," he said. "Right, girls, follow me…!"

After the last girl had left, Cynthia turned to Mr Cranmore.

"That went better than I expected," she said. "Only two masters against. The odds on our side seem rather overwhelming."

"Except Mr Kent and Mr Smith have stormed out of the room to telephone the police, I expect."

"No," said Cynthia, "they have stormed out of the room to stare at your desk, where the telephone used to be. Next, they will go to the surgery, which is likewise devoid of a telephone. Then they will run up the lane to where a pretend broken-down van is blocking the way. This place is completely isolated from the rest of England until we have a satisfactory resolution. You understand our only enemies are the hippopotamus snoggers and, it seems, Mr Kent and Mr Smith."

Cynthia reached into her rucksack and pulled out a walkie-talkie. "Moses to Egypt base three," she said.

"Receiving," crackled the reply.

"Two masters AWOL," said Cynthia. "The rest have seen sense."

"That's better than you expected," said the radio. "The two masters are in the back of the van. We are just about to leave for the seaside."

*

At the girls' home, things were less complicated. Beryl had no problem in persuading the old mistresses to lock themselves in the library, where tea and biscuits were provided. Meanwhile, on the ground floor the hippopotamus snoggers regrouped, and, after surveying the dining room, advanced on the weakest specimen of boy to surround him.

"Boy," snapped the commandant, "who is your leader, and what is the meaning of this?"

The boy quivered in terror, but said nothing.

The commandant nodded to Matron, who grabbed his wrist and held his hand outwards. The boy tried to wriggle free, but the caretaker quickly reached out to hold his shoulders firm. The commandant swished her cane through the air.

"I will ask you one more time," she said. "Who is your leader, and what is going on in your evil little minds?"

The boy began to sniff back the tears. "I will never tell," he said.

"Oh, I think you will," said the commandant.

She nodded to the caretaker, who turned his hand to present the back of his fingers. The cane swished down with such force, it appeared to be a serious attempt to shatter bone. At the moment of impact, her eyes became blinded by a series of flashes. As the boy slumped to the floor, she looked around to discover the children were now passing two cameras towards the window.

"What is the meaning of this?" screeched the commandant.

A boy on the next table stood up. "The newspapers would not believe your brutality," he said, "so we got them pictures. Also, I have been asked to point out that this boy has not been formally given to your care. Caning him is therefore common assault. Our solicitor will be contacting you shortly."

"You're just a boy," screamed the commandant. "Boys do not have solicitors!"

"Our leader knows many important grown-ups," said the boy. Then he sat down, trembling with fear, but also overwhelmed by the knowledge that Cynthia was certain to like him better.

The commandant looked about the hall of evil, smug boys. She knew it was stupid, but the boy was right: she could not cane a child who had not formally been handed into her care. "Get the cameras!" she demanded.

But a boy had already climbed out of the window, and was running across the grounds.

"Well, after him!" shrieked the commandant. "He can't get out!"

The hippopotamus snoggers raced out of the door, only to discover the boy was already standing before the coils of razor wire that kept him ten feet back from the fence. A lady standing in the woods beyond was holding a fishing rod over the top, the cameras hanging from the hook. The catch was quickly recovered, allowing the lady to point a camera at the approaching warriors.

"You lay one hand on that boy," she said, "and I'll shoot."

"Who the hell are you?" screamed a hippopotamus snogger.

"My name is not important. The important thing is, that the fence you have used to imprison the girls cages you also. The cameras are over here, you are not."

The lady then spoke into the walkie-talkie. "Patrol sector eight, we have the film."

"Good," crackled a voice. "The girls have managed to take over the boys' home."

"Wahaa!" said the lady.

"They're there, aren't they?" replied the walkie-talkie.

"Affirmative."

"Damnation."

The boy on the roof gazed through the binoculars, then tried to give his report to Cynthia in a deep, manly voice. "They've taken the bait," he said.

*

The hippopotamus snoggers marched out of the gates, their noses twitching at the unpleasant smell drifting in the air.

"Fire!" came a cry.

Looking around to see where the shout had come from, they saw the terrifying sight of five 'space aliens' hiding in the trees. They had enormous eyes, and great big proboscises; then came five brown splodges, followed by a sharp stinging sensation in their eyes, caused by rotting ammonia.

"Fire at will!" came a cry.

The artillery had got their reloading time down to three seconds, and they had five sacks of ammunition to get rid of.

The commandant stared at her followers stumbling around, bumping into each other under a continuous bombardment of foul-smelling nappies that flew from the bushes. Then Matron's assistant fell into the ditch, her scream causing the others to panic, but the lane was becoming increasingly slippery, one doing the splits, to be hit by the others who were sliding on their backs.

Miss Hodson clutched her nose; the smell was unbearable. She took flight, running into the boys' home, gulping for air. The remaining five stumbled blindly back in the direction of their home. On reaching the inner gate, the caretaker fiddled with the lock.

"It's broken!" she screamed.

"Or," said a grown-up voice, "it could be a new lock, for which you need a different key, like the one in my hand."

The hippopotamus snoggers tried to squint through their blurred vision, and just about managed to make out a human form.

"You stink," it said. "Have you ever thought about taking a bath more than once a year?"

"Just open the lock, bitch!"

"Sorry," said the woman, "this way's closed. You will soon discover the outer gate is now also closed, and secured with a new padlock. I expect you now want to run about your cage, clawing at the bars, and generally being silly. When you've finished doing that, I shall be back to see you again, because there are some letters I want you to sign. But, whatever you do, don't kick over the shoe boxes lying on the ground. They contain thousands of flies, who all want to worship you. Though, if we need to speed things up, I have assistants to prod the boxes with sticks, and what fun that will be, bitch!"

*

At the boys' home, Cynthia's walkie-talkie crackled into life. "Chief HS on her way…all backup eliminated."

Mr Cranmore got confused with real war, and went to hide under a table. Then came the report that the commandant had tried to disrupt the Geography lesson, but Mr Hill was having none of it. To him, teaching double Geography was now a fundamental human right.

It was with a much-deflated ego that the commandant crashed into the dining hall. She stared at Cynthia.

"You!" she gasped. "I might have known you were behind this!"

"Behind what?"

"This…everything."

"You mean the girls finding sanctuary in this great place of learning because of your cruel and ruthless treatment?"

"I teach the girls respect, you know that."

"The photograph of you teaching a little boy respect came out very well. The newspapers will be very impressed by all your muscles!"

The commandant paced across the floor, stopping only when she realised Cynthia was making no sign of retreat. She looked down at Mr Cranmore, hiding beneath the table.

"And you," she rasped, "snivelling little toad, get your boys out of my home this instant!"

"Mr Cranmore is a real flower petal," said Cynthia. "He is my hero."

"Flower petal? Surely you are not going to let this slut speak to you like that! You know she's been working the streets?"

"But I ran away to college."

"Huh, we all know you wanted to wander in and out of the gates, so as to drop your knickers to the boys over here!"

Cynthia picked up five pieces of paper from the table, and handed them to the commandant.

"What are these?" she snapped.

"Photocopies of my 'O' level certificates. You will notice I got a grade A in Human Biology. I'm already registered for my 'A' levels."

"But you are fourteen," stammered the commandant.

"Thereabouts."

"Which means you are still in my care, and that is where you will remain for the next year!"

"How very silly of you. At midday my friends on the outside are going to start alerting the television companies as to what has happened here. Just another scandal at a children's home? I think not. The tunnel was quite a nice touch, don't you think? We could have cut the fence with bolt croppers much easier, but it didn't have the same 'pizazz' as girls tunnelling to safety."

Cynthia saw the uncontrolled rage in the commandant's piggy eyes. The consequent punch was uncoordinated and, being expected, quite easy to dodge. This coincided with a blinding flash, and the commandant turned to see a woman holding a fancy-looking camera. The woman gave a happy wave.

"*Daily Post*," she called. "Now can I have a photo of you kicking the nice gentleman underneath the table? I need to emphasise the raw brutality."

The commandant looked down at Mr Cranmore. "You are going along with this?" she snapped.

"Hippopotamus," he muttered.

"What?"

"You snog hippopotamuses."

"Have you lost all reason?"

"Then I bet you get down on all fours, and let them do it. 'Oh, more,' you scream, 'I promise not to take this sack off my head if you keep doing it!' Whoops, I've farted, like I did in church. Oh, what a stink!"

This was Mr Cranmore acting on his own initiative, and while Cynthia generally approved of his regression into childhood, she did not want unrehearsed scenes happening at such a crucial part of her play.

"Enough!" she said. "She knows it is over. There is nothing to be gained by tormenting her anymore."

"Ah, but I want to take her to the zoo, just to watch the hippopotamuses running away, when she tries to snog them."

The commandant stared at him. She had no idea how to deal with his madness. In fact, she no longer had any idea how to deal with Cynthia, or the 150 girls sitting in diverse classrooms. Getting them back over the lane on her own would be impossible. Anyway, the boys were over there, so it would mean 300 horrible children all meeting in the same place.

Cynthia saw the self-doubt in her eyes, and circled towards the exit. When standing at the door, she used the arm behind her back to signal to the special effects department waiting on the veranda. Well, it was meant to be entirely special effects, but one of the sisterhood owned a horse, so they did not need the coconuts. Cynthia opened her palm…

There was an almighty clap of thunder, and the wartime blackout shutters crashed down. The lighting engineer jiggled the fuses, before removing them completely, putting the room into near darkness. Then a horse came galloping along the veranda to stop outside the door. The rider landed on the boards with a solid clump of lead boots.

Cynthia had got the local amateur dramatics society to teach her how to speak deeply from the diaphragm, and though not entirely convincing, given the terror already generated by the special effects department, it would do. Also, the captain had taught her twelve assorted words in Welsh. She had no idea what they meant, or in which order they should go, but the combination of her skills had caused the audience to shiver, even though she had been rehearsing on the stage of the village hall, in broad daylight.

"*Llwyddiannus,*" said a dark voice from inside the girl, "*cyrhaeddiad imynyddig llfrgellydd.*"

Three plates, pulled by fishing lines, flew across the room to smash near the windows, which to anyone not realising they were in a play, would be quite terrifying – as demonstrated by the commandant, whose bladder decided to empty itself without bothering to consult her brain.

Cynthia rolled her eyes. "*Poblogaidd,*" she screamed, pointing a finger at the commandant's chest.

The commandant threw out her arms in the shape of a cross. "Be gone, Devil," she wailed. "Leave this child!"

The *Daily Post* reporter carefully placed her camera on the table, then, with a blood-curdling scream, fell to the floor.

"Now look what you've done," said Cynthia, in her best sweet, innocent voice. "My master has gone to live in whoever she is…was."

Mr Cranmore remained underneath the table, reflecting on the beautiful language of his childhood, and the general mystery of why the girl had said something about the public library. Then he realised what she was doing, and became mildly upset that his native tongue had been used for such a purpose. Fortunately, like most schoolmasters of his generation, he knew Latin, which he was fairly certain the ill-bred hippopotamus snogger did not.

"*Pro regina de olidus flatus,*" he proclaimed, "*tormentum ad ipse nusus. Ille odoratus inanis eclesia vos antiquus equus aqua.*"

The commandant spun around. For a moment, even Cynthia was confused. Having no idea what Mr Cranmore had just said, she needed to improvise.

"Oh, master," she said, "I understand your command,

and will obey!" She turned to the commandant. "My master wants me to prepare you for his entry," she said, "so please bend over and take down your knickers."

The commandant fell into a pit of unimaginable fear, as well as the pool of urine in which she was now kneeling. "I believe in the Lord!" she cried.

"So does my master, but that is no concern of yours. After my master claims you with anal sex, your place in his kingdom is guaranteed. But don't keep him waiting, because it makes him very cross, and you might find when the time comes, he simply prefers using your mouth as a toilet for all eternity!"

The commandant had gone through all the stages of a complete nervous breakdown in a matter of seconds. The girl, Mr Cranmore, and the Devil all seemed to be dancing around her. When a pen and paper appeared from the darkness, she offered no resistance.

"You are to write exactly what I say," said Cynthia. "Then I shall beg my master to pass you by, if it is what you wish."

"Yes…yes…anything…is he still here?"

Cynthia looked at Mr Cranmore. "Master?" she asked.

Feeling overwhelmingly powerful, Mr Cranmore crawled from his hiding place and advanced, mumbling to himself in Latin.

"Yes, master," said Cynthia, "but I can deliver you twenty virgins, none of whom have such a problem with flatulence. If you take her to your kingdom, you are risking a terrible explosion."

The commandant only had one thought: to get away from this place of evil without the Devil possessing her soul. If writing helped, then she would not question it.

"Memo to Matron," dictated Cynthia. "It has come to my attention that the Prince of Darkness has entered some of our girls. Why are you not making them use the carrots, as I instructed? I have slept with a carrot inserted down below for many years, and it has never done me any harm. Also, what is wrong with the purple hair dye I gave you? The other night, I was looking about the bath-house, and there was not a purple pubic hair to be seen anywhere. Have I not told you that the Prince of Darkness hates the colour purple? Yours faithfully, Miss Hodson."

Cynthia looked at the note.

"You do realise," she said, "that those who see my master are never believed, and usually get locked away in mental institutions. However, I have a little black box, and your letter will never see the light of day, so long as you and your relatives do what I say. Your time here is over, do you understand?"

Cynthia then gave her the letter that Anna had typed at work.

"This is your letter of resignation," said Cynthia, "asking Mr Cranmore to act on your behalf, until something can be sorted out. Please sign it."

Cynthia took the signed letter, then handed it to Mr Cranmore. "Congratulations," she said, "you are now in charge of both homes." Then she returned to the trembling commandant.

"If you ever think about a counter-attack," she said, "just remember what you have written about the purple dye, and prepare to be taken away by the men in white coats. You and your relatives have an hour and a half to be out of the county, do you understand?"

But the commandant did not reply; she was too busy running out of the door.

The *Daily Post* reporter sat up to give a round of applause. Mr Cranmore looked blankly at his letter. Now the excitement was over, he came back to Earth with a bump.

"I can't do it," he said, "I mean, control the girls."

"Oh, Beryl does all that sort of stuff, all you have to do is be a theoretical headmaster to keep the nuns happy, and, of course, pick up the extra wage packet. All the girls want in return is a disco once a month, and a game of football on Saturday mornings."

"Except for the reporter," said Mr Cranmore, "I do not think the nuns are going to be impressed when they read in the paper that I called Miss Hodson a hippopotamus snogger."

"Oh, I'm one of Cynthia's friends," said the pretend reporter, "and a member of the am-dram society. The photo was just for backup, if things went wrong."

"You are still forgetting about the masters who escaped," said Mr Cranmore. "They will return with the police."

"When they wake up tomorrow morning, they will be stowaways on a Panamanian-registered freighter! Now, aren't you glad you decided to be my friend? China's not a place I would like to go without a passport."

Inexplicably, Mr Cranmore sat down, placed his head on a table, and started to sob.

"Do not distress yourself," said Cynthia. "You let me live in this place of sensibility for two years, do you really think I would now let bad things happen to you?"

But Mr Cranmore was not sobbing for the future, rather for a time, forty years earlier, when his ex-girlfriend had dumped him after his bank balance had hit zero. Her parting words had controlled his brain ever since: "Your father is a much better shag anyway," she had said. What he had just witnessed was a similar level of deceit, only now used for good. If only, when young, he had fallen in love with somebody like the girl now standing in front of him, and not the lying cow he had met during the war, how different things would have been. Instead his life had been wasted, and was now almost over... crying for this did not make him weak, merely human. Having thought all this, he got up and shuffled from the room.

How long Mr Cranmore stood in his shabby room, to study the door, he could not say; it terrified him so much that his brain had turned itself off. That door represented a future he could not comprehend.

Eventually, his gaze turned the open suitcase lying on his bed. It was half empty, yet it contained everything he owned. He did not have any savings, and was sure what had happened today would forfeit his pension.

On hearing a knock on the door, he turned to discover the girl had already entered, and was now looking down at his suitcase.

"Going on holiday?" she asked.

"For me it is over," he replied.

"What nonsense. I have already explained that you are vital to our plans. Tell you what, how do you fancy changing your holiday to a big orange ship? Once onboard, the captain and...his girlfriend will find great pleasure in helping you adjust to your life."

Mr Cranmore thought the girl was trying to suppress a smile, but could not imagine why.

"You are grounded," she continued, "and to make certain,

I am now going to take the starting handle from your Jowett. You can take me down to the boat village this evening… presumably at about 30mph, so I'll bring a picnic, for a stop on the way."

Without any further explanation, she then took the suitcase from his bed, and walked out of the room, turning towards the lopsided stairs, down which she disappeared with all his worldly possessions.

*

Later that afternoon, Cynthia walked to the girls' home, then up to the library. After giving the prearranged secret knock, Beryl unlocked the door. Cynthia glanced at the terrified mistresses huddled in the corner. They had been at the home since its foundation in 1941, and no longer had any understanding of the outside world. As a result, they had been bullied mercilessly by the commandant, who had threatened to send them into exile if they did not do their exact bidding.

"It is over," said Cynthia. "The hippopotamus snoggers have gone!"

"And can we stay?" asked Miss Jones. "We will do anything…"

"…Anything," they all chorused. "We are so sorry about what happened on stage, looking the other way…"

"And was not Jesus nailed to a cross so that his followers might be saved?"

"Yes…yes!"

"There you go, then, do not concern yourself with the trivialities of life."

The three mistresses fell to their knees, and reached out to almost touch her.

"But," continued Cynthia, "you must understand that what happened here today never happened. After all, nothing illegal has taken place, with the possible exception of showering the hippopotamus snoggers with baby poo!"

The mistresses giggled, then clapped their hands in delight.

"Also," continued Cynthia, "you will be pleased to hear that there are to be no new appointments. Mr Cranmore has agreed to be the theoretical headmaster."

"A ma…man?"

"All the masters who proved themselves willing to adapt will be teaching the older girls, together with yourselves. The younger children will be taught by stay-overs."

Cynthia pointed to the ceiling. "Up there," she said, "is an attic. It will be turned into a dormitory for the college girls. The boys' Woodwork class will be here shortly to cut a hole in the ceiling, then drop down a rope ladder for access. It was made by the captain."

"Boys…captain…M…M…in the attic. What will become of us!"

They began to flap around like frightened chickens, at which point Cynthia led Beryl away from the library, then along the passages, to inspect the rooms abandoned by the commandant thirty minutes earlier. They were very 1940s and smelled awfully of stale perfume. It was also very hot, the antique gas fire having been left on. Cynthia turned it off, then threw open the heavy brown curtains to look across the grounds.

"These OK for you, Beryl?" asked Cynthia.

"What for?" responded Beryl.

"Your new apartment!"

Beryl laughed. "I've got a screen in the senior dormitory," she said.

"The spoils of war," said Cynthia, "and, given all the flapping in the library, the mistresses will be wanting you to deal with all the necessary 'man things' for some time to come."

*

The following week a luxurious motor car swept up the drive to park before the main entrance. A less salubrious vehicle came from behind to flank it, the driver, bodyguard, and two male secretaries spreading out in a defensive ring. Even so, it was with great anxiety that the nuns emerged from the Bentley; they still remembered the dark cloud of evil that had fallen on this place during the final days of Miss Buckley's reign. And now, Miss Hodson had inexplicably resigned. It was surely the Devil's work!

After crossing themselves, the nuns made their way to the entrance steps on which three girls were sitting.

"Oh, how delightful," said one of the girls, passing over her Wordsworth poetry book to another.

In the foyer, the nuns discovered a team of girls working the floor with huge mops. On seeing the visitors, they curtsied, then stepped aside to let them pass. Instead, the nuns merely stared in astonishment, until one of them asked what was happening.

The girls curtsied. "If you please, Mother," replied the lead actress, "the caretaker has left. We have been asked to do the cleaning, for which we get a whole apple – each!"

The mother superior looked at the path that had been cleared for them, then pointed to a side corridor. "I rather think we will go this way," she said.

Silently, wearing pumps, a girl scampered ahead, opening all relevant doors, and giving a hand signal. In one room, the Geography teacher stopped telling the girls about his travels around Somerset on a bicycle, to mark his twelfth birthday, and pointed to the blackboard.

"...Dolomitic Conglomerate," he was saying as the door opened.

All hands shot up.

"Yes, Lucy," he said.

She began a well-rehearsed speech, describing how Dolomitic Conglomerate was formed, only stopping when the nuns interrupted.

"Surely," said one, looking at the Geography teacher, "you are a man!"

"From the boys' home, yes, I have been told to teach the over tens at both homes. The younger children are taught by suitable fifth formers." He lowered his voice. "I believe," he said, "Miss Hodson went considerably over budget with the fencing, and it is necessary to make savings."

The nuns withdrew, and presently found Mr Cranmore in the office normally occupied by Beryl. He presented them with a report on joining the two homes under one administration, using stay-overs to teach the younger children, in return for college fees. Then, the proceedings were interrupted by a knock on the door.

"I beg your pardon," said the girl, "I did not know you had visitors. I shall just amend the tea trolley."

The nuns inwardly groaned. They knew this meant tea

made with lukewarm water from the urn, and possibly two digestive biscuits that had to be dunked to make them edible. Hence, they were very surprised when, two minutes later, a tea trolley was pushed in. In the middle was a pewter teapot, and to one side, five plates containing cream horns. The girl did her act of tea pouring – based on an etiquette book of the 1940s – then curtsied, and left. A few minutes later, all conversation had ceased, the nuns staring at the cream horns from which they had each taken one bite. Mr Cranmore happily munched away on his.

"The cookery class make them," he said. "The ingredients cost 2p, but it is cheaper than buying biscuits."

The nuns stared out of the window – an idyllic scene, with a mistress teaching the girls to play croquet, while an older child seemed to be doing 'caretaker things' with a white line marker.

The mother superior finished her cream horn, then turned to kneel before the statue in the little alcove.

"Dear Lord," she whispered, "thank you for sending us Mr Cranmore to show your children the path to righteousness…"

Mr Cranmore also closed his eyes, though not in prayer. He now realised that Cynthia's plan of asking for an additional half-pay to cover the girls' home was quite realistic. And, if his retirement was to be spent at the boat village, he did not need a great deal of money. Two years of saving was enough…just to keep Beryl's seat warm until she was ready to take over officially.

SIXTEEN

Victoria had been a State Registered Nurse for one week, and now sat in her favourite armchair with a rather strange look on her face. Rosie, squatting by her feet, was gazing upwards with dreamy eyes.

"Oh, I do love you," she breathed. "I think about you all the time."

Cynthia looked up from her book, then went into the bedroom. She returned, dragging her camp bed.

"I do like happy endings," she said. "There is nothing I need from my room, my college stuff is in the hall."

Rosie stood up, and came across. "You will make a wonderful daughter," she said.

"I accept, but don't you have to consummate the marriage first?"

Anna and Janet ran across to congratulate them. "Party!" they cried.

After all the fuss had died down, Rosie turned to find an empty armchair. Happily, she walked to the bedroom, but came out frowning.

"Victoria's not there," she said.

Soon, the girls had searched the flat, and stood shrugging their shoulders. Rosie began to cry, causing Cynthia to rush across to comfort her.

"I expect…" she said, "…I don't know, but I'm sure she'll be back."

*

Victoria entered the 'emergency escape capsule' and drove for two hours, after which she pulled into a lay-by. Here she remained sitting in the driver's seat with the engine running. The fear of the lesbians giving chase meant her escape time needed to be immediate.

After an hour or so, the terror faded to the extent that she felt able to get up and go into the back. Here, she went around fussing with the curtains, paranoid there might be a gap through which people could look. Only then did she turn off the engine, and think about making supper…

But it felt wrong: before, when she stayed in the van, Cynthia had been sleeping in the opposite bed. Such weekend excursions had felt safe, but on her own, it all seemed very different. Her car might have been dreadful, but at least it was inconspicuous. A camper van, with electric light shining across the lay-by, let the whole world know she was in residence.

As the night wore on, the outside noises took on sinister meanings. A car stopping might be the police; or the rustle of an animal, the footsteps of a man looking for opportunities. At other times, she tried to come to terms with the way Cynthia had betrayed her. Fancy accepting Rosie as her mother, as if it were normal!

As the first light entered the sky, Victoria got up to make breakfast with the emergency provisions. While eating her porridge, she decided that a camper van in a lay-by was best suited to people who had been specially trained to do mad things. Idly, she flipped through the road atlas to see where a sensible person might go. There would be caravan parks, then she remembered the household gloss paint in pink and yellow. It would be too embarrassing! Next, she thought about her bank balance. The wage for a student nurse was not designed for grown-ups and, after a few months living at the lesbian flat, she had felt obliged to offer something for rent, and Cynthia's upkeep. Her bank balance was effectively zero and, in any event, she could not use her chequebook because of Twiglet...

Twiglet, what sort of name is that? It had come as a great shock when Cynthia explained that the bank manager got excited by being one of the girls.

Nervously, Victoria peered into every pocket of her purse to collect £62.59. This was the total of her wealth, considerably less than when she had left the orphanage eighteen months earlier.

Then she noticed a page of the atlas had been marked with a large red cross. It caused a great shiver to run through her body. The cross was by the side of a river; it could only be the location of the boat village. She tried to put the thought from her mind, but could not. The camper van was essentially a boat on wheels. The quay had two sides, one of which was used to park boats; the other was land where vehicles could go. Could she not find shelter beneath the trees? Was it compulsory to be mad to live at the boat village, or could ordinary people do it too?

By midday, she realised she had no choice; it was the only secluded place that she could think of where she could park for free. *And*, she thought, *now I have my qualifications, I can get a job anywhere in the country*. She did not have to tell her employers she was a gypsy. With everything else the boat people could do, she was sure they had worked out how to have an address.

Victoria threw her head into her hands. To do all this she would have to face George, and apologise to the mad purple witch...but anything was better than living in a lay-by, where it would soon become known she was a woman on her own.

At three in the afternoon, Victoria found her way to the lane where the cross was marked on the map, but nothing was as she remembered. The woods that she thought might lead to the quay were an army firing range.

Presently, she parked the van on a bit of scrubby ground opposite the woods, and made her way to a solid timber gate surrounded by a brick arch, above which coils of razor wire had been fixed. Either side of the gate pillars was a hedge, which was much too thick to see through, but she felt certain it must be the back garden of a grand house. The gate, she noted, had a hole for a particularly large key, the sort you found on dungeon doors. Clearly, whoever lived there did not like visitors.

She returned to the van to make her supper. Perhaps she would spend the night here, and review her various misfortunes in the morning. Then, halfway through eating a piece of toast, she saw two well-dressed gentlemen emerge from the gate arch, and approach an expensive-looking car parked in front. They seemed slightly alarmed when, still clutching the toast, she jumped out to confront them.

"Excuse me," she said, "I am looking for the boat village, but it seems to have disappeared."

They looked at her strangely, then even more so at the van from which she had emerged.

"Not around here," said one of the men, rather snobbishly.

They were just getting into their car, when Victoria remembered something about a code.

"I'm Gwendoline," she shrieked.

The men gave her an odd sort of look, then one of them walked back to unlock the gate. Why? She did not want to visit their house. Nervously, she stepped through the arch to find the gate closed and locked behind her. She bent down to look through the keyhole, and saw the expensive car driving away. With great fear, she turned around to find herself on a woodland path. Saying she was Gwendoline had brought her to this predicament, which meant it must be something to do with Mr Silver.

After a minute, she began to walk into the deep, dark woods, the terror fading as things became lighter, with shafts of sunlight flickering between the trees on her left. It was in the direction of the army firing range, but curiousity forced her to part two interlocking branches, which revealed a clearing with a diverse collection of tree stumps. It seemed a recent development, because the air was scented with newly sawn timber, the ground a patchwork of leaf mould and sawdust. A Shetland pony looked up and plodded towards her.

"Hello, boy," she said as the animal nuzzled her pocket. Curiously, she looked underneath – "girl," she corrected, stroking her mane.

The pony seemed unable to believe that she had come to visit without having something edible in her pockets. Victoria sat on the nearest tree stump, the animal following to take gentle tugs at her clothes.

"Sorry," she said, "I have nothing for you."

Slowly, the rhythmic stroking of the animal allowed her to feel calm, and she looked up to see a long-haired white rabbit with floppy ears watching her from about ten feet away. It took a little hop forwards to sniff the air. Then, thinking better of it, it turned around, and hopped towards a hutch, into which it disappeared. Then another pony wandered from the trees near the lane, and, without fear, trotted across to search her pockets too. She began to tell the animal all her troubles, in particular about the pink and yellow van that was her home.

Victoria became aware of a clucking noise, causing her to get up and make a zigzag path between the tree stumps to a wire enclosure. Two eggs were clearly visible, and she wondered how one went about buying them, or perhaps, in paradise, they were provided by God? Then she noticed a small antique pony trap at the far end of the clearing, and went to investigate. It looked well cared for, the curly springs to the axle giving the appearance of being recently black enamelled, and the single seat newly varnished. A little brass plate told her it was made by coach builders in 1908.

A little to her left, she noticed a path through the trees, the deep ruts of tractor wheels not yet filled by leaf fall. She followed this for thirty paces, where she came across a loose stone track. Ahead, the vegetation rose chaotically to a high chain-link fence, obviously the boundary of the army firing range. Turning right, she walked around the first bend to find herself staring at the boat village, or at least an imitation of it. The shed on top of the sunken boat had gone. Where? How? The orange ship was back, and towered above the quay. Many other assorted boats had arrived, all of which looked rather posh. Looking towards the land, she decided it was perfectly wide enough to park a camper van. Also, if anywhere in England had a zero crime rate, this would be it.

Then she found herself frowning; surely the captain should be in the Mediterranean, or off Wales, or something? It was what he did – travelled the world. He had no right to come back here and confuse everybody. Also, there was something very strange about his ship. There was no ladder down the side, or even a Tarzan swing hanging from the trees. Instead, there was a solid boarding ramp with two handrails. She broke cover and went to stand below the ramp.

"Captain," she shouted, "I have come to say sorry."

There was no reply, so timidly she walked up the ramp. Looking into the hold, she could see the markings of a squash court. It looked as if the children played here, but surely Mandy and David were at school in Holyhead?

"Captain," she shouted again, "I have come to say sorry."

Looking about the ship, she realised that where the captain's hatch had once been there was now a little guardhouse, with a front door in the middle. This eventually opened…and Hilda looked out.

It caught Victoria off balance. Indeed, Hilda seemed mildly surprised.

"I have come to apologise," said Victoria, "to you and the captain, and whoever else might be here. In fact, everyone."

Hilda nodded. "In that case," she said, "you'd better come in."

Victoria went into the guardhouse, and was surprised to see a flight of stairs going down to the living room below.

"What happened to the ladder?" asked Victoria.

"It was either me or the ladders," replied Hilda, "he couldn't keep us both. Thankfully, my captain liked me better."

The two stood in silence for a few seconds, both searching for something to say.

"Well," said Hilda eventually, "I must say I find this very uncomfortable. I was brought up to the old ways, and find it difficult to change my ideas."

Victoria looked about the cabin; now it had stairs, it looked really cosy; the wood-burning stove all clean, and ready for the Winter. She gasped; ever since living in the tent, she had been having weird thoughts.

"But it's lovely," she said.

Hilda seemed quite taken aback by this. Victoria thought of the next thing to say, practising the exact words in her head.

"What happened to George's chalet?" she asked.

"Cynthia organised him, got him to demolish his home, and buy a narrowboat."

George…narrowboat," stammered Victoria. "I don't understand, surely they cost a fortune?"

"He had been living rent free in that shed of his for fifteen years, so I can't imagine money being an issue. He already owned the land, of course."

"Land, how can you own where a sunken boat is?"

"Whoever owns the bank, owns the riverbed to the middle."

"But surely he does not own the quay?"

"Bought ten feet back from the river front some years ago," said Hilda. "Cynthia turned up with her bank manager friend last year to organise the rest. She used the existing ten feet as a deposit to buy the woods, all the way to the lane. Recently she turned up with some lumberjack friends – weird lot, dressed as if they were going into the Canadian backwoods. Anyway, they took enough timber for George to pay back the mortgage. He rents the moorings to city types. More money than sense, if you ask me, but it's the solitude and security they like. Of course, he lets me and Vera stay for free."

Victoria sat down in a state of shock. The bit of land where she wanted to park her van was owned by George. Now, if she apologised, he would think it was because she was after his property empire. And if she could not find sanctuary here, where else could she go with only £60 in her purse?

"Cynthia never told me," she mumbled. "I was only vaguely aware she ever came here."

"You never seemed interested in the boat village. I suppose she did not want to upset you."

Victoria averted her eyes and so noticed a shelf, on which a long line of postcards was propped. Nearly all had exotic pictures facing outwards, but there were only a couple of landmarks she recognised. One was of the Statue of Liberty, the other of a ship passing through the Panama Canal.

"You have been on your travels," said Victoria. "I would be much too nervous to undertake such adventures, even though I imagine it would be quite safe with the captain."

"It would," said Hilda, "but why would we be sending postcards to ourselves? Those are from Becky."

"Surely she works for the Irish Ferries?"

"That girl never stands still, always taking some course or other, got loads of certificates in things I don't understand. When we knew we were coming back here, my captain found her a place on a cargo ship leaving for New York. He looks after people, my captain does."

Hilda passed a postcard across, and Victoria flipped it over to read the back.

To David – have now seen the Amazon Delta – you do not want to go there on a canoe, it's really big, and there's many alligators who would like to eat you for dinner.

To Mandy – I am the only girl on the ship, so I've got my own cabin on the officer's deck. Just about to cross the Pacific, but the mean lot won't stop-over in Hawaii for clothes shopping, so I guess the next postcard will be from Japan!

Love Becky.

Victoria tried to equate this Becky with the little girl she had seen growing up at the home, but couldn't. So many things had changed without her knowledge. And why should they tell her what was going on? From Becky's point of view, there were no bonds between them, other than assistant and matron. Victoria so wanted a daughter who would keep in touch, and send her postcards. But she supposed what the captain had done for Becky was far greater than what she had done for Cynthia. In fact, Cynthia had achieved everything by her own efforts, helped by Anna and Janet, who had kept a roof over her head. She was quite worthless when it came to helping people.

"I see Becky addresses her card to the children," she said. "How are they?"

"Quite grown up now. Their various schools around the Mediterranean helped a great deal, and my captain taught them everything there is to know about Geography and Mathematics. It was for them we came back. They needed a settled period in their lives."

"But surely you should be in Wales – the ferries where the captain works. Don't the children go to school there?"

"The ferry company thought seventy was a good age for my captain to retire. Not that it's stopped him gallivanting. He's circumnavigating Ireland on Mr Silver's yacht at the moment. As for our children, they got into the local grammar school, easily, if only by speaking to the principal in four languages, and explaining how to do three-dimensional trigonometry. It suits us, because Vera does the school run with her lot."

"I take it Social Services are OK?"

"They were OK with me, on account of being a matron. What worried us most was Mandy. She will keep telling everybody that she and David are nearly married! Leaving them sleeping together in the crew quarters on their own was asking for trouble, though I don't expect you would understand that, given your…"

Hilda gave the impression she was searching for words, to explain something. In the end, she merely said, "Huh."

"Anyway," she continued, "George decided to adopt David, leaving Mandy with us. That's why he had to demolish his shed. Can't imagine a social worker even going across that rope swing to look inside. However, we made sure he got the sort of boat they would like – central heating, and that sort of thing – so I'm sure the adoption will go ahead. I mean, what is there not to like about George? But of course you would not understand that, either."

Hilda's search for words was interrupted by the sound of footsteps walking along the deck. Barely recognisable versions of Mandy and David walked down the stairs. They greeted Hilda with a hug, then turned to Victoria, but it was obvious they did not know who she was.

"This is Matron," said Hilda, "you know, the one who helped you to run away."

The children frowned. Victoria imagined them thinking that they had run away by their own efforts, and the last time they had met, she had been trying to take them prisoner.

"It was a long time ago," said Mandy. "I really don't remember much about the time before I came here. And now you are my mum, so they can never make me go back to the bad things."

"And George is my dad," said David, "so I can't go back either."

"That's right," said Hilda. "She has just come to say hello."

"That's OK then," said Mandy.

Both she and David hung their matching school blazers on the wall-mounted coat hooks.

"I'm just going to feed the animals," said Mandy.

"Oh, can I come?" asked Victoria.

"They are frightened of people they don't know," said Mandy. "It's best if you don't."

Hilda stepped forwards, as if to protect them, then followed them up the stairs. At the top, she turned around to look back down.

"I'm sorry," she said, "I can accept Janet and Anna because they are honest about their feelings, but I have no idea what is going on in your mind. I would ask you not to approach our children, unless I am there."

With that she walked off.

Victoria turned to stare at the gas stove that David had once used to make egg sandwiches, just after all the madness had started. How she longed to return to that distant age of innocence – a time before everybody believed she was like Janet and Anna. And if she told the truth now, after living among the lesbians for so long, people would simply think she was telling lies, to make her life easier.

Victoria could not cope with the situation any longer. She ran up the stairs and down the ramp, to sprint along the vehicle track (where she had acquired her puncture many years before). But the gate that should have let her escape to the lane had barbed wire coiled over the top. She just knew the sign on the other side told her that she was standing in an army firing range. Parked down here, she would have been so safe, with George to watch over her.

How long she gazed over the gate she could not say, but eventually she heard the sounds of an approaching lorry. Just in time, she jumped back to hide in the undergrowth. Peeping out, she watched the massive tractor cab park behind her own camper van.

"George," she mumbled. "What on Earth am I to do?"

But it was not George who climbed down from the cab, it was one of the lesbians…Jackie, the one who was always talking about her desire to drive lorrries. And now, that same woman had walked across to the brightly painted van, and was trying to find a gap in the curtains so she could peep inside.

Victoria ran back down the track to hide in the undergrowth, from where she could observe all the boats. Soon Jackie emerged, and stopped by a narrowboat.

"Victoria," she called, "are you here?"

Of course, all the lesbians knew what her van looked like. She turned and ran, her clothes becoming torn, hair frazzled, arms covered in bramble scratches. Then she came to a clump of bushes and dived into them, to hide like a frightened animal.

After her breathing slowed, Victoria began a long commando crawl to circumnavigate the clearing. On reaching the hedge that bounded the lane, she looked for an escape route, but there was none, and the arched gate was locked. She was completely imprisoned between this and the river. Then she heard George's voice, also calling "Victoria!" He must never see her like this – a wild woman, trespassing on his property, who had recently been living with the lesbians.

What was impenetrable under normal conditions became less so when being pursued by unimaginable horrors. She crawled into a muddy ditch and found a gap beneath the bushes, through which she could just about wriggle. Looking along the lane, she realised that her camper van was hidden between two tractor cabs. Soon, they would put a guard upon it, and she suspected a love-sick Rosie was already racing down to make her lesbian's arrest. There was not a moment to lose; she sneaked back, jumped in the driver's seat, and raced away as fast as her gears would allow.

After rounding a couple of bends, she saw a pony and trap coming towards her. She pulled onto the grass verge, so it could pass on the single-track lane. Then she realised Mandy was resting casually in the driving seat, the pony walking along without any instructions necessary. David sat by her side, holding a shopping bag.

Victoria was so astonished by the sight, that she jumped out of her van and frantically waved. Mandy immediately sat up straight, and shouted some instruction to the pony, which made him break into a dignified trot. David, his mouth open, turned to look at Victoria, until Mandy poked him in the ribs with an elbow. The trap rattled by, with both children looking straight ahead, like royalty of long ago, when they had the misfortune of coming across a peasant.

Victoria looked down at her torn, muddy clothes, then, unable to comprehend the horror of her appearance, she turned to lean against the van.

"Oh, George," she breathed, "I do not deserve you."

Victoria spun around, as if somebody else had spoken the words, but there was nobody. Then she realised the children would tell Jackie about their recent encounter, so she jumped into the driver's seat to drive…where did not matter; one lay-by was much the same as another.

Before supper, she took a brief shower, leaving herself covered in soap because the water tank had run dry halfway through. What a mess her life had become…but it was worse than that; if she applied for a job in a hospital, they would expect a reference, which would surely alert the 'Lesbian Mafia' to her new location. To be free of them, she would have to leave the country. Then she looked around her little house, that was neither constrained by convention or borders. In Ireland, she was fairly certain, being a lesbian was illegal.

The following day, she drove to Holyhead, where she intended to take some menial work to pay for her ferry crossing. Having no luck at the job centre, she went to the ferry terminal to ask what a sailing to Dublin would cost. Not a great deal, but it was more than she had in her purse. She tried to think how Cynthia would deal with such a difficulty... be creative with the truth, perhaps? After a few seconds to adjust to her new reality, she asked for the personnel office. Here, a man came to look at her uncertainly.

"I wondered," she said, "if you have any jobs going in your medical bay? I'm a State Registered Nurse."

The man looked a little embarrassed; he was going to turn her away, she knew it. Becky had studied surgery, and could keep people alive for days on end in the middle of an ocean. It was not the same as being a nurse, surrounded by all the backup facilities of a hospital. Then, thinking how she had got her job at the orphanage, many years before, she submissively bowed her head.

"I'll work for half-pay," she said, quietly.

The man coughed. "We are governed by merchant-shipping regulations," he said sternly. "We pay the going rate for the correct staff. May I suggest you try the local hospital. I trust you speak Welsh?"

It was the final straw. Victoria sat in the nearest chair and burst into tears. When she looked up, the man had gone, and a lady had entered with a box of tissues.

"Oh, don't worry," she said, "happens all the time. Bet you had a row with your boyfriend, and decided to run away to sea. It's not like that anymore, because you're not allowed to work a sailing until you've gone to naval college for training. These positions tend to be offered to those who just long for a life at sea, and come here to find out what college courses they need to get their first step on the ladder. Then he would have taken you seriously. Also, I'm afraid bursting into tears was pretty near fatal for your career prospects here. You need to have a strong personality to work on the crew side of things, just in case you're faced with an emergency situation."

The rejection caused Victoria to bow her head in despair. Then some survival instinct kicked in, making her remember her tent-dwelling period. That had happened because pride had prevented her from applying for any lower-qualified jobs, until it was too late to be considered for anything. But this time she was going to fight back, while she still had a full tummy and clothes that did not resemble the sort of rags to be found in a skip.

"You said the crew side of things," replied Victoria. "This suggests there is another side?"

"Well, yes, the canteen staff tend to come and go, so we sometimes take them with a basic crew training..."

"I'll take it!"

"What?"

"Whatever you just said, I'll take it! Then you have a State Registered Nurse on board for free. Also, I recently stayed on the captain's big orange ship. I just loved going out to sea!"

The girl nodded. "I know who you mean," she said. "We employed his daughter."

Victoria felt confused, but only for a moment. Then the Cynthia side of her brain fully activated.

"Oh," she said, "Becky, yes, very reliable, just like I intend to be!"

SEVENTEEN

Victoria was astonished to discover just how quickly her bank balance grew into something substantial – a combination of having a proper job and few expenses. Six months after joining the ferry company, she purchased a scrap of woodland with a central clearing, where she parked her 'house'. Six months later, she bought the adjacent field, which took her total holding to three acres – just sufficient for her to acquire two friendly donkeys. She then bought a dozen hens, who liked nothing better than pecking about underneath her house, which made it really difficult to start driving anywhere, so she abandoned the idea of moving, and bought an old Morris Minor that could be parked in the lane. The track to her clearing soon narrowed to a footpath, after which her dwelling effectively disappeared from the outside world. Then, one morning, she was sitting on her doorstep to feed the donkeys with apples, when she had a most horrible thought: she had subconsciously recreated what she had seen on her last visit to the quay!

Except here there was no river, no children, and no George to keep them all safe. Soon, her watery eyes made her surroundings go fuzzy...

Then, accepting this to be the new reality of her life, she went indoors to collect a sack of dirty washing, the afternoon to be spent at the launderette, where the locals all spoke a language she did not understand.

Given her non-existent social life, Victoria dedicated herself to work. It was thus, after six months' service, the ferry company had offered her a small promotion, putting her on the first rung of a well-established career ladder. After returning from her first residential college course, the hard work really began: that of learning how to walk about the decks without feeling silly, because of the two gold epaulette stripes on her shoulders.

Towards the end of her second year, this had increased to three stripes, allowing her to lean on the ship's rail to watch the lorries rumbling up the loading ramp, anyone who saw her assuming it to be part of her work. Really though, it was how she preferred to take her breaks. In particular, it allowed her mind to float idly through daydreams, mostly concerning how pleasing her life had become since going away to naval college, but occasionally frowning if some detail of her previous life got in the way. Then, on one such break, she suddenly found herself wide awake: it was George, with David and Mandy, in the cab!

"What to do, what to do?" she said, walking about in circles.

She had three and a half hours to make up her mind – less, probably, because lorry drivers generally went straight to the café for a meal, after which they might go to the men's loo, or take a shower. Her brain was so preoccupied by the complexities of her situation, that she failed to notice her legs had automatically started walking towards the café. Her senses returned just in time to make her jump sideways at the door. From here, she could peep around the edge of the frame. All three of them looked really happy…but George probably had a girlfriend by now. On the other hand, he might not!

"Right," she said to herself, "here goes!"

She smoothed down her uniform, fiddled with the gold epaulettes, then went across to their table.

"I'm down the sickbay, if you want me for anything," she said. After walking away for three paces, she turned to look over her shoulder. "You know how to ask for a plaster, don't you?" she called back.

She hoped George would come. She would so enjoy taking him back to her house, that just happened to be on wheels, and swayed slightly in sympathy with the trees on windy days.

*

Four years after the departure of the hippopotamus snoggers, two tramps with long bushy beards stumbled down the lane towards the boys' home. Tears were running down their cheeks; after a long, long time, they were coming home. Then they heard the laughter of children, and looked at each other uncertainly.

"Disobedience," said one.

"Yes," replied the other, "it needs correction."

On reaching the entrance to the home, they stopped, and began to make gargling noises in the back of their throats. Three girls were sitting on a bench beneath the shade of a large tree; a boy, standing no more than two feet away, was actually talking to them. Then he held out a tennis racket, which one of the creatures accepted. They walked away together in the direction of a newly built tennis court.

Presently, a long line of girls came walking up the lane with football boots hanging casually over their shoulders by the laces. They sauntered through the entrance, then onto the lower football pitch next to the drive. Here, one of the girls glanced back, and changed direction to walk towards the main buildings, without being arrested!

"It wasn't a nightmare," said one of the tramps, "they actually escaped."

The men shuffled sideways to hide behind the hedge at the side of the entrance. From here, they peered at the incomprehensible scene; girls were actually playing football, with boys, on the same team. The tramps hugged each other for support, as they had done many times before in foreign prisons, when the guards had come with electrical prods to get them to confess to something or other. Then, remembering this was England, they awkwardly withdrew to discover new hope, in the form of 'Old Clever Clogs', who was walking towards them. He would know what was happening, and probably have plans for a counter-offensive. When about five feet from the end of the drive, he stopped.

"This is private property," he said, "and though I can't stop you lurking in the bushes, the police generally remove men who want to watch girls running about in PE kits."

"But we are Mr Kent and Mr Smith," said one of the tramps, "surely you remember us?"

"Not that I recall."

"But we were here…the day the girls escaped."

"What are you talking about? No such thing ever happened."

The tramps looked at each other; this was not the

reception they had been expecting. Then the true horror of their situation dawned upon them: they had marched for two days without food to get home; it had never occurred to them that they would not be fed…and find sanctuary in their old rooms.

"We need to speak to Mr Cranmore," said one.

"Retired," said the English master. "I am the headmaster now."

Then they saw the new matron walking down the drive. She would remember them, and perhaps have something for their various ailments. She came to stand beside the English master.

"Are these the gentlemen looking at the girls?" she asked.

"We are Mr Kent and Mr Smith," said one of the tramps. "We remember you replaced the fat matron – no, there was one in between – anyway the English master can't remember who we are."

"Do you have identification?"

"No, all our papers are in our room. Don't you remember? The girls came, they were everywhere."

Matron looked at the tramps, perplexed.

"I have no idea what you are talking about," she said, "but I expect the white coat gives me away as something medical. Perhaps things might sound more convincing if you knew my name, or the name of the gentleman by my side?"

"You're just a matron," said one of the tramps, "and the English master was always known as Old Clever Clogs. You were given the monk's room to make you leave, don't you remember? The bed was made of scaffolding planks."

The tramps watched Old Clever Clogs walk to the edge of the football field, followed by the matron, who stood behind him on tiptoe so she could rest her chin on his shoulder. Then she put her arms around his waist…

The tramps gargled in horror. "It's like that book where space aliens take over a town," said one, "brainwashing the inhabitants, so they can't remember anything about it!"

"But we escaped with the knowledge," said the other, "though who will believe us?"

"No one," said a voice behind them. "In truth, you just want to watch girls running about in PE kits."

"We are masters here," said the tramps together.

"Yeah, right, and I'm the Queen of England!"

Beryl went to join Imogen and Andrew by the edge of the football field.

"Are we following Cynthia's emergency procedures?" she asked.

Andrew nodded, and Beryl walked onto the football pitch, which she always thought rather brave, since the girls often teased her by passing her the ball, expecting her to do something with it. Also, there was Nick, the Games master, a stay-over who had now reached the age of nineteen. His PE kit did little to hide his huge muscles, and it frequently made her feel peculiar. She went to stand beside him, looking away to an imaginary object in the distance.

"Smith and Kent are back," she said. "They are watching you from the gate. Tell the girls, they will know what to do."

Beryl returned to Imogen and Andrew, and nodded towards the tramps.

"They have lost their identity, it seems," she said. "They must have got back into the country as illegal immigrants."

Just then there was a cry of 'Foul!', and Nick blew his whistle.

"Ah, sir," said a girl.

Jane, the sixteen-year-old girl in question, marched off the pitch to stand a few yards from the tramps. Nick followed.

"You know the rules," he said. "You made a foul, now remove an item of clothing, immediately!"

Jane rounded on Nick. "Ever since I burned down the library, you've been picking on me!" she screamed.

"But you kicked a boy on the shins."

"He was trying to take the ball from me. What did you expect, that I should lie down and let him do me?" She spun around to face the tramps. "And what you looking at?" she screamed. "Go find some other bush to wank in!"

Then she threw the sort of tantrum few men ever get to see. The tramps staggered backwards, turning to make a panic retreat up the lane. Jane let out two ear-piercing screams, then dropped her arms onto Nick's shoulders and began panting.

"Orgasmic elocution," she breathed. "I teach it in my Sexology class. The screaming bit always leaves me drained. You'll have to give me a moment while I come down from the ceiling!"

Beryl pretended to watch the tramps as they tried to throw themselves over a hawthorn hedge. After crawling out of the ditch, they continued their hobbled escape to the first official stile, over which they rolled. Beryl threw a sideways glance, to see if Jane was still being a tart. Even more so; she now had her arms around Nick while looking over his shoulder to gaze adoringly at Andrew; both men were under her total control.

"Did I do OK?" she asked. "I'm sorry about the bad word, but masturbation seemed out of context so close to the verb phrase of 'letting a boy do me'!"

"It's called agreement..." began Andrew.

Imogen poked him in the ribs. "She's flirting with you," she said.

Jane changed her expression to the 'Doris Day' look she had copied from an old film.

"Just trying to increase my house points for dealing with the tramps," she said.

Under the new regime, these points could be traded for useful things like a visit to the ice cream parlour, or going to the picture house, so were strictly rationed.

"Two," said Andrew.

Imogen stepped behind him, and put her hands over his eyes.

"She's a girl," she said. "You cannot give her house points… only I can do that, when I'm over there as her matron, and Jane is behaving herself correctly."

Jane immediately turned all her attention to Nick, which was rather fortunate, since his legs were about to give way. She led him to face Beryl, then put his arms over her shoulders to keep him upright. Beryl looked down at her feet to prevent Nick seeing how red she had gone.

"Oh, look," said Jane, "the tramps are coming back."

Beryl was glad to have somewhere innocent to look, but, before she realised the tramps were nowhere to be seen, a hand pushed her firmly against Nick. She strongly suspected Jane had her other hand on Nick's back, because he made no attempt to escape the forced embrace.

"Can I have some house points for dealing with the tramps?" asked Jane.

Beryl understood there was an element of blackmail to the request, so decided to say 'yes' because this generally made life easier.

"One," she mumbled.

"Added to what Imogen is going to give me, that's enough to let me take you two to the pictures," said Jane.

"I can't imagine…" began Beryl.

She waited for Nick to provide the necessary excuse, but he remained silent.

"Oh, I'll sit somewhere else," said Jane. "It doesn't even have to be the same film. And afterwards, I can disappear to spend the night in Cynthia's flat."

Beryl found herself pulled away from Nick, Jane immediately taking her place.

"You will have to excuse Beryl," she said. "She grew up under the curse of Miss Buckley, and it takes years to recover. However, I am a disciple of Cynthia and fully qualified to deal with such disorders."

She embraced Nick in a 'twining of a creeper' position. What she whispered into his ear was largely meaningless, because Cynthia's elocution lessons included talking while breathing in. When Jane's chest was fully expanded, her tummy muscles went into rapid spasm, causing the air to escape intermittently through slightly open vocal chords.

"Oh," she breathed, "that feels so good." Then she stepped back to stare down at his PE shorts. "They are surely about to burst at the seams," she gasped. "Beryl, look at that, it's an absolutely enormous bulge!"

Then her voice became more authoritative.

"Now, Beryl," she said, "I want you to try that. First, take a firm hold of his buttocks then…Ah, but it seems we've had a little accident. Beryl, give the poor man your jumper, we can't have him walking back up the drive with a wet patch."

Beryl turned to look up the lane.

"Beryl," said Jane crossly, "don't be so cruel. Can't have all the girls knowing about his premature ejaculation."

Beryl took off her jumper and held it over her shoulder.

"No, no!" screamed Jane, overcome by genuine horror. "Remove your jumper nicely. Nick wants to believe your blouse buttons might come flying apart at any moment!"

But Beryl merely threw the jumper to the ground and clomped off down the lane.

"Honestly," said Jane, "that girl is so sexually frustrated. I think it's because she suffers from 'pulsating vagina syndrome'. Only one girl in 36,000 suffers from that!"

She knelt down to tie the jumper about Nick's waist, arranging the sleeves to hang casually over the wet patch.

"There you go," she said, "now get back to your room to sort yourself out. I'll pop up in ten minutes to begin instruction about how to control your PC muscles."

*

Beryl sat on her normal log to gaze across the boating lake. It was much the same as four years before, except the boathouse had been renovated, and George had bought a number of boats for the children to use. On hearing footsteps, she lowered her head to hide her tearful eyes. Then a set of trainers came to stand before her.

"I knew I would find you here," said Jane's voice. "Always the same fallen tree."

"Aw well, you know how it is."

"You only feel safe in familiar surroundings," said Jane. "Twenty years from now, you could be the daft old bat in the attic, with a telescope."

Beryl felt herself being pulled up, then forwards.

"You will find it easier to tell me things if we are not facing each other," said Jane.

"Or I might push you in!" said Beryl.

"That's the sort of silly thing people say when they don't feel able to talk about what is really on their mind," said Jane. "But don't worry, my Sexology course will soon boost your confidence. Oh, don't look so shocked, Psychology is a basic part of my Sexology course. You need it to know how people work."

Beryl found herself being led along the path, until it turned left to cross the dam, which, being more exposed than the woods, made her wish she had not discarded her jumper so casually. It was the only thing that disguised how fat she had become. Then, glancing up from her feet, she realised Jane was still wearing her football kit. How could the girl be so unashamed of her bare arms and legs? Arms and legs that had recently wrapped themselves around Nick. On reaching the middle of the dam, Jane stopped above the pipes that took the water away.

"Do you remember the night you led us girls to freedom," she said, "through these very pipes? I was twelve then, and it's been the best fun ever since. This is my way of saying thank you. In fact, all the girls have agreed to hold back on Nick to give you a free run."

"I want you to go away now."

Jane did not seem to understand the request. "When I go to university," she continued, "I want to study Psychology, then I can help you break free from the curse of Miss Buckley. For instance, why did you just clomp off when Nick was so clearly enjoying our company? It was most rude."

"I do not clomp!"

"Yes you do, and the way you took off your jumper was a disgrace."

"I took off my jumper the way…as Miss Buckley would have expected: privately."

"I see, and do you still wear the 1940s vest, with interlocking knickers?"

"Jane! What sort of question is that?"

"A psychological one – which you have just answered. I'm quite good at this, aren't I?"

"You are worse than Cynthia."

"But she lived in a brothel, had a flat share with a load of lesbians, and is now a qualified doctor. There is no way I will ever be so good as her, given all her diverse experience."

"That's not what I meant…"

"No, I understand. I'll give her a ring, she's much better than me at being cross when you are being silly."

Beryl had an awful flashback to the time she had been lashed naked to a chimney stack because she had been behaving…like Miss Buckley expected.

"That's blackmail!" she gasped.

"Of course," said Jane.

It occurred to Beryl that Cynthia had created a monster: the brain of a Sexology professor inside the body of a nymphet. Thankfully, there was no more talk about getting Dr Cynthia involved. Instead, Jane began to circle around her, all the time making a variety of hums, like a doctor examining a patient.

"You need to lose six kilograms from the hips," said Jane eventually, "but don't worry, your Kama Sutra exercises will sort that out for you. A kilogram a week is not unreasonable. That gives us six weeks to sort out the other stuff."

"I heard what you said to Nick," gasped Beryl, "about down below."

"It will give him something nice to think about," said Jane. "Six weeks is a long time to wait when you are his age."

"You made it quite clear you wanted to go to bed with him yourself," said Beryl.

"Beryl, really! That's scandalous, he is my student! I only took temporary control of his nervous system to show you what to do."

"Like I could ever be such a tart?"

"You misunderstand the arts of love. No matter, my Sexology course will soon bring you from the fog in which you hide, hoping men don't notice you."

Jane finally stopped her circling. "That's fine," she said, "I understand what needs to be done. Next time your vests go down to the laundry room, they will not be coming back, then we can work on your personal blouse-button settings. Nick needs the basic information to work out his night-time fantasies…"

"…About you," said Beryl.

Beryl felt two hands turn her around, then one hand pushing the back of her head, so she was looking down at the steeply angled stonework of the dam.

"About you," repeated Beryl, almost in tears.

But Jane would not be drawn into the argument, instead standing in silence as Beryl stared down the dam. Then Beryl had another flashback. Had she really led the girls to freedom down that? Next, she remembered splashing down the stream, where she met Cynthia leading the boys the other way – two well-disciplined armies going off to war, each side pretending not to be distracted by the other. It had been fun, as were the following weeks, but now she was falling back into her old ways. Without Cynthia forcing her to do brave things, she found it much more natural to deal with Mother Superior than the complications of her new life. It had already been suggested that she became a proper nun. Jane was right; twenty years from now, she would be wearing a habit to hide all her wobbly bits.

Then Beryl found herself turned back to face the real world.

"It is true," said Jane, "that Nick has only just started his journey into love, his mind focused entirely on your 'pulsating vagina syndrome', but it is how wedding bells begin, if that is what you wish."

Beryl then felt a determined tug on her arm, the walk continuing along the dam until it became a neat gravel path on the boys' side.

"...Of course," Jane was saying, "Sexology is the most demanding course there is. We will begin with your deportment. There is no mountain so high it cannot be climbed."

Beryl looked down to her battlefield shoes; she did clomp. Then she looked at Jane's trainers, which seemed to be floating effortlessly over the path.

For a brief moment, she wished she could be like her – sensibly play tennis in a PE kit, and walk places without wobbling – yet in reality, Beryl knew her destiny was to live alone on the top floor, each day becoming more and more like Miss Buckley. As for the girls, well last year not a single one had left to begin a dead-end job, most taking the bus that came down the lane to do their 'A' levels at college, the others going for important job interviews, and taking control of any room they entered by sheer force of personality. But Jane was the worst; if she decided something needed to be done, it was beyond her comprehension that anybody would try to stop her.

When the path came to a neat timber bridge across a little stream, Jane came to a halt.

"We will begin your Sexology lessons tomorrow," she said. "A most important part is strategic planning, like this."

Beryl realised that anything within Jane's wild imagination would have no relevance to her own life, so could be ignored. To pass the time, she turned to gaze across the lake, thinking how pretty it looked with its path meandering pleasantly between the shore and the woods. Then she saw a skiff leaving the boathouse to skim across the water. It was him!

She leapt behind Jane to hide, but then realised Nick would now see her outline as something that belonged to a huge, scary monster. Desperately, she looked for a better place to hide, but there was none. Turning back, she discovered Jane had gone. Then reality arrived…in the form of a skiff bumping against the bank just twenty yards up the path. Jane changed places with Nick, to row competently away; due to strategic planning, Beryl had been abandoned on the boys' side of the lake, without her jumper. She spun around, so Nick could only see her back. Then she heard the crunch of his trainers coming towards her on the neat gravel path…